KNOW YOUR ENEMY

Hugh Aldersey

Cover Design and Typeset by BookPOD
Cover images by iStockphoto

ISBN: 978-0-9941871-3-0
eISBN: 978-0-9941871-4-7

Sixth reprint 2020

CONTENTS

Chapter 1.	The Cable	5
Chapter 2.	Water	23
Chapter 3.	The Enemy Revealed	34
Chapter 4.	The Assignment	47
Chapter 5.	Back in the Bush	57
Chapter 6.	Auction Surprise	77
Chapter 7.	Just in Time	80
Chapter 8.	Opportunity	89
Chapter 9.	The Court Ruling	94
Chapter 10.	New Names	107
Chapter 11.	War	121
Chapter 12.	In the Trenches	127
Chapter 13.	The Field Hospital	143
Chapter 14.	On the Move	150
Chapter 15.	Recuperating	158
Chapter 16.	The beginning of the end	166
Chapter 17.	Aftermath	170
Chapter 18.	The Great Depression	197
Chapter 19.	Unwelcome Phoenix	231
Chapter 20.	Bending the Beams	241
Chapter 21.	Diverse War	268
Chapter 22.	'Overlord'	331
Chapter 23.	A fight to the Finish	352

Chapter 1

THE CABLE

The cable arrived on a Saturday afternoon while Mark and Sasha were holding a birthday party for their son, William.

Twelve excited children were being brought inside from their games in the garden for the birthday tea when the telephone rang and was answered by Sasha in the study.

Sasha's face went deathly white as she listened to the operator at the local exchange reading out the message. (Which they are not supposed to do, but if the local operator thought the message was important they usually read it out over the phone as the written copy would not be delivered till the next day.)

> Oakhill Hall,
> Cheshire. England.
> Telephone Brockington 65
>
> 'MacIntyre farm attacked ten days ago. Alice killed.
> Gillie wounded but held off attackers till help arrived.
> Gillie recovering in the quarters.
> Writing.
> Love. A & G'.

As soon as Sasha had hung up the phone she called Mark into the study and between sobs gave him the sad news and then said.

"We can't spoil the children's party so we must try to keep up appearances till they have all gone home."

Mark said.

"Yes Dear, that's right, perhaps I can help with the games. That is terrible about Alice, the poor dear was so well and almost fully recovered from TB in the better climate out there in South Africa.

George has done the right thing by bringing Gillie back from their remote farm and putting him into the quarters at SATCO to recover as this attack sounds like some more Boar reprisal activity and the farm would not be safe for him any more.

After our last visit to SATCO two years ago, I felt that all was running smoothly and that the rush to develop the mines and industry was keeping everyone busy, but I suppose Gillie was still a marked man after his involvement in rounding up the last of the known Boar terrorist groups at the time of our wedding and now it appears that some latent Boer hatred may have surfaced again."

Marg. Brooks, the mother of two of the visiting children and a close friend of Sasha, came into the study and saw mark trying to console Sasha who was obviously in a state of shock and still wiping away her tears.

"What ever is wrong, what has happened?"

Sasha said. "We have just had a cable advising that Gillie's wife, Alice, of whom you have heard me speak, has been murdered on their farm in South Africa. Alice was a very dear friend and was almost like a mother to me before we were married."

"Don't worry, I can organize cutting the cake and look after the children for a while if you like"

"Would you, please Marg? I could not be jolly with the children just at the moment."

Marg went off to play hostess as Mark and Sasha tried to adjust to the terrible news about Alice and Gillie.

When the last of the visitors had left and their own children, William and Amy, aged three and two, were in bed, Mark and Sasha were able to discuss the situation at the dinner table.

Mark said. "I did not realize that there could still be deep seated racial hatred that would manifest itself after such a long time. During our last, very rushed visit to SATCO. there was so much activity with all the rapid developments that I was oblivious to any changes in the political situation.

I always thought that Gillie and Alice were perfectly safe quietly farming in the bush.

What few doubts that I still had about security were only for the business of SATCO. but as the Boers seem to have become dependent on SATCO as a supplier of essential goods and services they don't risk damaging a vital link in the chain to their further development and prosperity.

It looks as though I must go and assess the situation first hand as soon as possible, would you like to come with me?"

"Oh, Darling Mark I hate the thought of you going to SATCO, on your own, particularly if it is now a trouble spot, but I think that I should stay here and look after our children.

What do you think Gillie will want to do now that he is on his own. Do you think he would want to come back to England?"

"Yes, I think that you are right, and that he would probably like to come back, but it must be his decision. I understand that you would prefer to stay with our children this time, as it is important that one of us is safe at home with them.

If Gillie wants to come back, I will sell the farm and make over any increase in value to him as he has made so many improvements.

Then there is the safety of sister Anne and George and all the SATCO staff to think about as well.

Depending on what I find out on arrival in Johannesburg, we may have to consider selling SATCO if there is a major security risk for the staff and the future of the business.

Thanks to the SATCO staff and George's subsidiary company success the total value of the enterprise must have increased several times over by now.

If there is a resurgence of anti British sentiment and Boer terrorist activity it could be the right time to get out while the going is still good. But who would want to buy into an economy that might become unstable at any moment?"

"Mark, we must not prejudge the situation, perhaps we should keep an open mind and be ready to move quickly in whichever direction that is necessary, even if this does mean selling and getting out as soon as possible.

What do you think we should do about the staff if we have to sell? Do you think that they would want to stay on with a new owner or do you think that some of them would want to come to England?"

"I had not thought that far ahead yet Sasha, but you are right, we have to think about each member of the staff so it would be necessary to cater for each person's individual wishes.

The Boers previously always vented their anger on not only the British, but anyone who worked for, or did business with the British, so all the staff could be in danger of reprisals.

I wonder what our friend Colonel Wilkinson from BHQ in Johannesburg knows about the true situation, he was always very well informed on the South African scene.

It is a good thing that we have kept up contact with him, even if it has been only one visit and exchanging Christmas cards and a bit of news. We have his home address now that he is retired and back in England. Perhaps I should write to him as soon as possible."

"Yes that is an excellent idea, you must do that tomorrow and catch the first post on Monday."

As soon as breakfast was finished on the Sunday, Mark went to the Study and started to write to Colonel Wilkinson.

Oakhill Hall
Cheshire.
Telephone Brockington 65

Dear Colonel Wilkinson,

We hope that you and Rachel are both keeping well and enjoying being back in your own home in Sussex.

There was a distressing cable yesterday from my sister Anne and brother in law, George Bridgeman, in Johannesburg.

You will no doubt remember ex sergeant major Mc Tavish, 'Gillie,' and his wife Alice?

Their farm was attacked twelve days ago. Alice was killed and Gillie was wounded but was able to hold off the attackers till help arrived and is now recovering at SATCO.

We were wondering if you have any up to date intelligence on the current political situation in South Africa that would help us to make decisions about the future of SATCO and the staff?

As could be expected, I am planning on going out to asses the situation first hand on the first available ship.

With kindest regards,

Mark and Sasha.

When Mark had finished the letter he looked for Sasha, who was playing with the children in the garden, and she came over and they sat on a garden seat under a tree.

"Sasha, while I was writing, I thought about our other friends like John and May Ashcroft at the Glendarvel shamba and their two girls, who are now at college most of the time. Then there are Mike and Sheila Burgess at the British Coffee Estate (BCE) with their small children who could become targets for Boer reprisals if there is any increase in terrorist activity."

"Yes that is right, but we don't know how well they have been able to keep an ear to the ground for any change in the political situation, which I suppose would be difficult out in the bush with poor communications. Perhaps we should ask George to let them know about Alice and Gillie and keep them fully informed?

You need to send a reply cable to George on Monday and could add a bit about keeping the others informed."

Mark went into the study and drafted out a cable for George and Anne.

Oakhill Hall
Cheshire.
Telephone. Brockington 65

To Bridgeman
SATCO
Johannesburg. South Africa.

'Cable received.
Condolences and a speedy recovery for visitor.
Glad he is relocated.
Need to check reason.
Please keep Glendarvel and BCE. informed.
Plan to come soonest.
Will advise ETA. Love. M and S.'

Three days later Mark and Sasha had just finished dinner when Colonel Wilkinson telephoned.

"Hello Mark, how are you both?"

"Good evening Colonel, we are all well here thank you. I hope that you and Rachel are both well."

"Yes we are both well thank you. Mark, it is very timely that you wrote as we could do with your help if you are going to South Africa, but firstly, yes we can give you some important background and up to date information.

When have you booked your passage to go to Durban?"

"The first ship available leaves in 9 days from Tilbury docks in London."

"That is good as there is time to post you the background of the colony which will help to explain the reasons for the continuing difficult situation. Then if you still have any queries you could phone me before you leave.

Although I have retired from the Army, I am still working on some 'special projects' and South Africa is one of them.

Would you be prepared to do some field work for me while you are over there?"

"Yes certainly, provided it can be done fairly quickly."

Two days later a large envelope arrived and Mark and Sasha started to read the documents.

SOUTH AFRICA.
Confidential.

In order to understand the current social and political situation it is necessary to go back to 1814 when 'Britain purchased The Cape of Good Hope' from the Dutch Government for 6,000,000 pounds and made it a British Colony because it was a vital supply port and strategic base necessary for the ships servicing Britain's interests in the Far East.

The Dutch settlers / farmers, or Boers as they are called, were infuriated and did not accept that their land had literally 'been sold from under their feet', by their own Government to Britain and became very, very angry and ill feeling started between the Boers and the British settlers. The Boers were pushed back inland and started their own republics of Natal, Orange Free State and Transvaal.

Later, gold was found at Witwatersrand in 1886 and Johannesburg was founded and grew very rapidly.

Thousands of mostly British prospectors and settlers rushed in to the republics to claim the new wealth which further antagonized the Boers who then imposed very heavy State taxes on them and removed their voting rites.

The British settlers, or 'Uitlanders' as the Boers called them, revolted against the Boer Government, the British Governor then formed an army.

The Boer commander, Paul Kruger, issued an ultimatum that if the army was not withdrawn immediately, war would result, and when this did not happen the Boers declared war on October 12th 1899.

Sasha said. "That was soon after you went out to rescue SATCO, when the manager had deserted, became involved, was wounded and helped to re-start the railway and we met and fell in love!"

"Yes, Darling that was the most wonderful event in my life and you have made me so happy ever since." They kissed and then continued reading.

The Boers won most of the early battles, and later the British won back the major cities and the British Commander returned home assuming the war was over, but the Boers were in no way defeated and fought on in small groups. They did not wear uniforms thus making it impossible to determine who was an enemy and who was a friend.

Lord Kitchener was then appointed British commander and introduced very harsh measures to defeat the Boers but this only caused more anger among the Boers and even caused dissent in the British parliament.

The treaty of Vereeniging was hastily signed on the 31st of May 1902 but this did not stop small independent groups of Boers still fighting on as terrorists.

The loss of life during the war was very heavy on both sides with Britain and her allies loosing 28,000 men, the Boers loosing 4,000 soldiers and 20,000 civilian fighters. There were also 12,000 black Africans killed.

There has since been very rapid development of the mines and now there is rising pressure for the formation of the independent 'Union of South Africa'.

The flow on effects of a new regime are unknown at this stage and could range from stabilization and consolidation of the Boer Government and solid business growth, to unstable, and or, dictatorial government and a doubtful future for foreign owned businesses and foreign residents.

There are still isolated terrorist attacks on people who were involved with the latter stages of the Boer's defeat and it appears that there are some unknown terrorist leader(s), with a long memory, who are directing the terrorist operations.

A complete update of the situation is now urgently required.

They then went on to read the colonel's letter.

'Dear Mark and Sasha,

In my new position, the instructions come from the highest level and the information that I obtain is highly confidential and is discussed at regular meetings.

I have very limited resources, so sometimes I have to use trusted associates, like your selves, to gather information.

Our intelligence gathering is done independently to provide a second opinion to that gathered by the traditional professionals, which is often politicized on the way through and can't be used to make decisions of national importance, and therefore our operation must be in complete secrecy.

Now that you have read the background, you will see why that there has been so much hostility and ongoing terrorist activity in South Africa.

We are vitally interested in the current situation because we now have to decide, whether or not, to agree to the formation of an independent 'Union of South Africa'.

In particular, we are interested in the likely flow on effects if the 'Union of South Africa' is approved and formed in about one year.

The information that we urgently need is also pertinent to your situation.

Questions.
What is the current breakdown of large company ownership by country.

If the 'Union of South Africa' is formed within the next year or so:

What will happen to foreign owned businesses?

Will foreigners have voting rites?

How will black people be classified and treated by a Boer government?

Who is orchestrating current terrorist activity?

Would a new Union Government have permanent armed forces?

Perhaps we can discuss your findings in London when you return.

Regards W.

Mark discussed the document and letter with Sasha and she had mixed feelings about Mark being involved with 'espionage', but had complete confidence in Colonel Wilkinson's integrity and felt that they were still deeply indebted to him for his previous help before they were married in Johannesburg in 1902.

Mark said.

"Now that we have the complete history on the Boer hostilities, it just shows how in '99 I rushed headlong into saving SATCO, when the manager had disappeared, and being involved with the railway without fully understanding what it was all about.

I should have followed Ghillie's training and applied the principle of 'Know Your Enemy'!

But the most important result of my first trip to Africa was meeting you my darling girl!"

When Mark arrived in Durban he was met, as usual, by Gustav Petersen, the owner of a timber, shipping and forwarding company, The Durban Forwarding Company, who was a good friend and confidant and stayed the night with his family. It was also good to see his wife, Anna, and their two teenage girls again.

Gustav and Mark sat up till very late discussing business, but Mark was also able to work most of the questions for his assignment into the conversation.

Gustav's answers were reserved about the future because he suspected that an independent Government of South Africa would assume more power and could make business more difficult for foreign owners and that there would be more segregation and exploitation of the black workers which would cause more trouble later on.

Gustav's many international business connections gave him a wide source of information and he said.

"We are now getting reports of the business men in Europe talking about 'Gold Fever in South Africa', so there is a rush of foreign fortune hunters already coming over, which is sending prices up and will open up more mines. There is also secret talk about the discovery of diamonds."

The next morning Mark started the train journey to Johannesburg and arrived in the late afternoon.

SOUTH AFRICAN TRADING COMPANY

As soon as Mark's cab arrived at SATCO he was greeted by the manager, Abdul Suliman, and all the staff and then went up to the 'quarters', over the office, to see Gillie who was sitting with one bandaged and tension splinted leg propped up on a stool.

"I am verr'a pleased to see you Mark, and how are Sasha and the children."

"It is good to see you recovering Gillie, and all at home are well, thank you. We are very sad and sorry about the loss of Alice and offer our deepest sympathy.

How do you feel now that you are all strapped up and resting."

"It is verra sore at temes, but I am stronger every day noo. Mjuba is looking after me verra weel, she is a verra capable lass."

"What do you think was behind the attack?"

"I ha' bin aware of a bit of possessiveness and more of a kind of superior attitude among the Boers of late. They act as though all others are inferior and of course they wilna' accept the blacks and keep them repressed all the teme because they are scared that the black majority will tak' a 'waw, their power.

The attack at the farm was mid morning and Alice was in her much loved garden and I was working in the barn with the boss boy, Makede.

There was just one rifle shot so I sent Makede to warn the native shamba, grabbed an old rifle that I keep hidden in the barn and then crawled round to where the shot came from and found Alice, poor lass was dead before I got to her, then they started shooting at me, there were at least four of them. I could not see where they were at first, then I got two before I was shot in the leg.

I was able to crawl back to the barn, dragging ma' leg, and climb up to the loft and shoot at them from above and keep them pinned down.

It then became a stalemate. I had them pinned down and I could not move as my leg had lost a lot of blood and was verr'a sore. I was able to cut some strips off me' trous' to bind up ma' leg and then just wait it 'oot.

Late in the afternoon there was some screaming and commotion from where the Boers were hiding and a few shots, then silence.

Later a group of young hunters from the shamba and Makede came into the barn and called me.

Makede explained what had happened. The group of young hunters had been off looking for game since dawn, had speared a young impala and were bringing it back to their shamba when they saw the 'signal bird' that Makede had put on the top of the end hut. This was a crude system that they had developed when the slavers were out hunting for slaves among the native villages.

The chief told them to make a 'bird' out of wood and woven reeds with a few feathers and when there was any threat they put it on top of the most prominent hut in the shamba as a warning to any of the men, who were out hunting, of the danger.

Makede met up with the hunters and told them what was happening so the hunters had crept up to where the Boers were hiding and attacked them from behind with bows, arrows and spears.

A wounded Boer shot one hunter before he was speared to death.

The poor hunter lad died later.

After eight days, I felt strong enough to put some gear together and asked Makede to help me to ride back to Pietersburg and help me on my home made crutches onto the train and then back to Johannesburg and hospital.

Raymond took Makede back to the farm a few days later and helped to sort out any problems and he also went on to Major John Ashcroft's shamba at Glendarvel and told him what was happening.

Major Ashcroft said that there was a lot more Boer activity around his shamba and Mike Burgess, the manager at BCE, was complaining that his native workmen have been threatened again if they continue working for BCE. He thinks that the BCE. big boss may sell the whole operation if there is any more violence.

I was verr'a lucky, the bullet went through my thigh muscle but did not hit the bone so I just have to wait till it recovers."

"That was good that Makede is reliable and knew what to do in an emergency.

Did the doctor at the hospital say how long you will be laid up?"

"He said I must stay strapped up for noo and then he will want to operate again in about three weeks to get the muscles working."

"I must go and see Abdul and catch up on what is happening in the business and then I will come up and have dinner with you."

Mark went down and met Abdul and they went on a complete tour of inspection of the whole SATCO. complex and then the branch store which was now managed by Abdul's son, Hassan.

Mark was most impressed with the many new products added to the range of merchandise since his last visit and the considerable increase in turnover.

Abdul had a very keen sense of merchandising (And improving his profit share.) and all the staff seemed to be working well under his leadership, but there was now the all important decision to make about the future of the business, which of course he could not discuss with Abdul at this stage.

After Abdul had gone home, Mark went to check on the two men who were employed as night guards. They were lounging around in their hut at the rear of the compound and were very surprised to see anyone in the compound after 'lock up' and became very nervous.

Mark said. "When did you last patrol the area?"

"One hour ago, Bwana"

"Where is your log book?"

A well thumbed book was produced which had columns of times, which were much too regular to be real, and there were no entries in the remarks columns.

"We need to vary the times that you patrol the compound and you must note down all irregularities and after hours visitors in the remarks column. I will see Mr. Suliman in the morning."

Mjuba was mostly of English parentage and only one quarter Kenyan, from her grandmother, and had started as the housekeeper for the quarters and part time assistant in the front shop.

Now that she was nearly thirty, she had matured and was doing an excellent job of housekeeping for Gillie and prepared a tasty evening meal which was served for all of them in the large upstairs sitting room of the quarters.

When they were all seated at the table, Gillie asked.

"What is the news from home?"

"Well, firstly at Glencairn all seems to be going well, we have visited a few times, usually in the better weather. My Aunt Mary is running the estate, now that my uncle has died, and they have a new foreman for the home farm, who is living in your old house. He is keen to use all the new farming methods. But as he comes from down in the south of England has to learn to adapt to the different climate in Scotland.

My Cousin Elizabeth is off and married and has at least one child already.

At home, Sasha and I have been busy with developing the home farm and cheese making business, which is now paying well. We also have been busy with improvements to all the tenanted farms and cottages and rebuilding the dairy and beef cattle herds after the foot and mouth disease wiped most of them out a few years ago.

Sasha is a wonderful wife and has fitted into the lifestyle perfectly and has made many friends in the area. We have enjoyed starting a family and have two wonderful children who are adored by Sasha. I hope that she does not spoil them and lets them learn to stand on their own two feet.

Your part in blasting out the stumps after we felled the great wood has made the cable plowing by two steam engines, and then the replanting, much easier. The young trees are growing well now and in another 40 or 50 years we will have another stand of fine oaks.

There are more and more of the new engine driven trucks and motor cars on the roads and we even have a motor car now, but it is very temperamental in the cold weather.

Now in total secrecy, I must tell you about an assignment that I have been given by Colonel Wilkinson to undertake while I am here and I need your help. You will of course remember the Colonel?"

"Och ay', I remember him verra' well and I am used to handling confidential military material at the HQ in India with your uncle, and will be pleased to help, as much as this leg will let me."

"Firstly I will give you this background report and the colonel's letter to read and then we can discuss how we can get the information that he wants."

Gillie moved his position and got more comfortable before starting to read while Mark asked Mjuba to make some coffee.

When they had finished their coffee Gillie said.

"Now that I have read that report and have a better idea of what the situation is, I was thinking that we should get the two guards to help move me to the big room over the archway so that I wilna' disturb you and I will be able to see more of what is going on in the SATCO. compound."

"That sounds like an excellent idea, we can do it now and Mjuba can make up your bed by the window."

The two guards soon had Gillie rolled onto a stretcher, 'borrowed' from the store, and carried across to the large room over the archway where Mjuba was already making up his bed.

As soon as Gillie was sitting comfortably on the bed he said.

"Could you please get me a rifle and some ammo from the store as I have a feeling that we may be in for some more trouble now that it is probably already known that I am here and I seem to be a marked mon at the moment".

"Yes, I think that you are right Gillie, I will also get a rifle for myself and a revolver for each of us. I will keep my weapons in the Quarters. The trouble is we can't use firearms too much in the city area now that the war is supposed to be over.

So both of them went to bed with a loaded rifle and revolver close at hand.

Chapter 2

WATER

The night was uneventful and Mark's sister, Anne, came down from their new house up on the hill, early on the next morning, to see Mark and as they sat at the table in the sitting room in the quarters, they exchanged news about what had happened in their respective lives since they had last met during Mark's rushed visit two years ago.

Anne now had a boy aged two and was expecting again.

George sent his apologies as he was still very busy with his consulting and construction business and would call in later.

Mark swore Anne to secrecy and then told her about the assignment that he had been given by Colonel Wilkinson and then let her read the report and the Colonel's letter and she was immediately very worried about news of the plans to form an independent 'Union of South Africa' and what would happen in the future, particularly now that she had one child and was expecting another.

Anne quickly realised that much of the information required for the assignment was also important in making decisions for their own future and became very keen to help.

George then arrived and had a long discussion with Mark and said that he would start immediately to look for the information required by the Colonel, and said that he must hurry back to his office as he had a visitor coming.

Anne and Mark had just started to put a few ideas on paper when Anne's housekeeper, Millie, hurried up the stairs and poured out a breathless account of a problem with two of their horses which were kept in a house paddock behind the big house up on the hill.

One horse was already dead and the other was very sick and looked about to die.

Mark immediately sent for the vet and then got Raymond to harness up some horses and they all rode up to Anne and George's house on the hill as fast as possible.

There was a very large water tank at the end of the garden which was supplied with water from the roof, and when necessary, water was pumped up from a deep bore by a large windmill nearby. This had all been installed by some Australians who had stayed on in Johannesburg after the end of the Boer war and were experts with deep bores and windmills.

Just over the garden fence into the house paddock there was a drinking trough which was supplied from the big tank.

The dead horse was lying close to the trough and the other horse was lying a few yards away and was writhing in pain with staring eyes and was frothing at the mouth.

Mark said. "Looks like poison, we should shoot that poor horse to put it out of it's misery but the vet should see it first to try to determine the cause.

"Raymond, please go quickly and alert everyone in the company houses lower down the hill that the water is probably poisoned and NOT to drink any or use it for any other purpose.

I will turn off the main tap but there will still be some water in the pipes.

Anne, as you know, the water for your house has to be pumped up into the tank in the attic every few days. When did you last pump up to the attic tank?"

"I think it was a few days ago, Millie, can you remember?"

The housekeeper looked alarmed and said. "Yes it was two days ago, we have not pumped up yet today"

"Thank God for that, at least we may have some safe water left in the attic tank, but we must test it first."

Mark then hurried off to close the main tap that controlled the flow of water to all the company houses further down the hill and then closed the tap that connected the pump that supplied water to the attic tank in the big house.

They all went up to the house and Anne suggested a cup of tea, but Mark said.

"Wait, we must check first, just to be sure, if there is poison in the big tank, we don't know if the house supply has been affected. Also tell the nanny to keep young Timothy well away from the garden and not to use any water till we are sure it is safe."

There was a knock at the door and the vet was let in and was then asked to follow Mark to the house paddock.

"Certainly looks like poison, look at the way that poor animal is contorting with the pain, I will get a gun from my saddle bag and shoot it".

The vet then took samples from both horses, the tank and trough.

Anne said.

"Could you also take a sample of the water in the house please, we want to be sure that the house supply has not been contaminated."

The vet got a sample from the house and said.

"I will do the tests as soon as possible and send a boy with the results to SATCO."

He put the samples in his saddle bags and hurried off to his surgery.

Raymond rode up at a gallop, dismounted, and went up to Mark.

"Bwana, we were too late for at least two women and several small children. Tad was off shift and was home so he started doing a careful house to house check, while I went to SATCO and got Abdul to send for the doctor."

"Thank you Raymond, can you get one of the men from the workshop to drain the horse trough to ensure that no other animals get poisoned and also drain the water from the pipes that supply the other houses by opening the garden taps at the lowest houses and use a hose to run the water into the drains?"

Mark and Anne rode slowly down the hill and met Tad who was coming out of one of the cottages on the lower slope.

"Hello Tad, what have you found so far?"

"Morning to yer' both. Terrible wot I found, two women and three small children dead already. Two more small children very sick and look like they'l die, poor little mites, screaming and all screwed up with pain. Wot a dastardly thing to do, who'd yer reckon done it?"

"At this stage we don't know Tad. Millie, have you seen anyone round the house and garden this morning?"

"There has only been the old peddler woman with her pack horses selling soap, mops, brooms and cleaning stuff. O yes, I just remembered, she asked if her horses could drink at the trough in the house paddock as they was very tired and thirsty after coming up the hill."

Mark said.

"She sounds like the prime suspect, does anyone know where she lives?"

Raymond said.

"She has been going round with her pack horses for years, but there were never any problems. Would you like me to go and start making enquires about where she lives?"

"Yes please Raymond, report back to the office when you find where she lives, but don't go in, because we don't know who else might be hiding there."

After Raymond had left, Mark, Anne and Tad went back up the hill and started searching round the tank and water trough for any clues.

There were the hoof prints of the pack horses and imprints of small size, well worn boots. Two large empty bottles with 'Clean Wiz' labels and the dregs of a brown liquid were found by Anne under some bushes near the tank. Mark shouted.

"Don't touch them! They probably will have some poison still in them, we must wrap them in paper and send them to the vet to be tested."

The bottles were wrapped, taken back to the office and sent with a stable boy to the vet's surgery.

Back at SATCO Mark made everyone wash very carefully.

The water supply at SATCO luckily came from the town supply. The pressure in the town supply was not sufficient to force the water up to the hill so SATCO had had to put in the separate water supply system.

Mark and Anne had lunch sent up to Gillie's room so that they could discuss the affair with him.

When Gillie had been brought up to date by Mark, he said.

"That is the most dastardly thing I have ever heard of, poor wee bairns and their mothers made to die a terrible death. Poisoning is the lowest form of killing anyone and is only used by the scum of the earth, may the culprit die a similar death in hell!

If the peddler woman was at the big house about nine o'clock that would be when the men were at work and the older children were at school, so only a few women and the small children were at home. The only exception being Tad who has to work shift hours to catch the mine captains for his sales calls. Fortunately he had had a meal earlier with his wife and they were sleeping.

You say Raymond has gone to find where the old peddler woman lives, but this sudden terrorist act seems out of character from what you say. She has probably been blackmailed into this by the arch terrorist, whoever he is. If we can question the peddler woman carefully we may get a description of him and some more details."

They talked on about the immediate need to take more security measures at SATCO and decided to take on two more guards for a day shift to give 24 hour coverage. The guards would also be armed with revolvers and given basic training on a local firing range.

"I cann'a, cover both the front drive and the inside of the compound sitting in one position, so I was wondering if you could get me a wheel chair so that I can push ma' sel quickly to cover both sides?"

Anne volunteered to pick up a wheel chair immediately.

The workshops made an attachment for the wheel chair so that Gillie's splinted and bandaged leg could be supported out in front of him and Gillie soon learned to propel himself rapidly round the large room to cover all the windows overlooking the compound and the front driveway. The loaded rifle was stowed in a leather 'boot' attached to the side of the wheel chair.

Late in the afternoon Raymond returned from finding out where the peddler woman lived and came up to Gillie's room, which had become an operations center, and said.

"Bwana, I have found where the peddler woman lives, it is an old, run down place out along the North road. There is a small house and a few sheds."

Mark said.

"I think we should plan to go tonight before she has a chance of disappearing."

"Yes I agree, and I suggest that at least three o' you go as we don't know who may still be there." Said Gillie.

"Raymond, Tad and myself can go before it gets dark, I will take a rifle and Tad and Raymond can have revolvers. We will need to leave in about an hour. Can you think of anything else that we should take?"

"Perhaps ye' should tak' some cord in case there are any prisoners to tie up and a lantern in case it tak's a wee bit longer than expected." Said Gillie.

Mjuba came in and said that the vet had arrived.

"Thank you Mjuba, would you bring him up please."

The vet was introduced to Gillie and then said.

"My findings were so alarming that I thought that I should come in person to explain the extreme danger that this has created.

Putting about two pints of arsenic into that tank is enough to kill half of the population!

The tank, trough and all the pipes will be contaminated and will have to be replaced, as it is not possible to remove all the poison from them.

The samples that I took from both horses were loaded with arsenic, so were the samples from the trough and tank, but the sample from the house supply was clear.

What did you find in the other houses?"

As Mark was explaining the tragedy that had been found in the houses to the vet, Mjuba brought in the doctor who still looked in a state of shock.

The vet and doctor then exchanged details of their respective findings.

The doctor said.

"You realize that as there is loss of life involved, that I am duty bound to report to the authorities. There are two women, and now five small children dead and two more children sent to the hospital for treatment, but they may also die."

Mark said.

"We understand, and thank you for coming so quickly, let's hope that you have saved the lives of the other two children. Please be ready to come very quickly if we have any more cases of poisoning. Is there any anti dote that we should have ready?"

"Sorry, there is nothing known for arsenic, it is very powerful and acts so quickly."

"We are planning on 'having no idea of how the poison got into the water supply,' to minimize any bureaucratic heavy handed response and rely on your discretion to do likewise. Based on your advice, the whole system will be replaced as soon as possible.

We will also put a locked cover on all tanks in future."

The doctor and vet were then shown out with more thanks for their fast responses.

Mark, Raymond and Tad then went to the stable and started to load up three horses with equipment ready for the raiding party.

Just as dusk was approaching, three riders dismounted and tethered their horses in a patch of scrub a short distance from the old house and quickly went along a fence line to the back of the house.

Raymond and Tad went to the back door and tried the handle while Mark covered them from one side. The door was unlocked and swung open. They went in with revolvers drawn and moved through the house but there was no one home.

They then went to the stable and cautiously approached the open door.

The two loaded pack horses were still tied up in their stalls and a pile of old clothes was just inside the door.

A muffled groan came from a vacant stall and on getting closer they found the old peddler woman, in just her ragged under wear, in a semi concussed state, tied up, gagged and with a still bleeding gash on her head and dried blood on her face and body, lying on the floor.

Tad sat her up leaning against the stall, cut her bonds, removed the gag and gave her some water in a tin mug.

"What happened to you, who beat you up?"

After a while she recovered a little and said.

"Get me a brandy from the kitchen cupboard first." Raymond complied and the old woman gradually recovered a bit more.

"That bitch jumped me, roughed me' up, left me' with a bleeding gash on the 'ead and took me' 'orses!"

When the old woman had had another drink and put her clothes on, and Tad and Raymond had bound up the gash on her head, Mark asked what had happened.

"I was just loaded up for me' rounds when this woman in a mask jumped me' from behind and beat me with a stick till I was knocked down, then she made me take me' clothes off, and tied that rag in me' mouth. I was then tied up.

The bitch then took her own clothes off and put my clothes on and took off with me' loaded 'orses.

The next thing that I remember was the bitch back in the stable and busy swapping her clothes again, I just pretended to be dead. The bitch even came and kicked me a few times, but I never moved. I think the bitch thought that she had killed me 'cos she called to someone and said. The old bag has chocked, we must get out fast, fetch our 'orses.

It was another Boer woman who answered, but I could not see her."

They helped the old woman into the house and helped her to prepare some food which she ate noisily and then Mark said.

"Did you get a chance to look at the woman's face, or is there anything else that you could tell us about her appearance?"

"There was a moment that she took the mask off while she was changing into my clothes and I saw her face, she is a Boer of about 40 with brown hair and a long, thin face, but I could not see how tall she is."

Mark then said.

"Thank you for helping us, we can't tell you at the moment what they did while they had your pack horses, but it was a very serious crime and we think that the idea was that you would get the blame, so we suggest that you 'know nothing."

"When there is any trouble I never know's nothink, I don't know who you are, but thank you for 'elping me, if you 'ad not come, I could have died 'cos I was still bleeding and I live on me' own so nobody comes to visit. I must go and see to the poor bloody 'orses 'cos they are still loaded and tied up."

Back at SATCO Gillie was given the details of the visit to the peddler woman's house and his comment was.

"Well, I had expected that she had been blackmailed into putting the poison into the tank, but the impersonation trick was a carefully planned move that must have been well researched. Do you think that the authorities will follow up and that she will get the blame?"

"If we say nothing about the peddler woman they will have no connection with her.

As we know, there is so much anti- British hatred among the Boer officials that they will either twist the facts to incriminate some innocent person or just ignore an attempt to poison a bunch of 'Uitlanders'. We must advise Millie to say nothing about the peddler woman."

Gillie said.

"Ye will remember when I was training you and your brother back in Scotland when we talked aboot the different types of terrorist?"

"Yes, but please refresh my memory, that was a long time ago."

"Well, there are three main types o' terrorist.

The first is the type who is retaliating against what they consider as some injustice or oppression, and of course, this is the case we have here because of the sale of the Dutch settler's land in The Cape of Good Hope from under their feet by their own Government to Britain for six million quid, back in 1814. That caused very deep seated hatred and vengeance that has lasted several generations already, and I don't think it will stop for a long time to come.

The second type of terrorist is the territory grabber fanatic usually backed by a 'would be' dictator or junta Government who manipulates the operatives in the field to achieve more power and or territory.

We have a new small component of this type here trying to apply leverage on Britain to hurry up and approve the formation of the new Union of South Africa so that the Boers can be boss of the land that they reckon is rightfully theirs, in spite of gladly accepting six million quid, cash for it.

The third type of terrorist is the most dangerous.

The religious fanatic who is selected, trained and manipulated, usually by religious leaders who are trying to gain power and or influence in their own country, or more often, in other countries as well. The operatives are selected, trained and brain washed so that they put their 'cause' or 'Jihad' (Holy war) before all else, even to the point of undertaking life sacrificing missions.

There have been many terrorist regimes based on religious fanaticism such as the persecution and mass murder of the Protestant Huguenots in France by the local Catholics and Papal armies, or the infiltration into developed countries by Muslim extremists trying to gain power and territory, as in the Austrian and Ottoman squabbles."

Fortunately we do not appear to have any of this type here."

"Thank you Gillie, now your training is coming back to me and it all starts to make sense and I can see who the enemy is and how he is motivated."

First thing next morning Mark engaged a plumbing contractor to replace the complete contaminated water system and fit a locked lid to a new tank.

A few days later two young policemen went to the big house and questioned Anne, then went and had a cursory look at the site where the tank and trough were being replaced.

Some notes were made in a book and they left without any comment.

Chapter 3

THE ENEMY REVEALED

A few days later Mark, Gillie and Anne were still piecing together the information required for the assignment. George had been very helpful in obtaining information from Government sources where he had many contacts in high places.

Several small nuisance type incidents at SATCO had kept everyone on high alert.

On one occasion two youths, who had been hiding in a covered wagon that came into the yard in the late afternoon, and then hidden in a stores area till the night guards were alerted about midnight. The guards blew a whistle and then gave chase with revolvers drawn.

Gillie awoke and was able to fire a few warning shots in the air as the youths tried to climb over the high side gate.

The guards then tied up the youths and Mark was called down to question them.

It appeared that the boys had been promised a few pounds to hide in a wagon going to pick up supplies, hide among some boxes, and then after dark cause as much trouble as possible by turning on the taps of the barrels of lamp oil, turpentine and any other liquids in the flammable goods shed.

Fortunately, when they entered the shed they had knocked over an empty oil drum with a clatter and alerted the guards.

Mark asked.

"Who paid you to do this and where do you work?"

"We don't know, we just got an envelope passed to us at work with a note and the promise of money, we work at the livery stables, the money will come in another envelope when we done the job, there would be a bonus if we started a fire."

Further questioning produced nothing more so the boys were released with threats of severe punishment if they were ever seen again anywhere near SATCO.

Gillie said.

"That was a very cunning way of getting your dirty work done without exposing yourself.

We have an enemy who thinks and plans every move and must have a lot of information about how SATCO operates.

Do you think that there could be a spy at SATCO?

"That is possible, but I can't think of any suspects, the staff all appear totally trustworthy."

Gillie said.

"Can we get the day guards to check all carts and covered wagons that come into the yard in an 'as inconspicuous a way' as possible?"

"Yes, that can be made part of their duties. Perhaps we can move their hut to just inside the entrance and they can go to greet each driver and have a good look inside every vehicle at the same time?

As you say, it does look as though they are getting a lot of information about SATCO.

If they had set fire to all that flammable liquid, it would have made a very hot fire immediately. We must put a padlock on the shed as soon as possible."

Mark supervised the guard hut being put onto two long baulks of timber, dragged across the yard by two horses and repositioned just inside the compound by the main entrance.

Over lunch, Mark and Gillie continued their discussion. Gillie said.

"Do we know the livery stable where the boys work?"

"I expect Raymond will know, I will ask Mjuba to fetch him."

When he had arrived, Raymond said that there was only one livery stable in the area which was owned by a very wealthy man who also had a cartage business.

Tad was called in as soon as he had finished visiting the mines for the day and given all the details.

"Do you think that you can find an excuse to visit the livery stables and have a chat with some of the lads working there? Perhaps you need help with moving some 'goods' or 'something'? If they are used to doing shady work they may open up and show their hand. You may then be able to find who delivered the envelope to the boys who came here and made trouble in the flammable goods shed."

"Yer' I can go and could say that I have some explosives to be moved, on the 'quiet' like. We could make up some boxes with old Dynamite wrappers filled with clay molded into shape, same as we used to do back home to confuse the customs men.

Just give me a day or two to make up the dummies and make a few more enquiries."

Mark then went to see Abdul and get more, in depth information on the business.

Abdul was pleased with the ever increasing demand for all their products and services which was in keeping with the growth of the area but he had been alerted by the staff to a number of instances where one or two well-dressed strangers came into the store and spent a long time observing everything and perhaps making just a token small purchase.

"It is as though they are doing a survey with view to a takeover or the establishment of a rival company.

The 'Gold Fever' foreigners go for any opportunity in the mines and keep buying existing mines or starting up new mines, but the clever ones, particularly the continentals, look for opportunities in the 'service industries supporting the mines' and this of course is where SATCO is placed where it is safer and less of a speculation risk.

I am tempted to go and talk to some of these men doing a survey, but expect that they would just deny that they are doing a survey as they would not want to show their hand.

What do you think they are up to?"

"Your guess is right, I am sure that this is proof that the whole area is developing very fast and we can expect more foreign investors to arrive, but I wonder if the newcomers realize that the whole structure of South Africa could change at any time. It is still a very fragile balance between the British and Boer government's respective policies.

George has found out that the local banks are getting greedy and are flooding the financial scene with loan money to ensure that they get the lion's share of the new found wealth coming from the mines.

The way that the Boers exploit the Black workers and keep them suppressed and in poverty, is a powder keg of frustration, anger and pent up racial hatred waiting to explode, but that may be a long way off yet."

Abdul said.

"Provided we continue to treat all our employees equally, regardless of colour, we should not have any problems from the black employees. But we are already under Boer threats because of our equal pay policy. Some of the Boer owned customers only buy from SATCO when there is no other supplier available."

Two days later Tad came up to the ops. room to report on his exploits with transporting the 'explosives' to an abandoned mine a few miles away with the 'cover story' that he had found 'another gold bearing seam that had been over looked and was going to do some exploratory blasting,' and then gave details of what had happened.

"After the dummy Dynamite had been delivered, I waited a few hours and then went into the old mine and set off a couple o' sticks of real stuff to make it look real and as I was about to come out of hiding, I saw two men riding away so I s'pose they will report to their boss woman that they saw the exploratory blast. I wonder if they will go in to see how good the seam is, actually there was quite a likely seam where I laid the charges!

Them at the stables are right into all sorts of 'odd jobs' and were very 'elpful. They tried to question me about getting more Dynamite a bit later on for some big job that they are planning, seems to be two women at the back o' this. They offer big cash payment for everything. So I said I can get more Dynamite, at a price!

Wanted to know all about SATCO, but I just said that I was new here and don't know much and don't want to be sent back to the old dart to face the music."

A clatter of wheels and horses hooves on the cobbled entry under the arch and children's voices made them all look down into the yard below.

Mark immediately recognized Mike and Sheila Burgess from the BCE coffee plantation, and went down to greet them.

Sheila was in tears and was looking very distressed. The children looked tired and disheveled and Mike looked exhausted.

"Hello to you all, how are you?"

"Hello Mark, we have come with sad news and to ask for your help."

"We are always pleased to help, but firstly come up to where Gillie is recovering and then you can tell us all about your problems."

Mike paid off the cab, rounded up his family and followed Mark up to Gillie's room.

Mjuba quickly provided coffee and food for the visitors and they all sat close to where Gillie sat in his wheel chair. Mjuba then took the children to Mark's sitting room to play.

"Firstly, we came here to give you the sad news about John and May Ashcroft.

Their shamba was raided two days ago and they were both killed and their shamba was burnt.

Our plantation had just been sold by the BCE area manager to a local consortium and we were given the option to stay on and continue to manage as before, or, BCE would give us three months' salary and our fare back to Britain.

With the renewed terrorist threats against our native workmen and considering our two small children's safety we decided to pack up and go as soon as possible.

We set off for Pietersburg with our cart loaded with a few trunks and boxes and on the way called in to say good by to John and May Ashcroft at Glendarvel.

As we approached their shamba we detected that horrible smell of burning huts and human bodies!

Sheila stayed with the cart and looked after the children while one of our porter boys came with me to investigate.

It was terrible, their hut had been burnt to the ground and their charred bodies were among the ashes. The native village close by had also been burned down with many bodies in the ashes but there were a few young men there who had been off hunting during the raid and were still alive and in a state of fear. We offered to take them with us but they wanted to stay and try to put their lives together again in the only place that they knew even though they had lost their huts and all of their equipment.

We got to Pietersburg, dumped our luggage at the station, sold the horse and cart, paid off our porter boys and came on the next train to stay in a cheap hotel for a few days, till it is time to go to Durban to catch the ship, and to give you the sad news.

There is of course the grim task of informing the two Ashcroft girls about their parents. Fortunately the girls were at college here in Johannesburg at the time of the raid.

Can you give me moral support while the girls are given the sad news?"

"Yes of course. We are very shocked and saddened with the news about John and May and are sorry that you and your family are leaving, but these things have a way of turning out for the better, so you must look forward to a new start when you get back to Britain."

"Aye' that is verra' sad and I am truly sorry for the poor girls. Could I suggest that you, Mark, go and fetch the girls and gi' them the news here where they can be a wee bit private and no' with a crowd o, girls at college."

"Yes, I will go and see the principal immediately, we can ask Mjuba to get camp beds for them from the store and they can sleep in the sitting room.

If their parents were targets, then the terrorist's mind will also target their children so we will have to look after them very carefully."

Mark took a large cab to the college and asked the driver to wait.

The Principal was a middle aged woman with graying hair tied up in a bun. She greeted Mark warmly and asked him into her office. Mark had tried to plan what to say but was only able to put the facts bluntly.

"Thank you for seeing me at such short notice. I have come regarding a tragedy affecting the Ashcroft sisters.

Their parent's shamba was raided by terrorists, and both parents were killed and the house burnt to the ground a few days ago.

Some of their neighbors have just arrived at SATCO and given us the very sad news.

My life was saved with emergency surgery by the girl's father, Major John Ashcroft, and I lived with his family while I recovered and we have been close friends for many years. We would like the girls to be in a safe and familiar place when we give them the sad news.

We would then look after them, if that is what they would like. The only relative that we know of is John's 80 year old father living in Scotland.

Now that the parents have been targeted, it is usually the case that their children will also be targeted.

So it is essential that the girls are in a safe place. We have 24 hour armed guards at SATCO now."

The principal was visibly shocked and said.

"That is terrible Mr. Oakhill, the poor girls have lost everything. What are your plans now?"

"I am out here to sort out another tragedy and will be returning to England as soon as the other problems are resolved. Probably in another six to eight weeks."

"You realize that I am responsible for the borders but I can't see any alternative other than as you suggest. Do you plan to take the girls back to England with you?"

"Yes, if that is what they want. My wife is also a close friend of the girls and we have two small children of our own in England. If there are any fees or expenses from the college I will be happy to pay their account."

"Can you wait while I have a discussion with a collegue and then I will bring the girls?"

"Yes certainly."

After a long wait, the principal returned with Sally and Sarah who both rushed up to Mark and kissed him, but they then looked puzzled and sensed that there was some sinister purpose for the visit.

A college house matron and a manservant then arrived with the girl's luggage and the principal saw them off to the waiting cab.

While they traveled along the girls asked lots of questions about Mark's children and what was happening at SATCO, but it was obvious that they were trying to find out the real reason for their sudden move to SATCO.

As the girls walked into Mark's sitting room, Mike Burgess stepped forward and greeted them and they all sat down. Mark noticed that the Burgess children and their mother had been moved to Gillie's room.

Mike said.

"I am afraid that we have some very sad news for you.

When we called to see your parents on our way here, we found that their shamba had been raided, your parents killed and the house burned.

We are all very sad and sorry, please let us know if there is anything that we can do."

Sally and Sarah hugged each other and then came and sat each side of Mark while they sobbed.

The girls had always had devoted parents and had worked as a close family team so this sudden loss was a terrible shock for them.

Mike Burgess got up and as he left Mark asked him to send in Mjuba.

Mjuba brought in a tray of cups of tea and homemade short bread biscuits.

The girls went up to her and held her hands which reduced Mjuba to tears and they all sat down again.

Mark said.

"Sasha and I are more than pleased to make a home for you and have you as part of our family and provide all that you need. I will leave you now and Mjuba will look after you for a while."

Mark returned to the ops. room, as it was now called, and felt physically drained after the very sad and emotional experience with Sally and Sarah.

Gillie looked very distressed and said.

"I think we all need a wee dram after all that. Just to settle our nerves and help us to think straight."

Mark got a bottle of whisky and some glasses and poured the drinks.

Gillie asked.

"When does your ship leave Mike?"

"Gustav has us booked on a mixed cargo and passenger ship in four or five days' time from Durban to London via the Suez canal and the Med. The children are so excited at the idea of going on a ship. It will be a real experience for them.

We will have to stay with my parents at Henley on Thames at first till I can get a job and find a house. We are all very tired so please excuse us if we go now and call in again tomorrow before we go to catch the train. Good night."

After the Burgess family had left, Mjuba brought in the Ashcroft girls and suggested that she went out to get some more fresh food and then cook dinner for everyone.

The girls were struggling with their grief and were glad to have each other and close friends with them. Mark tried to think of suitable topics of conversation but could not come up with anything. Gillie talked about his life in Scotland.

Suddenly the bell cord at the main gate was pulled violently and there was calling from down below.

Gillie grabbed his rifle and went to the window overlooking the driveway.

Mark went carefully down the stairs and into the cobbled entrance under the archway with his revolver drawn to find two strong looking black men supporting Mjuba near the gate.

One man said. "Two white woman attack poor girl, so we broke their heads together and find where to go for her." Mark put the revolver in his pocket and opened the gate, let them in, locked the gate and asked them to take Mjuba to the room upstairs. Gillie was at the ready with his rifle so Mark signaled that it was alright and Gillie put his rifle away.

Mjuba was laid out on Gillie's bed and showed signs of recovery. Gillie wheeled himself alongside the bed and started to check on the cuts and bruises while Mark talked to the two men. Sally and Sarah had already got a bowl of hot water and a first aid kit and were soon bathing and bandaging the wounds.

The two black men were pleased to have been able to save Mjuba from serious harm and talked freely about the attack.

"Yes, two Boer white woman, all tall and strong with stick. They lie down now, longtime."

"Maybe them die?"

"We no kill, jus' knock head together, make lie down longtime."

Mark offered money which was not accepted so he got a few tins of ham from the store which were accepted gladly and off they went.

Mjuba was now sitting up and was talking to Gillie and the girls.

"Please tell us what happened."

"When I was about half way to the shops I was followed by two women, I tried to hide but they chased me into a laneway and stated to beat me and to question me while they held me down.

They wanted to know all about SATCO, who was living in the quarters, how many guards are there at night, where is the money kept and so on. When I would not tell them anything they hit me with sticks and knocked me down again, then the two good men came and banged their heads together till they were knocked out on the ground.

The two men then brought me here."

Mark asked.

"Did you see the women clearly enough to describe them?"

"They were both Africaner women, one about 40 and the other a lot older, both fairly tall and skinny. I could not see too much in the poor light."

Gillie said. "Sounds like the women who attacked the peddler. I wonder if one of them is the leader of the local terrorists. They must be getting desperate to show themselves just to try to get information."

Mjuba was getting tired so she was helped to get into her bed in the next room.

Sally and Sarah made up their camp beds in Mark's sitting room.

Gillie had just gone to sleep that night when he was awoken by Mjuba calling out from the next room. He struggled out of bed and limped into the room with his revolver drawn expecting to find an intruder, and found that Mjuba was having a violent nightmare.

He gently shook her shoulder till she woke up but she was still living the fear of the dream and said. "I am sure that they are following me all the time. Please take me with you to England, I don't want to be left here with the Boers everywhere."

Gillie tried to console her and had to agree that now Mjuba had been attacked that she was likely to be marked as a target for obtaining information again.

They talked on about what a move to England would involve and Gillie was aware that in spite of the recent loss of

Alice, he had become dependent on Mjuba and was starting to become very fond of her, so agreed to take her with him. Mjuba was so pleased that she drew back the bed clothes so that he could get in beside her.

After a while, Gillie suggested that it would be a good idea if she changed her name to something more English. Mjuba said that she had been forced to use the tribal name given to her by her grandmother after her parents had been taken from the family business by the slavers and that she had always liked the name Jill but had not been allowed to use it, but would be pleased to change her name as soon as possible, if this was allowed by the government.

Gillie liked the name Jill and said that he would talk it over with Mark.

Chapter 4

THE ASSIGNMENT

Mark went to his bedroom, sat at the desk and started to draft out a cable to Sasha. He must be very careful on how the cable was to be worded due to the 'open' nature of cables.

> SATCO.
> Johannesburg
> South Africa.
>
> Oakhill Hall
> Cheshire UK.
> Telephone Brockington 65
>
> 'Visitor recovering well.
>
> BCE. sold and boss returning home.
>
> Both at Glendarvel same as Alice.
>
> S and S coming home with me.
>
> Best option firming as plan B
>
> Please phone south.
>
> Xxx. M.

Gillie returned after three days in hospital for minor surgery on his leg and he was now doing exercises every day. He was even able to use crutches to walk a little more each day.

George and Anne came to the ops. room for a meeting to finalize the data for the assignment.

All the information was summarized on separate slips of paper and arranged in the order of the relevant question and the results entered up.

~~~~~~

Q. What is the current breakdown of large companies by country of ownership?

	%
A. South Africa.	40
Britain.	30
Holland.	15
Germany.	5
Others.	10

IF THE INDEPENDENT UNION OF SOUTH AFRICA IS FORMED.

Q. what will happen to foreign owned businesses?

A. Local banks are getting greedy and are making plenty of poorly secured money available to ensure that they get the lion's share of the wealth coming from the mines and new businesses.

Thus the local ownership (With a lot of bank money.) is increasing rapidly.

The Africaners also need as much support and numbers of white owners (regardless of nationality) to strengthen their position over the black majority, so foreign owned businesses will be supported in the short term, particularly if there is a part local ownership. In the longer term it is expected that foreign owners could be squeezed out.

Q. Will foreigners have voting rights?

A. Yes, almost certainly, all whites will continue to get the vote to maximize on numbers of total whites, but the blacks will never get the vote under an Africaner Government.

Q. How will black people be classed and treated.

A. The Africaners are very much aware of the threat to their power by the vast majority of black people and will continue to treat them as inferiors and keep them segregated and in poverty.

All people of mixed race, even quarter casts or people with lesser coloured heritage, are classed as black.

There is, however, a twist in Africaner law which allows some coloured people to be classed as 'temporary whites' when there is some political or financial advantage! For example, Asians investing large sums of money into local businesses are classed as 'temporary whites'.

Q. Who is orchestrating the current terrorist attacks?

A. Current terrorist activity is mostly confined to reprisal type attacks against anyone who was involved in the last stages of the war, particularly if they have British connections.

We have had renewed, targeted, terrorist attacks at SATCO since I arrived which appear to be planned and executed by two middle aged women.

The raids in remote areas have been carried out by groups of up to twenty men attacking only target rural properties. We have not yet been able to get any details.

There is a new type of terrorist activity which is based on the Boer's theory that strategic attacks are a very strong form of leverage to make Britain hurry up and sign the agreement for the Independent Union of South Africa to be formed.

Q. Will a new government have permanent armed forces?

A. Yes. We also find that they plan to have the maximum possible number of armaments manufactured locally and will be seeking access to design and manufacture technology from overseas companies. eg. Small arms and ammunition manufacturers.

Q. What is the likely relationship between a Union of South Africa and Britain?

A. There is a realization of a need to get as much strategic help as possible to protect the local high value resources, and the territory of course, so it is felt that they will be happy to build defense ties with Britain.

There is a fairly strong German community in the Eastern area which will probably side with Germany in the event of any conflict.

We add these comments.

Due to the gross exploitation of the black workers, particularly in the mines, there is an increasing cohesion among the black workers and they are now demanding safer working conditions (The death rate in the mines is appalling.) higher wages and the freedom to live under better conditions.

These demands by the black workers have strengthened the Africaner's resolve to keep all black people suppressed and in poverty and they are in the process of drafting draconian laws to enforce their policy.

We have also noticed a number of business men in Johannesburg conducting clandestine surveys, presumably with view to buying existing businesses or setting up new businesses.

The talk of 'Gold Fever in South Africa' is widespread in Europe and is attracting takeovers and the start of new mines.

The discovery of diamonds is rumored and reports suggest that they have found very high quality stones which can be mined by fairly simple methods.

Mark said to Gillie.

"Do you think that it is safe to post this report to Sasha, so that she can forward it on to the Colonel?"

"Yes, but I suggest that you put pages of some other letters between the pages of the report and make sure that the envelope is flat and normal looking."

So the assignment was soon on its way to Sasha.

Back at Oakhill Hall, Sasha was outside playing with the children when the telephone rang and a cable was read out by the operator. Sasha's interpretation was:

The cable was from Mark to say that John and May Ashcroft had been murdered at their shamba, but their two girls are safe. The Burgess family, who live close to the Ashcrofts, are leaving their coffee plantation and are returning to Britain.

It looks as though Mark will have to sell up and I presume that it is likely that his sister, Anne, and her husband George will also decide to come back to England.

I have to advise Colonel Wilkinson immediately.

Sasha left the children with the nanny and Mark's mother and went into the study and booked a call to Colonel Wilkinson.

"Hello Colonel, This is Sasha. I hope you are both well. We have had a cable from Mark."

"Hello and I hope that both you and Mark are well, perhaps he has sent some interesting news?"

"Yes, he has given some masked information. I will give you my interpretation.

Major John Ashcroft, the ex-Army doctor, who saved Mark's life, and his wife May have been murdered at their Shamba in the bush, some distance North of Pietersburg.

The BCE coffee plantation nearby has been sold and the English manager is returning home.

It looks as though Mark will have to sell SATCO.

Do you think that I should reply?"

"Yes certainly, and I know you will be careful with what you say. You might like to tell him that I recommend that if he decides to sell that he cables 'Warringtons of London.' They are the best international commercial brokers, have an office in Cape Town, and usually get the best results quickly.

Thank you for keeping me informed and I look forward to meeting Mark in London when he returns.

All this information is very important and is helping us to keep up to date.

Thank you both very much, you are providing vital information.

Oh yes, I have a sister who lives at Neston in the Wirral just the other side of Chester, quite close to you and we are overdue to visit her so perhaps we can call in next time we are in the area?"

"Yes, we will be delighted to see you both again. You are always welcome, just let us know when you are coming and we will meet you off the train.

Kindest regards to you both. Goodbye."

Sasha went to the drawing room and sat down and tried to put her thoughts together.

When Mark comes home he will be bringing the two Ashcroft, now orphaned, teenage daughters with him.

They are delightful girls and having been raised at John's shamba in the bush are very mature and resourceful. They have been at a new girl's college in Johannesburg for a short time and must be about fourteen and thirteen, I think.

It is also very likely that Gillie will decide to return to Britain, but he will need somewhere to live now that there is a farm manager living in his old house at Glencairn.

When Mark sells SATCO. I wonder what he will do with the proceeds of the sale?

There should be a fortune if the sale goes well!

The housekeeper came in and said.

"Young Jack Dutton has come to the back door to ask for someone to come quickly as his grandfather, old Bill Huxley at the lodge is very sick and he thinks that he is dying."

"Tell Jack that I will come as soon as possible."

Sasha put on her hat and coat and hurried down the drive to the lodge and was met by young Jack who just ushered her into the house.

Old Bill was sitting slumped forward in his favorite chair by the fireside.

Sasha felt for a pulse, but there was nothing. She then closed his eyelids and sat him up in the chair.

Jack just looked on.

"Jack, your grandfather has died peacefully and he will suffer no more. Can you go home and tell your mother. I will stay here till she arrives."

Jack hurried off on his bicycle and Sasha was left alone with the black cat which kept rubbing against her legs so she picked it up and stroked it. It seemed to know that the old man was dead and it wanted human contact and comforting.

Eventually Bill's daughter arrived and Sasha was able to go home.

As soon as Sasha got home she wrote out a cable to send to Mark.

> 'Cable received.
> South recommends you cable Cape Town office of Warringtons of London.
> Best international brokers with fast results.
> Lodge now vacant.
> S and S very welcome.
> All well here.
> Xxx Sasha.

When the cable arrived, Abdul took it up to the ops. room where Mark, Anne, George and Gillie were about to start the vital discussion about the future of SATCO.

"Thank you Abdul.

We need you to join us as we are about to discuss the current situation affecting the future of SATCO."

Abdul sat down and Mark continued.

"The time has come when we have to take a perspective look at the future of SATCO.

We are being targeted by Boer terrorists again and this is putting the staff and business at risk.

The poisoned water and the attempted arson attack are thought to be the start of ongoing trouble, particularly as we are a British owned company. Also Gillie's and my involvement in finishing off the Boers at the end of the war are contributing factors.

We also expect major changes in Government policy very soon.

Now that we have gathered some more information we have to make a decision on the future of SATCO and the staff.

Now I need to know what Anne and George, Gillie, you Abdul, and later, all the staff, want to do if we sell the business.

My thoughts are firming towards selling, but I welcome your thoughts and plans if we sell."

"I think that we should sell, Anne and I have talked it over and we would like to sell our business and return to England, particularly now that we have started a family." Said George.

Abdul looked a bit shocked and said.

"I have made SATCO my life for nearly 20 years and would find it hard to start again anywhere else so I would stay on and see what the new owners are like to work for before making a decision to leave. Also, we have family here so we would stay in Johannesburg anyway."

Gillie said.

"Noo' that I have lost Alice, my life has been totally changed and I would not want to live at the MacIntyre farm with the sad memories any more. I am like a fish out o' water in a city so I want to 'gang heme', when I have two good legs again, and get somewhere in the country."

"Well, that looks as though selling is an acceptable option. Now we can cable a business broker and get the ball rolling to see what it is worth,"

They chatted on for a long time about how each one would be affected and could not come up with any serious alternative suggestions.

Mark said.

"I think it is too early to say anything to the rest of the staff so please keep this strictly to yourselves at this stage.

We have a 'secure tenancy plan' for those living in company houses and the details will be available shortly."

Mark went to his sitting room where the girls were sorting out their luggage.

"The loss of John and May is a terrible shock and very sad for all of us and we want to help you to adjust and put your lives together as soon as possible. I have cabled Sasha and she sends her love and would be happy to have you as part of our family in England.

Perhaps you can let me know what you would like to do when you have had time to think about the future."

Without hesitation both girls went over to Mark and held his hands while the tears rolled down their cheeks.

"Mum and Papa always treated you like one of the family while you were recovering from the wounding and we looked to you as a sort of brother or uncle and we love Sasha, so yes we will be pleased to come and live as part of your family." Said Sally.

Sarah just nodded in agreement as she was too overcome with grief to speak.

"Well, that is what we hoped that you would want to do, so now you just settle in here while I sort out selling the business and the MacIntyre farm and then we can book a passage. Gillie also wants to return to England so he will be coming with us.

George and Anne want to return to England but may have to stay on for a while to sell their business."

Mark gave each a hug and then started to write out a cable to Warrington's office in Cape Town.

Within an hour there was a reply cable.

'Thank you for your valued request for our services.

Sending a leading broker to stay Johannesburg for duration of negotiations.

William Collins will contact you on arrival tomorrow.

Kindest regards. Reginald Barker. manager.

Warringtons of London. Cape Town.

Chapter 5

BACK IN THE BUSH

As Gillie was not yet mobile enough to go back to the farm, he prepared a list of what he wanted brought back.

Mark and Raymond set off on the train to Pietersburg, picked up horses from the livery stable and headed for the farm.

It was decided to go to the depression out in the veldt first and use the binoculars to check on the farm before going up to the house.

The house and barn looked the same, the irrigation area seemed to be flourishing and all looked normal.

They tethered their horses in some scrub at the end of the irrigation and walked towards the buildings.

When they arrived at the native shamba down by the irrigation area they were met by a number of the resident natives who greeted them warmly.

When Makede appeared, Mark quickly confirmed what had happened at Glendarvel and that there had been more Boer attacks at SATCO.

"Have you seen any Boers round here recently?"

"Bwana, plenty Boers near mos' time. Come again soon maybe. We no like Boers come. Take plenty food and hurt young girls."

Two young native boys ran up to Makede and said that there was a group of Boers riding up to the shamba.

Mark arranged that Makede and the other natives quickly went to their huts while he went into the barn with Raymond and took up position to observe and fight if necessary.

Four horsemen rode up through the house paddock in a confident manner and on reaching the native shamba started to demand young girls and food.

When no girls or food appeared one man went into a hut and dragged out a terrified girl of about eighteen and held a gun to her head while he grinned and made lewd signs and suggestions and then tore her clothes open and touched her intimately.

Mark applied all Gillie's training and his own experience and aimed his rifle at the man's thigh and fired.

The man was thrown backwards by the impact and then collapsed. The other three Boers were taken completely by surprise but reacted quickly, took cover, started looking to find where the shot had come from and soon started shooting back.

Raymond had taken up a position just inside one of the open windows in the side of the barn while Mark had climbed up to the loft and was lying just inside the large opening designed for loading hay.

Mark remembered the list of items that Gillie wanted brought back and that the cache of weapons should be hidden in a pocket in the thatch just above his head.

Gillie had got Makede to help him to hide two rifles, a double barrel shot gun, a revolver and some ammunition wrapped in a tarpaulin in the pocket in the thatch when he was lying wounded in the loft after Alice had been shot.

This was the same place where Mark had hidden with Jean MacIntyre when he was wounded about eight years previously. On that occasion they had had to stay hidden in the pocket in the thatch for a long time while a party of Boer soldiers had camped in the barn overnight.

Raymond was now firing a few shots from down below so Mark took the opportunity to slide the bundle of weapons out of the pocket, loaded the rifles and shotgun, then laid them out within easy reach.

Movement out on the veld caught Mark's eye and he saw a group of about ten men galloping towards the barn. By their clothing and their fast response, they must be more Boers alerted by the gunfire and were coming to help their friends hiding down in the irrigation area.

While the horsemen were tethering their horses at the end of the irrigation, Mark opened fire as quickly as possible with each rifle, then the shot gun loaded with number 4 shot. He then reloaded and hoped that his ruse of using a range of weapons in quick succession would give the impression that there were many 'Uitlanders' in the barn.

Several of the Boers were down and the rest took cover.

Mark and Raymond were hopelessly out numbered with only a limited supply of ammunition.

Mark used Gillie's snap shooting training and his own experience to shoot two more Boers and Raymond was sure that he had 'winged' a couple so there were still about seven or eight Boers, who are some of the best bush trained riflemen in the world, surrounding the barn with darkness only about an hour away.

Mark called to Raymond and asked him to come up to the loft where they had a better view from both of the hay loading openings.

Now that the Boers were fully preoccupied, Makede was able to crawl out of the back of his hut with some of the shamba's best hunters armed with knives, bows and spears.

Darkness was rapidly falling and Mark was becoming worried that they could be rushed in the darkness and easily overcome by a group of Boers. He was weighing up the options of staying put or creeping away when it was fully dark.

Sometime later, there was a series of native calls and screams in the direction of the irrigation, a few shots and then silence.

Raymond said.

"That was our tribal call to attack, so should we go and help?"

"It is much too risky in the dark, we would not know who we were shooting at. We must wait till Makede comes back."

After a long time, Makede called from below and then explained how the natives had crept up to the Boer's position and attacked with spears and knives in the dark, but that two or three Boers had escaped into the darkness. They would find that their Horses had been quietly led away and hidden so the Boers would have gone off on foot.

"We mus' follow track when light coming."

Mark and Raymond were glad to get a few hours' sleep in the loft.

As soon as it was light enough Mark, Raymond and a native tracker set off on horseback following the tracks left in the soft ground. The tracker told Raymond that there were three men and that one had a 'sick' leg and was slowing them down.

They had been traveling for about an hour when the tracker held up his hand and then made the sleeping sign and pointed to a rocky area some distance ahead.

Mark had a discussion with Raymond and the tracker and a plan was formed.

Raymond would start shooting at all the likely hiding places among the rocks while Mark and the tracker moved closer and took cover in a fold in the ground, then Mark would start shooting so that Raymond could move to a position over to the left hand side.

When they were in their new positions and had placed a few well aimed shots the Boers started firing back erratically.

Mark could see that the rocks did not provide complete protection for the Boers and was able to apply his skill in snap shooting as the Boers moved round trying to find safer positions among the rocks, and shot two of them.

There was then a long period without any return fire or movement.

Finally, a rifle was raised with a dirty white handkerchief tied round the barrel.

Mark and Raymond advanced with rifles at the ready and found that the last Boer was out of ammunition and was wounded in the leg. He was the man who the tracker had identified as having a 'sick' leg.

Mark took the bolts out of the Boers rifles and put them in his pocket and then gave the wounded man a water bottle and a horse and told him to be on his way South.

Raymond and the tracker doubled up on one horse and they then rode back to the farm.

Mark packed all Gillie's weapons and ammunition in canvas again and put the package back in the pocket in the thatch, to be picked up on their return from Glendarvel.

Early the next morning Mark and Raymond rode off, with one of the Boer's horses as a pack horse, to Glendarvel with sad thoughts about what they would find there.

Raymond started giving native calls as they approached the native shamba and was immediately answered by the young hunters.

A lengthy and emotional discussion was held in Swahili and then Raymond gave Mark the translation which confirmed what Mike Burgess had said when he had arrived at SATCO.

Raymond stayed at the native shamba and gave the young hunters the few essential items that they had brought on the pack horse.

Mark went up to the site of the burnt down Ashcroft shamba with much dread and sorrow.

There were just a few blackened metal and china items among the ashes and a lot of brass cartridge cases of several calibers including 0.577, as normally used in John's, Rigby Express, large bore rifle for elephant and buffalo. He wondered what one of those huge caliber bullets would do to a man!

Presumably John had run out of smaller caliber ammunition and had had to use whatever was available.

Judging by the number of cartridge cases, the Boer terrorists must have had a very hard fight while trying to murder John and May and would have had very many casualties.

John was a very experienced marksman and rarely missed his target!

Mark became aware of a presence behind him!

As he was about to turn with his rifle aimed, he almost subconsciously, recognized a familiar smell.

"Couja harper, Sheeba."

A fully grown lioness was standing a few feet away.

Sheeba rose up on her hind legs and placed her front paws on Marks shoulders and licked his forehead affectionately. Mark talked to her and ran his hand down the length of her back and Sheeba purred.

Mark was amazed that Sheeba had recognized him after all this time and that she was still living in the place where she had been reared from an orphan cub as the Ashcroft's family pet.

John Ashcroft had rescued her when she had been left to starve to death by some German game hunters who had shot her mother and left the cub to die.

When Mark had been brought to John's shamba by Jean for life saving emergency surgery during the Boer war, he had lived for many months as part of the Ashcroft 'family,' which had included Sheeba, while he recovered from major wounding and surgery.

Mark used to go for walks with Sheeba when he was getting stronger after the surgery on his chest and leg and a close bond had developed between them.

Sheeba became very demanding for attention and kept licking his hand and rolling on her back to have her chin and chest rubbed and stayed a long time. It was absolutely wonderful that Sheeba had remembered him and was looking healthy. Judging by her nipples, she was probably still feeding a litter of cubs.

Finally, Sheeba gave a loud call, which Mark thought was to alert her pride that she was returning. She then went across the river and up by the cave where she had kept her first cubs after she had moved them from their birth place in the cellar under John's hut.

It was in front of that same cave where Sheeba had mauled the ex-manager of SATCO, Henk van de Brecht to death when he had gone too close to the cave where the cubs were hidden. That had been while Henk spied on the shamba when he was implementing his vendetta against Mark and SATCO.

It was amazing that Sheeba had recognized Mark and made a 'social' visit after all this time.

The Ashcroft girls will be delighted when I tell them. It was also very probable that Sheeba had her pride living close to the place where she grew up in the care of the Ashcroft family.

Two small mounds with wooden crosses marked the place where Mike Burgess and the porter boy had buried John and May.

As Mark stood by the graves he made a solemn vow to himself to make a lasting memorial for them at a later date. The Ashcroft family had not only saved his life but had become very close and respected friends.

Now that they had visited Glendarvel and given the hunters some essentials to replace those lost in the fire, and had a very welcome surprise visit by Sheeba, Mark was keen to get back to SATCO as soon as possible.

Just an overnight stop at the farm and then the pickup of Gillie's weapons was all that was necessary before heading back to Pietersburg and the train to Johannesburg.

While traveling on the train, Mark thought about how to sell the farm, but this may be difficult. Who would want to buy a remote farm that had been targeted by the Boers?

One option was to sell it to Makede, but the natives had little or no money as they mostly lived off the land and only did the occasional barter or sale for cash to buy tools and essentials.

He seemed to remember that blacks were not allowed to own land under the Africaner laws, or was it that there were some complications that made it very difficult, if not impossible.

Perhaps he could form a small company and lease the farm to Makede and his tribe on a token rental?

He would talk it over with Gillie on his return to SATCO.

William Collins arrived at SATCO and asked for Mr. Oakhill, but was referred to Abdul and Gillie as Mark was away visiting the farm and Glendarvel for the next week or so.

Abdul took William on a complete tour of all the SATCO properties including the main complex, the branch store on the other side of town, the shops and workshops across the road and the company houses on Commando Hill.

Gillie arranged for a desk to be set up in the ops room for William, so that the purpose of his visit would remain confidential at this early stage.

William immediately got to work.

Firstly, he made a summary of the last three years trading from Abdul's account books, then he made a detailed list of all the land and buildings together with an inventory of all the stock on hand.

He then composed a cable, written mostly in company coded abbreviations, which was sent to his Cape Town, London and Paris offices. This took two whole days to complete.

Each office, including his local one in Johannesburg, would then produce a sales catalog for circulation in their area so that prospective buyers could put in preliminary expressions of interest through a local agent who would then check the details on site and advise their client accordingly.

Mark and Raymond arrived at SATCO and went up to the ops room to give the package of weapons and ammunition to Gillie who was delighted to see his beloved weapons and started to check them over right away.

Sally and Sarah had heard Mark return and came into the ops room to greet him and Jill (As Mjuba was now called.) brought in coffee for everyone.

"When I was at Glendarvel I had a very welcome visitor!

I became aware that Sheeba was standing behind me! She then greeted me with all her usual affection and stayed for a long time. I think that she has cubs and a pride of her own living very close."

"That is absolutely wonderful that she remembered you and was still wanting affection, you are very lucky, I am so pleased that she is still living near her old home". Said Sally.

Sarah was overcome with happiness and said.

"I am so glad that Sheeba is still living at our shamba, maybe she feels that she still has to look after and guard the shamba. We had so much pleasure rearing her and seeing her grow up and have her first cubs. I am delighted that she remembered you after all this time. She must have very fond memories of the time that you were living at our shamba. Animals often have remarkable memories, based on familiar smells and sounds in many instances."

William Collins came in with his bundle of books and a note pad. Mark was then introduced to William by Gillie.

"I am very pleased to meet you, and I see that you have already started working on our project.

Have you been able to get an idea of the estimated value yet?"

"Yes, but did you know that you are literally sitting on a gold mine?"

"No, that is news to me. Please explain more."

"Now that we have distributed the catalogs, we have already had one expression of interest from a newly formed local company, which has French backing, at 1.2 million pounds, which is just below where I had put the valuation. I have been told by my informant that the Johannesburg Mining Company, or JMC as they are called, have found that there is a gold bearing seam that has been exposed near the company houses on the lower slope of Commando Hill.

They have even secretly taken samples and had them assayed and the results were excellent, according to my informant.

I was told that the plumbing contractor that you engaged to replace the water system on Commando Hill after the poisoning, decided to leave some of the old contaminated pipes in the ground and put the new pipes in better locations to suit the new street layout.

He is an ex mine captain and recognized the seam as gold bearing immediately when he had to dig deep to go under a road. He has a brother working as a manager for JMC and they were very excited about the potential and immediately arranged for the samples to be taken and an assay to be done in complete secrecy.

They have all been sworn to secrecy of course, but one of my contacts is keeping me informed!"

"Well, that is a total surprise, I wonder if JMC will keep out bidding all others at the auction till they have secured the property?

Abdul has done a 'shirt tail' calculation and thought the value would be around 1.3 million pounds, but if this gold seam is proven what will happen?"

"That will depend on whether another bidder gets the 'smell' of a gold seam and they then bid against each other, these miners can't resist a challenge, particularly if there is gold in the picture!

I agree with Abdul's estimate."

Tad had been following up on the two women and their use of the livery stable and had found that the two 'bombs' (Made up as dummies.) that they had 'ordered' via the boys in the livery stable complete with 3 minute fuses, were to be delivered that same night. The Ashcroft girls had helped Tad to make up the dummies with clay and talcum powder carefully formed into the shape of sticks of Dynamite and then carefully covered them with old Dynamite wrappers. Tad had later added small slices of Dynamite, 'Just to make a bang'.

The 'drop' for the two 'bombs' was to be at midnight at the back gate of the livery stable, so Tad arranged, with a suitable payment, that he could use the front window of the house opposite the livery stables to watch the pick up by the two women, scheduled for one o'clock, with Gillie's powerful binoculars.

Tad delivered the two 'bombs' at midnight and was paid the ten pounds, as promised, and then moved the spring cart to the street behind the house to be used for observation and went into the front room to wait.

It was after one o'clock when a horse drawn van arrived at the back gate of the livery stable and the two boxes were quickly loaded. An envelope was given to someone in the shadows and as the van was about to move off Tad was able to see the outline of a painted over sign by the light of the lamp on the van.

Mark, Gillie and Jill, were anxiously waiting for Tad to return and report on his exploits.

As soon as Tad arrived he said.

"I was able to read part of a sign with your glasses on the pickup van but it had been painted over like, so all I saw was '... de Brecht   Butchers.

Could this be any connection with Henk van de Brecht the ex-manager of SATCO?"

"That is certainly possible, you go and get some sleep and perhaps Jill can ask some of the older employees in the morning."

Before Tad had left the room a series of explosions and a lot of white 'smoke' at the rear of the compound had the night guards running towards the flammable goods shed brandishing fire extinguishers and revolvers.

"Jesus, the bastards did not waste any time planting the first 'bomb'. I will go with one of the guards to check outside the back wall". Said Mark.

Tad went to the flammable goods shed and found that, as planned, all the drama was outside.

Mark used a lamp to check for wheel tracks at the back of the compound but the hard gravel road surface did not have any indication of which way the van had gone.

Tad arrived and checked on the performance of his dummy bomb and explained that the talc powder gave the appearance of 'smoke' from a distance.

There was no damage to the wall and just a few soot stains where the 'bomb' had gone off.

Jill asked around in the morning and found that a fitter in the workshops had done some repair work on Henk van de

Brecht's house a long time ago and remembered that Henks father had had a butchers shop but that he had died many years ago.

While he worked at SATCO Henk had lived with his mother and sister, and the fitter said that he could recognise the house but could not remember the street number.

Mark thanked Jill for obtaining the information so quickly and then discussed the next move with Gillie.

Abdul was becoming very worried about the absence of the chief clerk, Robert Mckenzie, and went in a spring cart to his house to investigate.

The front door was not locked so he called and went inside. The living room was a shambles but there was nobody home.

When Abdul told Gillie about his visit to Robert's house, Gillie said that he would like Jill to help him to have another look. They went in the spring cart and Jill helped Gillie get down from the cart and use his crutches. The house was still unoccupied and they checked every room carefully for clues. Gillie then went to the back door and said.

"I smell trouble." He told Jill not to follow him and headed for the privy in the back garden.

When the door was opened, there was Robert's tied up and rapidly decaying body with obvious signs of torture, finger nails pulled out, burns and bruises.

They hurried back to SATCO and Gillie said that they must quickly find Robert's wife and daughter because they had probably been abducted and used to blackmail Robert into giving information about SATCO.

A raid was planned for the de Brecht house and the fitter was given basic information.

Mark, Tad and the fitter set off in the spring cart and went slowly down the street, as remembered by the fitter, and half way along the street, the de Brecht's house was recognized so they drove slowly round into the street at the back. The fitter stayed with the cart, Tad went to the back door and Mark went to the front door and knocked.

As there was no answer he knocked again but there was still no response. Mark gave a whistle and Tad broke in through the back door and quickly checked inside before letting Mark in through the front door. There was nobody in the house but there was a lean too at the back which was probably a laundry. Tad soon had the locked door prized open with his jemmy bar and they went inside.

Robert's wife and daughter were both securely gagged and bound lying on the floor.

When the two women were released they were so dehydrated and starved that it took a long time to revive them sufficiently to answer questions.

When the two women were sitting in the kitchen having had water and some food Mark asked them what had happened to them.

"We answered the door and two Africaner women rushed in and threatened us with knives and a revolver. They then bound and gagged us. We were later forced into a van at knife point and brought here. That was several days ago, we were given some water and food the first day, but we have not seen them since."

Tad took the women home in the cart while Mark and The fitter walked back to SATCO.

As Tad stopped the cart outside Robert's front door, the woman from next door rushed out and said that she had looked in the back garden to find the reason for the bad smell and had found a rotting body in the privy. She had called the police and they had arranged for the body to be removed, but had made no comment.

Tad stayed and helped the women to get back to a semblance of normality for a while and then drove back to SATCO.

The de Brecht women had singled out the largest British owned gold mine in the area, which was the Rand Mining Company, or RMC.

They had then investigated the feasibility of placing a bomb in the most vulnerable place, which was the 'head works,' or winding gear, near the mine office. But this was swarming with men 24 hours a day so it would not be possible to place a bomb there undetected. So they had to select somewhere else that would cause the maximum disruption to the mine.

As soon as the fuse of the bomb placed against the back wall at SATCO had been lit, they jumped into the van and thrashed the horse to hurry to the top of the ventilation shaft at the end of the longest RMC underground drive.

Looking back they could see a cloud of white smoke at the back of the SATCO compound.

At the top of the vertical air shaft there was just a huge single cylinder Ruston oil engine chugging away, driving a large fan which forced fresh air down into the underground workings to keep the underground conditions above survival level for the hundreds of sweating and straining black miners.

Alongside the machinery there was a small shed to give some protection for the duty engine man.

On arriving, the women hid the horse and van in some scrub nearby and crept up to the machinery. The duty engine man was refilling the fuel tank as it was nearly the end of his shift and as he stooped to lift a container the younger woman hit him on the head with an iron bar. The blow was so violent that he was killed instantly.

The body was then dragged to the back of the fan and the women went to fetch the horse and van. The bomb was placed as close as possible to the engine and the younger woman then knelt down to light the fuse.

As it was nearly time for a shift change, the relief engine man was already sitting in the hut having a meal and when he had finished his meal he ambled over to chat with the duty man.

He saw a woman lighting a fuse beside the engine, and being a mining man immediately realized what was about to happen, so he kicked the lighted fuse away from the unusual looking box and hit the woman on the head with a broom handle. The other woman was trying to pull a revolver out of the waistband of her skirt so he jabbed her in the stomach with the broom handle and she doubled up with pain and dropped the weapon.

The relief engine man soon had the two women tied up and went looking for the duty engine man and found his body behind the fan and the tracks leading to the van.

As the fuel tank had just been refilled, it was safe to leave the engine unattended for a short time so the relief engine man retied the women more securely and locked them in the shed and drove off in the van to report to his manager.

Two days later Abdul went up to the ops room early in the morning and handed Gillie a copy of the local daily newspaper with a marked news item.

FAN DAMAGE FOILED.

An attempt to blow up the machinery operating the vital ventilation air supply at the end of the RMC long drive was foiled by the relief engine man coming on shift yesterday.

Two women had allegedly murdered the duty engine man and placed a bomb alongside the engine and had already lit the fuse when the relieving engine man arrived and was able to remove the lighted fuse and overpower the two women.

RMC have issued a statement and say that they will continue to enforce high level security at all above ground and underground installations and will vigorously prosecute all offenders with the full force of the law.

The alleged offenders are believed to be Mrs. and Miss van de Brecht who are being held in custody pending further investigations.

"Well now we know why the de Brecht women disappeared. Let us hope that they are put out of circulation for a very long time, if not permanently." Said Mark.

"Och aye, but the women were doing exactly what is the Boers usual way of trying to gain leverage so do you think that they could be let off on some 'technicality' by the biased Government officials."

"I think that RMC has the money and influence to get a full prosecution, as they have indicated in their statement to the press, so I think that the women will receive the full force of the law.

RMC will also want to take the opportunity to make an example of the two women."

Jill rushed in excitedly and handed Mark a letter addressed in a very familiar hand and said.

"A letter from Sasha, I hope it is all good news."

"Thank you Jill, Could you please get me a cup of coffee while I read the letter."

Mark sat down near the window and started to read.

Oakhill Hall

Dearest Mark,

The children have gone to have a picnic lunch down by the lake with your mother so I have the chance to write an overdue letter to you.

As you will remember, Nanny Ferguson is a fully trained governess as well and has started to give William preschool lessons every day now.

Amy is growing so fast that she is nearly as tall as William and joins in with some of the lessons already.

I have visited Marg. Brooks several times recently and we have been out riding, and one day we went to the now deserted Barden Park estate.

Such a shame as it is an absolutely wonderful place.

There is just the shell of the old house left after the fire and the estate is totally neglected and going to ruin without any maintenance. There is not even any stock in the home farm fields or the park to keep the grass eaten down. The tenant farmers are complaining that they get no response from the lawyers who are supposed to be managing the estate.

Marg. also says that the rents are not being collected properly and that the estate is badly in debt.

One day when Marg. called in here for lunch and there was more time, she explained what happened to the Marshbank family, who own the property, and I will give you a short version.

Old Harold Marshbank was married to Enid and had two sons and a daughter.

The two sons were killed in the Boer war and the daughter, Rosemary, is the sole heir to the very large estate.

Enid was suddenly taken very ill and died and Harold married Priscilla almost immediately. Priscilla already had a son, born out of wedlock, who she claims is the love child of an affair she had with Harold while he was married to Enid.

Harold had a heart attack and died about two years ago and Priscilla had Rosemary certified as insane and she was kept locked in an attic.

There was then that terrible fire and Rosemary was still locked in the attic, but was rescued at the last minute and has shocking burns to her legs.

Priscilla now claims that her bastard son, Justin, is the rightful heir because Rosemary is insane and she has challenged Harold's will. (Apparently Justin looks nothing like Harold! So heaven knows who his real father is?)

The beautiful old house, built out of locally quarried sandstone blocks, now just has the outside walls standing. One of the two stable blocks was lightly damaged by the fire at the end nearest the house but is otherwise undamaged.

I took the children up there one day in the spring cart and they had a wonderful time exploring and found a big manmade lake higher up a small valley. We had our picnic lunch by the lake.

The lawyers handling the Marshbank affairs had a large area of fine oak trees harvested recently to pay off some of the huge debt (And some of their own overdue fees no doubt.) and now there is a large cleared plateau a lot further up the hill behind the old house. Now that the trees have gone, there is the most wonderful view from the plateau and you can see for miles on a clear day.

All the farms here are doing well with the good season, plenty of hay was made and we are having good milk yields with all the lush grass. The home farm cheese making continues to improve and we have plenty of orders now that our 'Red Cheshire Cheese' is getting better known farther afield. We should do some advertising and have a better label.

Old Bill Huxley died recently and the lodge is now vacant. Would this be a suitable place for Gillie to live if he decides to come back to Britain?

Your mother is amazing, she has started a Red Cross branch based on this house and holds regular meetings and fund raising functions.

The children keep asking 'when is Daddy coming home' I hope it will be soon. I miss you too!

With all our love. Sasha. Xxx

Chapter 6

AUCTION SURPRISE

The day before the auction William had a large marquee erected at the front of SATCO and a caterer started to set up his equipment in a service tent.

Mark's excitement and apprehension started to increase as the time of the auction approached.

On the day of the auction all the agents and buyers were served exotic food and drinks by scantily clad waitresses for an hour before William went up to the rostrum and started extolling the virtues of SATCO.

The first bid came from an unknown agent at 1.2 million pounds and this was soon raised to 1.3 and then to 1.4 million by the agent acting for JMC.

William dragged the price up in small increments to 1.5 million and it became stuck at 1.5 million with the JMC agent.

So it looked as though the 'gold seam influence' was going to be a non-event.

William raised his gavel and said.

"Are you all done? I ask you, once! I ask you Twice! There was a dreaded pause before a hand was raised by a different unknown agent and the price quickly went to 1.6 million.

There was then lively bidding in a three way contest between the agents up to 2.4 million where the bidding stagnated again. The crowd had gasped at each of the last few bids.

The last bid was from the second unknown agent so Mark nudged Gillie and shrugged.

William was about to raise his gavel again when the bidding started between the first unknown agent and the JMC agent.

William reduced the increment for a bid and dragged the two agents up to 2.9 million with the last bid coming from the unknown agent.

The JMC agent then put in a bid at 2.95 million and William realized that as this was probably the limit given to their agent by JMC, he quickly knocked it down to the bid from the JMC agent.

The crowd clapped and applauded when the JMC agent went up and shook William's hand to confirm the sale.

George's consulting and construction business was then put up for auction and fetched well over the expected price.

The scantily clad waitresses appeared again and started serving more champagne and exotic food in an almost party atmosphere.

Some of the guests were starting to get very merry and Mark could see that there could be some wild drunken behavior if the champagne continued to flow like water, so he went to find the head caterer in the service tent, set up at one side of the marquee, to find out how long William had arranged for the champagne to keep flowing.

As he went through the tent flap he saw that two of the agents were each already wrapped round a waitress, who seemed to be enjoying the attention.

One particularly attractive girl quickly pulled the agent behind a stack of crates of empty bottles and was very soon making moans of rapture indicating that she was enjoying her greatest pleasure.

When Mark finally found the head caterer, he said that the party would end as soon as the champagne ran out and that they were down to the last two bottles already.

William sat at a small table and organized payment of the 10 % deposits, the signing of the contracts of sale and the hand over procedure in seven days' time, on payment of the balances.

When William had completed the formalities, Mark went over and congratulated him on a truly remarkable result. William gave him a knowing wink and they shook hands.

Mark thanked all the SATCO staff for their help and cooperation prior to the auction and then went to his bed room and sat at his desk to draft out a cable to Sasha with just the basic information on the auction results.

Now that SATCO had been sold there was a lot to do, like packing up some personal items to be sent to Gustav for shipment and the all-important task of transferring the proceeds of the sale to his bank in Chester.

Chapter 7

JUST IN TIME

After discussion with Gillie, it was decided to form the MacIntyre farm into a small company, jointly owned by Mark and Gillie, which would then lease the farm to Makede and his tribe for a nominal one pound a year rental. This was quickly arranged by William Collins.

Mark then asked Sally and Sarah if they knew where their father had had his bank account and Sally said.

"Yes we know because we have an arrangement to draw pocket money from the account each month while we are at college."

An appointment was made and Mark took the girls with him to see the bank manager.

John Ashcroft had a considerable portfolio of investments which was producing a steady income and all the documents were given to Mark so that he could get William to set up a trust company, based in England for the girls, with Sasha and Mark as directors till the girls were both over twenty one. The dividends would be made available for the girls immediately, so that they could draw pocket money.

Gustav confirmed that he had booked a passage on a mixed cargo and passenger ship for Mark, Gillie, Jill, Sally and Sarah and cables were sent to Sasha and Colonel Wilkinson advising the ships name and their ETA in London.

The new owners of SATCO, JMC, appointed a tubby little Frenchman, Monsieur Jacques, as the general manager and with his good English and friendly, jovial manner he was soon accepted by the staff and customers.

Abdul was appointed as operations manager and Hassan kept his position as manager of the branch store and the rest of the staff decided to keep their positions.

George and Anne had to stay on for another month or so to hand over their business to the new owners, and would then make their own arrangements for returning to England.

Mark realised that as Raymond and Tad had been involved in helping to defeat the Boers that they were both prime targets for reprisals, so he called them into the office, explained that it would be safer for them and their families to go to England. He offered to pay for their passage to England, compensate them for any furniture left in the company houses, pay a bonus and provide a house and a job in England.

Tad agreed without hesitation, but Raymond was hesitant and wanted to talk it over with his family. The next day Raymond told Mark that he had talked it over with his wife and that he would be happy to wait till Tad was ready to go in a few weeks' time and that they would then go together.

Mark thought that Tad must have talked to Raymond and his wife and had persuaded them to move.

On the day of departure all the SATCO staff, together with George and Anne, assembled under the archway and there were emotional handshakes and kisses all round.

Monsieur Jacques insisted on kissing all the girls and then kissed Mark on both cheeks, as only the French can, with much aplomb.

During the train journey to Durban the three girls asked lots of questions about life in England and Mark and Gillie answered with as much detail as possible.

Gustav met them off the train in Durban and said that he had booked them into a small hotel close to his office for the overnight stop.

As soon as they were settled into the hotel, Anna, Gustav's wife, arrived in a cab driven by a trusted friend, who always had a loaded revolver tucked into his belt, and took the girls on a sightseeing trip round the city and Gustav's timber business down on the wharf where the old slave barracoons were located.

When the driver explained how the slaves were kept in the barracoons and then auctioned off to the masters of the slave ships for transport to America, the Ashcroft girls were shocked, but Jill already knew all too well about the way that slaves had been captured and shipped to America, or more recently, sold in the Middle Eastern countries.

Mark, Gustav and Gillie went to a café close by because Gillie was still restricted by having to use crutches.

When they were seated at an outside table and the drinks had arrived, Mark gave a brief summary of the sale to Gustav who was a little skeptical about the gold seam, but did not ask any questions.

Gustav said that he had a reliable contact working in a senior position in the Government offices who had seen draft legislation for the prevention of capital being taken out of South Africa by individuals or companies, so he asked if Mark was sure that the transfer of the proceeds of the sale to England was fully completed.

Mark became very anxious and checked the bank transfers in his brief case. All was in order and he was sure that his transfer was complete, but he remembered that George had not yet made a transfer, so he then hurried off to the nearest cable office and sent a cable to George. He also sent a cable to William Collins with masked information.

The ship sailed early the next morning and the three girls shared a cabin and Mark and Gillie each had separate cabins.

When the ship approached El Suez, Mark explained to the girls how the canal was first started in 1300 BC when Egyptian Kings used slave labour to join several salt water lagoons together to make a shallow waterway that could be navigated by the Arab feluccas with their lateen sails for about 50 miles to the North as far as Lake Timsah.

The present 101 mile long canal was built by a joint French and Egyptian company headed by a French Diplomat and engineer, Ferdinand de Lesseps, and was completed in 1888.

Egypt had already sold its half share to Britain in 1875 on a lease that would expire in 1956.

When the ship reached Lake Timsah it had to move out of the shipping lane to allow a number of South bound vessels to pass.

While they were waiting at anchor in Lake Timsah, the strange smell of cooking fires fueled with dried camel dung wafted across the water from the city of Ismailiya and Mark pointed out where the 'Sweet Water' Canal came into the lake.

"Why is it called the Sweet Water Canal, when it all is very smelly?" asked Sally,

"Good question, the Sweet Water Canal runs from West to East, with the Western end joining up with the River Nile near Cairo. It is therefore the fresh, or 'sweet', water from the Nile that flows down to Lake Timsah. This fresh water is also used for irrigation all along its length. Crude counter balance devices called a shadouf are used to raise the water to higher levels for irrigation.

Feluccas can also navigate the sweet water canal with the aid of locks. The whole system is hundreds if not thousands of years old!"

The ship then moved into the shipping lane and started up the Northern part of the Suez Canal past the, 'bitter,' or salt water, lakes.

As soon as the ship left Port Said and entered the Mediterranean, a violent storm blew up and huge green waves crashed against the side of the ship causing it to roll violently and many of the passengers retired to their cabins suffering from 'la mal de mer.'

By the next morning the sea was calm as a mill pond and the ship sailed through beautiful blue water towards Gibraltar.

There was another storm as they went through The Bay of Biscay and it was then a smooth trip through the Channel to London docks.

As Mark and his party stood on deck, while the tugs were pushing the ship up to the quay in London, he was pleasantly surprised to see Colonel Wilkinson waiting where the gang plank would be placed on the quay.

There were greetings and introductions all round as they stepped off the gang plank before the Colonel directed them into two motor taxis that he had waiting.

They drove to a small private hotel in Curzon Mews where they were met by Rachel Wilkinson.

When they had checked into the hotel, Rachel took the girls on a sightseeing tour of London in a motor taxi for the rest of the day.

Reginald Wilkinson asked Mark and Gillie to follow him and then used a key to enter a small room where a tall young man dressed in a business suit was seated at a desk. The young man immediately stood to attention and treated the Colonel with the deference due to a superior officer.

Mark and Gillie then had to sign copies of the Official Secrets Act and were searched for concealed weapons.

Reginald explained that this was always done as a standard security precaution.

The young man then released a hidden catch and slid back a section of one wall to reveal a conference room set up with a large table, a black board and rows of chairs.

They all sat down at the table and a distinguished looking man came in and sat at the head of the table. He was introduced just as Richard. He then distributed copies of the report on South Africa that Mark had sent to Reginald, via Sasha, and these were then used as the basis of discussion.

Richard led the discussion and asked a lot of questions and then asked if there were any recent developments.

Mark explained about Gustav's inside information regarding the draft legislation to prevent money from leaving South Africa. This caused considerable consternation and Richard hurried off to start telephoning.

A sandwich lunch and coffee were served before two, obviously semi- retired Army officers, came in and joined in the discussion which they then focused on troubles in Europe.

They said that the 'Hague Conference' in 1907 had been just a lot of talk without any sincerity from the delegates and did nothing to defuse the mounting tensions in Europe.

Germany, Austria / Hungary and sometimes Italy, were sabre rattling against Britain, France and Russia.

Alliances were being sought and the arms race was gaining momentum.

Small outbreaks of hostility had occurred in Morocco with Germany siding with Morocco against the French and there was ongoing trouble in the Balkans. France had increased National Service from two years to three years while Germany was building more armaments as fast as possible.

It had also been discovered that German companies with outstanding accounts for goods that had been exported, were told by their Government to discount their debtors accounts for prompt payment in gold bullion, as it was expected that some currencies would become worthless in the event of war and Germany would need the gold to buy essential raw materials such as iron ore, coal and rubber.

Britain had the largest navy in Europe and Germany was aiming to equal the British tonnage of naval ships as soon as possible.

So, if Mark was going to Europe in the near future he would probably be asked to gather information. Mark said that he had no reason to go to Europe in the immediate future.

By late afternoon Mark and Gillie were glad to get out of the stuffy room and wait in the lobby for Rachel to return with the girls.

Mark told Gillie that the lodge was vacant and that Sasha had got it ready for Jill and himself to move into and that he could live there till he found some where more suitable.

Gillie said that it sounded perfect and that he would be glad to move in.

Reginald came and joined them and Mark asked if there was a connection between Reginald's secret organization and the Hotel.

"The 'boss' owns the hotel and pays all our overhead expenses. The hotel is available for all our associates and their immediate families to use at reduced rates as this provides the 'cover' for a normal private hotel. We have armed guards in civies here all the time and we do not tell even our families that it is a secret meeting place for gathering and discussing information."

Mark checked on the train times and sent a cable to Sasha advising their ETA, at Chester on the next day.

Rachel and the girls got back to the hotel after six o'clock and as the hotel only served a buffet breakfast and a sandwich lunch they all went to a small restaurant that was recommended by the Colonel.

Over dinner they exchanged the usual news about each of their families and Reginald talked about his son Phillip who was expected to join them for coffee later on.

Phillip arrived as they were having coffee in the lounge and was introduced and said that he had just received a letter from Oxford University advising that he had passed his graduation exams so Mark called for champagne to celebrate his achievement and they all drank a toast to his future success.

During the train journey Northwards on the next day Mark and Gillie used the passing scenery to explain to the girls about the various farm crops and animals in the fields. With their rural upbringing the girls soon started to understand how farms were operated in England.

Mark's brother Hugh and his wife Margret met them off the train in Chester and they all went for a quick cup of tea and a chat in the station restaurant before going out into the station yard where Arthur Phillips, the home farm foreman, was waiting with the car.

The girls were fascinated by the old Roman walls in the city of Chester, the timbered houses and shops and the quaint narrow streets.

As the car came up the long drive to Oakhill Hall, Sasha held on to the excited children till the car had stopped and Mark had got out. They rushed up to Mark and were picked up for a quick cuddle. Sasha then stepped forward and embraced Mark and then kissed the girls and Gillie and welcomed them into the house to relax in the drawing room before dinner.

Mark's mother, Agnes, joined them and was delighted to meet the Ashcroft girls, Jill and Gillie.

Mark arranged for Gillie and Jill to take the spring cart to the lodge after dinner and keep it there as his means of transport because Gillie was still recovering from the wounding and his leg was still painful at times.

"When you have settled in, say by the day after tomorrow, would you please come up to the house at about nine and we can 'do the rounds' of the home farm and all the tenanted farms together."

The children had grown and were developing quickly and Sasha had difficulty in controlling their excitement at having Daddy home.

They kept on asking. "Daddy. Daddy. Please can we have another picnic at the place we found by the burnt house and the lake?"

"Yes we can go as soon as we are all ready, and it is a nice day."

Gillie and Mark set off in the family car to go to every part of the home farm and found it was in good condition. Gillie was most impressed with the cheese making rooms attached to the home farm dairy and asked lots of questions. He then said.

"You seem to have too much work for the existing cheese making rooms, what will you do if you get more business?"

"Well, I suppose we will have to think about building a purpose designed factory, I will have to talk it over with George when he gets back."

All the tenant farmers were pleased to see Mark and were introduced to Gillie.

The recent improvements to the farm houses and farm buildings were very much appreciated by the tenants.

Mark asked Gillie how he was settling into the lodge with Jill.

"Och, it is a fine wee hoose and there is even a resident black cat for Jill to fuss over. Apparently it belonged to the previous tenant and was kept fed by your house keeper, Annie, till we arrived.

Chapter 8

OPPORTUNITY

On the following Saturday the whole extended family squeezed into the car and drove up to a farm track close to the Barden Park estate and met Gillie and Jill, who had driven up in the spring cart as arranged.

As the old mansion house was just a burnt out shell, the main gates locked and the twin lodges deserted they had had to gain access from the nearest farm track and walk into the abandoned park.

The children took the girls to see the burnt house and the stables while Mark and Sasha carried the picnic basket up to the lake. Gillie followed with the help of his stick but he kept stopping to take in the view. He felt at home as he got higher up the hill which was partly covered with bracken and heather.

Just like the lowlands of Scotland!

Sasha allowed Sally and Sarah to take the children to have a paddle in the lake before they all sat under a tree for lunch.

After lunch the children and the girls went off 'exploring' while Sasha, Mark and Gillie moved to the plateau above the old house.

Sasha said.

"You will remember what I told you in the letter about the problems with the Marshbank family? Well, I was wondering if they want to sell?

This is the most wonderful place to build a house, Just look at that view now that the trees have been cut down!

Imagine a comfortable manor house with this view from all the main rooms!

From the first time that I came up here with Marg.Brooks I have thought about having a house here. Do you think we could see if it is for sale?"

"You have taken me completely by surprise, as I have not had time to think about what would be involved, but yes it is certainly a wonderful place to have a house.

You wonderful girl, you always see things that I would probably miss."

Gillie squeezed Jill's hand and smiled at her and she looked overcome with happiness.

"I seem to remember my father saying that the Barden Park estate is more than 60,000 acres but that a large part of it is too hilly and is just used for hill grazing. The property goes back over the whole of this range of hills and includes many farms and small holdings as well as the village of Upper Barden.

The entire village of Upper Barden is built out of the same red sandstone blocks as the original mansion house and is a real showplace village. There is also a sandstone church and school in the village.

From what you said in the letter that you sent to me at SATCO, the estate is bankrupt and in the hands of the Marshbank's lawyers.

Are you serious about wanting to build here if it is for sale?"

"Yes, I am very serious, and I know that we can make it into a marvelous home and fix up the estate."

"It is certainly the most wonderful place, and I like a challenge. We can start investigating, but we should not make direct contact with the Marshbank's Lawyers and show our hand, it should be done through an agent. After the excellent performance by William Collins, I wonder if he would consider acting for us again?"

"Perhaps you could telephone his London office on Monday?"

"What do you think Gillie?"

"Sasha has seen the potential and I agree that it is a perfect place to build a hoose, it reminds me of the lowlands of Scotland with the rolling hills covered with heather and bracken, and all the sandstone buildings give it a lot of character."

Jill said.

"I hope that they want to sell, because there is such a marvelous view from up here and I love the old sandstone buildings."

Mark booked a call to Waringtons London office at nine o'clock on the Monday morning and was put through to a Mr, Martin Simpson who said that William Collins was actually on a ship coming back to London for some well-earned leave and would arrive in London in about a week.

However, in the meantime he would contact the Marshbank's lawyers in Chester and see if they want to sell. He said that he would also see if William Collins would consider postponing his leave to undertake this assignment as it was company policy for each broker to continue to service his established clients.

A few days later Martin Simpson telephoned and told Mark that he had made contact with the Marshbank's Lawyers in Chester and that they would be pleased to start negotiating a quick sale for a cash buyer, but that there was a problem to be overcome first.

Harold Marshbank's daughter, Rosemary, was the sole surviving heir to the estate, but the will was being challenged by Priscilla, Harold's second wife, so the matter would have to go to court for a ruling before a sale could be made.

By making further enquiries he had found that the Marshbank lawyers had been reluctant to go to court to get a ruling on Priscilla's challenge up to now because of the huge debts and the nonpayment of their expenses and that there was no cash available to pay the court fees necessary to have a court rule on the inheritance.

But now that there was a cash buyer available, they were very keen to recommend an early sale to both Rosemary and Priscilla, as a quick sale to a cash buyer was the answer to all the problems.

William Collins telephoned a week later from London and said that he was now back in London, would be honored to continue to look after Mark's affairs and that he had already booked into the Grosvenor Hotel in Chester and would hire a car on arrival.

Two days later William phoned to say that he had visited Rosemary and that she wanted to sell as she had no income while the estate was in limbo and was having to live on the charity of an ancient aunt in Chester.

William had also visited Priscilla, Harold's second wife, and found that she was adamant that her son, Justin, would be awarded 100 % of the estate because Rosemary had been certified as insane and that Justin was the sole surviving child. She definitely wanted to sell as soon as possible.

William confirmed that old Harold Marshbank had not made a new will to include Priscilla but now that he had met Priscilla it was obvious that she was obsessed with hatred and greed and was likely go berserk if the court ruled in favour of Rosemary.

He considered that the most that Priscilla could expect was 95 % to Rosemary and 5% to Priscilla. The claim that Justin was Harold's bastard son would not affect the ruling.

Rosemary had a very competent young lawyer who was using all the leverage available to maximize her inheritance.

If mark was agreeable, William would grease a few palms to get an early court hearing and that they should now make a firm offer to the Marshbank's lawyers, effective for a limited time, to prevent the lawyers going to auction.

He then explained his formula for estimating the value of the property.

A search of the title showed that the area of the very large property was 67,600 acres and that the going price for large properties in the area was around 30 pounds per acre, but as a large part of the land was hilly, with only some of the hill land suitable for hill grazing, and also that there was no mansion house, the overall value should be based on no more than 20 pounds per acre. Thus the value was about 1.35 million pounds.

Chapter 9

THE COURT RULING

Mark talked over William's suggestions with Sasha and they agreed for him to put in a firm offer of 1.3 million pounds, for settlement within six weeks, and to go ahead with his plans for an early court session.

A few days later William called with documents to sign and said that the court session was booked for the first week in next month. He said that as there were likely to be 'fireworks' in the court when a ruling was given in favour of Rosemary, it would be better if none of the family attended court and that he would attend the court to represent the 'cash buyer' and confirmed that a firm cash offer of 1.3 million had already been made to the Marshbank's lawyers.

The day after the court session, William arrived at Oakhill Hall early in the morning, as arranged, and explained what had happened in court.

"All the relevant facts were presented and I was asked to confirm that I had documentary proof that I had received a firm cash offer of 1.3 million pounds and produced your offer to the clerk of the court for the record.

The ruling was then given as 95 % to Rosemary and 5 % to Priscilla, with all court costs, expenses, and legal fees awarded 50 / 50 to Rosemary and Priscilla. (The considerable costs were likely to consume a large part of Priscilla's 5 % share of the estate!)

When the Judge gave the ruling, Priscilla had jumped up and started shouting obscenities at the judge and got Justin to stand on the seat beside her and claimed that he was the only sane child and was entitled to the entire estate!

The judge rapped the rostrum with his gavel and ruled contempt of court and Priscilla was dragged from the court still screaming obscenities and fighting like a wild cat.

She was later sentenced to one month in prison for contempt of court."

William then said that he had an appointment with both of the lawyers representing Rosemary and Priscilla that afternoon so he asked Mark to meet him at his bank and draw a bank cheque for 1.3 million pounds, payable to the Marshbank Lawyer's trust account, later in the morning.

Mark and Sasha hurried into Chester, picked up the bank cheque and met William and then later went to the office of Rosemary's lawyer to complete the documents and within one hour they had the signed contract of sale and the title deed in their hands!

Sasha was so excited that she kissed Mark, then the Lawyer and William and said

"We must hurry home and start working on this project, tres vite, mon cheri."

Mark's father's foresight in establishing SATCO at a time when the gold mine boom was just starting in Johannesburg, Marks rescue of SATCO when the manager had deserted, his recovery from wounding and determination, the solid work put in by Abdul and the staff, the cunning and skill of Tad and Raymond, and the skill and acumen of William Collins had all culminated in a fantastic sale and now they were the proud owners of a 67,600 acre property that had been selected by Sasha as 'a suitable place to build a home', and there was still money in the bank!

The challenge lay ahead.

George and Anne were due to arrive in another week and George would be put to work immediately to start designing the new house and supervising the construction.

William Collins had found that the keys for the main gate, the stables and the two lodges were being held by the village blacksmith at Upper Barden, so Mark and Sasha drove up to collect them.

The blacksmith, Jack Darlington, was a huge man with hands and arms twice the normal size, but was quietly spoken and very polite.

"I be very pleased to see a fine young family coming to Barden Park with plans to build a new house.

For 'tis too long since the fire and them useless lawyer men letting the place ruin while poor Miss Rosemary went without a penny, and with those terrible burns.

That was a terrible cruel thing to do, locking up a perfectly normal girl, and I should know, 'cos I shod her horse many times when she rode up to me' smithy and she talked to me' wife and me, perfect' normal and well 'edicated' she is.

T'was lucky that I was repairing a farm machine close by and went to 'elp at the fire.

When I got there someone said that Miss Rosemary was still locked in the attic. I wrapped me'self in wet bags, as we have to do some times when we are working with a big red hot piece in the forge, and got her down, 'ad to break the locked door down with just me' bare 'ands."

"You did a wonderful job in saving her life and thank you for looking after the keys.

We will soon require your services again when we start building."

Sasha said.

"I am pleased to meet you and as you say, it is a shame to see the place abandoned and going to ruin, so now we have a big challenge ahead to build a house and put the estate back in order".

"Good day to you both."

Mark bought a motor wagonette for Gillie and a car for Sasha and then Arthur Phillips taught them to drive.

The day after George and Anne had arrived, they all went to the proposed house site in the two cars.

Mark, Gillie, Jill, and George went to the stables first and Mark asked George if it was possible to convert the two stable buildings into two, double story, comfortable homes.

After a quick inspection George said that it could be done by just using the outside walls and the roof.

Mark asked Gillie if he would like to live in one of them.

"Yes please, I am sure that we could be very happy here, what do you think Jill?"

"Oh yes, but can we have those little windows that stick out upstairs?"

George smiled and said.

"Yes of course, if you mean 'Dormer' windows. That is a good idea as they would help to give them some character."

Mark said.

"Well, you decide which one you prefer and we will give it priority in conversion"

George nodded in agreement and said.

"There is so much to be done on site here that I would like to use one stable block as a temporary office, engage two draftsmen and a secretary and connect a telephone so that we can eliminate traveling to and from a city office all the time."

"Yes, certainly, you are more than welcome to use the stable block, that is not being converted for Gillie and Jill, as your temporary office.

Have you had any thoughts about a workforce?"

"No, I have not planned that far ahead yet, but if we re use the stone from the old mansion we will need some skilled stone masons as well as carpenters and labourers and other trades."

They then walked up to the proposed house site where Sasha and the girls were busy discussing the possible layout of the house.

George had carried up a sack of little white pegs and a mallet so that they could peg out a rough layout of the proposed house.

It was decided to position the house towards the back of the plateau and that the house would be a long building running East to West as this would maximize the view and the winter sun.

A four or five car garage, a workshop and a small stable were to be included in the design.

They soon had a pattern of pegs roughed out and these were then moved around to incorporate other features that were being suggested.

By lunchtime they had arrived at a layout that seemed to appeal to everyone, including the Ashcroft girls who excitedly joined in with the planning and had some interesting ideas about adding cellars with underground passages to the stables and a summerhouse in the garden.

George also wanted to check on the feasibility of using the water in the lake up in the higher valley to supply water to the house, the converted stables and the lodges. He said.

"It may also be possible to use the flow of water to generate electricity like they do in the Lake District. There is a company up there that makes and installs complete systems."

When the family was having dinner that evening Sasha said.

"We must remember that Tad and Raymond are due to arrive in about two weeks so we must get the lodges ready for them. Would you like me to buy some furniture and household things or do you think that Jill and Gillie would do a better job?"

"I am sure that you would do a very good job Darling, but perhaps Jill and Gillie would like to be involved, they can go into Chester and order the furniture to be delivered and bring back the small stuff in their wagon."

So during the next few days Jill and Gillie visited many of the shops in Chester and brought back loads of the smaller items. Jill then offered to arrange for both lodges to be cleaned and painted inside by a contractor who lived in the village and Mark agreed.

The twin lodges had been built on each side of the impressive wrought iron front gates.

Each lodge consisted of a large cylinder made out of stone blocks with a domed roof and had a front door and windows. The cylinder was just one large room inside. Behind the cylinder there was a very comfortable single story two bedroom house attached.

Mark commissioned the black smith, Jack Darlington, to make and install a cattle grid at one side of the main gate for use by the cars so that he could put some cattle into the park and that it would no longer be necessary stop and open the gates every time.

Mark and Gillie visited each of the tenanted farms and small holdings and met with the tenants and listened to their ideas for improving the houses, farm buildings and the land. They also asked for ideas on increasing the area of good pasture by encroaching onto the hill land.

All the ideas and requests were noted down for future action.

Mark's mother, Agnes, was holding a monthly Red Cross meeting in the dining room and she asked the delegates if Sally and Sarah could come in and observe. This was quickly agreed to and the girls came in and were introduced.

The first item to be discussed was the problem created by the nearby Handley quarry suddenly flooding, when the blasting had exposed an underground waterway, and putting about fifty men out of work. There were now fifty local families who had been dependent on regular income from the quarry with no income and no work available.

There were several suggestions for fund raising or the collection of fruit and vegetables but this would only provide minimal short term help.

Sally nudged Sarah and whispered "Building?"

Sarah nodded, so Sally put up her hand.

Agnes invited her to speak.

"Would the men have the right sort of experience to build a stone house?"

Yes, I think that they would, that is an excellent idea. We can ask Mark and George and find out if he thinks that they can do the work. Well done girls."

At dinner that night, Agnes put Sally's suggestion to George and he was immediately enthusiastic with the idea and set up an informal meeting for the men in the Handley pub for the following evening.

George, Gillie, Mark, Sasha, Jill and Agnes arrived early and went into the bar which had a low beamed ceiling and was decorated with many horse brasses and local memorabilia.

The publican came over and greeted them and said that the proposal was 'manna from Heaven' and that the men he had spoken to so far were keen to start as soon as possible. The men would be coming in very soon and he offered drinks on the house all round while they waited.

There was the rumble of many voices outside and then men started to pour into the bar.

The publican introduced Mark and Agnes and explained that Mrs. Agnes Oakhill, President of the local branch of the Red Cross, was aware of the problem that the closure of the Handley quarry had caused and was trying to find a solution.

He then explained that Mr. Mark Oakhill was about to start building at Barden Park and had brought his construction manager, Mr. George Bridgeman, to discuss his need for skilled men.

George gave a quick description of the work required and said that he would be pleased to interview men at the work site tomorrow morning from ten o'clock onwards.

Mark shouted for drinks all round and then his group said good night and went home.

Long before ten o'clock the next morning a long line of men was waiting outside George's temporary office.

Gillie could see that he could help by forming the men into a separate line for each trade and this hastened the process of assessing the men to fill the vacancies for the building project.

By noon George had selected all the men and allocated them into their trades and appointed the ex-quarry foreman as supervisor of the building site.

The first job was to remove all the tree stumps from the building area and dig out for the foundations, the cellars and underground passages.

While this was being done Mark contacted the steam plowing contractor, Harry Hough who had worked for him before, and asked if he could use his steam cable plowing engines to remove the stumps from the rest of the plateau area.

Harry had a quick look at the site and said that he could do the job and was able to start in a few days. The contract was confirmed and included leveling an area for the front and back gardens and removing all the fallen trees and rocks from the 1,000 acre park, which Mark was already using for grazing cattle.

Tad and Raymond arrived with their families and were shown to the lodges by Gillie and Jill. They were delighted and tossed up on who had the first choice, left or right.

Tad won the toss and chose the left lodge and they were left to settle in with their families.

Mark went down the next morning and welcomed them and when he had got Tad on his own asked him what he knew about the 'gold seam' find!

"Well, when I saw that the plumbing contractor had exposed a likely seam I got Raymond to help me to get some fines from under the big rock crusher in the best producing mine that we visited on our sales calls and we winnowed the fines to remove most o' the rock dust, then we 'salted' the likely seam and put out the 'word'.

The plumbing contractor fell for the story and got 'is brother from JMC involved. They even took samples for assay and got good results, and from then on all I had to do was salt a bit more each time they was about to take samples and then leak the word for another mine's agent to hear.

After the sale, I had to stay on for a bit to keep salting so that the seam did not run out too quick like, but funny thing, when I had run out o' fines, they still got fairly good assay results!

So they may have a weak seam after all. They must have the Devil's luck!"

"Thank you Tad. As you know, this must remain our secret. There will be a special bonus for you and Raymond."

"Oh ye'r, must tell ee', them rotten de Brecht women was in court for two murders and was hanged just before we left. Serves the bitches right, for killin' poor old Mackenzie and that engine man, an' not forgettin' all the women an' kids, with tha'r poison in the water."

"I am glad that they got what they deserved. That should close off the de Brecht vendetta against SATCO and my family.

Now we must allocate jobs for you and Raymond so would you please call him over?"

Tad suggested going to his 'round' sitting room, of which he was very proud, and when they were seated Mark said that he would like Raymond to take charge of gate keeping and general security and he would like Tad to take charge of salvaging the stone blocks from the old house, removing the rubble and ash, and ensuring that the stone masons were kept supplied with good stone. They both accepted their new jobs with enthusiasm.

Mark told Gillie about his little talk with Tad and he said.

"Cunning as a wagon load of monkeys, and full o' the tricks that he picked up in the Cornish tin mines, that one, but he has a heart of gold and will follow you and Sasha to the end of the earth.

Raymond is very reliable and the gate keeper and security job is ideal now that he has limited use of that leg.

I am very sure that we did the right thing by bringing them back as they were both likely to be targeted by the terrorists and they will be very useful here.

That is good news about the de Brecht women being hanged. It closes off a chapter of hatred and reprisals that could have continued for years."

Four months later, the outside walls for the new house were waist high and the whole site was a hive of activity.

Gillie had a large marquee erected as a mess tent close to George's office and engaged two ex-army cooks who served over sixty people with lunch, tea and coffee every day.

Sally and Sarah had been taught to drive and used Sasha's car or a spring cart to run messages and pick up small items and also started to attend Red Cross training classes in Chester one day per month.

One day when Mark, Gillie and Jill were standing admiring the conversion of a stable into a very comfortable looking two story home, they heard a horse and spring cart approaching up the drive from the front gate and looked round to see a smartly dressed young woman approaching them.

"Good morning, I am Rosemary Marshbank and I would like see Mr, Mark Oakhill."

"Good morning, I am Mark Oakhill and I am pleased to meet you. This is Mr. Mac Tavish and Jill. How can we help you?"

"Now that the sale is completed, and I have been able to afford some more surgery for the burns, I would like to discuss the purchase of some land close to Upper Barden village where I would like to have a riding school.

Would you consider discussing the proposal?"

"Yes certainly, how about we go into the mess tent and have a cup of tea or coffee?"

Sasha was working in the mess tent with her lists of planned furniture and fittings for the house, so Rosemary was introduced and they all sat at one of the long tables. The cooks served coffee.

"I have always wanted to teach riding and now that I have the opportunity I would like to have a riding school on part of the old family property and would like it to be near the Upper Barden Village. I did not mention this before the sale because the lawyers would have taken ages and charged a fortune to separate and retain a few acres."

Mark said.

"Would it suit you to meet in the village, say one day next week, and we can then look at the area that you have in mind. We could also have our agent, William Collins, present and he could record the details and start the formalities immediately, if you are agreeable?

There is of course our preferred option that the estate builds a house and the riding school buildings for you, to your requirements, and then leases them to you together with the land that you will need.

You may prefer to lease custom designed buildings rather than buy and build.

This would be much quicker to arrange as there would not be any land transfers involved.

We could arrange for George Bridgeman to design what you want and then supervise the construction, as he is doing for the mansion house.

How would next Wednesday at ten o'clock suit you?"

"Yes that sounds fine, I am pleased to meet you all and will see you by the Upper Barden church on Wednesday.

Oh yes, there is something else that I have been meaning to discuss with you for a long time.

Now that I have the proceeds from the sale of the estate, it is far more than I will ever need so I would like to build a village hall, with all the amenities, in the village as a sort of memorial to my family.

Do you think that George would design and build a village hall?"

"Yes I am sure that he would be pleased to do that for you and we can check that there is still stone available from the original quarry which we could supply free of charge."

"That is very kind of you, but if it is available, I would like to pay you for it, as it is my project and I would like to give something of lasting value to the community."

"Yes we can do it that way, as you wish. How soon would you like to start?"

"The sooner the better, to fit in with your other building plans."

Tad had realized that as some of the stone blocks were fire damaged that they would need to cut some more from the quarry near Upper Barden Village where the original stone had been quarried, so he went with the foreman from the Handley quarry to investigate. There was also the additional stone required for the village hall, as soon as George had worked out the quantities.

Even though the quarry had been unused for many years, they found that there was still an apparently unlimited supply of top quality stone and soon had new stone being delivered to the building site.

Mark got Harry Hough to build a good all weather track from the quarry to the house site and a proper road from the quarry to Upper Barden Village.

Word soon got round that good quality stone was available to replace the supply from the now flooded Handley quarry and unsolicited orders started to come in from all over the area, which were then delivered by Harry in his new Sentinel steam truck. Tad was made manager of the quarry as it was now a small sideline business.

Rosemary was already waiting at the church when Mark, Sasha, and William Collins arrived. She got into the car and they drove up a lane behind the village for about half a mile and stopped.

Rosemary pointed out a level area alongside the road and said that she would need about 200 acres. William put in some pegs as directed by Rosemary, made some calculations and notes and said that he would arrange for a surveyor to mark out the area and he would then draw up a contract for lease or purchase as required.

Mark suggested that Rosemary should meet George at his temporary office as soon as possible to discuss her requirements for the house and riding school.

Rosemary said that she was very impressed with George's work on the new house and would contact him very soon to discuss her requirements and was now thinking that leasing may be a lot better for her as she had no experience in designing or building.

Chapter 10

New Names

Nearly two years later, Mark and Sasha's house was ready for them to move in.

Mark's mother, Agnes, had decided that she would like to live in the new house, so a ground floor, self-contained suit of rooms with a conservatory had been included in the design for Agnes, and Annie, the live in house keeper.

Sasha, Agnes, and usually the girls had searched for furniture suitable for the house and the family lifestyle and it was now all in place.

Anne and George had decided to stay at Oakhill Hall which was now separated into two parts. Half to be used by Hugh and Margret and half to be used by Anne and George because now that Hugh and George both had cars it was simple for them to live in the comfort of the original family home and drive to their respective offices each day.

Jill and Gillie had been married at the Upper Barden church the year before and were enjoying living in their new house with the black cat and Jill was expecting a baby.

The steady increase in business at the cheese making facility, as observed by Gillie, had reached crisis point and Mark had sent George on a study tour of cheese factories and machinery makers before he designed a large purpose built factory and fitted it out with all the latest plant and equipment. The sandstone factory, in keeping with the style of the rest of the village, was built near Upper Barden, and was within a ten minute walk from the houses so that it would provide much needed female employment in the area.

Four new sandstone cottages were then added adjacent to the village green, one of which was to be used by the girl's grandfather, The Reverent Angus Ashcroft, and his housekeeper so that Sally and Sarah could keep an eye on him.

Mark wanted to create a new image for the estate now that his family was in residence and decided that a new name would be appropriate so asked for suggestions. There was much discussion but nothing was suggested that seemed to be appropriate.

Mark then remembered his vow to make a memorial for John and May Ashcroft and thought that 'Glendarvel' would be suitable, much to the delight of Sasha and the girls.

Mark commissioned Jack Darlington to make a pair of new front gates with the new name, 'Glendarvel', formed in large wrought iron letters built into the design of the gates.

Then, at the suggestion of Sally and Sarah, they had a profile of Sheeba made into a bronze casting which was then mounted below the name.

A naming ceremony was planned and John Ashcroft's father, The Reverent Angus Ashcroft, was asked to perform the ceremony and was brought down from the village by Sally and Sarah in Sasha's car.

All the staff, the builders and the local people were invited and when Angus drew back the red velvet curtain from the new gates there was a cheer and Jack Darlington stepped forward and welcomed the new squire and his family on behalf of the local community.

Sally and Sarah were crying with emotion and grief.

Mark thanked Jack Darlington for the welcome and explained that the name was chosen as a memorial to Sally and Sarah's parents who had been murdered by terrorists at a place in the African bush called Glendarvel and that their parents, Major John Ashcroft and his wife May, had saved his life with emergency surgery after he was wounded during the Boer war.

Everyone was invited to join the family for food and drinks in the mess tent which had been decorated with photographs and memorabilia from the African bush for the occasion.

Rosemary went up to Sasha and the Ashcroft girls and said that she had been unaware that Mark had been wounded and had his life saved by the girl's parents and had found the naming and memorial very touching and appropriate. Sasha thanked her and they chatted for a while before moving round to mix with the local people.

A few days later, Mark and Sasha had just got into bed when the doorbell rang. Mark slipped on a dressing gown and answered the door.

Colonel Wilkinson's son, Phillip, was standing on the step, he was unshaven and was wearing badly fitting, dirty old clothes.

"Hello Phillip, please come in, what has happened?"

"Please excuse my appearance, but Mum and Dad are in serious trouble and suggested that you may be able to help them."

"Come into the sitting room while I fetch Sasha"

Sasha arrived and they all sat down.

"A few days ago Mum and Dad returned home in the car to find the front door blown to pieces and their house keeper's body lying in the hall.

It appears that one of Dad's Irish contacts, who he had visited when he was in Ireland recently, was a double agent all the time, working for the Irish Republican extremists and had planted a homemade bomb that was triggered by the front door handle. But instead of killing Dad, the housekeeper must have returned from shopping or something, and was the one killed.

Dad contacted his friends in London and they sent a large van which picked them up in total darkness. The driver left one man to supervise the operation and two tailors dummies wrapped in blood stained blankets. The police and an ambulance were called and three, 'corpses' wrapped in blood stained blankets were seen by the local press photographer being loaded into an ambulance and a reporter wrote a dramatic article for the paper about a bomb blast killing three people.

Dad phoned me, at my digs in Oxford, from a phone box the next day and gave me the rough outline but said that I must not go home or try to contact him. He said that the place where they have been put is no longer safe and they need to move to a new location very soon. They were only allowed to bring one suitcase with them.

Dad gave me a phone number and two code words which would indicate if you can have them here, or not. The call should be made from a phone box as far away as possible."

Mark looked at Sasha and she nodded, so he told Phillip that yes they can come but that the move must be in total secrecy.

Sasha asked Phillip if he had been followed and he said that he had not come by a direct route and had borrowed the old clothes as a disguise. He had checked many times but had not seen anyone following.

Sasha asked if Phillip would like some food and said that she would prepare a room for him upstairs at the end of the passage. Phillip said that he was starving as he had not eaten all day.

Sasha went to prepare a meal and Mark said.

"You must realize that you will have to stay in your room and keep out of sight till we can give you and your parents a 'new persona.'"

Mark then called Gillie on the 'house phone', (which could also be connected to Raymond's lodge, Gillie's house or the stable.) and asked Gillie to come up to the house.

A few minutes later Gillie and Jill arrived and Mark explained what had happened.

Jill went to help Sasha in the kitchen.

Mark said.

"I was wondering what to do with the other converted stable, but now we may have a tenant sooner than expected!

The trouble is that the other stable conversion was given a low priority in the building programme due to George's office and the priority given to the double story extensions that we added to the lodges for Tad and Raymond's growing families. It will be essential that the Wilkinson family all stay in the house and keep out of sight till they have a new persona and can move in as 'bona fide tenants' for the second converted stable".

Gillie and Jill got the phone number and yes code word from Phillip and drove to the seaside resort town of Llandudno in North Wales on the next Saturday and used a phone box to send the 'yes' code word.

A few days later Raymond rang from the lodge, late in the afternoon, to say that a van load of furniture from Hastings in Sussex had arrived and where should he send it.

There was no furniture expected but the reference to Hastings in Sussex indicated to Mark what to expect, but he must still take precautions as it may be a trick to get access to the house.

He told Raymond to tell the driver to come up to the house and back up to the open garage door.

Mark alerted Sasha and Gillie and opened one garage door in a bay that was empty, put a loaded revolver in his pocket and waited in the adjoining bay.

The van drove up slowly, slewed round and backed up to the open door and the driver got out and walked into the garage.

Mark said.

"Hello, what have you got to deliver?"

"Good evening Sir, there are two items from Hastings for Mr. Mark Oakhill"

"Yes, that is alright, we are expecting them."

The driver tapped twice on the door and there was a two tap answer so he opened the door and helped Reginald and Rachel to get down with their one suitcase.

After greetings and introduction of the driver as Sergeant Morgan they all went into the kitchen and Sasha and Jill prepared some coffee.

"We have been traveling for about thirty six hours with just snacks picked up along the way so we are starting to get tired.

It was Sergeant Morgan who picked us up in this van after the bombing and he knows the whole sorry saga. He has worked for us for a long time and knows a few tricks like carrying several sets of different screw-on trade signs to put on the sides of the van and an assortment of number plates that can be changed as necessary and having plenty of spare fuel in cans. We had a few 'identity changes' along the way in case we were being followed, but saw nothing suspicious!"

"You had better back the van right into the garage for the night so that we can close the door and I expect you all want a bed as soon as possible.

Sasha, Jill and the girls organized a quick meal for the weary travellers and then a bed for everyone. Gillie and Jill then went home.

The van was checked, put in the garage, and then the door was closed.

Sergeant Morgan left very early the next morning.

After breakfast there was an impromptu meeting in the sitting room to create a new persona for the Wilkinson family and decide how best to 'bring them to life'.

They could not just pop up like mushrooms, they had to have a plausible background that would be difficult, or preferably impossible, to check.

Sasha came up with the idea of the 'retired manager of a small family owned import and export business in Bombay, India,' as the records in that country were not good and this would be difficult to check. This suggestion was accepted and then embellished till it was complete in every detail.

They then had to be given names!

There was a lot of discussion and finally they chose Mr. Geoffrey Baker, his wife Florence and their son Andrew.

Mark said that he could get William Collins to advertise in London for a tenant, for the second converted stable block, and then negotiate a lease with a Mr. Geoffrey Baker and his family who would reply to the advertisement and could then be met off the train at Brockington station by Gillie in his wagonette. The Baker family having been taken to Chester lying on the floor of the family car.

On discussion with the building site foreman, Mark found that there was still about three weeks work required to finish the conversion of the second stable block, so that was ideal.

The absence of any furniture belonging to the Bakers was explained by the move from India.

Gillie was able to give Geoffrey and Rachel some tuition on some of the Anglo Indian words used in India such as 'Pucka Sahib,' for good boss, 'Mem Sahib',for the wife of the boss, 'Wallah', for workman and so on.

Geoffrey had been told that his house in Hastings, his car and furniture would be sold and that the proceeds would appear in his new bank account in Chester via a devious route.

Jill and Gillie made a detailed list of the furniture required by the Baker family and went into Chester and ordered it to be delivered. They brought back the small items in the wagonette. Everything was paid for in cash, provided by Mark, on the understanding that he would be repaid when the Baker's house money arrived in their new account.

The painters were still finishing off in the last two bedrooms when William Collins telephoned to say that he had found a tenant and negotiated a rental for Mr. and Mrs. Baker and that they would telephone Mark direct to confirm when they could move in.

A few days later, Mark took the Baker family, lying on the floor of his car under a rug, into Chester and dropped them and their extensive hand luggage, suitably plastered with shipping line labels, at Chester station.

Gillie drove to Brockington station and was early for the train which gave him time to chat with the station porter, as planned. He talked about the weather and then just mentioned that he had come to pick up the new tenants for the vacant converted stable.

Gillie put on a show of having to identify his passengers when they got off the train and then took them to his wagonette in the station yard.

As the Baker family had not been able to venture out of Mark and Sasha's house till they had 'officially arrived', they were delighted when they saw the house for the first time and the choice of furniture that had been bought by Jill and Gillie for them, and started to settle in.

Mark left the Bakers to settle in, with assistance by Jill and Gillie, for the first week and then suggested a meeting in their house.

As Sasha and Jill already knew about the intelligence gathering, they also were asked to come to the meeting being held in the Baker's dining room.

Mark opened the meeting by saying.

"I think that we need to establish some ground rules to keep your operation secure and to make your work as effective as possible, and I would like to run through a list of suggestions that I have jotted down.

Have a direct telephone line connected to this house in your own new name.

We will have your study connected to our house telephone system which gives you access to Raymond, our gate man who lives in the right hand front lodge, Gillie's house, the stable and our study.

There are already spare telephone wires buried in the ground.

When you come to our house in connection with your work, please always come via the stable and the underground passage. We will give you a key for the concealed door in the stable.

When you visit socially, please use the front door!

As you plan on having a car, we will arrange for George to have a garage built, similar to the one that is attached to Gillie's house.

Have you thought about having house servants? Or, perhaps we should discuss that later.

George is in the process of installing an electricity supply system, which will be connected to your house very soon.

Gillie and I have discussed our possible involvement with your work, if required, and we can undertake some small local jobs that could be worked in with our work on the property.

We need to discuss the question of your associates visiting you at home. Has this been necessary in the past?"

"That is a very valid point, and we have had a very strict rule that we only meet associates at the London facility, or if there are just two people involved, at some random, neutral place such as a restaurant or cafe in a nearby town and that rule would most certainly be applied here.

This rule was established to protect the homes and families of associates as well as for general security.

As you will have already guessed, we found that the Irish contact, who turned out to be a double agent, traced me to my real name and address.

There is a civil war raging in Ireland over the partition of the mostly Protestant North and the mostly Catholic South, which has triggered violence and reprisals to flash point and I was over there gathering information for London. Quite by chance, I came across a nest of leading players in the Irish Republican extremist movement and we arranged for the local police to round them up after I had left.

The Irish contact who was working for me had found a dry cleaners label in my jacket pocket while I was getting changed after we got drowned in a heavy rainstorm. He had then phoned the dry cleaner to say that he had found a jacket with the job number ticket still in the pocket and where should he send the jacket?

And of course, the dry cleaner was very obliging and gave him my name and address.

So that emphasizes some of the rules of espionage!

The Irish double agent has since been picked up and is in prison on rape charges."

"Perhaps, when you are ready, we can have a meeting for you to bring us up to date on the situation in Europe."

"Yes certainly, but because there is so much happening at the moment, I need to go to London for a few days and get all the latest information, which I fear will not be good news."

Mark and Sasha's children, William and Amy, were doing very well at Rosemary's riding school and were entered in a 'bending race' which was the main event at the school's annual gymkhana on the next Saturday and William was expected to win.

Priscilla was living in a nearby village with her son, Justin, who also attended the riding school and was entered in the bending race, but he was fat and not a very good rider, so was not expected to do very well.

The bending race was the main event. The course started with a long strait to spread the riders out, followed by 'the bends' comprising a series of staggered flags, a U turn, then back through more 'bends' and a long straight back to the start, cum finish line.

Some of the parents and spectators were gathered near the U turn to see the ponies and riders go through the 'bends', but most of the spectators were gathered at the start cum finish line.

At the drop of the starter's flag the young riders galloped down the straight and into the first 'bends' with William leading and Amy in about fourth place.

Priscilla was standing at the U turn and touched the paper fuse of a 'rick rack' firework, concealed in a paper bag, with her cigarette and dropped it into a metal rubbish bin and sauntered off towards the finish line.

The leading group of riders went through the first bends and rounded the U turn and were going through the second set of bends when the 'rick rack' started banging and jumping in the bin, so it was the last riders, including Justin who was trailing behind, who were close to the bin when the firework went off and frightened their ponies.

Most of the leading group of ponies stayed on course, with the odd flag passed on the wrong side and went on to finish but the last three ponies were terrified and bolted in all directions!

After crossing the finish line in first place, William slowed to a halt, and was turning to see the other riders finish when he saw his friend, Julia, clamped down and hanging on to a terrified pony's neck, charging towards him.

He turned his pony and took off after her and tried to get close enough to turn the terrified animal but it was not till they had got nearly to the back fence before he was able to get hold of the rains and pull the pony to a halt. Julia was shaking with fear and tumbled off the pony and held on to William's saddle. They then walked back to the finish line leading their ponies behind them.

Justin had been thrown from his pony near the U turn and had a suspected broken collar bone and another boy had had a hair raising ride till he was thrown off against a fence, but was apparently not injured.

Mark, Sasha and the girls had been standing near the finish line, so had not seen how the rick rack was put in the bin but immediately went to the U turn and asked around.

The mother of one rider had been standing close to the bin and had seen a woman throw some rubbish into the bin and had thought nothing of it, till the firework went off, but by that time there was nobody standing near the bin. She could only describe the woman who threw the rubbish as being 'thirty to forty and smartly dressed'.

Rosemary was angry, embarrassed and humiliated as she awarded the cups to William and the winners of the other events.

Mark found Rosemary among the crowd and invited her for coffee that evening so that they could discuss the incident. Sasha suggested that Gillie and Jill should also be present and Mark agreed.

It was half past seven when Jill and Gillie arrived and Rosemary arrived a few minutes later.

As usual for all family matters, Sally and Sarah were also present.

"I am so glad to have you as responsible neighbours and that you have offered to help me.

I was so angry that someone would want to spoil the children's gymkhana and I feel very responsible for the children that got hurt. Do you have any idea on who, and or why, they would do such a horrid thing?"

Mark said.

"I think that we both know that it was almost certainly Priscilla, but that her timing went wrong and it was Justin who was the one most seriously hurt, and not our children who I am sure were the planned targets.

As there do not appear to be any reliable witnesses we can only work on the assumption that it was Priscilla, or it is remotely possible that it was someone working for her, and act accordingly.

What do you think Gillie?"

"Aye,'ye will understand that the mind of a wicked person often targets a spouse, and or, children as a means of getting revenge on their real enemy.

Noo, in this case, with due respects, Priscilla's real target is you, Miss Rosemary, so by disrupting the gymkhana and hurting the children she damages the reputation of the riding school and at the same teme had a chance of injuring the children of the family who are now in the position that she likes to think, in her twisted spiteful way, is rightfully hers."

"As usual, our expert military strategist has put his finger on the purpose of the attack and why it was done in that way."

"Yes that sounds right, I think that there must be still a lot of hatred and pent up greed and anger coming from Priscilla, so we will have to be very careful in future. What do you suggest?"

"Och noo, there is only so much that we can do. We must always be thinking ahead aboot what she is likely to do next and not leave any opportunities for her to make trouble.

I suggest that we get together and exchange information every so often and make sure that she knows that we are watching her every move. Perhaps when you have another gymkhana I can come and keep an eye on her and it would be better if ye' can arrange for her son to leave the riding school as he can be manipulated into making trouble now he is getting older. Perhaps ye' can say that ye' can't be responsible for his safety any longer?

We must give Raymond at the lodge more up to date instructions and get him to watch out for Priscilla. He already has the newspaper photographs of her taken at the teme of the court fracas."

Chapter 11

WAR

Geoffrey Baker returned from London a few weeks later and told Mark that he had been given all the latest news about the European troubles and could explain the situation as soon as it was convenient.

Sasha invited the Baker family, Jill and Gillie to dinner for the following evening.

William and Amy joined them and then they all moved into the large comfortably furnished sitting room.

Mark said to Geoffrey.

"We operate as a complete family whenever possible, so would you be agreeable for my mother, Agnes, Sasha, Andrew, Sally and Sarah, William and Amy as well as Florence of course, and Jill and Gillie to be present while you tell us all the latest information about the troubles in Europe."

"Yes, as they are already partly involved it is better that we all share information on the strict understanding that it remains secret, do you all give me your word that you agree?"

There were assurances all round.

"A lot of what I am about to tell you has not yet been given to the newspapers so is still on the secret list.

Europe has become divided into two main hostile groups over the last few years as a result of a number of minor conflicts, some misunderstandings and a number of longstanding grievances. The two main groups comprise;

Germany, Austria / Hungary, Turkey and Bulgaria, versus Britain, France, Russia, and sometimes Italy. It also includes the United States of America in a more remote way.

Each European country has started making armaments and forming armies, and tensions have been escalating for some years, so now it will only take one minor incident to trigger the start of a major war in Europe.

Germany is rapidly building naval shipping to try to equal the size of the British navy and Alfred Von Turpitz is secretly building submarines for the German navy.

There has just been an 'incident' in the city of Sarajevo in Bosnia Herzegovina, and that it looks likely that this incident will lead to war!

On the 28 th of July, Archduke Francis Ferdinand, Heir presumptive to the Austrian and Hungarian thrones, and his wife, were assassinated by a Serbian Nationalist, Gavrilo Princip.

As a result of the assassinations, Austria declared war on Serbia on July the 28th.

Germany declared war on Russia on the 1st of August and is now expected to declare war on France any day now.

If Germany does declare war on France, Britain is honour bound, under the 'Entente Cordial' agreement to join in and help France.

So we are on the brink of war, and as usual, are not prepared.

There is a lot of propaganda both in Germany and Britain that if there is war it will only be very short, but I think that it could last for a number of years because there would be so many countries involved over a huge area, possibly with a number of 'fronts'.

Perhaps we should be ready to meet again, if there is news of a major development."

Mark said.

"Thank you for giving us the latest news, and yes we certainly need to meet again if you get more important news particularly now that a declaration of war appears imminent.

Now, how about port and coffee all round."

Sasha Said.

"Thank goodness we are in England if there is going to be a war, at least we should not have terrorists in civilian clothes living amongst us, like there were in Africa. What can we do to get prepared?"

"Och ther' will be a lot to do but the first will be getting trained men to the front, so as some of us are getting older or have been wounded, training would be the best way that we can contribute to the war effort."

The next day Geoffrey phoned on the house phone to say that he had just received more important information and would like to come up to the house, via the stable and the tunnel, and see the family group as before.

Mark got the group together and they assembled in the sitting room

Geoffrey said.

"Firstly, Germany declared war on France yesterday and Britain is in the process of declaring war on Germany, right now, as I speak.

I have been recalled to London, for a series of high level meetings.

As Gillie has said, the first priority is getting trained men into the front line, so you may like to think about how you could contribute to a training programme for small numbers of Special Forces personnel.

Now that we are on a war footing, I plan to arrange for Sergeant James Morgan to move into our house with us, as my full time assistant for improved security and to provide service when I am away. He was badly wounded in the Boer war so can't go on active service."

"Once again, thank you for the news, even if it is not what we wanted to hear, and you have a safe trip to London."

Six months after the declaration of war, Andrew had volunteered for the Army and had completed a very rushed officer training course and was home on two days embarkation leave.

Sally and Sarah had volunteered for the nursing service and had had intensive training in a London hospital and were awaiting their posting to a field hospital in France.

Mark had attended a course in Aldershot and was appointed to the position of civilian instructor / administrator for the proposed Special Forces Training Unit.

Jill and Anne were both the proud mother of new babies and were involved with some of the Red Cross activities.

George had been directed into a civilian position to control the construction of shore defenses and gun emplacements along the South coast of England.

Geoffrey had been given a special warrant to establish a small Special Forces Training Unit, (SFTU.) which was to be set up as a tented camp in the hills behind the Quarry.

Gillie had had to go to the Special Forces HQ in the South of England, where he received intensive training to bring him up to date as a civilian small arms instructor. He was then appointed the chief instructor for the 'SFTU' in the tented camp in the hills behind Upper Barden village, but he was allowed to live at home, much to Jill's relief and delight.

Andrew was seen off on the train in his full uniform by the family and expected to be at the Western Front, somewhere close to the Belgian border, in about three weeks.

The girls telephoned from London to say that they would be leaving in a few days and would be working in a field hospital somewhere in France.

Andrew crossed the channel on a very old cargo ship with the company of men who would be under his command in France and they landed at Le Havre. They then went to a transit camp for two weeks familiarization before being sent to where the Cheshire Regiment was stationed at the front.

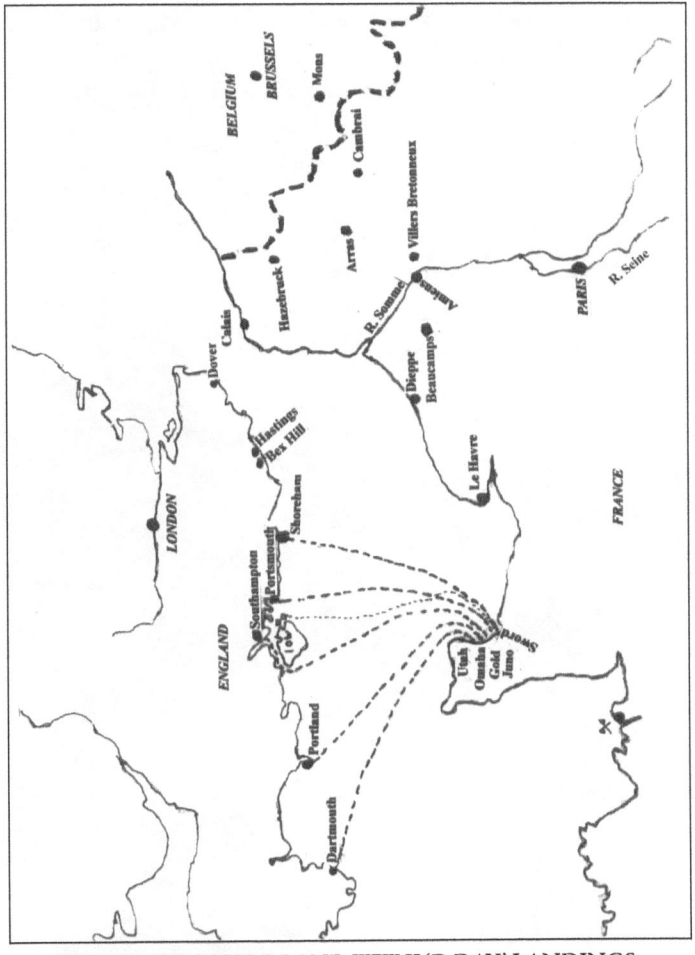

WWI BATTLE FIELDS AND WW II 'D DAY' LANDINGS.

As they marched along a narrow French road towards the Belgian border near the village of Hazebrouch, Andrew's Company had their first experience of being shelled.

When he heard the first shell whistling overhead, Andrew gave a quick hand signal and they all took cover in the ditch as the pattern of falling shells slowly moved along the road.

Several men at the rear of the column were killed and some were wounded. The wounded were soon picked up by motor ambulances and they continued towards the front.

Chapter 12

IN THE TRENCHES

On arriving at the communications trench serving their area, Andrew and his men were met by Major Smith who gave Andrew orders to deploy his men in a support trench and to be ready to move forward later that night and relieve the company of men from the 'fire', or front, trench.

Andrew was amazed that men were living in trenches, often with a foot of putrid mud and water in the bottom and only having rations of stale bread or hard biscuits, bully beef, jam, tinned beans and the occasional apple or tin of fruit or vegetables and large quantities of tea, with sweetened condensed milk, if you were lucky.

All supplies of water, food, ammunition, shoring timber and sand bags had to manhandled, often at night, through the communications trenches to the support trenches from the dumps farther back which were kept supplied by the motor transport units and numerous horse drawn wagons.

All the supplies had to be shipped from Britain on small freighters, which had to dodge the German U boats and mines, to be landed at Le Havre.

When Andrew's Company moved forward into the 'fire trenches' he realized that they were just low level walls of sand bags, often hastily built at night, above ground level and were not entirely bullet proof!

What was more amazing, was the fact that the German trenches were so close to the fire trenches, often only twenty to one hundred yards away and in places within range of hand grenades and of course the British two inch trench mortars or the German 75 mm mortars.

Andrew was shown to the 'Company HQ' which was a small dug out on the side of the fire trench.

There was just enough room for two sleeping bags, a packing case used as a table and a hand cranked field telephone.

The officer in charge of the previous company in the fire trench stayed behind to explain the layout of the trenches and their duties.

"I am John Peters, pleased to meet you and good luck. Our fire trench is only seventy five yards from the Bosch at the Southern end and over ninety five yards at the Northern end and is about five hundred yards long.

Just a small part of five hundred miles of trenches reaching from Switzerland to the sea!

We have been digging every night to deepen the fire trench so that part of it is already well below ground level at the Southern end, but the men get tired and you have to push them and work with them to keep up morale.

There is a supply party that brings up rations and ammo each night but you will probably have to send your own extra supply party on some nights if you run short.

Do you have any snipers in your company?"

"Yes we have two and are training two more. Do you think we need more?"

"You can never have enough because the attrition rate is high and you need to have enough trained snipers to rotate them frequently. We have about ten and rotate them every two hours. You also have to keep moving the loop holes because once Jerry finds where the shots are coming from he starts giving them buggery with wiz bangs, grenades, mortars and machine gun fire.

We had a 2nd Lt. as second in command of our three platoons and our 2 inch mortar section till we had to do a night attack on a Bosch machine gun post, on that small hill over to the South end of our run, and lost about twenty men. We think that some may have been taken prisoner in the dark. The Bosch must have worked very quickly because the machine gun position was only out of action for a few days and is now a major threat to our lines again. The 'Skipper', Major Smith, is planning to have a night raid to put it out of action again.

Must get back to my men, may see you at the next change in about seven to ten days."

The next morning Andrew called the three platoon sergeants in for a meeting and they worked out the areas of enemy lines to be covered by each platoon and rosters for snipers and 'scope' men.

The 'scope' men had an attachment clamped onto the butt of their rifles so that a loaded and cocked rifle could be placed in a small groove on top of the parapet and a system of mirrors was then used to aim the rifle which was fired by an extension to the trigger. Not very accurate but it made Jerry keep his head down and had accounted for some German machine gunners who were over confident and sprayed the fire trench with bullets till their muzzle flashes had been located and the scope men got to work and systematically shot up the German machine gun post.

Andrew started a routine of patrolling the 500 yards of trench accompanied by the relevant platoon sergeant for each section at random times of day and night. Sometimes he went up to a loop hole with his personal snipers rifle, built up and sighted in by Gillie, and waited for a target to appear.

The German trenches were very deep and often had a deeper trench behind the front trench so you only ever saw their riflemen up at their loop holes or their machine gunner's heads in a machine gun post, but if the sun light was from behind, the telescopic sight on Andrew's snipers rifle could pick out much of the detail and Andrew was able to 'score' quite often. He made a rule of closing the loop hole and moving as soon as he had scored so that the source of the accurate sniping could not be identified.

An order came on the field telephone that as the Germans were thought to be using carrier pidgins to convey messages, all pidgins were therefore to be shot and if possible the message fastened to their leg was to be taken to the 'I corps' officer for translation.

This of course led to a lot of hilarity and every time a pidgin, or any bird, flew over there was a volley of rifle fire and usually the bird flew on unscathed. However, on one occasion a heron flew over with it's slow relaxed style of flight and was hit and dropped close to the fire trench.

As it was Sunday some joker suggested roast heron for lunch!

After much improvisation, a sort of oven made out of flattened out biscuit tins, was used to cook the heron and Andrew was ceremoniously given a small piece. It was tough, flavoured with mud and had an oily texture. Different, but not his choice of menu.

Because the opposing trenches were so close together neither side risked shelling the front line trenches but the Bosch did a lot of night shelling of the communication trenches and service area well behind the lines. Very often a pattern of shells landed where the men were 'resting' after a stint in the lines.

Andrew met the 'I Corps' officer for their sector who calculated that well over 50 % of total casualties was caused by shelling. He explained to Andrew the importance of morale and discipline in the trenches as there could be an enemy raid at any time, but particularly after shelling which was used to 'soften up the enemy' prior to an assault.

Andrew soon found that shelling was the worst part of trench warfare because it could start anytime, day or night, without warning and the open top trenches gave no protection from above.

The range of the shelling could go back into the so called rest areas, often some distance away.

Very often 'resting' consisted of forming supply units to carry supplies up to the forward trenches and the men had to struggle around new shell holes, often in the dark, and take cover when they heard a shell overhead.

Even though the lines were almost static for many months, the continuous shelling, rifle and machine gun fire plus several grenade and mortar bombardments prior to infantry charges by both sides, all accounted for dreadful numbers of dead and wounded.

Each time Andrew's company withdrew from the lines to the rest area they had to pick up more men as replacements, if they were available, but these new men were usually not fully trained and became a burden on the company in the front line for the first few weeks.

Many of the men had dysentery which was very easily spread and could reduce men to skin and bones in a few weeks and put them in hospital. Body lice were a constant problem and the men used to run a candle flame along the seams of their clothes to kill the lice and eggs. You could hear them popping with the heat of the flame!

The lack of proper sanitation, corpses of men and horses half buried in the mud attracted huge colonies of rats.

Large, hungry rats would even attack a sleeping man and were constantly stealing any food left out for more than a few minutes. The medics warned that the rats carried all sorts of disease but there was not much that could be done to stop them.

Sometimes a section of trench was sealed off and the men had a 'rat shoot' as target practice and to relieve the boredom of living in a confined space. There was usually much betting on the results and Andrew consistently had the best score.

Some of the local French people had stayed in their farms, shops and homes farther back from the fighting and Andrew was sometimes able to get a billet in a house when his company was 'resting' and he found the French people very friendly and helpful. They were very grateful for the efforts of the English troops trying to push the Germans out of their beloved France.

On one occasion Andrew and two other young officers were billeted in a partly damaged and deserted farm house about half a mile out of a village when at about midnight a pattern of German shells started moving along the road nearby. The farm house was hit and the front part was destroyed.

Andrew was covered in rubble where he was sleeping near the kitchen stove and was partly concussed, he pushed off the fallen timbers and plaster and slowly stood up choking in the dust. As he stumbled round trying to find a lamp or a candle and matches he heard someone else choking in the dust, but it sounded like a child.

He went towards the sound and contacted a small body that jumped with shock at his touch and called out in French.

Judging by the well-formed breast that he had contacted, the other survivor was a young girl!

Andrew only had basic school boy French so he said.

"Je chercher l'allumettes" (I look for the Matches)

"Je trouver pour vous Monsieur."

After a lot of stumbling about in the dark and removing a lot of debris they found the matches and some candles in the remains of a kitchen cupboard.

When two candles had been lit they went to look for "Les deux soldats." who had been sleeping in the front room, but there was just a jumble of stone blocks from the chimney and a large shell hole left with no sign of any human remains.

They found Andrew's pack half buried in the the kitchen and his supply of bully beef and dry biscuits and used a tin of condensed milk to make some coffee which the girl heated on the kitchen wood stove. The girl said that she was "Tres faim." (Very hungry.) So she made some soup with bully beef and turnips.

The result looked terrible, but she ate it all.

The girl's name was Michelle and she was dix-huit ans. (18 years old)

They used Andrew's field dressing kit to clean up their cuts and a gash on Andrew's leg and then applied the antiseptic ointment.

As only part of the kitchen roof remained they went to the barn across the yard where Michelle was living and settled down in a hay loft to sleep till first light.

Michelle was awake as dawn was breaking and went to the stable to wash and get some water so when Andrew woke and found her gone he became very worried that she had left some time in the night and may not return.

He was delighted to see Michelle coming from the stables carrying a bucket, part filled with water, and a bundle of fire wood.

Michelle lit the wood stove in the kitchen and made some coffee while Andrew opened the last tin of bully beef and found the remains of the ration biscuits.

Andrew was not due back at the assembly point to take his men back to the lines till the following morning so he asked Michelle if it was possible to have a wash and she showed him where there was a simple bucket shower set up in a stable and offered to heat up some water on the kitchen stove for him.

When the hot water was transferred into the bucket shower and Andrew was stripping off his clothes he became aware that Michelle was watching him.

As Andrew was getting dressed he saw that Michelle was still sitting on an old stool in a shaft of sunlight by the stable door. She had her skirt pulled up so that the sun was warming her very shapely legs.

He was surprised and delighted to think that he was apparently being seduced by this exciting, young French girl.

His excitement was mounting when he kissed her and felt her taut body pressed tightly against him.

Michelle was becoming flushed with excitement.

Andrew ran his hands over her and could feel that she was starting to tremble with excitement.

Michelle then started climbing into the hay loft and said.

"Venez ici, depechez-vous! (Come here, hurry up!)

The old rugs were still on the hay where they had slept during the night.

They slowly undressed each other and there was much intimate kissing. This was a totally new experience for Andrew and the aroma and feel of her beautiful young body sent him wild.

After a few minutes Michelle said.

"Maintenant!"

Andrew felt the heat of her young body and the intimate contact soon made them come together.

Michelle clung onto him for a long time while she kept on convulsing and squeezing him with pleasure.

Andrew said.

"I love you Michelle you are the most wonderful girl and I want to see you every time I come out of the lines. Will you be safe if you wait for me here?"

Michelle kissed and hugged him and said.

"Je t'aime aussi. Je attendre pour vous ici."

He told Michelle in his stumbling French that he would go to the supply depot in the village and pick up some more rations and supplies and would be back in two or three hours.

Andrew had found out that Michelle had learned English at school and was slowly starting to remember the language but had trouble with the pronunciation.

He had to report the death of the other two officers, who came from a different infantry Regiment, at the next opportunity.

The supply depot was out of condensed milk but had some tinned plums so he loaded up his pack with an assortment of tinned food and filled a sand bag with ration biscuits, candles, coffee, sugar, socks, a shirt and some chocolate that he was able to buy at an elevated price from a small shop that was still open in the village.

Andrew was anxious to get back to Michelle at the farm as soon as possible and hurried up the slope towards the farm.

Even though the air was still cool, Andrew got hot as he toiled up to the farm house loaded with his pack and the sand bag full of food.

Michelle was sitting in the barn and watched him as he came up the hill and when she saw how much food Andrew had brought she said excitedly.

"C'est merveilleux!" and kissed and hugged him passionately.

They resurrected the fire in the kitchen stove and made some coffee which they drank sitting in the winter sun in the doorway of the barn.

Andrew was falling in love with this tall,very beautiful, French girl and was enjoying her company and started to try to find out more about her as they became more relaxed.

She had lived with her family in a chateau which was on a large property near Arras but when the Germans had made their first fast sweep into Luxemburg, through Belgium and over the border into France everything had suddenly changed. There had then been the devastating loss of Mons, in the first few days of the war, and when the Germans crossed the border from Belgium and invaded France, their chateau had been shelled to a pile of rubble, her parents and brothers probably killed and she was the only member of the family to survive, as far as she knew, because she had been sent to visit a cousin, where it was supposed to be safer at that time, but the cousin's house had also been shelled and she was apparently the sole survivor from that house.

This farm was owned by one of Michelle's uncles so she had moved here to be with family, but her aunt and uncle had recently been killed by a stray bomb dropped from a German aeroplane, while they were at the local village market selling some produce.

During the stilted French and English conversation, Michelle admitted that she had crept up to the house, where the three men were billeted, to steal (Voler.) some food as she was starving and that was why she had been in the house at the time that the shell landed.

She said that previous men billeted in the house had stripped the garden of anything that was edible, killed and eaten the chickens, stolen the potatoes and wine that were stored in the cellar and taken most of the fodder in the barn to feed their horses. So she was living on turnips from a nearby field, apples from the orchard and porridge made out of oats that she had to beat flat before cooking. There was no milk because the cows had all been stolen a long time ago and there were no eggs now that the chickens had been killed and eaten. She kept in hiding because she was scared of being raped by the soldiers who kept on whistling and chasing her.

Andrew just said that he came from a Military family and had volunteered soon after he had finished at the university.

Michelle was keen to be involved in beating the much hated Bosch occupying and ransacking France, and asked if he could help her to join up with a British or French medical unit further behind the lines. Andrew said that he would make enquiries and let her know as soon as he found anything suitable when he next came out of the lines to the rest area.

That night Andrew and Michelle went to bed in the barn, and soon they were making passionate love and then slept still entwined together.

The next morning Andrew kissed Michelle good bye and she responded with a lingering kiss and a hug and he walked back to the assembly point and arrived well before the assembly time of ten o'clock.

His company was in need of ten or twelve replacements so he went to the transit camp and was surprised to see one of his men who had been badly wounded and had gone back to the field hospital a few months ago and was now recovered and back ready for duty.

"Good to see you recovered and back again. The field hospital must have done a very good job."

"Thank you Sir. Yes the 'African Angels', as we called the two senior nurses, did the job themselves as they are better than that old piss pot doctor in stitching up flesh wounds.

The great gash on me' back, caused by shrapnel from that shell that landed in our trench, is all neat as nine pence now."

"Did you know the nurses names?"

"Yer', they was Sister Sally and Sister Sarah, as I remembers Sir."

"That is amazing, I know them and would like to get a message to them. Next time we have wounded going back to the field hospital, perhaps I can send a message?"

As Andrew was going back to the fire trench it started to pour with rain and the whole trench system took on another form of misery, flooded trenches, wet clothing, wet feet, stinking mud, more mud, latrine buckets awash and overflowing. Poor visibility making the enemy very hard to see, but Jerry kept up rifle and mortar fire and the shelling never stopped.

The planned attack on the German machine gun post was postponed pending better weather.

A Lewis gun section was added to the company and would be used to keep firing at the German machine gun post over the heads of the assaulting troops till, the last moment.

The weather improved two days later and the attack was confirmed for one hour before first light on the next morning.

Andrew was to deploy two platoons in the darkness with one advancing in a curve to the left and one advancing in a curve to the right with the Lewis gun firing up the middle as soon as it was light enough. The third platoon was to stand by as a reserve if needed.

Cutting the German barbed wire in the dark was always a problem because it was thicker and stronger (High tensile.) than the British wire. It also had more barbs which were longer.

The English troops hung jam tins with a few stones in them along their wire to help detect wire cutting at night, but the Germans claimed to have a system of listening devices attached to their wire, but they were never found. This was probably just propaganda.

Andrew was to lead the right hand assault platoon and had a good supply of Mills grenades to lob into the gun emplacement as soon as they were close enough.

On a signal from the Major the troops crossed over their own parapet and released the opening in their own wire and quickly crossed 'no mans' land, cut the German wire and waited in a fold in the ground for dawn and the Lewis gun to start firing.

On the first burst of fire from the Lewis gun, Andrews's men started forward and approached the gun emplacement from two different angles. The bullets from the Lewis gun smashed into the sand bag walls of the machine gun emplacement and climbed up to the parapet where the gunners heads were visible at their loop hole.

There was another long burst and then the Lewis gun ceased firing.

Andrew and a platoon Sergeant started lobbing Mills grenades over the parapet and after four or five had exploded inside they ordered the troops to rush in and secure the emplacement.

As soon as the machine gun emplacement was secure Andrew ordered the men to move along the German trench in an almost hand to hand type of fighting.

Jerry was caught still half asleep with only a few sentries awake and armed so the first few minutes went according to plan but then more German troops started to come up from their 'deep' trenches.

Andrew then ordered the platoon sergeants who still had plenty of grenades to start rolling them down the access tunnels leading to the 'deep' trenches into the lines of Bosch starting to rush out.

Within half an hour they had overrun the machine gun emplacement and the supporting trench system, so a flag signal was given to the other two companies waiting to use the same assault path and fan out to take the rest of that whole section of Jerry lines.

To ensure that they were not cut off from their own lines, two companies of Sappers were ready to quickly join up the original fire trenches with the captured German trenches.

Mortars were brought up and the German supply trenches were systematically pounded with two inch and three inch mortar bombs to ensure that the captured trenches were secure from attack from along the German supply trenches.

They had gained about one hundred yards at one end and may be two hundred at the other end, but what was more important, they were now on some slightly higher ground!

They also found some food, cooking utensils and more comfortable covered dug outs for sleeping.

The British 'Top Brass' were frustrated and annoyed that the whole Western Front had been literally bogged down in the trenches for years and were prepared to try any means of pushing the Germans back.

Trench warfare caused a terrible manpower attrition rate on both sides, used vast quantities of small arms and artillery ammunition and supplies, kept the men in a permanent state of being under fire, due to shelling and small arms fire, and the rate of advance was usually only a few hundred yards, if you were lucky after another 'Over the top' assault with the inevitable high number of casualties.

One idea to improve trench warfare was the 'Magnall-Irving Thrust Borer' which comprised a see-saw hand pump and a hydraulic ram which forced screwed steel rods from British trenches, under no man's land, to within a few yards of the enemy trenches.

This whole system was developed and manufactured by The Hydraulic Engineering Company in Chester. As the steel rods were forced out, more rods were screwed on till the end was within about two yards of the enemy trench and then withdrawn. Explosive charges were then pushed to the end of the hole and detonated electrically.

On one occasion a pattern of holes had been made up to an enemy trench, then charged with explosives and wired up so that they could be detonated all at once to get maximum effect.

Immediately after the massive explosion a shower of red fleshy matter rained down and word went round that they had blown up a concentration of Bosch troops who were about to do an assault!

It was then realised that the explosion had gone off under the edge of a field of beetroot!

But the explosion had destroyed a section of enemy trenches and killed or wounded everyone in the area and a successful assault was then made.

The system was considered effective but too slow.

Another idea that had started back at the 'SFTU' where, under Geoffery's instruction, Tad had trained small groups of sappers in underground tunneling and these men were later employed on the Somme where many tunnels were dug and charged with many tons of explosives and old unexploded shells.

At 0730 Hrs on the 1st of July 1916 all the charges in a series of tunnels went off within 30 seconds and the devastation, blast and shock was terrifying and had a major demoralising effect on the Germans.

The troops who were waiting to do an assault after the explosion were told that they would be able to advance without any opposition. But they soon came under machine gun fire from a second defense line. However, a considerable advance was made but this was then driven back by German machine gunners in a few days.

It was apparent that trench warfare was not fully understood by some older senior officers and one example was when a Field Marshall reputedly said. "The machine gun is a much overrated weapon and two per battalion is sufficient."

The Germans had crack 'Maschinengewehr' units which were a constant threat and accounted for vast numbers of dead and wounded.

The French had replaced their Saint- Etiennre Model 07 Hotchkiss with the new improved 'Model 1914', machine gun which was an immediate success.

On one ten day period during a prolonged German attack on the French fortress city of Verdun a section of two Hotchkiss model 1914, air cooled machine guns were in almost constant use and fired the amazing number of more than one hundred and fifty thousand rounds with only minor stoppages!

This was an amazing performance by air cooled machine guns and gave the French an advantage because of their almost constant rate of fire.

The first Americans to arrive in France did not have enough machine guns and were supplied with 'Model 1914' Hotchkiss 8 mm. calibre weapons and immediately put them to good use.

Chapter 13

THE FIELD HOSPITAL

Sally and Sarah were exhausted by the almost continuous stream of casualties being brought in by the stretcher bearers and motor ambulances, plus the walking wounded who usually arrived in twos or threes, helping each other.

Many of the stretcher cases had been lying in putrid mud and water for a long time before they could be picked up and almost all of these had wounds that had become septic and or turned gangrenous. The mortality rate of this type of patient was over 80 % unless affected limbs could be quickly amputated and the stumps disinfected before the gangrene was able to spread.

Body wounds and stomach wounds nearly always proved fatal due to infection or the lack of major surgery facilities for internal operations.

The matron of the field hospital was a middle aged spinster who drove the orderlies and the girls day and night.

The doctor was a lecherous old drunk who was none too fussy about sterilization of the instruments and was very inept at tying off blood vessels and muscles when performing an amputation with the result that most of them required further surgery, if the patient lived that long.

With the girls training by their father and mother at the shamba and the London Hospital they were horrified at the poor standards and often performed part of an operation themselves when the doctor had stopped to have a rest (and a swig of whisky from his flask,) and the matron was not around.

Even though the field hospital was nearly ten miles behind the lines there was one German gun that had been christened 'Big Bertha,' which fired the occasional shell into the supply area close to the field hospital.

The shells from Big Bertha could be heard whistling overhead quite clearly before there was a huge explosion which shook the ground. So far the shells had all landed close to, or in the supply depot, which had apparently been located by a German spotter plane.

A young English officer with a badly damaged and infected arm was being prepared by Sally and Sarah for an amputation when one of Big Bertha's shells was heard very close overhead.

The matron and doctor were in the improvised kitchen tent having a cup of tea before starting to operate and were closest to where the shell landed and were killed instantly. Sally and Sarah had heard the shell coming and as it sounded closer than usual dragged their patient off the operating table and they all literally fell into the small dug out just behind the operating area. There was an earth shattering explosion and shrapnel and a hot blast ripped over their heads making them temporally deaf.

When the debris had stopped falling, the girls climbed out of the dugout, put their patient on an improvised assessment table and surveyed the damage.

The whole hospital tent had disappeared, the patients who had been bedded down on the floor were scattered in various states of distress over a large area, all of the equipment and instruments were damaged or missing and the orderlies were nowhere to be seen.

A motor ambulance drove up and two men got out.

"What a bloody mess, and a field 'ospital too. Bloody Bosch have no respec' for that bloody great red cross on the roof."

"Come on Charlie we must give those two nurses an 'and to clean up. You never know your luck, eh'?" A large supply truck arrived and four men and a sergeant got out. The sergeant took charge of cleaning up and reinstating what was left of the field hospital.

Two hours of back breaking work had the tent dragged back to it's original position by the truck, and with the one end that was not ripped, re- erected, the patients who were still alive carried into the half tent, some of the equipment collected and then the girls and the ambulance men started to re-asses the patients.

Only the young officer waiting for an amputation and five post op. patients were still alive.

Sally went over to the officer and said.

"Hello, my name is Sally and this is my younger sister Sarah who assists me. After the shelling, I seem to be the most senior person around. Your wound is badly infected and we were about to remove the infected part of your arm before the shell landed, do you wish to go back to another field hospital for the operation or do you trust me to do the operation because speed is essential if we are going to stop the infection spreading?"

"I will lose the arm anyway, but are you competent to do the job?"

"I am not a qualified surgeon but have worked with my father doing this type of operation many times and have finished off the operation and sewn up the wound for many of the operations done here."

"Well you sound confident, so go ahead and take care."

Sally set up the operating table and Sarah collected and sterilized a set of instruments and the ambulance driver stood by to administer the anaesthetic.

As soon as the patient was 'out' sally checked to find the limit of the infection and marked a line.

She then performed her first 'solo' amputation with great care and sewed up the flap of skin to neatly cover the stump.

"Jesus, you are a real 'African Angel,' you do a much better job than that old whisky sot of a doctor used to do!"

Said the ambulance driver, and his mate nodded in agreement.

Three days later the field hospital site had been moved about half a mile farther away from the supply depot, which had seemed to attract shells from Big Bertha.

A new hospital tent had been erected and there was more new equipment and medical supplies available.

The young officer with the amputated arm was recovering well and the other post op. patients seemed to be surviving after being thrown about by the blast from the shell. The fact that they were on the ground had saved them from most of the shrapnel but they had been caught by the blast.

After two more hectic days of running the hospital on their own, Sally and Sarah were relieved to see an ambulance arriving with the new doctor and matron, straight out from England. The girls then had to slowly teach them what it was like to run a field hospital in wartime.

There had been a particularly bloody battle a few months later and the hospital was inundated with casualties, many of whom died soon after arrival and Sarah was on night shift with the new Matron.

Sarah was going round checking on the patients when she heard a grown coming from the pile of corpses outside the back of the tent waiting for the burial party in the morning.

"Matron, I just heard a groan coming from one of the corpses outside, I will go and check."

"Don't worry Dear, it is just the gas you know."

Sarah was not satisfied and went out with a lamp to check.

There were two of the sleekest, fattest rats she had ever seen licking up the blood and gnawing the edge of a flesh wound on the protruding arm of one of the corpses.

Sarah realised that if there was blood flowing that the man must be still alive!

She chased the rats away and felt the protruding arm, it was warm!

The man was quickly pulled out of the pile and wheeled into the tent. He was definitely alive and had a strong pulse.

It appeared that the man had been very badly concussed and had just minor flesh wounds to his arms, face and upper body and as there must have been a lot of blood, he had been mistakenly put out with the corpses by one of the orderlies.

Sarah spent a long time cleaning up the patient and eventually he was able to speak a little.

She found that his name was Robert Hastings and that he came from near Shrewsbury in Shropshire. He then lapsed into a sort of sleep or coma for a while.

When he came awake again he said that he had just been promoted to Captain and had been in France since a few days after the war started and most of his unit had been killed during a major offensive near Verdun and he was on his way back to Arras when he was caught in a barrage of night shelling.

By the morning Sarah was very tired but still continued to provide intensive care and asked Sally to help her stitch up his numerous flesh wounds. This was done early in the morning under anaesthetic and then the patient continued to sleep.

As Sarah was off shift and was sleeping, Sally went to check on Robert Hastings about noon. He was awake and wanted to know where he was and how he had got there. Sally told him that he had been brought in by ambulance about six o' clock the previous evening and that as he was badly concussed he had been mistakenly put outside by one of the orderlies.

"My sister Sarah heard you groaning and brought you in and revived you and saved your life!

I stitched up most of your surface wounds this morning and it is now the middle of the day.

So you can just relax and let the wounds heal. We will need to check your dressings about four times a day."

Sarah came back on duty at 1800 Hrs. and went to check on Robert Hastings. He had been sleeping again and had just woken up.

"Your sister told me that you saved my life and thank you. You are a very sweet girl and you have looked after me so well. I would like to ask you out some time. Please come and tell me about yourself."

"I can't at the moment, but perhaps I can later when the other patients are sleeping."

Robert was fascinated by this beautiful young girl with a lovely skin colour who was so practical and confident. He could not place her accent, it seemed to be Scotish but there was also some other background language that he could not place.

By 2000 Hrs. the patients had been fed, checked and bedded down for the night so Sarah was able to go and sit by Robert's bed.

"How are you feeling?"

"Much better thank you, especially now that you have come to tell me about yourself."

"It is difficult to know where to start but I will just give you the outline."

She started by explaining about how her father had set up the shamba and she and her sister had grown up living in the African bush. Robert was amazed that they had reared a wild lion cub and that she had remembered Mark so many years later. Sarah became emotional as she told him about how her parents had been murdered by the Boers in a reprisal raid. She then explained how Mark had come for emergency surgery during the Boer war and lived with them while he recovered and that the sisters were now living as part of Mark's family in England.

Robert then started to understand why the two girls were so resourceful and competent.

The next day two badly wounded men arrived in the back of a truck, being looked after by a young French girl. The men said that they were in Captain Andrew Baker's company and had been asked to ensure that Michelle got safely to the field hospital as Andrew and the girl had become friends when they had met in the village that they used as a rest area.

The men were quickly checked and had their wounds assessed for surgery while Michelle waited and then said in her broken French and English that she had a letter from Andrew for them.

Sally opened the letter and started to read.

> Dear Sally and Sarah,
>
> Michelle has asked me to help her to volunteer to work anywhere that will assist in winning the war so when I found that you are at the field hospital I suggested that she might join you and she agreed so I have sent her with two of my wounded men. Please look after her as we have become very close friends.
>
> I think that I will be moving to a new location soon.
>
> Please take care and love to you both. Andrew.

Sally took the letter to the Matron who was not sure what to do but finally agreed to have Michelle as a 'Volunteer Nursing Aid' attached to the hospital staff.

Chapter 14

ON THE MOVE

Andrew's company was ordered to be ready to lead an assault deep into the German lines.

It had been found by questioning German prisoners that their supplies had not got through and that they had run out of food and were reputedly starving. The 'I' corps officer said that there had even been a German mutiny due to a lack of food a long way to the South where the lines were held by the French Army.

Andrew and Major Smith knew that an assault would mean fighting their way through a well-established system of German trenches as the lines had been static for many months so there would be stiff resistance, particularly from their deep second line of trenches.

Andrew and his most reliable platoon sergeant decided to go on a night 'recce' and find out what sort of opposition they were likely to meet.

They set off armed only with revolvers, bayonets, wire cutters and compasses and crawled up to the enemy lines. The first line of trenches appeared to be deserted so they got into the trench and explored along for some way till they saw the outline of a large redoubt with a single sentry sitting on a box with his rifle across his knees.

The sentry appeared to be asleep as the outline of his helmet was tilted forward and he made no move.

They decided to bayonet the sentry so that they could explore farther and crept forward. The plan was that the sergeant would cut his throat and Andrew was to remove the helmet and club him with the butt end of his bayonet.

But as the razor sharp edge of the bayonet sliced across, there was no throat to cut!

There was only a bag stuffed with rags where the head should have been!

The body was human and in German uniform alright, but the headless body was being held upright by a broom handle forced through the body and down into the ground. They suspected a booby trap like a string tied to the pin of a grenade or something similar and retreated for a few minutes. When all was quiet they continued along the trench and could not see or hear any Germans till they found a small tunnel leading to a system of deep trenches with muffled voices and the smell of cigarettes.

Jerry was at home and would come out of the deep trenches like angry ants at the first sign of trouble.

Back at the 'Company HQ'. Andrew telephoned the Major and reported his findings.

"You silly buggers could have got yourselves killed but at least you have got some information.

Did you get any idea of how many men they have in their deep trenches?"

"No sir, they seemed to be relaxing with just the dummy sentry on duty. If we do an assault we would need plenty of grenades for the front men to throw into the deep trenches before they can come out to man their front trenches."

"I will let you know if we decide to go ahead with an assault"

It was decided to do the assault two days later, as a dawn raid.

Andrew's company was to lead and hold the front enemy trench while two more companies were to follow immediately and attack the deep trenches with grenades.

The plan worked till the second and third companies found that there were machine guns set up in the tunnels leading to the deep trenches and there was a massacre. Some of the first grenades had put one machine gun out of action but there were two more which pumped lead into the mass of assaulting men.

As soon as Andrew realised what was happening he ordered a withdrawal and all the surviving men scrambled back out of the front line trench and raced for their own trenches. Andrew shot two Germans with his revolver as they appeared in the trench from the tunnel and then came out last and started back at a run but was shot in the leg. As he stumbled and fell a platoon sergeant and another man helped him up and dragged him back to their own trench hopping on one leg. They fell into the trench in a heap and Andrew passed out with the pain of the shattered pieces of bone grinding together and shock. He came to a few minutes later and a first aid man bound up his leg to stop the bleeding.

That night Andrew started on a terrible stretcher trip, with the stretcher bearers stumbling through the trenches in the dark, often with a foot of water and mud in the bottom to eventually reach an ambulance pick up point on a road.

The stretcher bearers had to go back to pick up more wounded so he was just left at the side of the road in a small dug out in the dark wondering whether an ambulance would ever come!

Andrew lay there in pain, was cold, wet and hungry as he became less confident that he would ever get to a field hospital.

Just as it was getting light, an ambulance arrived and he was shoved in with four other wounded men.

The ambulance got stuck in a shell hole after traveling a few miles and had to be pulled out by about a dozen men with ropes and then continued on its erratic journey with every bump making Andrew wince with pain. His knee felt as though it was packed with sharp stones which were grinding together.

When the ambulance eventually got to the field hospital there was just a deserted and empty tent with the flaps blowing in the wind!

There was a scrawled sign pinned to the tent flap.

Field Hospital No 6 has moved - ask MP.

"Bloody 'red caps' 'ave fucked us up again. SNAFU."(Situation normal all fucked up.) Said the angry driver as he turned round to go back to the nearest road intersection where there should be a red cap on duty.

Eventually they did find an MP and were directed to cross the River Somme at Amiens and go to Beaucamps where they would be redirected to the new location of Field Hospital Number 6.

The driver then said to the Military Police Sergeant.

"S'pose this means another withdrawal is expected, Sergeant?"

"Can't say, just ordered to evacuate the hospital last night. On your way driver and don't ask questions 'cos you might learn too much!"

The driver then realised that there was not enough petrol to go as far as Beaucamps so had to turn back and fill up at a transport depot which was down to the last few tins of petrol, reserved for ambulances only.

The journey took nearly six hours to travel some thirty miles and the patients were in a bad way when they eventually arrived at No 6 Field Hospital, in its new location near Beaucamps.

The matron went to receive the new arrivals as usual and supervised their transfer into the tent for assessment.

Andrew was on the assessment table when he saw Sally and Sarah coming to strip off the field dressings from his leg. They immediately recognised him and kissed him before starting to attend to his leg. They then told him that there was a surprise waiting for him!

Andrew hoped that the surprise would be Michelle and started to forget his pain and discomfort.

Michelle was helping to sterilise the instruments for surgery on the new patients when Sarah said "Go and see who has just come in." She did not fully understand but from the tone of voice and excited expression on Sarah's face she guessed what was meant and hurried to the assessment area.

There was Andrew with his shattered leg being cleaned up by Sally.

She held his hand and kissed him, "Mon pauve cheri vous avez un grand blessure. Mais nous sommes ensemble!" (My poor darling you have a big wound. But we are together!)

The evacuation of the field hospital had only just been in time as there was a major enemy advance as far as the River Somme and the old trenches by the river were reoccupied and became static again.

The British intelligence had found through one of their informants and reports from spotter planes that there was a massing of enemy men and supplies for a push to Amiens and just had time to evacuate the supply areas and plan a night withdrawal of the remaining front line troops before the 'softening up intensive shelling' started prior to the enemy assault.

Most of the first shells had landed immediately after the front line troops had left and the shelling pattern had then advanced and chased them as they retreated. The shelling lasted for about fifteen minutes and caused a lot of casualties.

Sally and Sarah were long overdue for return to Britain as they had been in the field hospital for nearly three years without a break and the matron had reluctantly applied for their replacement so that they could return to Britain for some leave or transfer to a local hospital.

Eventually the replacement nurses arrived with movement orders for Sally, Sarah, and Michelle to go to Le Havre with a convoy of ambulances and trucks.

The plan was that the nurses would provide medical support for as many wounded as possible during the journey. They must evacuate as many patients, needing more surgery in Britain, as could be packed into the vehicles. They would then be shipped back to Southhampton or Portsmouth on a returning supply ship as soon as possible.

Two days later the convoy of vehicles started to arrive. There were only two ambulances and eleven trucks of varying types and sizes.

It was suggested by Sarah that the open stake sided trucks have the sides covered with tarpaulins to reduce the draft and mud and this was soon done. It was also suggested that as many patients as possible should travel in a sitting position to nearly double the number carried as this could be the last chance of patient evacuation for some time.

Six of the most critical patients were loaded into the two ambulances and nearly 200 other patients were loaded into the trucks, packed in like sardines, with those requiring most attention in the two trucks under the care of Sally and Michelle was to travel with Sarah, Andrew, Robert and the boxes of medical supplies required during the journey.

The convoy started off early the next morning on the 80 mile journey to Le Havre and stopped at about two hour intervals so that the patients could be checked.

It was an exhausting trip for the girls with many of the patients complaining of bleeding wounds aggravated by the jolting, which then needed attention.

The harbour master at Le Havre said that they would have to wait till their ship had finished unloading which could take another 10 hours or so!

The convoy of trucks and ambulances was committed to return immediately, so the nurses and patients were off loaded into a large shed on the wharf.

There was no food, water or toilet facilities available so Michelle offered to go and find the essentials.

Half an hour later she returned with some empty buckets, also some tins of bully beef and then went off again.

Michelle made several trips and each time she came back with a trolly loaded with old packing cases, to be used as firewood, and an assortment of tinned food and ration biscuits.

Several clean buckets were half filled with water from a distant tap, a fire was lighted outside the shed and Michelle then made a stew of bully beef and 'tinned everything else.'

They only had a few tin mugs and empty tins to serve the stew in but with much banter they all managed to have a hot meal which raised morale.

Sally asked Michelle how she got the tinned food and ration biscuits.

She said that she had recognized the labels in a warehouse and used a piece of iron to break open the boxes full of tinned food.

They were just settling down after the meal when they heard the stuttering engine of an aeroplane approaching and looked up to see a German eindecker (Monoplane.) approaching at a low altitude.

The gunner was hanging over the side of the cockpit with a shining steel cylinder in his hand and as the plane came closer a company of men who had just disembarked from another ship was ordered to open fire on the plane and volley after volley of rifle fire was aimed at the plane.

The plane appeared to be hit but kept coming and as it was nearly overhead the engine spluttered and stopped and the plane burst into flames and spiraled down to crash into the harbour.

A loud cheer went up as the plane sank almost immediately.

The harbour master sent out a work boat with two armed men to pick up the two Germans struggling in the water.

Two military policemen took control of the Germans as soon as the boat came back to the wharf.

The supply ship eventually finished unloading and the harbour master sent over some men with trollies to move the patients to the ship and help them get on board.

There was very limited accommodation on board, designed for just the crew, so the patients were put under a temporary shelter made out of a tarpaulin slung across the after deck and the ship sailed almost immediately.

The crossing to Southampton was fairly smooth but the wind was cold and there were no spare blankets.

Chapter 15

Recuperating

On landing at Southampton everyone was taken to a clearing hospital.

Sally asked if Andrew and Robert could be sent to the Chester infirmary for surgery.

A telephone enquiry was made to see if they could be accepted and as the answer was yes, Sally said that they would take care of the two patients on the train journey and could also arrange for accommodation while they recuperated after surgery. This was readily agreed to as all the Southern hospitals were already overflowing.

That meant that they could return to Glendarvel and Andrew and Robert could recover at their own homes with their parents, when they came out of hospital.

Sasha and Jill met the train at Chester station with the two cars and had an ambulance waiting to take Andrew and Robert to the infirmary.

Sasha and Michelle talked in French as they drove home.

Sally was very excited as they drove through the memorial gates and got Sasha to explain to Michelle, in French, about the reason for the name.

Mark was waiting at the front door as they drove up and he kissed and hugged the girls on their safe return. He was then introduced to Michelle who was crying with emotion. She was sad and grieving for the loss of her family, happy to be with a loving family and in love with Andrew all at the same time.

The girls took Michelle up to a spare room and helped her to settle in.

Sasha decided to have an early dinner as the travelers were all tired and hungry so dinner was to be at half past six.

Mark phoned Geoffrey who was at home for a short rest, as he had been working in London for the last year, and asked if he and Florence would like to come up for coffee and meet Andrew's friend Michelle. Yes, they would and could be there about seven o'clock.

Michelle was very nervous about meeting Andrew's parents, especially as he was not there, but Sasha helped her with translation and tried to give her confidence and she gradually gained confidence and became more relaxed.

Geoffrey was itching to question the girls about the conditions in France and Belgium but this was not the time or place.

Florence said that she would telephone the Chester infirmary in the morning to find when it would be suitable to visit Andrew.

The Bakers said good night and left and everyone else went to bed soon afterwards.

Mark and Gillie had training at the 'SFTU' going full bore with a new intake of men selected to be trained as snipers every two weeks. Tad had failed his medical to join the army as the doctor had found that he had the start of silicosis from years of working in the tin mines in Cornwall. He was working with Gillie and running training courses on the use of explosives, precision tunnelling and detonating charges electrically.

Mark administered the SFTU and planned the arrival, departure and testing of all trainees.

There was also a camp staff who provided all the domestic services and physical endurance training for the students on the nearby hills.

Gillie had a full time armourer working in a small hut at the camp who selected and built up an SMLE. Mk III snipers rifle with telescopic sights for each trainee and then 'shot them in' for him.

"Ye will guard that rifle with your life laddie, and make shore that ye' check the aim regularly and good luck" Said Gillie to each sniper that completed the course and then shook his hand firmly.

Sasha and Agnes kept the home running smoothly and worked for the local Red Cross branch, which was now based in the new Village hall, which had a separate room for use by the Red Cross.

As the war dragged on, more and more of the everyday items became in short supply or just unobtainable, but the usual use by the family and estate employees of home grown meat and market garden produce kept the larders supplied except for sugar, flour and imported items.

Andrew came out of hospital to recuperate at his parents' home but the doctors had said that his knee was very badly damaged and could not be repaired without extensive surgery and that it would have to be kept straight for the time being. He was therefore not fit for active duty. After another two months he was posted to a training unit near Reading.

Michelle joined in with all family activities and started to become fluent in English but was becoming more worried about what had happened to her family in France. Geoffrey tried to get information but as there had been several battles around Arras and he was told that there were virtually no buildings left standing he could not get any meaningful information.

Andrew and Michelle were able to meet occasionally when Andrew could get some leave.

Sarah went to stay with Robert's family near Shrewsbury when he came out of hospital and after three months he was called for a medical, in readiness for being sent back to France. His posting for return to his unit came a few days later and Sarah was crying as she saw him off on the train.

Sasha had taken them to Chester station and tried to console her, but she was beyond consolation because she had lived in France, and knew the appalling conditions and the chances of survival for the men at the front.

Geoffrey and his organisation were collecting information from all the Allied fronts, the Western front in France, the Eastern front with Russia and the Southern front in the Balkans, as well as from Naval sources.

The German 'U' boats were taking a heavy toll of British shipping, but Britain was still blockading all German supply ships in the channel which was slowly strangling the German war machine to death.

It was widely known that, due to the British naval blockade, the Germans were running out of food for their front line troops, also raw materials for making munitions.

In particular, the Krupp steel works in the Rhur Valley at Essen was short of good quality iron ore for making steel which was curbing their shipbuilding and heavy armaments programme.

Having their fronts so far apart meant that the Germans used a lot of their very limited supply of fuel and resources in transporting men and supplies.

The British introduction of battle tanks had started to establish a new element to warfare as in the first major tank attack at Cambrai in the winter of 1917 where 400 tanks drove a five mile breakthrough into German lines. The rate of advance was much faster than expected and resulted in a lack of follow up support thus causing the loss of the ground gained, a short time later.

However, the unreliability, constant need for fuel in a battle zone and the terrain of trenches, shell holes and mud, and more mud, reduced the usefulness of tanks so they were only used sparingly after the battle at Cambrai.

Since America had entered the war in April 1917 increasing numbers of American troops were contributing to the Allied pressure on Germany.

Mark could see that the three girls had been through absolute hell and needed to get away somewhere to completely relax, so he arranged with his Aunt Mary that Michelle, Sally and Sarah went to stay at Glencairn in Scotland for two weeks to help them to recover after their traumatic experiences in France. He knew that Aunt Mary would treat them like daughters and enjoy their company at Glencairn for two weeks.

As the girls were volunteers and had been in a field hospital for three years under enemy fire without a break they could either retire or be relocated to a local military hospital.

A few days before the girls were due to return from Glencairn Robert's mother telephoned to say that there had been a mix up with the result of Robert's medical examination and that he had been recalled from France for more surgery in a London hospital. The blast from the shell had affected one eye socket and he had failed the peripheral vision test but that this had been overlooked in the rush to get men back to the front.

Two months later Robert was back home on leave. The eye surgeon could not fit in the very complicated operation as he was overloaded with more simple operations that could quickly get men back into the lines, so Robert would have to wait till he was called and was to stay on sick leave to await a call for specialised surgery to restore peripheral vision in one eye.

Sasha suggested that Robert came to live at Glendarvel so that he could help Sarah to recover from her distressed state and save the travelling to visit him, and this was soon arranged.

Geoffrey came home for leave at the end of July 1918 and gave his usual update on the war.

"The German high command finally realised a few months ago that they can't rely on submarines to win the war and made a last desperate, aggressive approach on the Western front with frightful losses on both sides.

Despite being very over reached, with almost no follow up supplies, in March the Germans pushed our lines back 40 miles, South of Arras.

General Foch had been appointed 'C in C Allied Forces' and this single command is now working very well. This should have been done years ago and could have saved a lot of the confused orders coming from the various military leaders.

I have just received news that there had been a surprise German attack pushing our lines back to the River Marne and in one place they got to within 37 miles of Paris!

This has frightened the hell out of the French Government even though they had evacuated themselves to Bordeaux, soon after the start of war.

Foch immediately ordered a counter attack and forced the enemy back over the River Marne and the German forces are now paying the penalty of being very over stretched, with no proper supply lines, and if we can keep up the initiative we can keep them on the run back to Berlin.

I have to go back to London tomorrow and hope to hear that 'the beginning of the end' has started!

The 'Butchers bill' so far, is thought to be well into six figures on both sides and the final count will be absolutely frightful."

Raymond telephoned on the house line very early one Sunday morning to say that a milk lorry had run into a herd of Mark's cattle, that were loose in the road and at least one had been killed. The cattle had apparently escaped from the park through a hole cut in the wire fence in a small lane and were now being rounded up by the herdsman.

Mark immediately suspected Priscilla and advised Gillie who agreed that this sounded like her revenge tactics and said that he would go with Tad to investigate.

Firstly, Gillie and Tad went to the hole in the fence and carefully checked the cut ends of wire to see what sort of tool had been used and then drove to within a few hundred yards of Priscilla's house, in a nearby village, and walked along the lane at the back.

Sure enough, there was a small garden shed adjacent to the back fence.

Tad climbed over the fence and went into the shed. There was a new pair of heavy duty wire cutters hidden under the bench with marks on the cutting edges of having been recently used.

He took the cutters to Gillie who smiled and said.

"I think that I will go to the front door and ask her if she dropped them somewhere last night and watch her face. It should be interesting."

They drove round to the front and knocked on the door.

The door was answered by Priscilla, who was still in a dressing gown.

As Gillie moved the wire cutters from behind his back into sight he said.

"Did you happen to drop a pair of wire cutters somewhere last night?"

Priscilla's face said it all. She was shocked, unsure whether she had dropped them, confused, and then put on a show of being innocent and knowing nothing.

Gillie said.

"We found that the wire had been cut in the back lane to allow cattle to get onto the road and checked on what was used to cut the wire.

With your history of revenge, we thought that we should come and have a look.

We just happened to find these new wire cutters in your shed with the marks of being used very recently which makes you a prime suspect.

Furthermore, your reaction on seeing the cutters has confirmed your guilt.

You have also been seen hanging round the cheese factory recently so now we have warned all the employees to watch out for you and they will report to us immediately if you are seen again.

We are now going to visit the local hardware shops to find out who bought the wire cutters.

Just ye' remember, that there is a war on and it is 'open season on vermin like you,' so leave the district before you are caught again doing something stupid and 'afore ye' have a nasty accident."

They left Priscilla spluttering with rage and shouting obscenities.

Chapter 16

THE BEGINNING OF THE END

Geoffrey arrived back in the London hotel to find that there was a plethora of confused information coming in which had to be quickly sorted out before the next meeting.

Russia had signed the treaty of Brest-Litovsk with Germany, which would take the pressure off their Eastern front and would probably release some German troops for their other fronts.

Romania had signed the treaty of Bucharest which conceded some territory and gave Germany access to the Rumanian oil wells which was vitally important for the German oil starved war machine.

In the Balkans, a force of 700,000 Allied troops comprising British, French, Greek, Serbian and Italian had been so successful in beating the Axis forces in Serbia that the Rumanian Government decided to enter the war again on the side of the Allies, thus negating the concessions recently given to Germany.

The rout of the Axis forces was continuing on the Southern front which was all very positive and was making Germany use a lot of her resources on the Southern front and was thus relieving some of the pressure from the Western front.

In Egypt and Palestine the Allies were gaining the advantage over the Turks with the aid of an Arab force, which was led by an amazing English officer, Colonel Laurence, who had lived among the Arabs and had gained their confidence.

These combined forces were expected to soon drive the Turks out of Palestine and back across the Dardanelles which would give the British access to that vital seaway.

The real Allied success on the Western Front had started in early August at Amiens when the British started a push which caused the second battle of the Somme, the fifth battle of Arras and continued on towards the German heavily fortified 'Hindenburg line.'

Huge numbers of German battle weary and starving prisoners were being taken and became a massive problem.

An unusual report came in from an English officer who had handed over many thousands of battle weary, half starved, German prisoners to be guarded by a small French unit and asked the French officer how he intended to keep them secure and was told.

"Monsieur, nous   couper tous les bouton enlever le pantalon et couper les ceintures, alors!

Tres occupe sauver le pantalon, tous les temps. Plaisanterie de Francais! Mais ils arret les Bosches!"

(Sir, we cut off all the buttons holding up the trousers and cut the belts, so. Very busy saving the trousers all the time. French Joke. But it stops the Bosche!)

As autumn approached more encouraging reports came in.

The German Government was seeking an armistice but this failed when the American President, Woodrow Wilson, insisted on only negotiating with a recognised democratic Government.

The German Navy mutinied, and there was an uprising in Bavaria.

The British were advancing across Belgium and the Hindenburg Line was broken and the remaining German forces were retreating rapidly.

Germany was proclaimed a Republic on November the 9th and the terms for an armistice were drawn up by the Allies and an armistice was signed, in a railway coach, at 0500 Hrs on November the 11th.

Hostilities officially ceased at 1100 hrs the same day.

The eleventh hour of the eleventh day of the eleventh month!

Geoffrey was asked to stay on in London as the 'Boss' wanted to personally thank all the associates for their dedicated contribution to winning the war.

As there were so many associates they would be called up in small groups each day.

A group of five taxis came to pick up the first twenty associates and drove them to Buckingham Palace Mews.

Geoffrey and his friends were ushered into an anti-room where they were met by a palace Aid de Camp who greeted each of them and said that His Majesty King George V was on his way.

The King came in and was announced and then spoke for a few minutes.

"We set up this second line of information gathering at the suggestion of Mr. Winston Churchill, to ensure that when I discussed matters of vital national importance with the war cabinet that I had been given independent information beforehand. This has been of immense value and on behalf of the people of Great Britain, I give you my heartfelt thanks and congratulations for a job well done."

The King then shook the hand of each member and departed.

Geoffrey was glad to return home to his family, but would still have to go back to work out the dreadful statistics at some later date.

Chapter 17

AFTERMATH

By early January of 1919, huge numbers of men were being demobilised and reunited with their families, often behaving like strangers in their own homes after sometimes years of living in the trenches under fire, in the most appalling conditions.

There were also huge numbers of men who had lost limbs or were incapacitated in some way and would find it difficult if not impossible to get a job.

Then there were tens of thousands of men with 'Trench Feet' which was a chronic form of arthritis caused by prolonged exposure to wet and cold feet in the trenches. Their ankles swelled up and would no longer flex and you could pick them out everywhere by their shuffling walk.

Very gradually the nations of Europe started to recover physically but the cost of running four years of war had left many nations bankrupt, Britain included.

Inflation in Europe went off the scale.

Germany, Hungary and Poland reputedly had over two thousand percent inflation, while Britain struggled with one of the lowest, at just twenty five percent.

Mark and Sasha had only just been able to maintain the status quo for the property during the war due to an almost total lack of manpower and materials, plus their own nearly total involvement in the war effort.

The SFTU was closed down and the camp staff returned to their depots. Much of the camp equipment had been abandoned as there was no official system for cleaning up a tented camp site.

Mark, Gillie, Andrew and Robert were all demobilised and the girls were officially retired from the nursing service.

Mark appointed Gillie as estate overseer of both properties so that he could delegate much of the day to day supervision to him and have more time to spend with the family and on the new projects.

It took all Geoffrey's influence in high places to get Robert into the London hospital for the specialist to restore full sight in the damaged eye, as had been promised. Sarah went down to London with him and stayed at the Curzon Mews private hotel for the week that he was in hospital and was able to visit him every day.

A week after returning home, Sarah carefully took the dressing off Robert's eye and he was able to see normally, but they had been told to only remove the dressing for short periods at first to let his eye muscles build up strength again. The sight was fully restored but there was still the permanent loss of his peripheral vision in one eye.

Geoffrey also tried to get an appointment for a specialist to check on Andrew's knee to see if it could be repaired and finally found a specialist in Liverpool who claimed that he could restore some, or maybe all, movement after several operations so he was booked in for the series of operations.

Mark and Geoffrey met in the garden one morning and started up conversation. There was a question that had been worrying Mark for a long time so he asked.

"Who is the 'Boss' of your organisation?"

"That is supposed to be our closest kept secret but you can deduct who he is if I tell you that we went to Buckingham Palace to be officially thanked for our service during the war."

"That confirms what I thought, as his family does own parts of London, like Curzon Mews."

They shook hands to seal their silence and Geoffrey said.

"I have just heard that the 'Treaty of Versailles' was signed on the 7th of June 1919, but we think that it was badly drafted and will allow Germany to have financial freedom and the ability to re-arm. Churchill is furious that the wording, insisted upon by 'other' nations, does not block loans or financial movements.

The 'armchair experts' have no comprehension of the real world and can't see beyond their distended navels!

We will have to be extra vigilant and continue to monitor the situation.

America took over from Britain as the leading bankers and financial centre of the world during the war and their financiers are behaving like undisciplined cowboys.

We are advised that their manufacturers are implementing mass production methods, like assembly lines for cars and canned food processing, which has cut their costs, so they are now able to export. They have also introduced 'broad acre mechanized farming', which cuts costs, but also cuts out thousands of jobs.

Canada and Australia are also changing to mechanized broad acre farming as it suits their huge farms and sparse populations."

Later in the morning Mark met Gillie who suggested that he could get Harry Hough to use his steam engines to clear and level the SFTU camp site and Tad's tunneling and test blasting area and then move the two buildings that had been left behind.

The two buildings could then be converted into a club house and a covered firing position for a rifle club range. Mark was impressed with the idea and said.

"Go ahead and let us form the 'Glendarvel Gun Club' and see if we can get the locals to join and ensure that we have a nucleus of trained men ready for whatever happens next.

Any way, you and I can use it to teach the children now that they are older."

Gillie was delighted and had work started right away.

There must have been many like-minded people in Britain because rifle clubs were springing up all over the country.

Were there still feelings of national insecurity even though the war was supposed over?

Mark could see that the post war period was going to be very different, and difficult, with industry run down, men exhausted and disoriented and having difficulty in adjusting to civilian life, huge national debts to pay off, possible food shortages and the threat of mass unemployment resulting in abject poverty.

When all the men had been demobilised and the effect of collapsing economies started to be felt around the world there could be serious trouble.

Mark and Sasha discussed the pending problems and decided that they should use more of the proceeds of the SATCO sale to get the Glendarvel property fully improved and productive so that they were in a strong position to ride out any future troubles.

The building programme at Glendarvel had stopped during the war and most of the men from the village and Handley quarry had been in the trenches, with only about half of them returning home in one piece, but these men were now looking for work again so Mark got George to enlarge the village green, add an ornamental lake and start building more houses in the village.

Mark asked Gillie to come over to discuss the list of improvements and suggestions that they had recorded when they had visited all the tenants on the Glendarvel estate before the war.

The largest tenanted farm on the estate, Valley Farm, had provided a long list of suggested improvements so Mark and Gillie drove over to see the tenant. The whole place looked neglected and run down and they were met by a middle aged woman, Mrs. Pickering.

They were told that Mr. Pickering had been killed at Ypres and that their son was killed at Arras.

So now there was only a teen age daughter left to try to work the farm. There was one sixty year old farm hand, who was a relative and a bit simple and needed constant supervision. They had had to put off the other two men because of the poor returns from the farm.

It was obvious that they were not able to run the farm without the husband and son and the two farm hands who had been laid off.

Mark listened carefully and then asked the widow what she would like to do.

"We cann'a manage without the men and we 'ave just been 'anging on 'opeing that suma't'll turn up. We cann'a keep paying rent with next to naught coming in!"

"Well, would you consider terminating the tenancy of the farm and being compensated for your stock and farm machinery?"

"Yer,' that sounds fine and would get us out of this place, but where could we go?"

"We have started to build more houses in the Village and they will soon need more people to work in the cheese factory. Does that idea appeal to you?"

"How soon can we stop paying the rent and when could we move into a house?"

"We can terminate the tenancy agreement for Valley Farm at the end of this month, or any month, and as we have started to build already, it will be about six months before there is a house ready. Could you stay with relatives or friends for a few months?"

"I think we could stay with me' mum for a bit."

"Well, if you want to go ahead and terminate the lease please let me know as soon as possible so that we can make the arrangements."

As they were driving back Gillie said.

"That sad situation that we have just seen will probably be the first of many. The war has killed off nearly half of the men. The losses are devastating for the country people where the farms are dependent on all the family members surviving. You did a very fine thing by offering to stop the lease for that farm, and buy the stock and machinery and reserve a house for the widow.

Have you thought about who you can put in the farm?"

"As I was speaking, I had a thought that Sarah and Robert might like to take on the farm, it includes several thousand acres of good flat land as well as a huge area of hill land. If we do up the house and buildings and help them to get started it could suit them very well. What do you think?"

"Och' 'ay it could suit them verra' well as Robert comes from a farming family and Sarah is a real country lass."

On returning home Mark asked Robert and Sarah if they would be interested in having their own farm.

Sarah's eyes lit up and she said.

"Yes, that is a wonderful idea as we both like the country but how can we start without any money?"

"Well, there could be a very large farm becoming vacant soon, so I thought that if you are interested I would give you first option on it."

Robert said.

"I have always wanted to have a farm of my own, but as my elder brother will inherit Dad's farm I could never see how I could get my own place without some help to get started.

Would we need much money to get started at that farm? Now that my eye is nearly fully recovered I feel confident that I can take on the challenge."

"We are waiting for the current tenant to confirm that they want to move out, and if so, when.

And yes, we could help you to get started. I will let you know as soon as there is any news."

Within a week Mrs. Pickering and her Daughter arrived at the lodge and were sent up to the house by Raymond.

Mark, Gillie and Sasha took them into the study.

"I 'ave talked to 'me mum and we can move in to doss down on the floor any time so could we finish up at the end of this month?"

"Yes certainly, that can be arranged.

We will get an agent to value your livestock and machinery right away and you can walk away with a cheque in your hand at the end of this month. It would then be necessary for you to sign a lease to reserve a new cottage in the Village, if that is what you want to do."

William Collins had been using an agent in Chester who he had found reliable, so Mark asked Stan Millard to come over and do the valuation. Mark and Gillie would then arrange the termination of the lease for Valley Farm.

Sarah and Robert were married in the Village Church and there was a big reception in the mess tent on the front lawn at the house afterwords for nearly one hundred guests.

The young couple then had a short honey moon in Cornwall and were looking forward to moving into Valley Farm as soon as the renovations were completed.

Mark took George and Gillie to Valley Farm to assess what needed to be done to renovate the house and farm buildings. As there had been no maintenance for many years, there was a lot to be done and George suggested some improvements as well. The whole job would take about six months and could give employment for up to ten men.

As soon as the Pickering family had moved out Mark took Sarah and Robert over and they drove round the farm and he then asked them what they thought about the place.

Robert said.

"Yes, I can see that it has been a very good farm, but has been let go back during the war, so there is an immediate opportunity to bring it back to its full potential, probably take about two years. I am sure that we can make a go of it. What do you think Sarah?"

"As you know, I am not used to this country yet, but it is much better land than the land that we used to use to grow our small crops at the shamba. I am sure that we will be very happy in that beautiful old sandstone house when it has been renovated."

"George has already assessed what needs to be done to the house and buildings and will start in a few days and if there is anything extra that you want done just let him know.

For example, if you want a conservatory to be added or landscaping for the garden just let him know."

Sarah took Sasha and her children to see the farm on the next day and they all drove round the tracks and then went through the house together. Sasha was impressed by the size of the farm and was sure that it was capable of producing a comfortable income for a family and was very happy to think that one of the Ashcroft girls was already married and about to settle down close by.

Mark bought a car for Sarah so that she could go to the farm each day with Robert and start working the farm. The stock and machinery were left in place to help them get started. It would be rent free till they had got the farm in full production and then be at half the usual rate.

Michelle and Andrew were married in the Village Church and Mark gave away the beautiful young French bride. There was another reception in the mess tent on the lawn and the young couple moved into a specially built, large new house by the Village green.

Geoffrey provided the furniture for the new house and gave Andrew a car.

Mark appointed Andrew as the general manager of the cheese factory and had the company re-registered as The Glendarvel Dairy Company.

The idea was that they could expand the cheese making into fresh milk supplies and other dairy products as well.

Sasha and Mark were relaxing one evening and were discussing what future plans Sally had and Sasha said.

"Sally has many friends but I don't know of any particular boyfriend yet, perhaps she would like to go on a trip."

"Yes that could be good, and let her meet more people."

"Michelle is still very worried about what happened to her family and their land near Arras. Do you think that we should help her to go and find out? But I don't think that she should go on her own"

"Well that gives me the idea of combining the two and the opportunity for me to take you on a long overdue holiday. Would it be possible for us to take Sally and Michelle on a holiday to France and spend some time at Arras for Michelle to find out what has happened to her family and their land?"

"That sounds like a very good idea but would it be too distressing for them to go back to where all those frightful things happened?"

"We can ask them, and if there is any doubt it may be necessary to change our plans."

Mark and Sasha drove to the Village and called on Michelle and Andrew and discussed the plan.

Michelle was very enthusiastic about the opportunity of going back to the place where she grew up and see her old home again, even if it was in ruins, and said that she would try writing to some of their friends in the area to get some advance information, but was not confident of getting any replies, as Arras had been fought over at least five times during the war.

Sally said that she would like to go back and see France again as they had been too busy in the field hospital to get a chance to appreciate what the country would be like in peacetime and it would be lovely to see Paris.

The bookings were made for a week in Paris and then to stay at a hotel in Amiens.

There were no replies during the next month to Michelle's letters, just one letter marked 'return to sender' sent back by the post office in Amiens.

Mark thought about the problem of sorting out Michelle's family land in war torn France and phoned William Collins and asked if he had any ideas.

"Yes we are happy to take on an assignment but it would be better if it is done by our Paris office as the French property laws are very different and local knowledge is important. I will put you in touch with a competent man in Paris."

The ship landed at Le Havre and after some delay Mark emerged from the car hire company office with a much lighter wallet. He had had to pay a 'black mail' price to hire a car because there were very few reliable cars available.

Michelle acted as 'chauffeuse' in Paris and took them to most of the famous places like the Arc de Triumph, the Eifel Tower, the Louvre, a fashion shopping area, a theater show and 'La Moulin Rouge' night club with its famous bare breasted dancing girls.

It was very good that Paris had not been occupied and then fought over as there were so many historic buildings which could never be replaced.

The hotel in Amiens was close to the river Somme and still had damage from shelling.

The next morning they traveled the thirty five miles to Arras with Michelle driving along the still shell pocked roads.

Mark and Sasha started to get an idea of what it must have been like by the shell holes everywhere, the patterns of trenches and dug outs, the stinking mud and the few remaining ruins of houses. Even the trees were just stumps or a grotesque silhouette on the skyline.

Michelle then took them to the village close to her old home and they stopped and got out and walked round what had been a thriving community.

There were only a few very badly damaged buildings left, the rest were still just piles of rubble.

There did not appear to be anyone living in the village and no attempt had been made to do any reconstruction.

While they were standing by the car looking at the scene of devastation, a battered old truck drove up, and the driver walked over to them.

Michelle immediately recognised the man and they embraced each other and started an emotional conversation with much gesticulating and sadness.

When there was a pause, Michelle introduced the man as Monsieur Henri Gidget, who was the former owner of the general store in the village. He was one of only three survivors from the village, the other two were children who had been evacuated to the South of France to stay with relatives.

There could be no immediate plans to rebuild anywhere in the village as the ownership of the land was confused and in dispute.

Henri had seen their car stop from where he was living with his parents on the hill and had come to see if they were more land agents trying to put claims on the land in the village.

Michelle had asked him what he knew about her family and their land. He confirmed that there were no survivors from her family. He suspected that there would already have been many attempts to put in false claims of ownership for their land, as was happening among the shop and house sites in the village. Most of the title deeds were missing or destroyed, due to the war, and greedy agents and city people were trying to take advantage of the situation. Most of the local people had been killed and their surviving relatives were confused and many were destitute.

Mark could see that if nothing was done very quickly, Michelle's family property could be virtually stolen out of the confusion and explained that he had already contacted Warringtons man in Paris and proposed to telephone him as soon as possible.

Sasha explained to Michelle and Monsieur Gidget what Mark was planning and they both became very keen to get an expert to sort out the volatile situation.

There were no telephones working in the village, so it was arranged to call at the house where Henri Gidget was living as soon as a meeting could be set up with Warringtons man.

Mark asked Michelle if she would like to go to see her old family home and through her tears she nodded and said.

"Oui, s' il vous plait."

Sally comforted Michelle as they drove slowly to where the chateau had once stood on a small hill.

There were so many shell holes along the drive that Michelle had to stop.

They got out and walked up to the ruins.

The shelling must have been so concentrated on the building that even the cellars were in ruins and there was hardly one stone still left on top of another.

Mark looked in the cellars and found piles of spent brass cartridge cases which confirmed that there must have been a very fierce defensive battle, or battles, possibly a battle unto death.

The cartridge cases included the distinctive French bottle shaped 8mm as used in their Lebel rifles and the parallel cases as used in the 8 mm. French Hotchkiss machine guns.

There were also British 0.303 cartridge cases as used in rifles and machine guns. He did not comment on his findings as it was too sensitive a subject at the moment.

Michelle was weeping on Sally's shoulder as they walked round the ruins and said that she was sure that the chateau must have been used as a refuge by her family and the French Army and then was shelled till it did not exist anymore.

They had difficulty in finding somewhere to have lunch in Arras. When they did find a cafe, it was in fact the only building that had been partly rebuilt and showing any signs of life. So they had a light lunch before returning to Amiens.

Mark then telephoned the Paris office of Warringtons and asked for Monsieur Georges Petallot.

After a long wait, Georges came on the line and said that he could meet them at the cafe in Arras on the following morning.

Sally said.

"Why don't some of us go back to the village near Arras this afternoon and let Henri know that we have arranged to meet Georges tomorrow as there may be a lot of other people who want to be involved with sorting out their land?"

Mark and Michelle went back to Arras while Sally and Sasha went shopping.

Henri was working in the garden as they drove up and was pleased that the meeting was to be so soon. He said that he would contact as many of the relatives of land owners as possible and get them to come along.

When they arrived at the cafe in Arras on the following morning there were already several strangers sitting at the outside tables with Henri who introduced them as some of the other property owner's relatives who were looking for a resolution to their problem.

Georges arrived and explained that he was acting for Michelle's family but could extend his investigations to include some, or all, of the properties in the village.

There was a general discussion and some concern was expressed about properties with no known surviving relatives.

Georges explained that it was very important to act quickly and assume ownership of all unclaimed land by a 'trust fund', which he would set up, which could then sell any unclaimed land and pay his expenses and that the balance must then be put towards a community project like a village hall or a water supply for the village, but the trust fund would have to guarantee to reimburse any bona fide claimants for five years.

He also explained that land that had no surviving owners or known relatives that was left vacant for more than one year could be taken over by the Government and sold!

An informal vote gave unanimous approval to go ahead for all the properties in the village and that they wanted any surplus funds to go towards a new water supply.

Henri Gidget was appointed chairman of the village reconstruction programme and he was to work with Georges to provide as much local information as possible.

When the meeting had broken up Georges had a discussion with Michelle and she said that she was thinking that she would sell the property as soon as her ownership had been confirmed and that was how she planned to pay Georges fee. Georges was agreeable and said that he would start immediately to check that the title deeds or other municipal records were still available and would keep her informed of his progress.

When they got back to the hotel and were having dinner Sasha asked Michelle if she had thought about keeping just a small part of the property as a memorial to her family.

"No I had not, but that would be a very nice idea, what part do you think it should be?"

"You may consider just the area of the house and garden. But you may want to remove the ruins of the house and plant some trees or something."

Michelle said that she would like to keep just the house site and garden area and could even use some of the proceeds to put up a memorial in the garden to her family who had died alongside the troops defending their home.

On each of the next two days they visited the sites where the Number 6 Field Hospital had been located. Mark and Sasha were horrified to think that the girls had worked in just a tent within range of enemy long range guns for three years and that they had performed lifesaving miracles with badly wounded and and often infected men under these dangerous and primitive conditions.

The farm owned by Michelle's Uncle was still just as she had last seen it with Andrew.

She thought that there was a relative of her Aunt who would inherit the farm but it would need to be sorted out by Monsieur Georges so she would ask him to add this to the list of properties to be claimed.

Mark said that he had promised Tad that he would go to the site of the battle of the Somme to see the effect of the huge blast engineered by the men who Tad had trained.

Michelle asked a group of locals for directions.

"Ou-est les grandes cavernes?"

There was much raising of eyebrows and gesticulating, and they made imitations of an explosion and then directed them to the area.

There were still all of the enormous craters clearly defined. Some were so big that a row of houses would be lost in them!

Reports estimated that 10,000 enemy troops were killed or wounded within 30 seconds! They were also directed to Messines Ridge where there were 19 huge craters made by the British Sappers exploding 450 tons of high explosives all at once with devastating effect.

The return trip was uneventful and they were all glad to be home, till Sarah came over and broke the sad news about Andrew.

They were all seated in the sitting room while Sarah explained that there had been an explosion at the Dairy Factory two days ago and Andrew and one other man had been killed.

Sarah said that she was told by the shift foreman that the boiler attendant had rushed into Andrew's office and said that there was trouble with the water level glass indicator on the boiler and that Andrew and the maintenance man had gone out to the boiler house to check and found that the water level indicator had been tampered with. The maintenance man, Billy Little, was just running out to get some tools when the boiler exploded, killing Andrew and the boiler attendant and injuring Billy Little.

Michelle was clinging to Sasha and sobbing piteously. Mark squeezed her hand and kissed the top of her head and went out to call Gillie.

Mark, Gillie and William immediately went up to the factory and looked out Billy Little who had his arm in a sling and bandages over the burns on his hands and face.

Billy took them to the boiler house at the back of the factory.

The whole of one end wall had been blown away and parts of the boiler were strewn across the yard. Mark said.

"Please tell us what you think caused this to happen."

"When Andrew and I come into the boiler house I could see that the water level glass was showing between the safe level marks, but I could tell that the boiler was running dry and was overheating. So I immediately tried to check the two valves that isolate the level glass but the valves were closed and the handles had been deliberately put on in the wrong position when the glass had been showing a safe level. So this means that the glass would show a safe level all the time regardless of what the actual level was.

I was going to get a wrench to open the safety valve and then douse down the fire when she blew."

BOILER WATER LEVEL GLASS AND VALVES.

"Do you have any idea of who would have enough knowledge to tamper with the level glass valves and set the boiler to blow up?"

"There only be the other boiler man, Sean Kelly, but he is off sick and we have a temporary man from some foreign place who was working on the other shift but he has disappeared and hasn't come to work since the explosion."

Mark thanked Billy and asked him to dismantle what was left of the old boiler and put all the pieces in a safe place as they could be required as evidence and that Gillie would arrange for two men to help him.

Billy said that George had taken all the details and had gone to negotiate the supply of a replacement boiler and had already found a boiler of the same size that had been made for another client who was not ready for delivery and was willing to wait while another boiler was made, so a replacement would arrive in a few days.

Mark, Gillie and William went to the office and the secretary brought them coffee.

Mark said.

"This has the appearances of a carefully planned act of sabotage, with Kelly conveniently off sick and a temporary 'foreign' man just happening to be available to fill the gap while he could tamper with the level control valves so that the boiler reaches a dangerous condition while he is off shift.

Do you think that is the likely sequence of events?"

"Aye' that be very likely because that foreign bloke was recommended by Kelly, and naturally Andrew was glad to find an experienced boiler man without delay."

"Have the police been informed?"

Gillie said.

"Och, aye', as there was loss of life, we immediately phoned the local police and they sent up some flat foot who made a lot of notes but I don't think that he got the message that it is a case of industrial sabotage resulting in the murder of two men and the wounding of another. We will have to go to a higher authority to get the right sort of response."

"Have Geoffrey and Florence been informed."

"Yes, we told Florence and she just went to pieces and Jill is looking after her. But Geoffrey is away on some secret mission and can't be contacted."

"Who do you think is behind this, Priscilla or the Boers?"

"At this stage I don't know, could even be some other party who we have not yet identified like one of the people who Geoffrey has encountered such as the people who blew up his house in Hastings now trying to get their revenge on Geoffrey through Andrew."

"I think that your last theory is the most likely so I will get in touch with Curzon Mews as soon as we get home. We must go and visit Kelly and see what he has got to say.

William, I am appointing you as the manager of the Dairy Company as of now, and you will only report to Sasha and me. You have worked here part time in your holidays so you must be familiar with a lot of the day to day workings. You must keep us fully informed of every detail till we think that you have gained enough experience. You will also have Michelle to help you as she has also helped Andrew from time to time and the staff here are experienced and reliable.

You must be ever vigilant about security and you must liase with Gillie and Raymond regularly and I will help you as necessary."

"Thank you Dad for putting your trust in me, I will run the company to the very best of my ability and will keep you fully informed."

"Congratulations William, I am sure that ye' can tak' over what Andrew has achieved and build on it and I am always here when needed." Gillie then shook William's hand.

"Now we will make a simple announcement to the staff and let you get down to work"

As Mark and Gillie drove back to the house Gillie said.

"The more I think aboot it, the more sure I am that this is the work of the more professional saboteurs from the Irish Republican extremists. That Priscilla woman would never think of sabotaging a boiler and would not have the contacts to get the right sort of men with the necessary experience.

How about we go and question Kelly, I got his address from the secretary at the factory."

The address was a small cottage a few miles away and the widow living there took in lodgers.

"You cann'a see Mr. Kelly 'cos 'ee 'as been gone a few days, even took all 'is stuff and walked to the station, but paid 'is rent first, 'ee did."

"Was Mr. Kelly sick for a few days before he left?"

"Oh no 'ee was in good 'ealth, even went out with 'is gun and shot me a rabbit for the pot."

"Thank you for your help."

As soon as they got home Mark booked a call to the Curzon Mews Hotel and left a message for Richard to call him.

Michelle moved into the house so that she could be looked after by the family and not be living on her own with all the sad memories.

The family had just finished dinner that evening when Richard returned Mark's call.

"Hello Mark we received your call and how can we help you?"

"There has been a repeat of the type of incident that happened in Hastings, but this time it was for the progeny and achieved their desired result.

We expect that there will be more of the same, so we think that you should be involved."

"Your message received and will get our urgent attention. Thank you for letting me know, it now appears to be following a pattern so please keep in close touch."

Mark returned to the sitting room and had just sat down when the house phone rang and Gillie said that he was coming up with Jill because Florence had not returned from a shopping trip in the afternoon.

Gillie and Jill emerged from the cellar and joined the family in the sitting room.

Jill explained that Florence had left in her car just after lunch to do her regular weekly local shopping for groceries. Jill had found that Florence had not returned when she had gone to check on her after dinner. There was no sign of Florence or her car.

This sounded ominous and they were considering telephoning the local police when Raymond rang to say that the local sergeant of police was at the gate and should he send him up to the house.

Mark answered the door and asked the sergeant to come into the study where Sasha,Gillie and Jill were waiting.

"I understand that Mrs Baker lives in one of the houses on this property. Is that correct?"

"Yes they live just down the drive a short way."

"Well, it is my sad duty to tell you that Mrs. Baker was found this afternoon, burned to death in her car, not far from the Tattenhall Grocers shop where she had just bought some groceries.

Our police arson experts came from Chester and found that some bottles of petrol had been wired onto the exhaust pipe and under the dash board which had caught alight soon after she had started to drive off showering her with burning petrol. The car ran off the road close to a nursery garden and they ran a hose out and put the fire out but it was too late to save Mrs. Baker. We found her hand bag and her driving license and got this address.

Does she have family living at home?"

"Yes she has family, but her husband is away on business at present and her married son lives in the Village, but he was killed in an industrial accident a few days ago."

The sergeant started looking puzzled and said.

"That is a bit of a coincidence isn't it!"

"I can't help you there because we have only just got back from the Western Front in France where we were sorting out some problems left by the war.

Any way, we are about to have coffee, would you like to join us?"

"Yes that would be grand, thank you"

They went through to the sitting room and everyone was introduced.

Poor Michelle was further distressed by the news about Florence and sat close to Sasha.

The sergeant asked what sort of work did Mr. Baker do and Mark said that he had retired but still carried on with his import and export business with some of his oldest customers now and again.

They chatted on for a while and the sergeant seemed to accept the situation and relaxed. He left shortly after wards.

Raymond rang through from the lodge early the next morning to say that a Mr. Richards and his assistant would like see Mark, so Mark asked him to send them up to the house.

Richard was accompanied by a small man with pebble glasses who he introduced as Dr. Clayton.

As soon as they were seated in the study Sasha came in and sat down.

Richard and Dr. Clayton were told about the sudden death of Florence and how it had happened.

Mark then outlined the 'accident' at the factory.

Richard's face remained impassive and Doc. Clayton just said. "That fits the pattern."

"Thank you for informing us so promptly. We can confirm that this all sounds like the work of the Irish Republican extremists who have a vendetta against Geoffrey because during his investigations he uncovered a nest of terrorists in Belfast and they were rounded up by the local police.

Now it is our turn to bring you the sad news concerning Geoffrey.

He was killed by a roadside bomb on a bridge near Londonderry last week. He was in a baker's van, as his cover, but the terrorists have their informers everywhere and had set a trap for him.

As you know, they usually target the whole family of anyone who upsets them.

So it would appear that as they have now murdered Geoffrey, his wife and son that should be the end of it.

But, there is a chance that they may extend their vendetta to the son's wife, and or, your family because you befriended Geoffrey. We don't know just how much, or how little, they know about your indirect involvement.

We would therefore suggest that we place some of our staff here for a while to see that nothing more can go wrong. We have two couples who are highly trained for this type of work and they are available now.

Could they move into the Baker's house as soon as I can arrange their transfer?"

"Yes, there are two houses available.

Michelle, the son's wife has already come to live with us, so it would be an idea for one couple to move into their house in the village, to keep a watch on Andrew's empty house, as well as the Baker's house, which is located just down the drive. There is a good all-weather track over the hill that you can use to drive between the two houses.

Have you got a suitable cover story for the sudden appearance of the two couples?"

"Yes we have already planned that they have credible cover stories which allow them to stay for some time if it is necessary.

We have therefore set them up as 'agricultural scientists researching improved farming methods.'

Now, would it be possible for Doc. Clayton to visit the place where Andrew was killed and also see Mrs. Baker's car?"

"Yes I can take you now, the factory is just over the hill at the back and Mrs. Baker's car is in the police station yard a few miles away. Do you want tea or coffee before we go?"

"No thank you, we must keep moving."

Mark drove up to the factory via the track to demonstrate the easy access and Billy Little met them in the yard where he was preparing to winch the old boiler out on rollers.

The Doc. produced his bag of test equipment and went to work while Billy repeated his explanation of events.

William was introduced and took Richard on a quick tour of the factory and then they went to see how the Doc. was progressing.

He had checked the remains of the water level control and confirmed that it had been tampered with by someone with engineering skills and a knowledge of boilers. There were all the usual signs of a boiler running dry causing it to rupture and explode violently, exactly confirming Billy's explanation.

The Doc. then said that this was exactly how many factories had been sabotaged in reprisal raids in both Ireland and England.

The fire damaged car had been towed to the police station yard and the Doc. got to work.

He found the wire that had been used to fasten the bottles of petrol to the exhaust pipe and under the dash board and some of the broken glass. He said that there would also have been petrol filled pieces of bicycle inner tube tied onto the exhaust pipe to start the fire but there were only sticky black marks where they had been.

This definitely was another case of the professional saboteur.

Richard said that it was very strict policy that no publicity was ever given to reprisal killings as this just gave the saboteurs more leverage for their cause and that he would send a very senior man from Scotland Yard to work quietly with the local police in sorting out the murders.

Mark explained that he had been with Gillie to question the other boiler man but had found that he had not been sick, as he had claimed, and had packed up and disappeared.

Richard and the Doc. stayed for a quick lunch and after Richard had made a phone call he confirmed that the two couples would arrive the next day, and then Richard and the Doc. departed.

Mark sent Gillie to buy seven revolvers, from as many different gun shops as possible, and he returned with four 0.455 Webley Mk. VI revolvers and three 0.22 very compact 'hand bag size' Belgian revolvers and plenty of ammunition.

Now that the reprisal murders of Geoffrey and his family had been discussed with Richard and extra precautions implemented, Mark had the opportunity to tell Gillie all that had happened on the trip to France.

Gillie said that the confusion and thieving of war damaged properties was something that he had never encountered before and could see that Mark had done the right thing by getting a local professional to sort it out before the land ownership was stolen or taken over by a cash strapped Government.

Tad was delighted that all the training that he had given to the Sappers had been put to good use and that the big blasts on the Somme and Messines Ridge had been so successful.

Restoration work at Valley Farm was proceeding well with all the structural repairs finished and all windows and doors already replaced.

Sarah had accepted Mark's offer to add a conservatory and landscape the garden so she discussed the design with George and included some of her own ideas.

Mark and Gillie visited all of the tenanted farms and checked on their viability and found two more that were in trouble.

The tenants just wanted to get out of the lease as soon as possible and find a job in a factory or a shop, not realising that unemployment was reaching plague proportions.

The widows had no confidence to continue now that a key family member had been lost in the war.

Those left were not able to manage the heavy work and the seasonal ups and downs of life on the land and were behind with their rent already.

They discussed the options available for the two farms and the first option was to 'find a new tenant' but this proved to be difficult so they decided to add the farms to the already very large home farm now being managed by Gillie and Mark.

Geoffrey's report about the use of 'broad acre mechanized farming' overseas gave Mark the idea that this could be used here now that they had such a huge area to manage.

Mark, George and Gillie went to several agricultural shows and trade demonstrations to find out what was available in the way of machines for broad acre farming.

There were many types of tractors available but the one that had about 75 % of the market was the Fordson model F which was made in Cork, Ireland and had a network of dealers for service and spare parts.

Mark bought two Fordson tractors and a range of plows and cultivating machines as well as two Australian made reaper and binders for harvesting corn.

The two farms that had been added to the home farm had all the internal fences removed and were to be used principally for growing large areas of wheat or oats with cattle grazing every few years to rest the land. There was also a new soil improver available called 'basic slag' made from the ground up slag from the steel works that was full of important minerals.

All the land from the two additional farms was plowed and sown with wheat and Dutch barns were built for storage of the grain crops before they were thrashed.

Chapter 18

THE GREAT DEPRESSION

The two now vacant farm houses were renovated and offered for lease as private residences and were very soon occupied by business people who had already lost their businesses and houses, as a result of the depression, and wanted to retire in the country and get away from the scenes of poverty and desperation in the cities.

All the new houses in the Village were occupied and the Dairy Company had been steadily expanding under Andrew's management. Many of the women living in the Village were now working at the Dairy Company. The demand for food was about the only commodity that was not affected by the depression. Andrew had implemented cash payment for everything to prevent any more bad debts.

A large envelope addressed to Michelle arrived with a progress report on sorting out the ownership of the land in France. As the letter was written in French by Georges, Sasha helped Michelle to understand the legal implications of the contents.

Georges had definitely established Michelle's ownership of her family property, as the sole survivor, and was in the process of having new title documents made out in her name and there were legal forms to be signed, witnessed and returned as soon as possible.

Many of the properties in the village were at a similar stage.

Her uncle's farm was also in the process of being granted a new title in the name of her aunt's surviving relatives living in Paris.

Michelle was relieved that Georges was able to achieve results so quickly and that it looked as though she would soon be able to arrange for the house site to be cleaned up and a memorial built.

The Glendarvel Estate had had a lot of new funds injected into it for repairs and improvements after years of neglect and mismanagement and was just starting to recover from the effects of the war, but now the world economy was getting worse by the hour.

One evening the family had finished dinner and was having coffee in the sitting room when Mark said.

"Now that we no longer have Geoffrey to keep us informed. I will try to give you a picture of what is happening, based on information still being provided by Geoffrey's organisation.

I will have to refer to the notes that they have sent, so please excuse me if there are some pauses.

This time the information covers a totally different area of concern, but never the less, has the potential to change the world, as we now know it, unless we can perform miracles.

The 'Gold Standard' was implemented in 1924 to ensure that all developed nations were on an even keel for international trading and this seemed to be working well with all members obliged to have a balanced budget.

Then the wealthy nations, like America, started getting greedy and offered cheap, not properly secured, credit to the struggling countries to try to create more customers, particularly for their mass produced goods, like cars and household appliances.

America loaned four billion Dollars to German industry and then American private financiers invested a further seventeen billion Dollars into European industry, including Germany.

This has enabled German and other European industries to update their industrial plant and dramatically increase their manufacturing capacity.

Thus, America has created a direct competitor for its own manufactured goods!

The Americans then 'Cried Foul'.

This exercise in stupidity and greed was reputedly referred to by Churchill as 'shooting yourself in the hip pocket'!

But what is worse, is that it is 'feeding the hand that will bite you a few years hence'.

It is difficult to comprehend how people could be so short sighted and stupid, or just plain greedy.

But, now the world has run out of customers who have any money, so there is no demand and the world economy is in a state of self-destruction.

Unemployment is rising rapidly and the German and Austrian Governments have already taken over their banks as an emergency measure.

America has put up interest rates to see if this will stop irresponsible loans followed by bankruptcies, but it looks as though the damage has been done already and it is too late.

Britain has 2.7 million people unemployed and there is the usual political blame game in progress as to the cause.

The Germans have 50 % youth unemployment and are blaming the Jews and the Gypsies (Just lame political excuses.) and here in many of the English cities, only one member of a family can have a full time job, without trade union intervention.

Some countries have abandoned the gold standard to give themselves freedom to take corrective action but they still can't create any 'real wealth' to get themselves out of debt.

The American Stock Exchange in Wall Street has become dependent on too much borrowed money and is in a very vulnerable condition which it has no apparent means of correcting.

So now the threat of a worldwide economic collapse is the 'new enemy' that we have to contend with."

Mark folded up the notes that he had received from London and said.

"We felt that things were going wrong and have been trying to get all the houses and buildings on the estate renovated and the farms in full production of essential foods so that we are in a strong position to ride out any problems, but from what we have just found out, the situation is much worse than we realised.

Do you have any ideas on what we should be doing to prepare for further economic problems?"

The family group discussed the subject at great length and some of the points that came out were:

Be prepared for English and foreign currencies to rapidly loose value, so place maximum funds in anything of 'real value' like land and gold.

Be prepared for unemployment to rise further which could cause civil unrest and general defaulting on payment of rents and other accounts.

The British Government may get out of the gold standard agreement which could cause all sorts of new problems.

Sasha said.

"As Mark has just said, we knew that there was trouble brewing but had not expected it to be so bad. Thank goodness we got out of South Africa when we did because the Boer Government will probably panic and make some drastic changes. But they should have the major advantage of being a gold producer which may help them to remain stable, if they manage their affairs properly."

After the rest of the family had gone to bed Mark and Sasha had a long discussion and decided to telephone William Collins in the morning and ask for his advice.

William said that he had never seen the world financial scene poised on the brink of a collapse before and he thought that putting any fluid funds into gold or silver bullion was the only way of minimising the effected of a sudden downturn.

He said that the Jews in Europe and London were buying up gold and silver like there is no tomorrow and that was a good indicator of what should be done.

William said that he could buy gold and silver bullion at wholesale prices for his clients and have it stored in a secure company vault. Later on Mark and Sasha had a quick discussion and rang William back and placed all their spare funds into gold, one quarter in coin and three quarters gold bullion.

William Collins then formed all family assets into one company and 'The Glendarvel Produce Company Limited' was established to ward off new taxes.

The Glendarvel Gun Club had been formed and local ex-service men were given free membership for five years to help to build the numbers. Gillie had bought some ex-army 0.303 rifles and ammunition to be used by members who did not have their own rifles.

Club shoots were held each Saturday, with Gillie acting as Range Warden, and the club became popular with the ex-service men who also encouraged their young family members to join.

Mark's son William was keen to become a marksman like his father so he was given special tuition by Gillie with some of the club's best marksmen in preparation for inter club matches. William, Raymond, Mark and Tad each had individual tuition in revolver shooting. Sasha and the girls had some practice shoots with their 'hand bag revolvers.'

The club provided a social meeting place for local families each Saturday and helped to develop a community awareness. Mark started to take Sasha and Amy on some Saturdays and they competed in the 0.22 shoots, which included snap shooting, on a separate part of the range.

The Ashcroft Girls were already excellent shots with rifle and shotgun, after years of experience in the African bush, and joined in the competitions.

As 1929 progressed the economic decline accelerated and the world was battening down for a storm expected to start in Europe.

Without any warning, the New York Stock Exchange in Wall Street collapsed in October and took the world financial system down with it.

Many currencies became worthless overnight.

Gold became the only true value currency.

Bankruptcies happened in pandemic numbers and soup kitchens were set up for the thousands of starving unemployed.

Lines of unemployed men snaked round buildings where unemployment benefits could be applied for and the survival money obtained.

Smash and grab raids for food and essentials escalated in the city shopping areas and fully paid accounts became a thing of the past.

As there was no end in sight, employers were loathe to spend their last cash reserves on trying to keep skilled men on because they may need every last penny for their own family's survival.

The city streets were full of destitute people looking for work or a soup kitchen that was still open.

Country people furiously grew vegetables and treated their livestock like Royalty.

But as could be expected, cattle and sheep 'duffing' and thieving of growing crops from the fields became a new nationwide problem.

Mark, Gillie, Tad, William and Raymond took it in turns to do night patrols round the home farm livestock and root crops.

One night Mark was driving slowly down a track without the lights on when he saw the outline of a small truck. He turned the lights on and saw three men loading a small truck with the roughly butchered major cuts of meat, from a bullock that they had killed close to the fence.

He went forward and stopped with his headlights illuminating the whole scene clearly.

Two men scrambled to get into the truck while the third was furiously winding the crank handle to start the engine.

Mark was able to write down the truck's number and then followed the truck down the track to the road and noted which way the truck went. He then went back to the lodge, alerted Raymond and asked him to go back to the scene and record the details. Mark then telephoned the police to give them the vehicle number and a summary of what he had seen.

A few days later the local police sergeant called to say that they had used the registration number to locate the truck's owner and had telephoned for a squad car to be sent as soon as possible. They had found the blood stained truck in a driveway about ten miles away and the men still finishing off cutting up and wrapping the meat in a shed. Charges had been laid. He said the operation was run on a commercial scale and that the meat was being sold at about one tenth of the normal price.

George and Arthur Phillips set up a similar roster at the Oakhill Hall property but never encountered any problems.

The state of depression dragged on to 1931 when Britain floated the pound sterling making the market value of the pound sterling drop by 30 % which immediately improved export opportunities and Britain's economic decline started to level out.

Mark and Sasha made a quick trip to London and Mark was given a preliminary report of the human tragedy statistics from the Great War.

When they returned home he gave a summary to the family group.

"I have put some of the figures on this large sheet of paper."

Country	Enlisted Men	Killed	Total Casualties inc. Prisoners	% total Cas. to Enlisted
Russia	12m	1.7m	9.15m	76.3%
British + Colonial	8.9m	0.908m	3.19m	35.8%
France	8.4m	1.357m	6.16m	73.3%
Italy	5.62m	0.65m	0.947m	39.1%
USA	4.35m	0.126m	0.35m	8.0%
(Plus all other Allied Nations not detailed here.)				
Total Allies	42.188m	5.152m	22.09m	52.3%
(In all theaters of war.)				
Total Axis	22.85m	3.39m	15.4m	67.4%
Grand Total	65.038m	8.538m	37.49m	57.6%
Total civilian deaths caused by the war is estimated at 10 million.				

"That is 'The Butchers Bill' as the troops call it.

Now we have some more general information."

Mark referred to his notes again.

"The estimated total cost to the 32 countries involved in the war, as calculated by American economists, was 186 Billion American Dollars.

Geoffrey had also listed some of the changes in military hardware during the war.

Battle tanks were first used by Britain but were never fully developed due to their unreliability and the difficult terrain of trenches, mud and shell holes on the Western Front.

Poison gas. Chlorine and mustard gas. First used by the Germans at Mons in Belgium which caused the agonising death of thousands of soldiers, on both sides, and also numerous civilians.

Deployment of poison gas was found to be too dependent on wind direction and many cases of self and or civilian deaths were reported.

There were also many tens of thousands of men and civilians with gas scarred lungs, often not apparent at the time, but who would be disabled for life.

Use of poison gas is being banned, but there is no guarantee that all counties will abide by the rules.

It is noted that Germany has very advanced chemical industries and is now capable of developing new products.

Greater dependence on the vastly improved machine guns which became a vitally important infantry weapon by both sides, particularly in the trenches.

Development and use of aeroplanes for bombing raids on military targets as well as munitions factories and essential services. They also proved to be invaluable in gathering information and photographs, often far from the battle zone. Use of machine guns from aeroplanes was also developed.

Aerial combat between opposing forces became an important part of warfare and is likely to become a future battle zone.

Development of the zeppelin by Germany for bombing raids. There were 60 zeppelin bombing raids on the South of England and London, mostly causing civilian casualties and property damage.

We considered that the slow moving gas balloon was too vulnerable from anti-aircraft fire and did not follow up the idea."

It was nearly six years later when Mark had the next opportunity to summarise events when the family group was together, and pass on the information still coming from London.

"Just summarizing recent major events, some of which, now represent a threat to Britain.

The German Nazi Party was formed in 1933 so that has progressively changed the focus from the economy to the emerging threat of a 'New German Nation' with its fanatical leader, Adolf Hitler.

Hitler was just a 'nobody' who dropped out of school and has been in jail for treason but he has the cheek of the devil and keeps gaining power and acceptance among the German people with his political rallies, Hitler youth movement, goose stepping army of brown shirts and wild promises of more land and prosperity.

Now that we have got the wireless we should get accurate news each evening, but I find that it doesn't give a lot of the important items, which are probably being kept on the restricted list, so I find it is still necessary to keep in touch with London.

As you know, on the 20th of January 1936 King George V died and was succeeded by Edward VIII who had a turbulent reign till he abdicated on the 10th of December the same year.

He was succeeded by George VI on the next day, much to the relief of the Royal Family, and I think most clear thinking people.

So now we have a King who is already presenting as a much respected figurehead capable of leading the nation and maintaining morale in time of trouble.

Edward has since married Mrs. Simpson in France and we hear that she is gadding round Europe with the besotted Edward still in tow.

Richard told me that they froze their operation during Edward's reign and kept him isolated from all items of national importance because the Simpson woman still fraternizes with her German friends.

There have been numerous detailed reports on how Germany started to seriously rearm in 1936 and that Hitler is now looking round on who he can call his friends, and who he would like to overrun first, like Czechoslovakia, Poland, France, Belgium and Britain for a start.

Richard has recently obtained the most amazing document giving instructions on how to prepare a country for takeover, reputedly issued by Hitler to his henchmen.

I will see if I can get a translated version for you to read."
Gillie said.

"So, you are now telling us that after all the terrible suffering and shocking loss of life during the Great War that there is a new and very real threat of 'all-out war from Germany', again!

What has happened to the good intentions of the Treaty of Versailles?"

"Apparently the Treaty of Versailles was full of loop holes, which were exploited by Hitler, and there was no proper follow up by the British, French or American Governments on the conditions laid down for Germany and the other Axis powers, and of course the injection of cheap loan money, principally from America, enabled Germany to re-equip the factories and overcome many of their problems.

Now referring to Richard's notes again.

Not only did the greedy financiers create their own direct commercial competitors, but they have made it possible for a 'Phoenix to rise from the ashes of war'!

All it needed was a fanatical leader, like Hitler, to appear at the right moment to whip up public sentiment and start building armaments.

Hitler preaches 'Lebensraum' or living space, anti- Semitic and anti- communist policies and claims that 'Fascism' is better than democracy, most of which appeals to the German masses.

Richard says here that German industrialists like Krupp now see rearmament as a heaven sent means of consolidating their businesses and an opportunity to build better and bigger factories. Consequently they covertly support Hitler's rearmament plans.

This means that Germany's prosperity has rapidly become dependent on the continuation of their war machine, which is a recipe guaranteed to result in another war because this gives support to Hitler's territory grabbing intentions and their likely access to more industrial raw materials.

Looking back a bit at the increasing influence of the Nazi Party in Germany.

In 1933 Hitler had a purge against mentally deficient and deformed children and they were all rounded up and sterilised. This was followed by the establishment of concentration camps and the murder of 400,000 Jews.

Hitler set himself up as the 'Fuhrer,' or absolute leader, and assumed he was able to make laws without reference to the

German Government and blatantly defied the disarmament intentions of the Treaty of Versailles, but there were only feeble bleats of protest from London, Paris and Washington.

Very surprisingly, the Catholic and Protestant churches in Germany both support Hitler's antics!"

Life at Glendarvel continued with a slow recovery from the depression for the next few years and Mark and Sasha were able take William and Amy to Europe for a good holiday that included a week in Paris, a week in Nice and then two day stops in Rome, Venice, Vienna, Zurich and Amsterdam.

Soon after their return home, Amy met the local vet when he came to attend to her horse and they started going out together and a serious romance started. They were married a year later and went to live in Tattenhall where David has his veterinary surgery.

Richard was still keeping Mark informed with much of the international inside news and occasionally came to visit.

During one visit he spoke to the family group as Geoffrey had done in the past.

"Hitler has become a fully-fledged fanatical dictator, has set up his henchmen and a ruthless punishment system. He then established his priorities for the takeover of other countries.

Just as though he was 'playing a board game'!

First. Czechoslovakia, and Poland.

Second. France and Britain.

Third. USSR. (Considered as a push over.)

Fourth. USA.

But as he was short of money his plans had to be put aside for a later date.

Shortage of money and raw materials led Germany to the development of synthetic rubber and synthetic oil plus numerous new plastics to replace conventional materials.

Hitler then courted the alliance of Italy and Japan and in 1936, he formed 'The Third Reich' which included Austria."

Gillie said.

"It is amazing that anyone could have such ill-considered grandiose plans for reshaping the World with the inevitable consequence of another major war. Surely the German people willna' support such crazy plans?"

"It appears that Hitler boasts that he can take over other countries with little or no opposition and preaches about the benefits of his 'New World Order'.

He also plans to have a massive propaganda programme to brainwash the population, and don't forget, he already has the support of the industries that have become dependent on making armaments.

There are now reports of secret police being used to silence objectors to his plans. One of his henchmen, Rohm, started to get too big for his boots so he was murdered along with 34 others and Hitler reputedly has 100,000 of mostly civilian objectors held as political prisoners."

Mark said.

"Thank you for keeping us informed, the supply of up to date information, still proves to be of great value to us."

Richard said.

"Oh, I forgot to tell you about another recent event. Chamberlain is going to sort out Germany's threats against Czechoslovakia, but I suspect that he will take the easy way out, he is as weak as water."

The group chatted on for a while and asked a lot of questions most of which Richard was able to answer.

The group then started to break up and say good night.

Georges had sent over all the documents from France, a long time ago, advising that he had finished sorting out Michelle's property and enclosed a copy of the title for Michelle's family land.

Michelle had then instructed him to sell all but the house and garden area, clean up the ruins and erect a monument in the garden with inscriptions as given on a list prepared with Sasha's help.

Georges then had sent a photograph of the site and a close up of the wording on the monument. There was also a letter from Henri Gidget with thanks and signatures from everyone in the village for initiating the process of re-establishing ownership of the properties in the village which was now rebuilt and starting to prosper. There was an open invitation to visit so that they could thank Michelle and Mark in person.

It was a bright sunny day so Mark, Sasha, William and Amy were working in the front garden when the two 'guards' from the Baker's house, Mike and Susan Cutland joined them, and they all sat on the terrace.

"How are your research plans going?"

"We are nearly ready to submit a final report thank you. We are very comfortable in the Baker's house and are keeping in constant touch with HQ.

It has been very convenient for us to have lived here for many years and used this as our base for all our operations in this part of England.

There is much going on in the rest of World and we can give you some of the news?"

"Yes that would be most interesting,"

"The news from the rest of the world includes.

The China – Japan war goes on and now the Japanese have occupied all the Chinese ports but we don't know what the Chinese will do in reply.

A recent re -appraisal of European military capabilities has shown that Germany has by far the largest and best equipped army, in spite of the restrictions imposed by the Treaty of Versailles.

America has passed a neutrality law forbidding assistance in any foreign conflicts. This appears to be just an internal political move.

Chamberlain implemented his minimum impact plan at Munich for Czechoslovakia to concede her Sudetenland (German speaking.) region to Germany on the understanding that Germany will cease all further claims, but we don't think that this will last very long.

Russia has signed a neutrality pact with Germany. Which seems to be Hitler desperately adding allies and preventing an attack through his back door.

Italy has overrun Ethiopia. Quite why the Italians want to go charging about in a very poor and desolate country remains a mystery, other than it boosts Mussolini's ego.

That is a brief summary of recent events."Sasha said.

"Thank you Mike, it always amazes me how you people keep abreast of all that is happening.

I don't like the sound of what that crazy Hitler is about to do next. Do you know if Richard was able to get a translation of Hitler's Manifesto?"

Susan said.

"I will go and get Richard's file as I am sure I have seen it in there."

She returned a few minutes later and put the document on the garden table and they each read it in turn.

MANIFESTO.
Preparing a country for take over. 1936

1/ Keep the population obsessed with sport and sex to divert their attention away from important national and international matters.

2/ Preach democracy all the time but covertly introduce autocratic restrictions by regulation.

3/ Be seen to promote and accept all religions and political factions to keep the population divided into small ineffective groups which spend all their energy competing with each other.

4/ Covertly gain access to all media and introduce a complacent atmosphere and unquestioning acceptance of a progressive loss of personal freedom.

5/ Obtain an inventory of all water, power and fuel installations, also food processing plants.

6/ Obtain an inventory of all defense equipment, military establishments and personnel.

7/ Praise and encourage all sedentary and inactive occupations and belittle all physically demanding occupations and physical fitness.

8/ Emasculate the justice system so that criminals and those preaching and or practicing treason are treated lightly by the courts or are let off on technical grounds.

9/ Confiscate all privately owned firearms, on the pretext of law and order, so that the population is incapable of resisting any armed attack.

Adolf Hitler
Fuhrer of The Third Reich.

Mark said, "Thank you for sharing that with us.

That just shows how Hitler was forming his land grabbing plans down to the last detail all along, on the grand assumption that he could convince the German people to follow his crazy plans."

Mike said.

"Sorry we forgot to keep you up to date with the local problems, with all the traveling to investigate recent reports from this area, we have been very busy.

As you know, we are also still fulfilling our role as 'agricultural scientists doing a study on modern farming methods', as our cover, and now that the university is wanting results, it is very demanding and takes a lot of our time.

Having a good working laboratory in the garage with all the usual glassware, and test equipment has made our job more effective, but it still takes time.

Our two replacement coworkers have just moved into Andrew's house in the village and will soon start to take some of the workload.

Taking field samples and questioning you and the farmers has given us freedom to move about as necessary.

Don't be surprised if the new couple turn up in white lab coats with some sample jars!"

Mike and Susan left and returned home, but within an hour they were back again with worried looks on their faces.

"We have just had an important message from Richard, and I will explain" said Mike as he joined the group in the garden.

You will recall that it was confirmed that the people who murdered the Bakers were all trained extremist operators sent from Ireland, because of Geoffrey's discovery of their headquarters followed by the arrest of the ringleaders and that they were definitely not locals.

They were then lying low while there was a hunt on after the reprisal murders of the Baker family, which had all followed the usual terrorist reprisal pattern.

Well, we have just been advised by Richard that there is renewed reprisal activity due the arrest of some more activists in Belfast and also because of political pressure coming from the Republic in the South.

It appears that they may have connected the indirect involvement of your family in the past, so the first warning that we are likely to see, would be any strangers moving into the area.

We have been told to expect them to make a move any day now, so we have to be extra vigilant."

"Thank you for the warning, we will let Gillie know and alert everyone."

Michelle came out with a tray loaded with mugs of coffee and sat down next to Sasha.

Mark said to Michelle.

"Mike and Susan Cutland have just advised that we need to be extra careful as there is more trouble expected. You know that they are still using their cover as agricultural scientists but keep in close contact with London and are well informed.

Michelle said.

"Are you really scientists or just pretending?"

"Actually, we both have science degrees in physics.

We have research grants from the university and also the Government is very interested in our project.

In particular, we are very interested in the mechanization of farming.

This estate is exactly the type of modernised property that we like to study.

We need to establish some more test plots alongside some of your large areas of crops?"

"Yes, we can arrange that. Do they need to be fenced off this time?"

"Only if there is a significant rabbit or bird problem."

"You can continue to liaise with Gillie and the home farm foreman for whatever you need.

We have seen a report that the same sort of broad acre mechanized farming methods are also being used in other parts of Britain.

Please continue to keep Sasha and me informed."

On the next Monday Michelle said at breakfast that she would like to go up to the house where she had lived with Andrew and get the last of her clothes and a few personal belongings that were still in the house.

Mark suggested that she went with William when he went to the factory so that he could help her.

On arrival at the house William backed his car up to the side door and they went inside.

The new replacement 'guard couple', Jack and Audrey, were still eating breakfast and when Michelle explained that she had called in to pick up the last of her clothes, they just nodded and said

"Yes, please go ahead," between mouthfuls.

It took several trips to carry all the items of clothing and ornaments out to the car and then Michelle went into each room to see if there were any other personal things that she wanted to take.

She found that there were some books and a few photographs that she wanted to take. There was an empty cardboard box in one bedroom and she put the books and photographs into it.

William then carried the box out to the car.

After a final check in each room Michelle said.

"Thank you, I have got everything." The couple just said.

"That is good. Now we will have more cupboard space and can finish unpacking!"

William and Michelle got into the car and drove to the factory and as they went into the office

William said.

"Would you like me to run you home as soon as I have seen the foreman for a few minutes, or would you like to stay here for the day?"

"I can stay here as it will give me a chance to go through the photographs and books."

The secretary came in and asked if they wanted tea or coffee.

"Yes please Jean, you know how we have it."

While the coffee was being prepared William carried in the cardboard box from the car and put it on the side table.

As soon as William had finished his coffee he started on his daily rounds of the factory with the foreman.

Several days production had been spoiled, while a machine was being replaced with a larger model, so the part processed material had been offered free to the local pig farmers who came each day with an assortment of vehicles and containers to collect it. There were several farm vehicles and their drivers in the yard waiting for the waste, part processed product to be pumped into their containers.

Billy, the maintenance man, had used the extra manpower, available in the yard, to finish moving the new machine into its final position.

"Morning Mr. William, all this extra help has put me ahead of schedule, so with any luck we should be back in production tomorrow morning."

"Well done, that is good news. We don't want to have to give any more spoiled product away to feed pigs!"

The foreman was using the downtime for all the production staff to give the factory a complete clean down and there were rubber booted women with brushes and mops everywhere.

Back in the office Michelle was busy putting her photographs into an album and Jean was helping her.

The foreman came into the office and was very interested in the photographs of France because his brother had been killed at Verdun. He said.

"I thought that you said that you lived in France and took some of these photos, but this box has a time table for the ferry from Belfast to Liverpool still in the bottom?"

William was coming through the door as the foreman was speaking and he was immediately suspicious and looked carefully at the date on the time table and then at the box.

The box had the printed name of a well-known brand of English washing powder but no address so could have come any one of their factories, but the time table had a current date which could have a sinister meaning!

He put the time table in his pocket and made no comment. Jean looked surprised but said nothing.

When they had finished their sandwich lunch William said that he needed to go home to do some research on a new process and asked Michelle if she would mind if they left in a few minutes.

"Yes, I can pack up and be ready very soon."

As they drove along William asked Michelle if she realised the significance of the ferry time table but she did not know where the towns were so he decided to wait till Sasha could explain to her in French and show her on a map.

Sasha was surprised to see William and Michelle coming home early and met them in the hall and asked if they were alright.

"Mum, we have found what could be a serious problem so please get Dad and Gillie as soon as you can."

He then showed the Time table to Sasha and explained that the ferry went from Belfast to Liverpool, Ireland to England, and Sasha then realised that this could indicate that the new tenants were two terrorists that had just been planted in their own 'back yard'!

Back at the Dairy Factory Jean was becoming desperate to contact Jack and Audrey, who had just moved into Andrew's house at the end of the village green and the only way of contacting them was to feign being suddenly taken ill and having to go home, so she put on a lot of powder with her make-up and wiped off her lipstick.

She then appeared for a moment in the foreman's office doorway and said that she was feeling sick and had to go home. He was busy writing and just smiled and nodded.

In her haste, she rode her bicycle directly to Andrew's house and knocked on the door which was quickly opened and she went inside.

When she had explained to Jack and Audrey that their Belfast to Liverpool ferry time table had been found in a box that they had left in the house and how that William had immediately reacted when he saw it. So this now meant that their true identity was almost certainly known.

Jack went berserk and started to beat Audrey to a pulp and would have murdered her if Jean had not intervened and got herself punched, thrown across the room and kicked in the face and stomach for her trouble.

Jean picked herself up and staggered out before she got another beating and cycled to her home, which was about a mile away, and started crying while she sat at the kitchen table with a cup of tea.

She then went to the bathroom and was horrified at what she saw in the mirror. She had a black eye and numerous cuts and bruises on her face and she felt as though she had a broken rib where she had been kicked. The bastard had beaten her up in an uncontrollable fit of rage. Just because Audrey had left the time table in the box, so there was no knowing what he would do next to her and the children.

Feeling utterly helpless, she realised that she was still blackmailed into doing things that were definitely not acceptable to her and could be accused of being a party to the murder of Andrew and the boiler man and if she continued to allow herself to be blackmailed, she could also be responsible for the murder of the French girl. She tried to grasp the extent of the danger that she and her children were in and decided that the only way was to go to William and ask for his help to get away before they had a chance to hurt the children.

Because she was still single and a widow, she had been picked out and blackmailed into becoming an unwilling informer for the Irish Republican Extremists with the threat that her children would be harmed if she did not comply with their instructions.

When Jack and Audrey had first forced their way into her house at night she had already provided a lot of information about Andrew's family and back ground but now she had been told to keep them informed about Mark and William Oakhill and Andrew's French wife who she found to be a very pleasant innocent young girl who would almost certainly be the next to be murdered because of some sort of revenge against the Baker family.

Jack and Audrey were now back again, but this time they were not creeping round at night and threatening her, they were in full view and posing as agricultural scientists sent to replace the other couple who had been living in Andrew's house!

Mark, Sasha, Gillie, William, Michelle and Sally were in the study working out how best to deal with the situation.

A list was made of all the options.

Inform Curzon Mews first, as both Geoffrey and Richard had said that they preferred to handle reprisal activity, as far as possible, without the police or the press being involved so that the terrorists did not get any publicity to further their cause.

Double check with Richard that Mike Cutland and Susan were not double agents and can be trusted.

Call Raymond and tell him to put the temporary gate across the cattle grid at the front gate and check before letting anyone in or out and to ask Tad to come up to the house as soon as possible.

Arm everyone with revolvers.

Tad to stay in the summer house and keep watch on the house and be kept in contact via the tunnel.

Mark, William and Gillie to drive over the moor to the factory and check with the night shift and the locals if they had seen the new guard couple, Jack and Audrey, going anywhere and then approach Andrew's house.

Mark phoned Curzon Mews and asked for Richard and was put through almost immediately.

"Good afternoon Richard, we hope you are well. There appear to be two strange wolves that have come across the sea to replace the originals in our upper hen house and need you to check on their parentage. We also need to recheck the possible duplicity for the couple at the lower hen house soonest."

"Just leave it with me and I will call you back. Please keep me informed."

Gillie had already called Raymond on the house phone and Tad was on his way up to the house and when he arrived Gillie gave him a rifle and ammunition and he went through the tunnel to the summer house.

Tad then set up the simple signaling system that they had used in the mines consisting of a length of string with a bell tied to each end. To send a signal you just jerked the string to make the bell ring at the other end and when there was an answering pull there was a code of various numbers of pulls for different situations.

Mark said to Sasha.

"I think that we should warn Sarah and Robert."

"I have just spoken to Sarah on the telephone and she will drive out to where Robert is working and tell him.

They will arm themselves and stay in the house till we give them the all clear."

Everyone had a loaded revolver and Sasha took the girls up stairs to the private 'Drawing Room with a View.' Agnes and Annie joined them.

Richard telephoned the Baker's number and Mike answered. Richard then started a low key informal conversation with some built in questions to recheck on Mike's true identity and after ten minutes he was satisfied that Mike's identity was correct. He then told Mike about the suspected imposters in Andrew's house and asked if he had met Jack and Audrey before this assignment.

"No, we had heard their names mentioned at some of the meetings but had not actually met them before."

"Well, as you had not met them before, it looks very likely that Jack and Audrey have been 'replaced' by two people from over the water so I want you to work very closely with Mark and his family and if possible round up the wolves in the top hen house. I will now ring Mark and confirm that you are part of the team and he will contact you shortly."

Mark answered the phone and Richard said that he had questioned Mike and was satisfied that he had been able to confirm that he definitely was one of the team and it was alright to work with Mike and Susan but definitely not the other two at the top location as they were unknown to Mike and Susan and were almost certainly imposters.

Mark rang Mike on the house phone and asked him to come up to the house with Susan.

When Mike and Susan arrived Mark took them into the study where Gillie and William were waiting.

William explained what had happened in the office at the factory and that it appeared that Jack and Audrey were imposters and could be armed and dangerous.

Mark took William in his car and Gillie went in Mike's car to the factory by the track over the moor.

The foreman had called off the afternoon shift as there was no production, but Billy and his two assistants were finishing off connecting up the new machine.

Billy had not seen Jack and Audrey since the day before when they had collected some samples and asked a lot of questions.

Jean was scared that Jack was so angry that he was likely to come to her house after dark so she decided that as soon as the children came back from school and had had a quick tea she would take them to the factory to see William and ask for help.

As Jean approached the factory with the children she saw the two cars parked by the boiler house and walked quickly in case they moved off before she got there.

William saw Jean and her two children approaching. It was obvious that Jean was in a very distressed state as she had numerous cuts and bruises and was limping.

"Whatever has happened to you?"

"I was made to do it or they would have harmed the children. I swear that I didn't know what they were going to do. I didn't mean no harm but they kept threatening me."

"Come in here and sit down while Billy makes you a cup of tea." Billy went off to make the tea.

"Now, who are 'they' and what did they want you to do?"

"It is that Jack and Audrey, as they now call themselves that started to come at night some time ago and threaten me to keep giving them information about Andrew or they would hurt the children. They were very pleased that Andrew had been killed and now have come back and told me to start giving them information about you, your father and mother and Andrew's wife.

I had to tell them that you had found that time table for the Irish ferry, or they would have killed me if they found out that they had not been told, as it was, Jack went berserk and half killed Audrey for being careless, and when I tried to stop him, he attacked me, so I escaped and waited at home till the children came home from school. I dare not stay at home now, so I came here where it is safer, and to warn you and ask for your help."

Mike stepped forward and said that he could take her and the children to their house and that Susan would look after them.

William confirmed that Mike and Susan were trusted friends and were still living in Geoffrey Baker's house, which is inside the park.

Mark and Gillie were discussing the best strategy to catch the two wolves.

Leave Jean and the children with Billy at the factory for the time being, take both cars to Andrew's house, but leave one back a bit, if Jack's car is still there, let one tyre down, go to the front and back and knock with revolvers drawn.

Mark and William stopped about 100 yards from the house and Mike went closer.

There was no car outside or in the garage.

Mike went to the front and knocked and Mark went to the back with William and Gillie.

Mike tried the door and it was not locked so he went in and checked each room and then opened the back door and let the others in.

They found Audrey in the kitchen lying in a pool of blood with her throat cut, but there was no sign of Jack, just the signs of a hasty departure.

Gillie said.

"Looks like you can only make one mistake if you work for fanatical terrorists!"

They went outside and discussed the options.

As this was now a case of murder, which was not a reprisal killing, it was probably time to call in the police, but Richard would have to be consulted first so they went back to the factory and Mark phoned Richard.

Richard agreed and said that he would talk to his contact at Scotland Yard and that he would instruct his contact to send a senior man to advise the locals immediately so that they could start their usual low key investigations . He would also see if the real Jack and Audrey had been murdered or were locked up somewhere. This would involve a general alert for all police stations.

As Jean and her children were to move in with Mike and Susan they got into Mike's car and picked up some essentials from Jean's house on the way.

On the way back to the house Gillie said to William that as Jack now knew that his cover was blown and was still on the loose that they would have to be extra vigilant.

"What do you think he will do? Which way would he go? Would he go through the village or would he take one of the tracks across the hill?" When they got home Mark said.

"I asked around and he was not seen going through the village so I think that he would have taken one of the hill tracks and may even shack up in one of the remote barns, used for the winter fodder, for a while and see if he can have a shot at one of us.

You are right, we definitely can't relax yet and we must keep Michelle and Sasha very safe.

We must get out the plans of the property and check on the tracks and the location of the remote barns, but we need some more men to do a proper sweeping search."

Gillie said.

"There are some ex-Army members of the gun club who are unemployed who might like a few days paid sport! What do you think?"

"That sounds perfect but what can we tell them? Anyway, we must keep Richard informed of what we are doing."

Mark made a quick call to Richard and told him what they had planned and he said that it was alright to go ahead as planned but if Jack was caught he must be handed over to the police and he would ensure that his man from Scotland Yard would be there in the morning to work with the local police.

Gillie went round to the selected members of the gun club and said that there was to be a 'deer shoot' and if they would like a few days paid sport they should meet at the gun club at six o'clock the next morning. They were all interested and agreed to join in the deer hunt.

Mark, William and Gillie were waiting when the men arrived.

Mark said.

"Good morning Gentlemen, we have brought you here supposedly for a deer shoot, but the animal that we are looking for only has two legs!

Andrew's young widow, who is now living under the protection of my family, has become the target of a foreign based vendetta because of work her family did during the war.

The man we are looking for, has just cut his own partner's throat because he found that she had left some incriminating evidence behind, so that gives you some idea of the sort of man that we are looking for.

While this man is still on the loose in the area, he is very likely to murder other innocent people so we need to find him as soon as possible and hand him over to the authorities.

Putting it bluntly, it is 'shoot to stop,' not, 'shoot to kill,' so fire warning shots or shout a warning to stop first, before you shoot to 'wing' him if he tries to run away, because we want him to be tried for murder.

He left the village yesterday afternoon in his blue Morris ten car. He was not seen going through the village so we think that he went by one of the tracks into the hills and he may be holed up in one of the remote barns or a farm building because he will need to hide his car.

Gillie has divided the area into sections and will give you the details.

If you decide to help us you will be paid twice the normal rate, or you are free to drop out now, if you wish. We ask that you stick to the 'deer hunt' story even with your families."

There was some discussion among the men and then they all went over to where Gillie had laid out the tracings of the maps, made by Sasha and Sally.

Mark, Gillie and William were to keep driving along the tracks and collect the reports from each group of men as the search progressed over the hills.

The search was nearly completed by late in the afternoon and Mark was beginning to think that Jack had left the area when he heard rifle fire coming from a remote barn at the head of a small valley.

Using his binoculars he could see three men lying prone on a hill overlooking a barn and shooting at the barn.

There was an occasional return of fire from a much smaller calibre weapon, probably a 0.22 rifle.

Mark drove closer, got out, lay on a small bank and checked with his binoculars again.

From this position he could see the low angle of the sun glinting on the windscreen of a vehicle parked in the barn thus indicating that they had probably found the right man.

Mark crawled forward a long way till he could get a long shot to disable the car to prevent an attempted get away.

He eventually had a clear view of the rear wheels and aimed at a rear tyre and fired.

The bullet glanced off the tyre and hit the fuel tank which burst into flames.

Within a few minutes the whole barn was burning fiercely and a burning figure staggered out and started rolling on the ground and crying out with pain.

The three men from the other side had already moved forward and helped to put out the flames by continuing to roll the man in the damp grass.

Mark had to drive back and then come up the other side of the valley to get to the barn.

Gillie had already arrived in his wagonette and Jack was being loaded into the back.

Jack had superficial burns to his legs, arms, hands and one side of his face. He was tied up, roughly patched up and one man agreed to travel in the back with him as Gillie took him to the police station.

Mark and William drove round sounding their horns to call off the search and take the men back to the gun club where Sasha and Jill had a hot meal ready.

Mark and Sasha located the three men who had first started shooting and asked them what had happened.

"We was going over the hill when we saw this bloke opening the barn door and starting to drive a blue car out so we fired a coupla' warning shots and shouted at him to stop but he backed into the barn and shut the door real fast and started shooting back at us with a small rifle. We was sure that he was your man 'cos o' the way he behaved after the warning shots and the shouting."

"Well done indeed, and thank you for your help, it is a very big relief to know that he has been caught before he was able to commit another reprisal murder. The police will now take over."

Sasha wrote down the names of all the men, shook their hands and thanked each one and said that their pay would be brought round as soon as possible.

One man said.

"I don't know as we deserve any money as we are glad to help and wos only doing our duty to rid the district of some vermin wot wos murdering and threatening local people, but I will accept it 'cos o' the kids. Thank you Missus."

When Gillie arrived at the police station the local police sergeant said that he had a man from Scotland Yard who wanted to see him.

Detective Inspector, Bill Jenkins introduced himself and as soon as the prisoner had been sent to hospital under police guard he asked Gillie to come into a private office and give him a summary of the events leading up to the capture of the prisoner.

Gillie checked that Detective Inspector Bill Jenkins was au fait with the work that Richard was doing and when he was sure that he was fully informed he gave a complete history of events with particular reference to the vendetta against the Baker family and now Geoffrey's daughter in law, Michelle, plus Mark, Sasha and William.

There was also the involvement of Jean due to her being under threat of blackmail which could mean that she could also be the subject of a 'silencing' murder.

Bill Jenkins said that the safest way was to relocate Jean and give her a new persona, subject to her approval, other wise she would have to take her chances and stay where she was.

The offer of relocation and a new persona was made to Jean, but now that Jack was behind bars and heading towards the hangman's noose she decided to stay, if she could keep her job at the factory.

Mark and William agreed to keep her job open on the strict understanding that if she was ever approached or threatened again that she would immediately tell them. Jean was very thankful and agreed without hesitation. As a widow with two children, it was vital that she kept her job as secretary at the factory.

Mike and Susan Cutland moved up to Andrew's house in the village as there was a bigger double garage and workshop with plenty of room for all their equipment.

Detective Inspector Bill Jenkins telephoned to say that he would like to call and see Mark and Gillie so it was arranged that he came up to the house right away and on his arrival they went into the study.

"Richard has asked me to tell you that the real Jack and Audrey have been found.

It appears that they were lured, or forced at gun point, to go into a railway shunting yard and shot. Their bodies had been put into an empty cattle truck and covered with straw and were found by a railway man two days ago."

Mark said.

"Thank you for keeping us informed. The callous murder of two people who they wanted to impersonate goes to show just how these extremists operate.

They are a very real 'enemy within'.

How is the prosecution of Jack progressing?"

"I don't know the details, as it is being handled in London by Special Branch so that it does not give the press a chance to make a 'story' involving local people and put you and your family further at risk."

Chapter 19

UNWELCOME PHOENIX

Life at Glendarvel settled down again and Mike and Susan got down to work on their project with test plots, soil samples, crop yields and even a record of fuel used and tractor hours spent in each stage of cultivation and harvesting. But they kept up their watch on all that went on in the area.

The 1939 summer was turning to autumn and there were more threats, incidents and unrest in South East Europe.

Hitler was asserting himself as a greedy and ruthless dictator with the largest and best equipped army in Europe and when he threatened Poland, Britain and France guaranteed to support Poland.

Early on the morning of the first of September, Germany invaded Poland with Hitler's new tactic of what he called a 'Blitzkrieg' or lightening war.

Britain and France surprised Hitler on the third of September by declaring war on Germany.

German Panzer tanks advanced rapidly in great sweeps across Poland with air strafing and bombing raids preceding each tank advance. Even though the Poles put up a very strong resistance, they were defeated by the end of September. Russia had also been attacking Poland from the East because Hitler had promised to carve up Poland and give Russia a part as a reward for their help.

Britain and France did not want a repeat of the First World War in the trenches and hoped that hostilities would remain in the Balkan and Scandinavian countries where Hitler seemed to be concentrating his efforts in this early stage of the war.

It was later discovered that part of Hitler's plan was to secure the supply of high quality iron ore from Sweden.

Britain moved a huge army into France and there was then a lull or 'Phoney War' with not much happening in central Europe.

London and other major cities in Britain evacuated their children into rural areas, anti-aircraft gun emplacements were built and as there was a fear that Hitler would drop gas bombs indiscriminately everyone had to carry a gas mask at all times.

William volunteered for the army and was soon selected to go to OCTU. (Officer Cadet Training Unit.) Sally took over as manager of the Dairy Company and proved to be a fair but strict boss with an obsession for hygiene and cleanliness. She introduced new packaging and started advertising which further increased demand. Amy started to look after sales and distribution.

George was again seconded to work in the South of England to design and supervise the construction of airfields, coastal defenses which included tank barriers, and gun emplacements.

All Commonwealth countries joined Britain by declaring war on Germany, with the notable exception of Ireland.

The American Ambassador to Britain, Joseph P. Kennedy, was found to be using his diplomatic position and immunity to access Britain's strategic defense and battle plans and was caught sending this highly confidential information to Germany, via the diplomatic bags!

Churchill was furious and had a difficult decision to make on how to stop the leak without upsetting the Americans. This would not be easy because Kennedy had used his Irish Catholic friends in Congress to get him the plum job of Ambassador, and in return, was already starting to help one of his anti- British, pacifist cronies in congress, to replace Roosevelt, which would be a disaster for Britain if he succeeded.

An order was issued by Churchill that Kennedy was to be totally by-passed and that he was not to have access to any important information, but Kennedy continued with his determination to sabotage Britain and started holding meetings to spread his defeatist and subversive ideas under the protection of his diplomatic immunity and status.

Hopefully, he would be diplomatically recalled to America before he did any more damage to the very real life or death situation in Britain.

This phoney war period allowed Britain to crank up armament production and increase badly needed aircraft production.

Chamberlain resigned and Churchill was made Prime Minister in May 1940 and there was a general boost to morale. Churchill then made the first of his legendary speeches which rallied every last drop of national pride and determination to defeat the evil enemy across the channel.

The German offensive started in Europe at this time with 300 German tanks sweeping across Holland, Belgium and through the Ardennes Forest to the French Maginot line with amazing speed.

The allied forces were forced to retreat as many French cities fell and it became a race to an RV at Dunkirk for evacuation across the channel. Most of the roads in Northern France were clogged with French people trying to escape from the fighting.

The German planes strafed the roads packed with French civilians and British military vehicles with machine gun fire and bombs with brutal ferocity.

The distinctive scream of a Stuka dive bomber became imprinted on the memories of the fleeing hordes of French civilians who regularly saw their countrymen, women and children being ruthlessly murdered in their thousands along the congested roads in Northern France. Among them were the evacuating British servicemen on their way to Dunkirk.

There were over 300,000 British troops to evacuate and only very limited shipping available.

A call was put out for owners of privately owned vessels to volunteer and to form a flotilla to help evacuate the men. Over 800 private vessels were hastily assembled, refueled and crossed the channel en mass. Many of the private vessels kept shuttling back and forth for days with loads of battle weary, and often wounded men.

The combined operation of Naval and private vessels was highly successful and over 330,000 men were returned to Britain.

Churchill referred to the Dunkirk evacuation as 'A Deliverance'.

The troops had had to dig in on the beach as they waited for evacuation because of continuous Stuka dive bomber attacks.

The RAF gave as much air support as possible and lost over 100 planes during the evacuation.

All British military vehicles and supplies had been 'disabled', and or burnt, as the troops moved down to the beaches and great columns of black smoke could be seen for miles.

Britain was now alone with the Germans only 21 miles away across the channel!

The RAF. Was short of pilots and started to train colonial pilots for combat in the spitfire fighter planes, designed by R. J. Mitchell, which had a powerful Rolls Royce V12 Merlin engine, two 0.5 inch canons and a machine gun, making it the superior fighter aircraft.

The first Battle of Britain, in the air, was in July 1940.

Up to this time, German bombing raids on Britain had been on air fields and military targets but in September 1940 Hitler changed his policy and the raids were directed onto civilians in London and provincial cities as a 'morale breaker', which was all part of Hitler's psychological warfare plan.

There were over half a million British civilian casualties in the first six months of Hitler's 'morale breaker' raids.

Germany occupied the Channel Islands, with only slight resistance, and started to use them as bases for U boats and patrol boats.

Mark and Gillie had an urgent request from Richard to go to London for two days as there was a new area that he wanted covered.

The Curzon Mews Private Hotel welcomed them like old friends and after the usual security check they went into the conference room for a high level meeting.

Richard was in the chair but there were three academic looking visitors sitting alongside him.

It was noted that there were some ladies present and all of the fifty or so people in the room had to swear an oath of complete secrecy in turn and then resume their seats.

Richard then said that the visitors would explain the purpose of the meeting.

A tall man with a bald head and horn rimmed glasses stood up.

"Good Evening Ladies and Gentlemen.

Today we are going to talk about the 'enemy within'.

We can sometimes pick up the transmissions of German secret agents in Britain communicating by wireless with their bases in Germany.

As these signals are encrypted it can take us several days to decode them but we now also have a means of using radio direction finders to locate them, and sometimes can pin point where the agents are transmitting from in this country.

Not only do we have enemy agents within our shores, but we have also found that there is a surprisingly strong 'Fifth Column' (For the benefit of the younger people present, that term originates from the Spanish wars when they marched in columns of four and the 'fifth column' was supposedly the enemy.) working in this country with the support and involvement of some apparently respectable and high ranking people!

The Germans have studied the science of what they call 'Mind Control' which is a very subtle, low key form of mental manipulation and they have set up groups in many cities which meet regularly and a senior member talks in a defeatist vein and uses such expressions as;

Why are we fighting a war that we are going to lose anyway?

We must be sure that we are in a position where we will be welcomed by our new masters as soon as they take over.

Whose war is it?

It is not our war, it only effects Europe.

Why are we fighting a war that is not necessary?

Is it necessary to sacrifice our wealth for a lost cause?

And so on.

There are a number of wealthy industrialists and even titled people who have given large sums of money to this subversive cause already and they have started to manipulate and bribe the industrial troublemakers in the munitions factories.

As we are 'at war', these clandestine meetings are considered to be verging on, or actually represent treason and must be treated as such.

Don't let us forget that we are literally fighting for our lives in a life or death situation and the slightest act of subversion or sabotage could tip the balance the wrong way.

Also, 'inciting treason' is a very serious crime and it could soon be necessary to round up the ringleaders so we need your help to learn all about them.

For example, we found one group that was calling itself 'The Feather Club' and was meeting in a private room at a hotel each Friday till they unknowingly enrolled a Jew whose family had been murdered by the Germans. The Jewish man was able to give us enough information to put in a special undercover agent to confirm their level of subversion and incitement of treason and then raid a meeting and round them up.

In that case we found that the group leader was a highly trained German agent equipped with a radio transmitter and bomb making facilities.

The club members included one left side Member of Parliament, a newspaper editor, several journalists, a secretary from the Foreign Office, a wealthy industrialist, several senior bureaucrats and some industrial troublemakers who had been planted in munitions factories, all involved in subversion and treason. They are now in prison awaiting to go before the courts.

We only want you to be our eyes and ears across the country and not, and I repeat, not, to become involved or you will lose your local status of an observer, so report back to us and we will send a specially trained person to investigate.

Now I will hand you over to the next speaker.

Thank you for your attention."

Another visitor stood up and he used the blackboard to set out the structure of the enemy agent's network of communications, and then continued.

"As my college has explained, these subversive cells are set up all over the country and it is our job to locate them and find out just how they operate and if they represent a threat to national security.

We find that there are several ways that we can get a lead to where a group is operating.

Look out for a regular meeting of men, and usually some women, from a wide range of social strata often in a private room at a hotel. There is usually an innocent sounding cover name for the meetings such as;

Progressive Research, Personal Development, Floral Club, and so on.

The agents manipulating industrial troublemakers are a weakness in their system because they have to stand out of the crowd in order to get their message across to their fellow workers and it is then possible to find who they associate with 'socially' and there is often 'talk' on the factory floor that can help.

Factory management are often alerted by evidence of sabotage, a falloff in production or worker attitude changes resulting from manipulation.

Don't be put off if your suspect appears to be of high social or financial standing or is seen to be doing good work for the war effort. This can be just a sham to give them a cover.

We are at war in a 'life or death balance' and any manipulation of the true facts or interruption to our munitions production could tip that delicate balance and must be stamped out and the perpetrators brought to justice.

From time to time we are able to intercept a wireless message and use direction finders to pin point the area where there is an agent operating and will be able to give you a lead on where to look.

I will now hand you over to our cipher expert"

The third visitor stood up and put a box of printed cards on the table.

"Ladies and Gentlemen I am sure you are aware that the enemy has agents, and victims of blackmail threats acting as agents, in the telephone and post office services, but it is necessary for us to have a reasonably secure and fast method of communicating with HQ.

As most of the risk in the event of an interception is primarily with the enemy agent, we do not need a time consuming elaborate system to maintain an adequate level of security.

We therefore will issue each of you with cards in a different series of rotating switch words which you can insert into a normal sounding conversation. These will be periodically changed. A crude but fast system based on the assumption that if the call is intercepted, by the time the enemy has worked out the real meaning the information will be out of date anyway.

There are twenty different telephone numbers at HQ and you must always pick a different one at random. All the lines can be connected to your usual contact internally.

You will see that the cards are in pairs so that we have a matching card for each of you in the initial issue. Please write your name and the name of your usual contact on the spare card and hand it back when they are distributed.

Thank you for your time and happy hunting."

Richard then opened the meeting for general discussion and several members said that they were already aware of subversive activity in their area.

On the return train journey Mark and Gillie were discussing the extra work load that they had been given and how they were going to fit it in with the Home Guard duties. Mark had been appointed commander of the local Home Guard battalion and Gillie was his 2/ IC.

There was a Sunday morning Home Guard parade each week for about twenty five men from the immediate area. Many of whom were old soldiers and there were a few younger men who had not been accepted for the services on medical grounds or had been wounded and classed as not fit for active service but were still fit enough to serve in the Home Guard.

The Home Guard was a collection of volunteers ranging from bank managers to farm labourers who were prepared to give up some of their leisure time to form the last line of defense during air raids or an invasion.

When the bombing raids started on specific targets in the area, like Liverpool docks, the Rolls Royce aero engine factory, aerodromes, railway junctions or the morale breaker attacks on civilian residential areas in major cities, the immediate HG duties became observation, reporting and patrolling for the duration of the raid.

In the event of a German bombing raid the observers on the South coast reported the number and type of enemy aircraft and their approximate flight path and arrival time at the estimated target area.

This information was then progressed by more observers as the planes flew inland and when the the target area was confirmed the details were phoned to the respective Home Guard contacts, which in this case was Gillie.

Gillie then called the four men on night duty in the Red Cross room at the village hall.

One man went into the church bell tower as a lookout and used a field telephone to keep in touch with his off-sider in the village hall close by. This man also manned the normal phone and the wireless.

The other two men used an old car to patrol the area and kept in touch with the look out and the village hall with number 38 wireless sets.

Their main duty was to look out for crashed planes and parachutists. There were also cases of unexplained indiscriminate bombing which landed on homes or farm buildings which sometimes caused a fire which had to be put out and reported.

Chapter 20

BENDING THE BEAMS

The most frequent targets in the area for the German bombers were Liverpool docks, Manchester civilians and the Rolls Royce Merlin engine works at Crewe.

Whenever possible a squadron of Spitfire fighter planes (With Rolls Royce Merlin engines) was sent up to attack the formation of bombers.

Some of the inexperienced, poorly trained or undisciplined German pilots just panicked when the Spitfires arrived, dumped their bombs wherever they were at the time, broke formation and fled back home thus becoming an easy target for a Spitfire pilot with his 0.50 cannons and machine guns as soon as the fleeing bomber did not have the covering fire available from the rest of the formation.

However, there were many bombers that reached their targets and there was much damage done.

The Rolls Royce engine works at Crewe was supposed to be protected by a ring of AA guns but these were not very effective against high altitude bombing.

The German bomber crews often had trouble locating their target and bombed a wrong area miles away. The secret service had even set up several dummy factories in rural areas close by which could be illuminated to simulate a factory fire during a raid so that successive waves of bomber pilots would use direct visual location to dump more bombs in the same wrong place.

Then there was a sudden change in the accuracy of the raids and the bombers started to locate the Rolls Royce factory easily, even if they had been previously scattered all over the sky!

Richard came to visit Mark and they had a long discussion on how the bomber pilots were being directed to the engine factory with such amazing accuracy even on dark and moonless nights.

It was concluded that there must be enemy agents along the flight path using some form of visual signaling devices like special lights or perhaps radio telephone 'talk along' like the system used to land planes in a thick fog, which was called 'talk down'.

Spotter planes were used in daylight to check for any markers or equipment on the ground, like aligned plow furrows, reflective signs painted on barn roofs or directional radio aerials, but found nothing.

Richard arranged for an order to be issued that for all future air raids there was to be a total HG turnout with every vehicle or pedestrian on the move during a raid to be stopped and checked and a careful look out for any suspicious lights or activity.

During the next bombing raid there was a 100% HG turnout with every man checking all possible ways that signals could be given to enemy aircraft.

The first alarm came when a light was seen coming from the top of a haystack and the two HG men on bicycle patrol called Gillie from the nearest house telephone for assistance to be sent as soon as possible.

Six men armed with ladders, revolvers, a rifle and torches stormed the haystack.

They found a very embarrassed, half dressed, courting couple!

The continuing supply of Rolls Royce Merlin aero engines, as used in the Spitfire fighter planes, was on the very top of the list of items of national importance, so Churchill's personal technical adviser was assigned to the task of finding the method used by the Germans to direct their planes with such amazing accuracy.

Richard phoned to say that he would be arriving the next morning with a very important visitor and Sasha suggested that it would be more convenient if they stayed in the house during the visit.

Mark met Richard and his visitor at Chester station and was introduced to a 'Cambridge physics professor'.

As soon as they arrived at Glendarvel the professor asked if he could set up his instruments and special aerials in a high place with all round uninterrupted views so they went up to the village hall and Billy, the maintenance man from the factory, was asked to set up the aerials as instructed on some high ground a short distance from the factory.

The professor then wanted to go to the old Norman castle on Beeston hill and he used his portable instruments to send signals to locations in the South of England.

There was no raid for the first two nights so Mark and Sasha were able to show the visitors round the area and then Mark drove them to the Rolls Royce engine works at Crewe so that they were familiar with the area and the professor took note of all tall buildings and landmarks.

On the third night there was an air raid warning just after midnight for a formation of enemy bombers heading a bit to the West of the direction of Crewe.

Gillie called a full turnout for the HG and all the men available went to their allotted areas.

Mark took the professor to the village hall and he was soon in constant telephone and radio communication with his other 'listening' positions and radio transmitters in the South of England.

He was also making frequent adjustments to his instruments and recording the results.

The bombers were within the range of the instruments for over half an hour and then the surviving bombers headed for home with a squadron of fighters attacking them as they went.

The professor then phoned his contact at the Rolls Royce engine factory and got a report that there had been a large formation of bombers in the area but that all the bombs had fallen some miles away in a rural area and the Prof. became excited and said.

"We have discovered how to bend their beams! Now we need to set up a more permanent system and we will bring up a team of our radio men to put in a more powerful system as soon as possible.

Would it be possible to fence off about an acre on the highest point of this hill preferably a short distance away from habitation, but we need an electric power supply?"

"Yes that can be arranged and I know just the place, it is close to our Dairy factory and a bit higher than where your first temporary aerials were erected, about two miles from here.

I can have the area fenced off first thing tomorrow morning. There is a heavy duty electricity supply at the factory that you can use when you need power."

"We will put up tents for the guards and technical operators in the fenced off area, and if possible connect to the phone system if there are any spare lines available."

After a quick visit to the area proposed for installation of the equipment, Mark drove the Prof. home where Richard was waiting.

The Prof. was excited as he explained to Richard that he had been able to bend the radio beams that the Germans were using to direct their planes.

"I did not realise at first that the German name for their system actually tells you how it is used.

The German name is Knickebein, which if translated literally, means 'Bent Leg'.

So we now think that the Germans shovel their bombers, with rookie air crews, into the air anywhere along the short 'base line of a triangle' on the French coast near Cleves.

The apex of the triangle is the old Norman castle at Beeston which is a major landmark close to their target.

As the planes fly Northwards, they have their special radios tuned to the 'beam frequency' and if they hear a predominance of dots they know that they are heading too far West, and if they hear a predominance of dashes they know that they are heading too far to the East, thus 'the beams kick them into the correct flight path,' exactly as the German name implies.

When the pilot hears equal strength dots and dashes he knows that he is at the turning point over Beeston castle and then flies on a simple compass bearing at a set speed for a very short given time and he is then over the target.

We have now found that we can either 'bend' the German beams or put up slightly off line beams to direct them away from strategic targets.

There has just been a signal from London advising that there is also a very urgent requirement to protect the Liverpool docks from bombing raids.

When you look at the map, it appears that we can deceive the bomber pilots into thinking they have reached Liverpool docks when in fact they have only got as far as the River Dee estuary which is a nearly parallel waterway some fifteen miles further south from the River Mersey and Liverpool docks.

I have the idea that we can make the River Dee estuary tidal mud flats look like Liverpool docks by installing a pattern of muted industrial lights and then bend the beams so that all the bombs land on the tidal mud flats well away from any habitation or any military establishments."

The next day several trucks of men and equipment arrived in the village and quickly set up their tents and radio masts in the fenced off area on the hill.

A team of men then dug trenches so that the men and delicate radio equipment could be kept safe during a raid.

Then another truck arrived with a 50 kVA generator and several reels of heavy cable. The generator was off loaded next to the boiler house at the factory and a cable was run out to the site on the hill. An electrician then put in a two way switch so that the radio site could normally use the mains power supply and in the event of a power failure could instantly be switched over to the generator because it was vital that the beams were 'bent' all the time during a raid. During a raid was of course the time when there was most likely to be a power failure.

The Prof. stayed on for a few more days till he was sure that all his 'beam bending equipment' was fully operational and then went back to London with Richard.

Many small boats were used on the River Dee mud flats, at high tide, to put up rows of short poles onto which 'blackout shaded' lights were attached. Several plywood and corrugated iron dummy 'buildings' were floated out on pontoons and secured to poles to represent dockside buildings.

The whole area was then cordoned off from fishing boats and sightseers.

There were two more raids which had been intended for the engine factory at Crewe and some nearby farmland with dummy buildings and lights was heavily bombed in a concentrated pattern.

Liverpool docks had been very severely damaged in numerous previous raids and there were several ships sunk at the wharves which were in a very critical stage in the process of being re-floated by teams of Navy divers. It was therefore essential that there was no more bomb damage or the whole port would become unable to service the ships bringing vital supplies from America or loading the ships taking men and munitions to the various battle zones.

When a raid was next directed towards the Liverpool docks, and the beams were being 'bent' by the Prof's system, the planes flew right over Glendarvel and Mark and Sasha went out to the summer house and could see the outline of a formation of bombers against the night sky and hear the loud drone of many powerful engines pulling their loads of bombs through the darkness. There were no attacking Spitfires in sight so they assumed that it was planned that the bombers would be allowed to drop all their bombs on the River Dee marshes before the fighters would appear and attack them on their way back.

About twenty minutes later the bombers started to return with Spitfires chasing them with cannons crashing and machine guns chattering. As one bomber was hit, Mark and Sasha could see the tracer bullets coming from the fighter and striking the rear gun turret of the bomber and raking along the fuselage up to the cockpit. The bomber lurched sideways and turned nose down with the engines still racing to crash into the hill about a mile away in a great ball of flame.

Mark estimated that the plane had crashed at about the top of the Valley Farm land so he phoned Robert and Sarah and asked them what they had seen.

Robert said that he had heard the crash and had got a line on the fire and confirmed that it was somewhere along his top boundary. Mark said that he would get Gillie to send some of his HG men up to investigate and report back.

In the meantime there were more returning bombers overhead being chased by Spitfires with their guns blazing. Some of the bombers were trying to jink from side to side to avoid the streams of tracer bullets arcing towards them but the heavy bombers response was far too slow to have any benefit.

Another bomber was hit and flew on with flames pouring out of one engine till flame engulfed the fuselage and it spiraled down to crash several miles away.

A Spitfire was hit by a stream of tracer coming from a rear gun turret on one of the bombers, the fighter's engine stopped and the fighter plane slowly flew round loosing height and appeared to land on a hill side but they could not see if the pilot had been able to land safely. Mark phoned Gillie and asked him to send out some HG men to look for the plane, but Gillie had already received a call from the Village hall and there was a car and four men on their way.

There appeared to be no more bombers left to return, but then a straggler could be heard, but the engine sound was different as though it was flying very low with fewer of its engines working.

As it was nearly overhead flames started to erupt from one wing and they could see the crew jumping out of a side door and their parachutes could be clearly seen as they were illuminated when the burning plane started to loose height and crash quite close by, probably somewhere near the village.

By dawn the HG had rescued the Spitfire pilot from the wreckage of his plane. The undercarriage of his plane had been damaged so the pilot had to do a 'belly landing' and had been able to keep the plane sliding over the heather till it had struck some uneven ground which had made the plane tip up on its nose trapping him in the cockpit with a few cuts and a broken arm.

The five crew members from the German bomber who had parachuted to the ground were rounded up. One had a sprained ankle, the rest were shaken but not injured.

Mark sent for Sally to come as soon as possible and take the spitfire pilot to the house to have first aid where she had all her medical supplies.

The German bomber crew were seated in the village hall under guard and given a hot drink before Mark and Gillie came to find if any of them spoke English.

They were all very young, probably only eighteen or possibly twenty and looked scared.

One of the crew answered, "Ja, I haf a leedle Englitch."

"Where did you go tonight?"

"Vee must no say."

"We will have to send you to be interrogated by a military intelligence officer, but it will help you if you answer a few questions now.

Are you the pilot?"

"Ja, I pilot, make much bombing Lilopool tree timez."

"That is better, now you are talking we can get you some food."

Gillie went to ask the Red Cross women on duty to make some breakfast for the prisoners.

"You must be a good pilot to have been on three raids, but how do you find your target?"

"Vee haf goot instrument, ja."

"It is very good that you speak English and if you continue to co-operate with us, we can make life more comfortable for you."

Mark decided that was enough questioning for now because it looked as though the pilot would continue to soften and could provide a lot more information if handled carefully. He must have a word with the I Corps officer before the prisoners were interrogated.

Breakfast was ready and the prisoners were moved to the Red Cross room with their two HG guards.

The smell of the prisoner's breakfast made Mark realise how hungry and tired he was so he asked Gillie if he had had any breakfast.

"Och' aye', the Red Cross lassies cooked me a bonny breakfast more than an hour ago. I ha' also phoned the red caps and they will send a truck to pick up the prisoners this afternoon."

"I think that I will go home for breakfast and have a word with the spitfire pilot and arrange for him to be returned to his unit."

Sally had re-aligned the pilot's broken arm and put it into a plaster cast and a sling and patched up the other cuts and was sitting in the garden talking to him when Mark arrived home.

The pilot, Angus Mackenzie, was introduced and he thanked Mark for organising his rescue from the crashed spitfire so quickly.

Angus had an unusual accent so Mark asked him where he came from.

"I was born in Scotland and went to Australia with my parents when I was six. I came over here soon after the start of the war to join the RAF, as I had always wanted to fly."

"Welcome back to Britain, and thank you for joining the RAF. We desperately need trained pilots."

Then giving Sally a big wink he said. "How is Sally looking after you?"

"The medical attention is very professional and the company is most charming!"

Sally blushed and said. "You only got what all the pilots get when they arrive on our doorstep, and you are welcome to stay till you are fully recovered, if you are allowed to."

Mark could see that there was an immediate attraction between the two young people so he excused himself and went to find Sasha.

"Hello Darling, it is good to see that Sally has made friends with the spitfire pilot already, so I left the young ones talking in the garden."

"They are not all that young, they are both over thirty. You must be hungry and tired, so come in and I will make you some breakfast and then you must go and have some sleep or you will fall asleep standing up, like horses do!"

"Bless you Darling that is just what I need, food, you and sleep."

They went into the kitchen and Mark sat at the table while Sasha cooked his breakfast.

"I started to question the German bomber crew, who had bailed out, and it looks as though the pilot, who speaks some English, will soften up some more and tell us all about how the beams are used, and confirm the Prof's theories. But I am sure that the Prof is right, because the Home Guard commander for the North Wales area has just phoned and told me that the Liverpool docks deception worked perfectly last night. The River Dee estuary mud flats were heavily bombed instead of the Liverpool docks, exactly as planned.

The German bomber pilot told me that it was his third raid on Liverpool, and apparently he had been completely taken in by the deception of the 'Bent Beams' and the false lights and buildings.

Richard and the Prof. will be delighted when I tell them.

I have not seen Jill much lately, how is she coping with running their household as well as working in the munitions factory?"

"She is getting very tired and says that some of the workers are talking about demanding higher wages and less pressure being put on them to meet production targets all the time. But Jill is a tough and determined girl and will keep going, unless she gets ill. Gillie is very good and does a lot round the house to help her. I was wondering if they would consider getting a woman from the village to do the housework to take some of the load off Jill?"

"That is an excellent idea and I will mention it to Gillie."

Sasha's comments about there being possible troublemakers in Jill's workplace rang a bell in Mark's half asleep state of mind and he wondered if there was any significance in them. He would discuss it with Gillie and find if it was worth investigating further.

Mark surfaced again at lunchtime and after a light meal went up to the village hall.

Rosemary met him at the door and told him that Gillie was still sleeping in the Red Cross rest room and said.

"Since the start of the war the patronage for the riding school has dropped off considerably, my best instructor was called up for the army and the other instructor is now working with the Home Guard a lot of the time, so I am seriously thinking of closing down as soon as possible and would like to do something more to help the war effort.

I am already working for the Red Cross here when they are busy but can you think of anything that I could use the riding school for?"

"That is a very patriotic sentiment but I can't think of anything just off the top of my head but why don't you drop in for dinner tonight and we can give some collective thought to your idea."

"Yes that would be very good. I can come around seven o'clock, and thank you"

Mark knew that if he did not phone Sasha right away he would forget, so he called her immediately and told her about Rosemary coming to dinner and about her decision to close the riding school.

By five o'clock the Military Police still had not collected the German prisoners, so Gillie called again and was told that due to trouble with munitions from the ships coming from America being stolen from the wharf in Liverpool they could not come till at least tomorrow afternoon, so the prisoners should be put in the nearest police cells for the time being.

Gillie called the local police, but they were not very pleased with the idea and reluctantly agreed to come and pick them up in about an hour.

William phoned to say that he had some embarkation leave and was coming home and would arrive at Chester around midnight and could someone please pick him up from the station because there were no trains on the branch line to Brockington at that time of night.

Michelle volunteered to go and meet William, if she could use Sasha's car.

"Yes of course you can, but don't forget that the head lights have those terrible 'black out' covers on them and you can't see any distance."

Sasha and Annie cooked a huge beef roast as there would be at least nine hungry people for dinner and Mark got some wine out of the cellar.

When Mark noticed that Sally skilfully arranged for Angus to sit next to her at the dinner table he looked at Sasha and gave a little nod in their direction and Sasha smiled.

When dinner was finished and they were all relaxing in the sitting room, Rosemary asked for ideas on the possible uses for the riding school that would help the war effort.

Several suggestions were put forward, including.

Training snipers similar to the last war, but it was then realised that snipers were not very important any more.

Some sort of factory for making munitions, but it was too remote and the buildings were not suitable.

Something secret that needed to be in a remote location, like training spies! Yes that was a possible but could the stables be converted into living quarters with all the manpower and building material shortages?

Mark said.

"That is definitely worth investigating so I will have a word with my contact in London.

I am sure that we could find some older local tradesmen and maybe some second hand building materials.

How do you feel about that idea Rosemary?"

"I have no problem with that idea but I don't know what I could contribute, other than cooking or administration."

Sasha said.

"Don't under estimate yourself, I am sure that you have some hidden talents that can be used, like languages or testing the agents for a complete change of persona right down to the brand of their buttons and cigarettes before they are sent into enemy territory."

The group decided that the spy school was the best option and Mark agreed to follow up with his contacts.

Angus had been impressed with the large acreage of wheat growing on the property as he was driven by Sally down the track from the village and now that they were seriously discussing the establishment of a highly secret military training unit, he was amazed at how much this one family was contributing to the war effort and said to Sally.

"Your family really impress me in the way that they take every opportunity to win the war. Your father is a natural military leader and your mother is very beautiful and so resourceful."

"Actually, Mark and Sasha are not my real parents. My sister Sarah and I were adopted by Mark and Sasha when our own parents were murdered by the Boers in South Africa and we are part of their family now.

We are very lucky because we are all very happy together. I will explain the details sometime."

"So where does the French girl, Michelle, fit in?"

"That is a long story. She came to work with us in a field hospital in France and her husband was recently killed when a boiler exploded at our dairy factory, not far from where your plane landed. Michelle was then put under the threat of a terrorist vendetta because of work her father in law had been doing, so we brought her here where it is safe.

How long will you be allowed to stay here? While your arm is in plaster, or longer?"

"I would be happy to stay here for as long as possible, but I must report to my unit first thing tomorrow morning and find out if I am allowed to recover here, if that is convenient?

I expect that I will have to go and have a checkup with the RAF. Doctor immediately I get back."

"Where is your base?"

"We are not supposed to tell anyone, but as you are 'very special' and you promise not to tell anyone, I will break the rules and tell you that I am based at Speke RAF. Base, which is not far from Chester, on the Welsh side, probably fifteen to twenty miles from here."

"Well, if they want you to go for a quick medical checkup, I can drive you there and wait while you are with the Doctor.

Because of the work that Mark does, he gets an almost unlimited petrol ration, so that is no problem."

"That is very kind of you, so let's hope that after a checkup I am allowed to recover here, because I want to get to know you better, you are a very wonderful girl."

"Thank you, as I am getting to know you, I am starting to think that you are a special sort of person and want to get to know you better, as well."

Michelle drove Sasha's car very carefully in the 'black out' with just the little slits of light from the head lights and arrived at the station well before midnight and waited in the station yard till it was nearly time for the train and then went onto the platform and stood under a shaded light.

The train was late and she was getting worried that there had been a problem with the air raids, but could not find anyone to ask when the train would arrive.

By one o'clock Michelle was becoming really worried and paced up and down to keep warm.

A clatter of wheels crossing points and a shriek of brakes finally told her that a train was coming!

Michelle peered along the dimly lit platform looking for William and saw him jump down and start walking towards her in his uniform and carrying a large kit bag.

William had not expected to be met by just Michelle, but was excited at the thought that she was sufficiently interested in him to venture out on her own, despite her reserved attitude towards him since Andrew's death, which on reflection, was probably just out of respect for her memory of Andrew.

Michelle hurried along the platform and threw her arms round his neck and kissed him and William felt her taut young body pressed firmly against him as he kissed and hugged her. She was a very beautiful, uninhibited, young girl who knew what she wanted and he felt honored to be favored with her affection.

They held hands as they walked back to the car and she asked William if he wanted to drive but he was very tired and not used to driving in the black out so he said.

"You drive please Darling, I am too tired after getting up at five and then having to stand while traveling most of the day."

"You called me 'Darling' that is wonderful 'mon Cheri!' Do you know where you are being sent after your leave?"

"We have not been told officially, but from the special training and issue of tropical clothing we assume it is somewhere in the East, probably Singapore or Burma. Steamy jungles with lots of snakes and tigers!"

"You make a joke, but that is not a healthy place to live. You must write and tell me where you are and what it is like. I will expect a letter every week and I will send one to you"

Sasha had waited up for them to arrive and met them in the hall and kissed William and said.

"You look very smart and mature in your uniform. Come into the sitting room and I will bring you some supper as I expect that you are hungry."

"Thank you Mum, you are right I am a bit peckish. I was very pleased to be met by Michelle as there are no taxis now and I would have had to 'hitch hike' and been lucky to have arrived home by morning."

"Your supper is ready now, so I will go to bed and leave you two to have your food. Good night."

When Michelle and William had finished the meal they held hands as they went upstairs and kissed before going to their respective rooms.

Angus telephoned his base early the next morning and spoke to his Wing Commander who said that he must return as soon as possible and then asked if he needed transport.

Angus explained that he was being looked after by the family who had organised his rescue from being trapped in his cockpit, provided professional medical treatment for his broken arm and that they could bring him back to Base and that they would be pleased to provide local accommodation while his arm was in plaster.

"You are a lucky son of a gun, you ditch your kite and fall on your feet all in one swift move, but you must come to Base this morning and see the MO. and if he agrees, you can go back to recuperate with your friends but you must give me their name, address and phone number so we can keep in touch with you. See you soon, and don't forget we need you back in the air as soon as possible."

Angus was so excited, that he put the phone down with a crash, quickly turned round and pulled Sally into an embrace and kissed her!

Sally was taken by surprise but responded to the kiss and hugged him.

When the phone line was free, Mark called Richard and gave him a coded version of the proposal for a spy school. Richard said that the 'new organisation' (Special Operations Executive – SOE.) was expanding and looking for remote sites to train operatives so he would discuss the idea with his colleges and let Mark know as soon as possible.

Sally drove Angus to his base at Speke and had to wait at the gate till the Wing Commander had issued a security pass for her to enter the base. He then told the duty sergeant to bring her to his office.

Angus was already on his way to see the doctor when Sally arrived at the wing commander's office.

The Wing Commander was surprised that Sally was a fully trained nurse and was able to set Angus's broken arm so quickly. He also found that she was au fait with many local defense matters.

Sally said that her 'father' was the local Home Guard Commander.

"With our chaps being operational over your area so much of the time, I would like to meet your father and have a chat to find out how he operates. Do you think that he would be available?"

"Yes I am sure that he will be pleased to meet you and I suggest that you telephone him and make a time to meet, as he is always very busy."

"We have to inspect where the planes crash and arrange the pick-up of the wreckage, so perhaps I can arrange to meet him at the same time."

Angus knocked and came into the office and from the look on his face Sally knew that the doctor had agreed for him to recover at home.

"What did the 'saw bones' say?"

"He gave me the once over and agreed for me to go and recover at the home of my new found friends and recommends six weeks sick leave, Sir."

"OK. Mackenzie, write down all the details of where you will be staying with phone numbers, and make sure that you look after this beautiful girl!

Off you go, and be careful."

"Thank you Sir."

As they walked back to the car Angus could not believe his luck, six weeks sick leave with the most beautiful girl he had ever seen, with all comforts provided.

Sally took him into Chester and parked in the Grosvenor Hotel car park, as usual, and showed him the famous 'Rows' and Roman Walls in the city.

The Rows were the most sensible idea that he had ever seen.

They comprised a normal pavement and street level shop fronts, but there was another walkway on top of the ground level shops and then another row of shop fronts set back behind the upper level walkway with the upper level walkway under cover. There were steps at intervals.

This meant that there were twice as many shops in a given length of street and if it was raining you could walk along on the higher level. Sally explained that the Rows had been developed by using parts of the old Roman walls, which were everywhere, and also completely encircled the city.

Sally did some shopping and took the stuff back to the car and then suggested some lunch.

They went to an old style restaurant built into the sandstone walls of the city and Sally suggested that Angus tried their home made herring roes with spaghetti. It was absolutely delicious.

On the way home they called in to see Anne at Oakhill Hall.

She was missing George very much now that he was working down on the South coast most of the time and said that she wanted to do more for the war effort and felt lonely, particularly now that Hugh had been called up and Margret had moved into the Morgrove house in Chester when Margret's father had died.

Hugh was in the army and had been posted to Singapore, but there had not been any letters from him for a long time, so Margret did not know how he was getting on.

Margret was running the family timber business and it was easier for her to be within a five minute bike ride to the sawmill and timber yard rather than having to travel by train now that there was no petrol available.

Mark, Gillie and Jill met that evening and talked about there being a possible threat from an enemy agent in the munitions factory where Jill worked.

Jill said that there was a man who she suspected and that the man did a lot of subversive talking and was always complaining about having to meet the production schedules. He was small and had reddish hair and often made rude passes at the girls, and sometimes patted their bottoms when he passed them in a passageway.

Gillie said.

"Do you know any more about him, like which pub he goes to or where he lives?"

"I don't know where he lives, but he has some cronies who go off with him when they leave from work most nights, but I don't know where they go."

"We don't want to put you at risk lass, so perhaps you can just point him out to us some time and we can take it from there."

Gillie went to pick up Jill from work a few times and on the fourth time they were just getting into the wagonette when Jill alerted Gillie and pointed out the man who had two friends walking alongside him on the pavement.

They waited a while and then moved off in the same direction and stopped.

The three men turned a corner and Gillie moved again just in time to see them going into a back street pub.

"That is enough for tonight, I now know what he looks like and where he goes with his friends."

Angus was keen to be involved and volunteered to help and after several 'no shows' of the men leaving the factory together, the suspects did appear and he was able to get out of Gillie's wagonette, follow them to the pub and sit at a small table near where the three men were standing at the bar.

The small man periodically looked at his watch, while they laughed and talked, indicating that they had some commitment in a short time.

The time checks became more frequent as it approached seven o'clock so Angus finished his drink and was ready to leave, preferably just before the small man and his friends.

Before Angus had time to go to the front door the three men walked purposefully to a side door and disappeared down a narrow lane.

Angus went out of the front door and quickly turned into the lane and hurried to keep the men just visible in the dim lighting of the black out.

Two streets away there was a Roman Catholic Church with a large Church hall alongside it and a lot of people were going into the hall.

A surprising number of the people had arrived in up market, well-kept cars, in spite of the very strict petrol rationing.

Angus waited in the shadows and about five past seven a large man in a black over coat came out of the door, looked round and then went in and Andrew heard the door bolts being locked.

There was a path beside the church leading to the vestry door and a small side door into the hall.

Angus was able to stand in the shadows by the side door of the hall and could just hear what one of the speakers was saying.

"We can't let this madness go on. We must stop using our valuable materials to be made into bombs and bullets while we can't even buy a table knife and fork or a safety pin.

The war factories can be slowed down and the wastage can be reduced with your help."

Another speaker started, but he must have been on the other side of the hall because Angus could not hear what was being said.

So he decided that with his 'chicken wing' he would come off second best in any confrontation, and that he had seen and heard enough, so he had better scarper before 'Mr. Over Coat' came out to do his rounds, if that was what he did while a meeting was in progress.

Angus was half way down the path when he heard the bolts of the side door being opened and he just had time to drop down behind some low bushes before 'Mr. Over Coat' came out with his torch shining along the path.

As Angus went back past the pub a familiar figure emerged from the shadows and Gillie said.

"I was getting concerned for ye' laddie when I found that all o' ye' had gone away from the pub.

We must get away 'afore they ken that we are following.

Did ye' see where they went?"

"Oh yes, it was a church hall and I will give you the details when we get back."

Gillie turned the wagon round and went through some side streets before heading home.

Angus and Gillie went through the tunnel from the stable and through the door leading into the house.

Mark met them and they went through to the sitting room.

Sally said.

"Would you like some tea or coffee Angus?"

"Yes, coffee please.

I am no expert, but what I have just seen and heard indicates that there is a real problem."

When Sally and Jill returned with tea and coffee, Mark Said.

"Please tell us every detail of exactly what happened."

Angus described his exploits in detail and then said.

"We have had security lectures at the Base about possible sabotage and subversion among the ground crew, or even among the air crews, and everyone is constantly on the alert but it is surprising to find it among wealthy civilians who stand be the biggest losers if Hitler wins the war."

Mark said.

"What you have witnessed tonight, exactly fits the pattern of what we were told to look out for.

It is imperative that us locals do not lose our status of apparent ignorance of their operation, so we must do no more and report to London so that they can send in an expert from the secret service."

A few days later Jill noticed that there was a new 'toolmaker / setter' who came from somewhere down South and was much more intelligent and helpful than the usual man in the capstan lathe shop where she worked at the munitions factory.

She soon became sure that he was the man sent to investigate. This suspicion was confirmed when he palled up with the little red head and started to go to the pub with him and his two mates.

When Jill and Gillie told Mark about the new man he said.

"The system seems to be working, so we must just wait and discretely observe.

It will be very interesting to see who gets caught in the net!"

William and Michelle spent as much time as possible together during his two days leave and when it was time to go and catch the train back to base camp, it was obvious that they were very much in love. The short leave before being separated had made them bolder in their approach to each other and they had already made a commitment to each other to get married.

Michelle took William to the station and they parted with much suppressed sadness, a hug and a lingering kiss with promises to write at least once a week.

There was an embarkation briefing as soon as William got to his Base camp and as the group of officers were seated in the lecture hall, the CO came in and told them that he could now reveal where each of them was being posted, but that this was still confidential.

He uncovered a drop sheet with a map of North Africa and went on to explain what was happening in the Middle East.

"This is the area where you are going Oakhill.

The Suez Canal is still very much a part of our 'Highway to the Far East' and Hitler has ideas of claiming North Africa, Egypt, Palestine, Iraq and Iran and gaining control of the whole of the Mediterranean to give him sea access to Southern Europe.

In particular, he desperately needs access to the Iranian oilfields via the Gulf.

Just to complicate matters, Mussolini has grand ideas of reclaiming all of the land that was once part of the Roman Empire, and as you know that includes most of North Africa and Egypt.

The Italians broke out of Benghazi on the 13th of September and 80,000 Italian troops, together with their tanks got nearly as far as Alexandria in Egypt.

The British Mediterranean Fleet is based in Alex, and also operates out of Valletta in Malta."

He pointed out all the places mentioned as he spoke and then pointed to the canal.

"We have since pushed the Italians back to just west of Tubruq.

Your first job Oakhill, is to help set up an improved defense system for the Suez Canal as this is the last barrier to stop the Italians and Germans crossing the canal and reaching the oilfields.

Oakhill, it is essential that your unit establishes every possible means of stopping any break through and that you know every road, mine field, salt pan, quick sand hole and desert short cut better than the back of your hand."

He then used the other drop sheets to detail the duties allocated to the other officers in the group.

"Each of you will be given a local briefing when you reach your respective areas, and good luck."

Richard arrived a few weeks later at Glendarvel and reported on the current situation.

"We can confirm that the MI 5 man got a job at the munitions factory where Gillie's wife works, was able to infiltrate the suspects, attended several of the clandestine meetings and note the level of subversion and incitement to commit treason and that then he had called for a full scale raid.

Several men had been hidden in the amenities area of the church hall long before the meeting was due to start on the night of the raid.

A number of small vans of armed men had been waiting for the meeting to start and then surrounded the building and broke in through the two doors and arrested all those inside.

The list of occupants included;

A local councilor.

Two journalists.

A titled gentleman and his de facto wife.

A senior official from the local branch of the Ministry of Defense.

A clerk from the ministry of food.

Several local business men and their wives.

Numerous troublemakers from munitions factories, including the red head and his mates.

A group of female agitators who were 'agin everything representing authority or the establishment.

A well dressed and well-spoken man who appeared to be the ring leader or a planted German agent.

They now have the opportunity to reflect on the folly of their ways in Brixton prison and some could soon have an appointment with a length of rope or a firing squad, depending on what the court discovers at their trials.

Our M I 5 man has also been able to link some sabotage on the railways and thefts from the munitions factories with the ring leader. When his home was searched they found a radio transmitter, an automatic pistol, bomb making supplies and a code book, so he is definitely a trained enemy agent and was a skillful and dangerous operator.

Oh yes, there was also a bonus find!

A large quantity of petrol ration cards, food ration cards and a large quantity of black market rationed items of food, all of which had been carried into the hall for sale during the meeting and we have been able to trace the source of much of the contraband and round up the suppliers as well.

The group called themselves, 'The Guardians of the Future,' and rented the hall from the church.

We suspect that the church must have had a pretty good idea of what they were doing in the hall, but can't prove anything yet.

Anyway, thank you and your team for a job well done and let us hope that this has plugged up another hole in our national security.

Now about your offer for a training site for some of our special friends. We would like to take you up immediately on the suggestion and will send up a group of our instructors right away to set up a tented camp to get training started even before you can convert the buildings."

Mark said.

"Since we last spoke another opportunity has come to light in the form of Oakhill Hall which is not fully occupied and is available for requisition as part of the school, if it is required. My sister is the only full time resident and may consider working in the establishment."

"We are so short of suitable premises that it is very likely that we will take up that offer as well.

I will contact you as soon as I have talked to my colleges."

Richard phoned the next day to say that he had been 'pipped at the post' by the Military Hospital Board who were already in the process of sending one of their associate directors to inspect the property and if found suitable, to negotiate a lease and requisition order.

"This will probably mean that we will have to have some of the school operation under canvas, but that could help us with security due to the remote location and not having to transport students between the two places all the time.

Anyway, thank you for the offer, and I expect that you will find that a Convalescent Hospital will make a very good tenant."

Chapter 21

DIVERSE WAR

Richard phoned and said.

"Now, there is another project that needs our attention and I will call in tomorrow and explain."

Richard was met off the train by Mark and he immediately explained what the problem was.

"Churchill and M I 5 have had a preliminary survey done to check out a theory on the reason why the German U boats that are playing buggery with our trans-Atlantic convoys, can stay at sea so long without going to their home port.

The theory is that they are being refueled and supplied somewhere on the Irish coast or in the Scottish Hebrides.

So far nothing has been found in the Hebrides but there could be some suspicious activity on the West coast of Ireland.

The U boats are playing merry hell with the Atlantic convoys and the loss of shipping has reached crisis point and finding a solution is top priority.

We are looking for ideas on how we can check for enemy activity and thought of your 'agricultural guardians', Mike and Susan Cutland, who are trained as our agents and also have scientific training.

Now that you have the Home Guard you are more self-sufficient, so we plan to send our two agents on a new mission.

They should be able to find out the quantities of diesel fuel allocated to the fishing fleets, farmers and local haulage contractors and then be able to pin point any discrepancy that could be used to supply German submarines."

"Yes you are right, the guards are not essential now and could be exactly the type of people you need. Would you like me to send for them?"

"Yes please."

When Mike and Susan were seated, Richard gave them the details of their new mission.

Mike said.

"Yes, we can use the fuel deliveries to lead us to the area but I have just had another Idea.

What if when we locate the refueling point that we substitute their fuel tanker trucks with trucks loaded with contaminated fuel that will allow the refueled U boats to return to sea and then after a few hours of use have total engine failure and leave them stranded in the Atlantic with no means of returning to base, once their batteries have gone flat! That way we can put a number of U boats out of action before the Germans work out what is happening. With any luck, the Germans will then vent their anger on the local suppliers!"

"Well done, excellent thinking that is what we will do. We could then use aircraft to find the drifting U boats and get the Navy to intercept them. We could then round up the collaborators on shore and destroy their facilities.

I must get Doc. Clayton working on how to contaminate the diesel fuel."

The Cutlands packed up all their equipment and left in the truck, provided by Richard, the next day, thus leaving an unoccupied, fully furnished house in the village.

Mark, Gillie and Tad met at the riding school to discuss the conversion of the stables.

Word had been passed round that they needed some retired or semi- retired tradesman and some men started to arrive to offer their services to set up an 'army barracks' as had been mentioned.

The idea was that the conversion was to be done using wood as far as possible to save time. As all the work was inside the buildings and this would not spoil the overall character of the sand stone village.

While the men were discussing the best way of doing the conversion, Mark went to the Factory to phone Margaret at Moregroves office and told her that they needed a lot of timber but that it could be second quality or second hand.

Margaret had a lot of timber that had been slightly damaged in an air raid and that more than half of it could still be used. Mark ordered a trial load to be sent right away.

Two hours later a large load of timber arrived and the men soon had it off loaded and checked.

The quality was adequate so more was ordered immediately.

It was decided to demolish the existing wooden stalls and loose boxes in the stables, put in a complete new timber floor to cover the original sloping, self-draining stable floor and then build partition walls as required for as many small bedrooms and bath rooms as possible in one stable block.

There was also to be a kitchen and mess hall in part of the other stable block.

Tents would still be required as training rooms.

Gillie suggested that they applied the old army trick used in India of pitching one large tent with the tent poles extended about one foot, on top of another tent of the same size with standard length tent poles thus giving a double wall tent which was cooler in summer and warmer in winter.

The electricity supply at the riding school was only adequate for lighting so Margaret used her contacts in the building trade to supply a commercial sized, wood fired kitchen stove, wood fired hot water services and room heaters.

Once the word spread round the area that there was temporary work available, more tradesmen wanted to join the workforce at the very high wages being offered and there were soon nearly twenty men working to meet the completion date.

Within three months there was accommodation, of a surprisingly good quality, for forty men, and or women ready to be furnished.

Rosemary was appointed as the domestic administrator and worked alongside the senior training officer.

The school was already operating under canvas at the far end of the riding school land with ten male and four female students who were eagerly watching the progress on the new accommodation.

Two truckloads of second hand furniture arrived and was put in place.

Some of the locals had ideas that there would be some civilian jobs available in 'another army camp' and were disappointed when they found that all the camp staff were to be military personnel.

The large pile of rejected timber would keep the camp supplied with fire wood for a long time.

Large tents were doubled up, as suggested by Gillie, and erected close to the new accommodation as training rooms, The staff and current batch of students then moved into their new quarters.

A new intake of another thirty students soon arrived and the school went into overdrive.

Mark, Gillie and Tad were asked to be available to give lectures on their specialised subjects.

The first time Mark was called and faced an audience of nearly fifty he was surprised at how young and dedicated the students were. He used his own experiences with terrorists in South Africa and in the immediate area to illustrate how terrorists infiltrate a community and become a significant force.

Gillie gave individual tuition in the use of small arms.

Tad gave practical training to small groups in the use of explosives.

Michelle had started to give individual tuition on French dialects.

Anne had had a visit by a Military Hospital Assistant Director who explained that they desperately needed large houses for use as convalescent hospitals and asked if he could look through the house immediately.

After an hour of checking and making notes the Assistant Director said that the house was acceptable and wanted her to sign a contract so Anne referred him to Mark as he was the owner.

Mark and Sasha came to meet the assistant director who said.

"As usual, I find that as the house was not built as a hospital it will be necessary to make some minor alterations, like wheel chair ramps and special shower rooms. The requirements of a Convalescent Hospital are fairly flexible and the house is acceptable and we are prepared to sign a contract right now. There is a flood of war wounded that are in urgent need of rehabilitation."

Anne said that she would like to move out and go to live in the now vacant house that had been built for the Bakers, which surprised Mark, but it did sound logical and it would be good to have her close to home. Any way, it would be very depressing to be surrounded by severely wounded men all the time.

Some of Anne's favorite pieces of furniture were transferred to the the Baker house and the surplus furniture was then transferred to the Hall during the next few days.

A week later the Hospital staff moved into Oakhill Hall and patients started to arrive, many of whom were very severely injured. Some of the stables and farm buildings were to be fitted out as exercise gyms and storage areas.

The wheel chair ramps were built and special shower rooms were added and the hospital became fully operational.

Within a few months Rosemary and the chief instructor at the 'Riding School', as it was still called, became engaged and were married soon afterwords.

After the rationing and restrictions in Britain, William found the atmosphere in Cairo, where he had been posted, like a nonstop party with plenty of everything, no rationing and the shop and restaurant prices were less than one quarter of those in Britain.

There was filth everywhere in the streets and beggars were on every corner but everyone was so busy enjoying themselves they did not seem to notice the stench and flies swarming over the rubbish.

The troops of the Eighth Army in combat in the Western desert were in a very different world, fighting their way back and forth across the desert with Churchill pushing for an immediate defeat of the Italians and General Wavell unwilling to confirm that he was ready for another assault, which infuriated Churchill.

William went to the BTE. (British Troops in Egypt.) HQ in Cairo which was responsible for guarding the canal and was posted to Ismailiya in a small unit which shared accommodation with the Royal Navy shore establishment at 'Avery Camp'.

Avery Camp was a collection of old stone buildings, Nissen huts and tents just south of the city of Ismailiya and across the Sweet Water Canal from the city.

Because the Navy had some WRENS working in their office, some joker had christened the place Avery Camp, and the name had stuck!

As William's unit was based in the middle of the 100 mile long canal he had to be highly mobile and in constant radio contact with all the defense positions, spread out 50 miles each way, North and South of Ismailiya.

EGYPT - NILE DELTA - SUEZ CANAL

There were token defenses at each of the control stations, which were placed at regular intervals along the canal to control the shipping. The control stations had been built by the canal company and looked like a small coast guard station sitting on the canal bank in front of a very comfortable colonial house and were operated by canal company staff.

Each of these stations was surrounded by a high wall with locked steel studded timber gates to stop thieving by the local 'clefty wallahs' (Thief men.) but there was no means of preventing an attack other than taking a long rifle shot at an enemy more than 200 yards away, from the sun deck on the roof of the house over the top of the wall. An army of men could stand close to the walls and remain out of sight from the sun deck on the roof of the house inside the walls.

William made a complete inspection of the area and found that four British Army guards were allocated to each control station for a week and then rotated to another station. The whole system was very lax and the men were only equipped with rifles.

The Germans had superior tanks with a better main armament which with one shot could blow down a section of the crumbling brick walls and a station could be assaulted and overrun in a few minutes.

The prime objective must be to prevent the tanks from getting within range of the control stations.

There were numerous small anti-tank mine fields round Alexandria and Cairo and there were areas of salt pan depressions out in the desert that were impassible for tanks, but once the tanks got onto the road running along beside the canal they could travel safely at speeds up twenty miles per hour and knock out control stations as they went. It would be like shooting toy ducks in a shooting gallery at a fair ground!

William realised that he could either accept the hopelessly inadequate system as it was or start jumping up and down till a completely new system was implemented. He decided to go back to the Colonel in Cairo and present the facts, even though this might be very unpopular.

He had noted that there was a large REME workshop at Tel el Kebir on the drive from Cairo to Ismailiya the week before, so he decided to call in on the way back to Cairo and check what sort of facilities they had in the workshops.

Service Bay REME Workshops Tel el Kebir.

Sweet Water Canal Ferry.

The Colonel was irritable and impatient and did not like his system being criticized and William was getting nowhere fast till a Brigadier came into the office, and much to William's surprise, joined in the discussion and asked a lot of questions about the existing system.

"Well, Oakhill, have you got any ideas on how we can improve the defenses with the very limited time and resources available?"

"Sir, it appears that the greatest threat would be from enemy tanks so it is important that we prevent a rapid German tank advance knocking out the control stations and gaining control of the shipping in the canal and use of the swing bridge just North of Ismailiya.

There are a large number of wrecked tank hulls at a dump in Tel el Kebir that we could use to blockade the roads, leaving just small openings that can be closed in the event of an enemy breakthrough. We could also mock up the old tank hulls to make them look operational and give them a coat of paint to cover the rust.

It would also be necessary to plant some anti- tank mine fields and if necessary to use some dummy mines to make up the numbers.

The control station walls need to have heavy steel plates, with small arms slits cut into them, recessed into the walls so that the men on duty can see what is happening at ground level close to the station and retaliate with at least BREN guns. Sir."

"Where did you learn to analyse a situation and work out a simple solution?"

William was taken by surprise, hesitated and then said.

"Sir, I was taught by my father and members of the family and friends."

"Your suggestions are all sound and I give you my authority to go ahead as quickly as possible.

My ADC. will give you the necessary works orders before you leave."

The Colonel was further angered by being overruled by a superior officer in front of William, but could not do or say anything. He just sat and fumed and William would not have been surprised to see smoke coming out of his ears!

William was afraid that his Army career was likely to start going rapidly backwards in future, but bugger it, he was not going to be frightened off from doing the right thing by a crusty old Colonel who had been asleep at his desk for the last twenty years while he had done nothing to stop Jerry from knocking out the control stations with the greatest of ease.

William waited till the paperwork was ready and then went back to Tel el Kebir 3 Base Workshops and asked to see the officer in charge.

"So, the top brass has finally listened to someone with common sense and is prepared to take action! Well done, it is good to see the old duffers being woken up.

We will be glad to get rid of the old tank hulls and can have them sent on tank carriers as soon as you are ready and put them in place for you.

You will need to draw up a plan for each location showing exactly where they are to be dropped.

From what you say, the steel plates need to be able to resist small arms fire and be about three feet wide by four feet high. We can also weld lintels across the top and bottom to make them easier to install. They can be ready in a few days and will be delivered to you in Ish."

William went to 3. BOD. (Base Ordinance Depot.) at Geneifa the next day and used a works order to arrange for a team of Sappers to build the steel plates into the walls surrounding the control stations as soon as they arrived.

He was also able to pick up twenty BREN guns to be used in the control stations.

During the next month William put his men through a training course on use of the BREN gun and how to erect the temporary barriers between the lines of tank hulls.

He had to get the help of an officer from the Company of Sappers at Geneifa to draw up plans of the tank hull blockades and the proposed anti-tank mine fields.

As expected, there were not enough anti-tank mines available, so they used old car tyres filled with painted concrete as dummies to fill the random gaps in the mine fields.

They were able to take advantage of natural salt pans and lagoons to block tanks in many places, which saved the need for minefields.

The new defense system was completed and had been in service for about a month when William got an urgent message that he was being transferred to GHQ. ME. in Cairo and to report to a Colonel Miles who was in charge of the defense of Alexandria and Cairo.

"Welcome to Cairo, you have been put on my staff as a result of your excellent performance on the canal defenses.

The situation here is suddenly becoming very different, because we did have the Italian army fighting raging battles to and fro in the Western Desert in Tunisia, with huge numbers of Italian prisoners being taken.

But now that the Germans are here in force under the command of Rommel the situation is totally different. He has better tanks and more of them and is called the 'Desert Fox' with good reason due to his cunning and aggressive tactics.

There can be another breakthrough at any time close to Alex. or Cairo.

Our job is to establish extended defense systems out into the desert to keep the enemy out of shelling range of the cities.

We have intercepted some of the German high command orders sent by wireless, so that sometimes gives us advance warning of where he is coming next, but the information is not complete or it takes too long to break their coded messages to be of any use.

We have found that there is an informer or German agent operating in Cairo who is informing the enemy of our battle plans and the location of our defenses.

Our counter espionage people are still trying to locate the agent, they even were able to listen to his wireless message on one occasion when he was giving the location of our gun emplacements.

Needless to say, the real guns were soon relocated and replaced with plywood dummies and a length of drain pipe sticking into the air, for the benefit of their aerial photography planes.

So, you see that we are in the business of real defenses and deception as well.

There are top secret maps of where our anti-tank minefields are and the location of the gun emplacements which we can study when you have settled in.

We are sure that the Germans use aerial photography to monitor all of our defenses, so we must make sure that they get some pretty pictures to keep them confused."

William immediately took a liking to Colonel Miles and could see that they would work well together.

Anne had just settled into the Baker house at Glendarvel when she had a phone call from George to say that he was coming home for a few days and would give her the details of his new assignment when he arrived.

George looked thinner and tired and needed a rest so Anne tried to get him to relax, enjoy some home cooking and spend time with their two children.

On the second day that George was home he went up to the house with Anne to find Mark and Sasha and they sat in the garden.

George said.

"I have been taken off the work down South and have been given a completely new project that is very 'hush hush' so you must not even think about telling anyone else.

It appears that our military strategists are already planning for the invasion of Europe and have realised after the lessons learned at the trial invasion at Dieppe that they can't rely on having deep sea ports available for the men and materials to be put ashore so have come up with a very clever alternative.

The idea is that we are to build some portable floating harbours made out of reinforced concrete that can be towed across the channel and positioned almost anywhere, even close to a gently sloping beach and then connected to shore by a floating roadway made in sections and mounted on pontoons.

The harbours are to be made in a number of standard modules, of various types, that can be assembled in the configuration necessary to provide a safe deep water dock for unloading men, vehicles including tanks and vast quantities of supplies from cargo ships.

A secret location has been selected on the mouth of the River Conway at Deganwy in North Wales for many of the modules to be built because of the local supplies of cement, crushed rock and skilled labour. Plus there is a firm sand beach with a suitable slope that can be used to build and side launch the modules.

I have been allocated accommodation in a requisitioned hotel in the town of Conway and should be able to come home from time to time for a few days.

Enough of that for now, so let's have your news."

Mark and Sasha gave him all the details of the recent events involving the beams, the murders of the other members of the Baker family and then told him why the 'agricultural guards' had been sent to Ireland.

"I hope they can find the traitors lair and 'fix' their diesel fuel.

I would love to see a whole lot of Jerry subs. drifting round in the Atlantic with engine failure waiting to be used for target practice by the Royal Navy!

I forgot to mention that there is another project that I am to be involved with, which again is very hush hush, so mum's the word.

The Jerries, and ourselves, seem to be getting tired of just shooting at each other and there is a new strategy coming into play. We are now attacking each other's water works and there is a boffin at the Teddington test laboratories who is coming up with some weird ideas, but they seem to work.

As I am sure you are aware, much of the water used in the Midland munitions factories, not to mention in the tens of thousands of homes in the area, is harvested and then stored in reservoirs in North and Central Wales making these reservoirs vulnerable strategic targets which are very difficult to defend.

All of the dams have a battery of AA. guns nearby and foot patrols on the dam walls but due to the reservoirs being located in steep mountain valleys, there is not much else that can be done against a bomb attack.

One theory is that bombs dropped into a reservoir anywhere near the dam wall will create shock waves that are capable of shattering the dam wall with catastrophic results.

Teddington has come up with the theory that if a curtain of air bubbles is released from the base of the dam that these will absorb the shock waves and prevent the wall being damaged.

As some of the dam walls are two hundred or more feet high, the water pressure at the base of the dam is already eighty to one hundred and twenty PSI, so the air pressure needs to be around one hundred and fifty PSI to create a curtain of bubbles. This would require huge high pressure air compressors with attendant fuel requirements and maintenance.

So much for the theories, it is now back to the drawing board of 'suck it and see'.

No one is prepared to do full scale tests on a dam wall, (I can't think why not!) so our job is to build some scale model dams that the boffins can use to test their theories on."

William was allocated a billet in an apartment block in Kasr el Nil Street which was about two minutes' walk from BHQ. ME and his tiny office was at the end of the passage on the same floor as Colonel Miles.

On the next morning William was called into the conference room by the colonel so that they could spread out the maps showing all the mine fields and defenses, on the big table. One senior Staff officer was also present for some of the time.

The Qattara Depression was about 150 miles West of Cairo and extended some some 150 miles North to South and 50 miles West to East with a gap between its Northern tip and the sea of some 20 miles. Thus, Rommel had the option of a 350 mile excursion round the South of the depression through uncharted desert, risk crossing the Qattara depression with a good chance of getting stuck in the salt pans and lagoons, or keeping to the 20 mile wide strip between the Northern end of the depression and the sea at El Alamein.

Thus the 20 mile wide strip and the city of El Alamein were crucial in the defense of Alex and Cairo.

There were already some mine fields round El Alamein and there were heavy gun emplacements out in the desert just north of the depression, but it was not possible to completely blockade the 20 mile wide strip. There were squadrons of British tanks in the area that could be brought in to challenge any assault on the gap but the British tanks were out gunned by the new German panzer tanks, so the gap was not 'watertight.'

Up to now, the risk of Alex and Cairo being attacked was considered as being remote so the defenses were low key, but now with Rommel's aggressive tactics to link up with Palestine and head for the Gulf oil fields, it was suddenly very different.

Colonel Miles had been advised of the German's intercepted orders to keep going East and capture the Gulf oil fields.

This meant that there must be more defenses some fifteen to twenty miles West of Cairo and Alex.

There were not the resources available to lay anti-tank mine fields or build gun emplacements to give complete protection so the only option was to have some real and some dummy defenses and find a way of feeding false information into the enemy to try to trap him into going into a real minefield or an impassible salt pan depression.

The River Nile delta started some fifteen miles downstream from Cairo where it divided into the Western stream or Rosetta and the Eastern stream or Damietta Rivers which were then criss crossed with a complex of minor rivers and numerous irrigation systems down to the sea. This comprised the very rich soil, boosted by silt from the annual floods and irrigated, where much of the world famous Egyptian cotton was grown.

So the Nile delta was a readymade blockade running North and South but it did not protect Cairo and Alex from the West.

There were some small minefields in geometric patterns close to the cities, which stood out like granny's tooth, and a few gun emplacements but nothing farther out into the desert.

William suggested doing a survey of the area and locating all the natural routs through the sand hills and rock formations which tank or vehicle drivers would tend to choose when going through the desert and plant just one real or dummy mine in each so that an area of 10 miles running North and South, by say ten miles from West to East could become one huge, low density, random minefield.

Just like setting snares in rabbit runs. No use putting them in regular patterns in the open, just put them in the runs that are likely to be used.

The idea being that there would be a high probability that some of the leading tanks would select the best natural routs through the parts of desert which provided some cover among patches of camel thorn, rocks and dunes and be disabled by mines, thus indicating a minefield. But when following tanks tried to estimate the extent of the minefield and took another route and struck mines a considerable distance away this should cause confusion among the tidy minded Germans expecting a regular minefield.

The staff officer present said the plan was totally inadequate and that the enemy tanks could be in Cairo in two or three days. He was right of course, but it was essential to make the best of what was available and add as much bluff and deception as possible to reduce the chances of the capture of Alex and Cairo and prevent Rommel charging farther East towards the oil fields.

Colonel Miles agreed that they did not have the resources to build an adequate defense system but could see the sense in Oakhill's suggestion and said.

"That idea of yours Oakhill, is worth considering and we may be able to use it in some areas, but I know that there are large flat areas without any rocks or dunes. Just flat expanses of sand.

We also have the RAF. Base at Fayid who can be called up to attack from the air, but it is not easy to bomb a tank traveling at up to twenty miles an hour. They can pepper the tanks with machine gun fire using tracer, but once Jerry has put his lid down, it is only going to scare the hell out of him and smash off his radio aerial.

I suppose that we could also peg out some conventional regular shaped mine fields in a few of the flat areas, and just use dummy mines, to keep up appearances for their aerial photography.

Your rabbit run mines probably could not be detected from the air so that may help in guiding Jerry to use the tracks in the cover of the broken ground.

Sir, I think that we should send Oakhill and a team of Sappers from Geniefa to do a survey as soon as possible. We will have to get the Sappers to lay the mines anyway."

There was agreement.

William and his team of enthusiastic Sappers made up a convoy of a Land Rover and small trucks and headed off into the desert with water, fuel, a radio and rations for two weeks.

They found that many of the tracks through the broken ground were used by the Bedu or nomadic desert Arab tribes following the sparse vegetation for their camels to eat, as had been their custom for thousands of years.

Mike and Susan Cutland had not been to Ireland before and wondered what sort of reception they would get. They each had adopted a new name and a change of appearance.

They decided that being on a camping holiday and interested in sea birds would give them freedom to move about in the more remote coastal areas where there was likely to be a submarine refueling and supply operation taking place.

While they were on the ferry from Liverpool to Belfast they studied the large scale hiker's maps of the West coast, while in their cabin.

On arrival in Belfast they were able to hire a car with a small quantity of petrol in the tank, but they had been given a liberal quantity of petrol coupons, to be used in small quantities at many different petrol stations.

The ministry of supply officials in England had provided sheets of figures representing quantities of bulk diesel fuel allocated to each area in Ireland and these should match with the quantities issued to the many users. It was a marathon task in numbers to find a discrepancy.

After many hours of diligent calculations they had found several places where the digits were correct but the decimal points had been moved making discrepancies of many thousands of gallons which should have given them a starting point, but the places where the discrepancies appeared were scattered over a large area and were over seventy miles apart.

There were many remote stretches of coastline and they reckoned that the sub base would definitely be within the Irish Republican area and probably high up on the West coast, closest to the subs hunting ground where they attacked the Atlantic convoys.

From the figures, it appeared that one or more fuel trucks were picking up fuel from a number of different bulk depots and taking it to a submarine base, or bases.

The position of each of the suspect fuel depots was then transferred onto a map and this narrowed down the delivery point to the West coast of County Mayo which was in the general area that they had expected it to be.

The next possible indicator could be the location of where the fishing boats were based and refueled.

Newport was the most active of the ports used by the fishing boats along that stretch of rugged coast and had a large fuel distributor with Bowsers on the wharf for refueling the fishing boats.

Mike and Susan decided to check into a small pub, which had accommodation, a few miles out of Newport and radiate out on daily 'bird watching' excursions with their bird books and binoculars.

Mike reckoned that if they could piece together the movements of the fuel trucks going in and out of the Newport fuel distributor that would be a start.

After a few days of careful checking, they had established that there were two trucks based at the distributor and one went to pick up fuel from the bulk supply depot, or depots, and kept the distributor's underground storage tanks topped up while the other did the detail daily deliveries to the larger customers.

But then there was a sudden change of routine for the larger truck which was used to pick up fuel from the bulk supply depots.

It went off very early one morning and did not return till late the next day. This was followed immediately by another pick up trip the next day to top up the underground tanks.

So it looked as though a whole load had been delivered direct from a bulk supply depot to a sub base.

Now that they had found which truck was being used, it was a matter of finding where it was making the deliveries.

Next time the large truck went off early, Susan was left close to the coast road going south and Mike went to a place on the coast road going north where he could observe all the traffic. Each of them had a bivouac and basic camping gear so that they could stay till late the next day.

When Mike picked up Susan late on the next day she definitely had not seen the fuel truck going South and Mike had seen the truck going North and returning some twenty two hours later, so it was confirmed that the drop point was to the North of Newport and that the fuel had been brought in on the road going inland, which fitted a likely pattern.

They decided to go along the North road the next day and see if there were any possible drop points in a hidden cove.

The road went to a small village about fifteen miles away with no possible drop points, then through a hilly section inland for another few miles, across a bridge over an arm of the sea onto an island and after the next village the road became a rough gravel track leading to the end of Saddle Headland, which was shown on their large scale map. The map only had a Celtic ruin marked on the headland.

One very significant thing that they noted was that the track was well used with no grass growing along the wheel ruts, despite its remoteness and that it appeared to lead nowhere! There was definitely no jetty and there were no buildings other than the Celtic ruins which were well away from the sea in the centre of the headland.

This place had definite possibilities so they did a few minutes bird watching and returned to Newport.

On recapping their day's work, they had confirmed that there was still an ancient Celtic ruin, as marked on the map, on a small hill that overlooked the last section of the track going down to Saddle Headland, which they decided could be used by a look out while a refueling operation was in progress or possibly for signaling with lights to vessels out to sea. There was no sign of any other buildings or a jetty, so if this was the correct place, it remained a mystery on just how the operation was undertaken.

In any case the location needed checking out again at night, and they would have to drive nearly to the last village and then hide the car and hike the last part in the dark.

Now that the high risk part of their operation had started they needed to advise Richard of their progress. The telephone was out of the question so they composed a fully coded letter, as would be expected to come from a young couple on a bird watching holiday, confirming that they had found how the fuel was delivered and a likely drop point. The letter, in Susan's schoolgirl handwriting, was posted from Castlebar, the next major town farther inland from Newport.

They had been obliged to discuss their bird watching activities with the owner of the pub where they were staying because he showed a lot of interest in the range of birds they had sighted and listed in their notes.

He then made some suggestions on where the nesting areas were likely to be, but made a point that there were no nesting areas on the island or remote headland because it was 'after being too exposed' which immediately alerted Mike and Susan that he was involved, or at least in the know about the refueling.

The owner then gave them advice about several nesting areas well away from the headland along the coast road going south, which confirmed their suspicions.

Mike decided that they would have to 'play the game' and be seen to be following the advice of the publican for a few days or their cover could be blown, which was a nuisance and might interfere with their plans to do the night hike trip next time the bulk truck went off early.

One option was to split up with Susan using the car for bird watching and Mike could buy or 'borrow' a bike for the night trip.

Sooner than expected, the bulk truck took off early the next morning so they both started off in the car and bought a much battered bike for a few pounds in another town and tied it on the back of the car and came back on another road and arrived back close to Newport and took the bike off the car.

Susan went off in the car bird watching along the coast road going south while Mike dressed as a local workman and rode off with some essentials in a knapsack towards the headland and stopped short of the last village and waited and watched.

There was no sign of the truck in daylight so as soon as it was dark he pushed the bike round the back of the village and joined the track where he started to ride slowly towards the headland.

When Mike was about half way he heard a motor bike coming up behind him so he quickly stopped and pulled the bike and himself well off the track and waited.

The ancient motor bike was being ridden by just one man who seemed to know the way with just a feeble slit of light to guide him on the rough track. When the motor bike reached a point opposite the Celtic ruins it turned up the slope to the ruins and disappeared inside.

Mike hurried up close to the ruins and waited.

About an hour later the fuel truck came grinding slowly up the track in a low gear and the motor bike man went down to meet it and talked to the driver for a few minutes. The truck then drove down the headland towards the sea but when it was close to the shore line it did a sharp left turn and disappeared, presumably along another track sloping down towards the beach. The motor bike man had then walked back up to the ruins.

Mike crawled closer to the ruins and could see the outline of the motor bike man using binoculars to scan the horizon out to sea.

After a while the man sprang into action and started the engine of his motor bike on its stand with the headlight pointing out to sea, took the blackout cover off the headlight and started flashing the light. There were acknowledging flashes from out to sea and after a few minutes the motor bike man rode down the track and disappeared onto the other track just as the fuel truck had done.

Mike hid his bike close to the track and took the short cut down to the lower track, stumbling through the rocks and heather in the dark.

When he reached an area overlooking the lower track Mike could see that the fuel truck had already turned round and was parked a short way from the bottom of the track and the two men were already connecting up a thick hose to the truck. The other end of the hose was already connected to the side of a mostly submerged submarine. After a flash of his torch the driver opened a valve on the side of the truck and Mike could hear the fuel gurgling as it flowed down the hose and into the submarine.

There must be a nearly vertical rock face and deep water immediately below the track.

A man who appeared to have some authority over the men who were standing on the deck of the submarine called to the men on shore and they went down and started talking and a package was handed to the men on the shore.

Mike was tempted to get the containers of chemicals out of his knapsack, that he had been given by Doc. Clayton to 'doctor' the fuel, but it was too risky as the men could return to the truck at any time so he must find another time when the truck was full of fuel and left unattended.

He now knew where and how the drop was made and some of the fuel trucks movements.

It did not need twenty hours to travel from the depot to the drop point, so there was a time slot in the operation between when the truck was loaded at a depot and it made the drop, during which it was probably parked for some eight to ten hours somewhere this side of Newport.

He relaxed as he started to cycle back down the track, but got a shock when he saw a large van coming up and just had time to get off the track before the slitted headlights swung round a bend.

He then realised that this would be the food supply for the sub which could be transferred while the fuel was still flowing down the hose.

He went back to see if his guess was correct. The food van had reversed down the last section of track and was close to the fuel truck. As he watched, two men pulled two sections of light weight industrial roller track out of the van and set them up with the center supported by folding legs. It was then a very simple operation to keep the cartons of food rolling down to the men passing them down into the conning tower of the sub.

The whole operation was possible because of the track leading to a very remote, natural deep water wharf and by daylight there would be nothing visible to indicate that enemy submarines were being supplied by a few locals collaborating with the Germans.

Mike waited till it was fully light and workmen were moving about before he went through Newport and became alarmed as he was approaching the pub where they were staying because there was no sign of Susan or the car so he kept on riding past and hid in a tumble down house and waited.

When all was quiet he left the bike in the old house and went through the pub kitchen and up to their room. The room looked normal but there was no sign of Susan so he left a coded note in a prearranged secret place, picked up a few items of clothing and left.

He cycled slowly along the Southern coast road where they had been told by the publican that there were sea bird nesting places and finally found where a car had left the road and plunged about ten feet down onto rocks below and had caught fire. He hid the bike and climbed down and looked into the charred wreck. It was definitely their hire car

There was no charred body in the car but still the remains of their camping gear indicating that Susan may be still alive and hiding somewhere.

William and the Captain from the Sapper unit reported to Colonel Miles as soon as they got back to Cairo and laid out the marked maps that they had made during their survey.

Several letters from Michelle were waiting for William when he called at the mess but he had to put them in his pocket to read and enjoy later. He had not been able to write very often but the forced separation was only making their love for each other stronger.

There were several meetings with the usual staff officer and a slightly modified version of William's plan was adopted and many truckloads of men and supplies of mines were sent off into the desert to implement the plan as fast as possible.

William also noted there were a number of highly mobile twenty five pounder units now available which had been moved up from the Southern end of the canal. They could travel to a new position and within a few minutes start firing anti-tank shells with excellent accuracy at a high rate of fire.

These consisted of a four wheel drive lightly armoured vehicle, known as a 'quad,' which towed a limber to carry the ammunition and a 25 pound field gun with a 'trail' which doubled as a draw bar.

William was glad to be back where he could have a shower, a change of clothes and food that wasn't out of a tin and 'murdered' on a camp stove consisting of a cut down petrol can, half filled with petrol and diesel fuel soaked sand. There were slots cut round the top from which black oily smoke belched and gave all the food the same 'flavour.'

That evening the other officers in the billet took him to a night club farther along the street and he had his first experience of the ways of the East.

He was taken into an inner restaurant and bar where there were some Army officers and civilians already seated at the tables or standing at the bar.

The waitresses were all beautiful and dressed in the most revealing outfits he had ever seen.

There was much joking and comment about the time and they said all, or it would be more accurate to say, half would be revealed at ten o 'clock.

Just before ten o'clock all the girls disappeared to return on the stroke of ten naked down to the waist! William's eyes nearly popped out of his head at the sight of the exquisite girls of many different races, Egyptian, English, Greek, Italian, French, African, and more, serving drinks and food with their perfectly formed breasts only inches away!

An excellent meal was served and there were plenty of wines and spirits available at amazingly low prices.

When the time approached eleven o'clock there was again much hilarity about another revelation.

This time the girls returned naked from the waist down.

At midnight the girls came in fully naked and some were taken upstairs for further revelations.

William could see that he could soon become seduced by the charms of the East and was disappointed when he was sent back into the desert to supervise implementation of his plan.

A month of living in the back of a truck, heavy work, only rough camp food out of tins and an occasional bucket sponge down, if you were lucky, soon had William hardened up to Desert life.

Several times they saw German planes flying repeatedly over the gap, presumably photographing the dummy mine fields, which they had put in first.

The R.E. Officer who was working with William suggested that they should put in a few anti-personnel mines round the edges of the dummy anti-tank mine fields and this was done as there were plenty available and it would add a little authenticity to the dummy mine fields.

The rabbit run plan was not quite complete when Rommel's tanks broke through the Western defenses and started bombarding El Alamein before swinging round and heading South along the West of the dummy minefields into the broken country.

As William's unit was not equipped for combat they made a hasty dash back towards Cairo and were shelled at a long range as they went. One truck was hit, and as it was still carrying some mines was blown to Kingdom come.

The tank leading the charge through the broken ground, and which was doing most of the shelling, struck a mine and threw a track and had a few damaged idlers which caused the rest of the tanks to halt assuming that they had entered a regular minefield. There was a pause in the German advance which gave William's unit time to increase the range but his truck was hit by shrapnel from a near miss and the driver killed so William had to drag the body across the cab and take over even though he had a damaged arm and some cuts from flying debris.

He found that driving a truck with one hand was not easy but managed to juggle the gears and steering well enough to get back to Cairo.

They had been saved by their own mines!

The German force was split into two and most of the German tanks went farther to the South and then started to cross the Qattara Depression about half way to the Southern end and many became bogged while the rest cautiously went through the gap along the coast avoiding the dummy mine fields. A fierce gun battle raged with El Alamein being a pivotal part of the battle.

While William was in hospital he heard that the Germans had got to within about thirty miles of Alex before being driven back with very fierce fighting at El 'Alamein.

There was a new British C in C. of the desert forces, General Montgomery, who was a real man's man and had an 'up and at em' approach, and led from the front, which put new life into the troops.

Now that 'Monty' was preventing any further push by the enemy to the East and was slowly wearing down a very overreached German army, the immediate pressure was off defenses and Colonel Miles was re-assigned to counter espionage and in particular finding the agent who was giving vital information to the Germans.

In one of the German agent's radio messages that had been intercepted he, or she, had signed off as 'Alex' but this could be just a code name or a location and gave no help.

The agent had access to top level, up to the moment information so had to be part of, or have access to, BHQ confidential material.

William asked Colonel Miles if they could attend the staff officers meetings as observers but this idea was not acceptable so he asked if they could interview the HQ staff but this was also not acceptable as it would be considered an insult to the integrity of those concerned.

They then drew up a complete list of all the people who had access to top security information and discussed each individual but could not find any suspects or possible 'leaks.'

So they must tackle the problem from the other end.

William remembered the beams and how it was possible to use a radio direction finder to locate a transmitter and asked signals for their help. Signals made up a system mounted on a small truck which could be driven round during a transmission and then use triangulation to locate the transmitter.

The agent seemed to have a regular call time of 2000 hrs when there was a message to be sent and the incoming messages came about the same time. The code used was very hard to break as the system was constantly changing.

William was to go in the radio truck each day for a week from 1930 hrs to 2100 hrs and wait for any signals. No signals were picked up on the usual frequency for two days so they tried hunting for signals on a whole band of frequencies and finally picked up 'Alex,' as he was known, on a different frequency and got one 'line' on him before he switched off.The line went through the central, older part of Cairo. Now they needed a second line to find the location.

The Colonel 'smelt blood' and was sure that they would corner the agent in a few days so William was ordered to keep up the vigil every evening.

There were several short messages on different frequencies but nothing long enough that they could get a line on, during the next week. It was as though Alex knew that his signals were being monitored and was just teasing them!

Colonel Bill Miles was getting more and more frustrated and asked for suggestions from William who said.

"Sir, if this agent is so smart that he thinks that he can play silly buggers with us, he must have some way of concealing his location that makes him very confident that we won't find him.

Also he appears to have immediate access to our confidential plans and may already know that we are using a radio detector van to track him down and is working on the assumption that we only have time to get one fix each night, which makes me wonder if Alex has his radio in a vehicle and keeps moving round Cairo.

What if we use two radio vans and only you and I know what we are doing so that we can get two lines at once and nail the bastard, even if he is mobile.

We need to give him a long and complicated 'bait' of some phantom plan that should make him stay on the air for long enough for our two detectors to get a line on him. They can then radio to each other and work out an exact fix which they can radio to us and we should be able to nab him."

"You have a devious mind William. You seem to be able to project yourself into his position, how did you learn to think like that?"

"My father was taught by a friend when he was involved with the Boer war fighting terrorists.

Both my father and his teacher have taught me how 'to know your enemy' and find out how they think."

"It seems to involve a lot of conjecture, but I am sure that your plan will work.

Now we need to work up a phantom battle plan as 'bait', decide where to plant it and get signals to supply a second radio detector to get a fix on him.

We also need a few experienced armed men to do the arrest who could travel in the second radio truck."

"Would it be possible to get hold of a civilian van to be used as the second vehicle so that we don't show our hand by using an army vehicle?"

"Yes that is an excellent idea and I know of a contractor who would oblige as he owes me a favor."

Colonel Bill Miles sat up most of the next night making a series of battle plans on 'drop sheets' as though they were to be used at a senior staff meeting and left them in his office.

The next day a medium sized delivery van, with a Cairo wine merchants signs on the sides, arrived and was fitted out with all the radio direction finding equipment and Signals provided a radio operator.

Bill Miles had a contact in a Military Police unit and they had a meeting in a restaurant and arranged for his MP contact and three colleges to travel in the second radio van in civilian clothes.

William was to travel in the first radio truck as before.

There were no signals on the first or second nights but on the third night there was a long signal on the original frequency which gave the two radio operators plenty of time to get a line on the transmission and use triangulation to pin point where the transmission was coming from.

The location was a sook, or market, in the old part of Cairo and after a radio message to the first truck, the two vehicles converged on the sook from different directions with William's Army truck stopping one street before the sook.

At one side of the sook there was a wide road where a number of delivery vehicles had backed up to the stalls and some of the vehicles were closed and some were still making deliveries.

As arranged, all the men mingled at random with the crowds of locals and a few off duty servicemen and ambled towards the parked vehicles and waited for a sign to move in as soon as a suspect vehicle or building was found.

William was with a radio operator who said there must be an aerial of some sort which should indicate which vehicle or building he was in.

They were walking slowly along the line of market stalls closest to the vehicles when the radio operator spotted a man reach up to the roof of his van and fold down a small metal grid like device and nudged William who raised one arm with the flat of his hand towards the van and then hurried round the intervening market stalls and arrived at the van just after two of the MP s had stormed into the van with revolvers drawn and there was crashing, shouting and then a shot from inside.

The men had been told to shoot to stop, not shoot to kill, so William hoped that the agent had not been killed and could be questioned but when he got to the door of the van, there was a very dead MP shot through the head and the other MP fighting with a man still holding an automatic pistol.

William aimed his revolver at the hand holding the pistol and fired.

The bullet hit the man's wrist which burst into a shower of blood and small splinters of bone with the pistol flying away to the back of the van.

The MP was then able to overcome the agent with William's assistance.

As they could not handcuff the prisoner normally they attached one manacle to the good wrist and the other to his ankle and threw him a rag to bind up his shattered wrist.

The MP then thanked William for his marksmanship and William mentally thanked Gillie for his dedicated personal tuition in revolver shooting at the Glendarvel Gun Club range.

"Sir, I think that we should call an ambulance and take this fellow to hospital under guard and they can also take my college to the morgue."

Then turning to the prisoner.

"Do you speak English?"

The prisoner shook his head and said.

"No Englisi."

William said. "I don't believe him because he can read documents and encode them so watch him very carefully. I suggest that you keep him handcuffed, even in hospital, he is a very clever operator and thank you for your service. I am very sorry that you lost your colleague."

The other two MP s arrived and the radio man called for an ambulance.

William waited till the ambulance had departed and then they went back to BHQ.

Colonel Miles was delighted with the result, but then wanted to know how the agent had been getting his information and told William to double check the total list of people with access to top secret files and the minutes of meetings.

After a lengthy and difficult process William found that one very senior officer always made copious notes at meetings and when he had read them through back in his office and transferred the parts that needed his personal action to a diary, he tore up the notes and threw them into the waste bin.

He kept the diary in his safe or carried it with him in a brief case.

This left opportunity for another staff member or cleaner to piece together the notes and pass the information to the agent.

Colonel Bill Miles said that he would arrange to work late and set up a small mirror on some items of Regimental memorabilia mounted on the passage wall opposite his office door, so that he could see anyone going into the office where the torn up notes were to be found.

In the early hours he saw a man in an officer's uniform furtively enter the office and drew his revolver and went to challenge the intruder.

The intruder must have heard him coming along the passage and as the Colonel entered the office he saw the man holding a chair and start to charge at him.

It took several shots from the Colonel's revolver to hit the man in the legs and stop the charge.

He recognised the intruder as a Major who worked in the cipher office down stairs and said.

"What the hell do you think you are doing up here in the middle of the night?"

"I have nothing to say."

"Oh, so you want to play silly buggers, but it won't help you. I will keep you covered till the red caps come."

The noise of the shooting had alerted the MP s on duty at the main entrance and they came running up the stairs and entered the office. They soon had the Major hand cuffed and sitting in a chair with his damaged leg patched up with a field dressing.

Colonel Miles explained to the MP s that there was a leak of confidential information and that he was working late to watch out for a possible intruder and had seen this man enter the office and that when he was discovered he had tried to charge him with a chair.

"Just leave it to us Sir, we will take him to the hospital and then lock him up"

"I nearly forgot, we think he has been taking important papers that have been torn up and thrown into the waste bin so will you please now search his pockets and put what you find in an envelope as evidence."

The intruders face said a lot and he started to struggle and tried to resist having his pockets turned out.

"Is this what you are looking for Sir?" said the Senior Sergeant MP as he held out a fist full of roughly torn up notes and documents.

"That is exactly what we expected to find in his pockets, so now please can you do a search of his office on the ground floor, in the cipher section, where I think you will find evidence of where he does the jijsaw puzzle act of pasting up the pieces of the documents that he has stolen."

Two MP s were delegated to search the Cipher office down stairs and half an hour later returned with a box full of incriminating evidence.

William was woken by someone loudly knocking on his door and was surprised to see Colonel Miles.

"Come in Sir, and take a seat while I get dressed, please tell me what has happened."

"The mirror trick worked and I went to challenge the intruder but he must have heard me and tried to charge me with a chair. It took several shots round the chair to wing him in the leg.

The MP s came and found his pockets full of torn up papers. He is a Major and works in the cypher office and the MPs found more evidence in his desk.

The question now is, why would a British officer, approaching retirement age, get involved in feeding secrets to the enemy? There must be a reason and we need to find it. When you are ready we must go to the office and start searching."

They went to the office and found that there was an MP sitting in the cypher office making sure that no evidence could be disturbed, which was good. He said that he would like to help search the office again and in particular find if the Major had any family who could have been taken as a hostage and were being used for blackmailing him into working for the enemy.

They did not find anything else incriminating but there was a photograph on a book case of who were probably his wife and daughter. The photograph was of just a normal looking mother and daughter standing in a garden that looked very English. When the photo was removed from the frame there was writing on the back.

Please come home soon.

Love Jenny and Phillipa. June 1940

The MP said.

"It looks like the wife and daughter could have been taken as hostages in England and are being used to blackmail the Major. We have encountered this sort of thing before."

The Colonel said.

"I must check with records branch as soon as they are available, get his address and have someone go round to his home in England as soon as possible, but I think it should be done by M I 5, very low key, or we may scare them off, and or, get the hostages killed, if that is the situation."

William said.

"Excuse me Sir, but my Father is in regular contact with M I 5 and can put you in touch with the right person who will know exactly what to do. Perhaps you would like to send a coded cable to my father and he will put you in touch with the right person."

"As I don't know anyone in M I 5 that could save time so give me the details and I will get a cable off right away."

Within two hours there was a coded reply cable from Richard asking for more details and a second cable was sent.

The next afternoon there was a coded cable from Richard advising that the wife and daughter had been kidnapped, were being held hostage at the agent's house, and that the agent controlling them had been put under a close watch.

It was suggested that there may be an opportunity to assume the 'wireless identity' of the Cairo agent and continue to receive the German messages and feed in harmless and or misleading information.

Richard said that he had been directed to use every possible opportunity to assume the Cairo agents identity and would allow the agent to continue to hold the hostages as long as necessary.

An experienced counter espionage agent was being sent by the next available flight via Spain to Fayid with instructions to check on the local situation and if possible to assume the wireless identity of the enemy agent. The ETA would be confirmed.

William was told to stand by, and be ready to go to Fayid to meet the M I 5 or M I 6 man as soon as the ETA was known.

Two days later a cable arrived advising the ETA, which was in the early hours, so William decided to go early on the previous morning and call on his friend at the REME workshops at Tel el Kebir and thank him for his prompt positioning of the tank hulls along the canal road and get any local news from that area.

"It was our pleasure to help, also we were glad to get rid of the ugly brutes of tank hulls that had been accumulating in the dump near the workshops."

"What is happening in the workshops now that Monty seems to be holding off the German advance at El Alamein?"

"We are still very busy with repairing tanks and trucks in the workshops.

As I am in charge of vehicle recovery, I have to go to the gravel pits on the canal road now, to supervise the recovery of a bogged truck. Would you like to follow me and we can continue our chat while the boys haul out the bogged truck?"

"Yes, I can follow you in my Bedford one tonner and then go on to Fayid from there.

The two young officers chatted at the side of the road and exchanged all the local news as they watched the recovery operation.

Close to the gravel pits there was an Army truck with a full load stuck in some soft sand at the side of the road which was carefully winched back onto the road by a Scammel 6 x 6 recovery vehicle. William saw his friend drive off and walked over to where some Egyptian road contractor's trucks were being loaded with gravel by men with long handled shovels. He noticed that one man filled the shovel at ground level and a second man standing in the truck had a rope tied to the shovel and helped to pull the loaded shovel up into the truck and asked the Boss man standing by the gate why they used the rope and was told.

"Why waste a good shovel on just one man."

William realised that he still had a lot to learn about the values and priorities of the Muslim people living in the desert, often only just above starvation level, and obsessed with their interpretation, or was it manipulation, of their Holy Book, the Koran.

He remembered the many times when he had seen local families traveling along a made road in the traditional 'marching order' with the dominant male riding a donkey, dressed in his fez and flowing white galabiah. The wives and children followed behind on foot, in ascending order of age and size of burden.

But when they took a short cut across the open desert the marching order was reversed with the oldest wife leading.

When he had asked one of his sergeants the reason for the change of marching order, he had been told. "One very good reason Sir. Land Mines!"

That said everything about their values and priorities, and particularly the value given to women, which appeared to be lower than that given to their livestock.

The flight was late due to engine oil leaks detected when the Wellington transport plane was refueling at Valletta, in Malta, so it was late evening when it landed at Fayid and William was called to the transit camp office to meet his contact.

As they were both tired they decided to stay the night and head off for Cairo early in the morning, but as usual, it was already very hot before eight o'clock.

During the trip back to Cairo, William was able to give Paul all the details of the agents arrest, how they had located the Major in the cypher section and then learn all about the happenings in England.

Paul said.

"We knew there was an agent operating near Reading, and had nearly got a fix on his radio transmissions a couple of times, but when you gave us the name and address of the Major it helped us to pinpoint the immediate area and found that the hostages had only been moved about a mile from their home. While the agent was at work the next day, we found that the hostages were being kept in a cellar in an old farm house.

Unfortunately we could not make direct contact with the hostages or this could have put them at risk or blown our cover.

So we now have a window of opportunity to assume the Cairo agent's radio identity and feed Jerry with some phantom plans to keep him busy chasing rainbows."

Paul spoke German like a native and proved to be a skilled operator and soon had the enemy avoiding phantom minefields and preparing for attacks that were only token air raids or long range shelling while the real attackers were being moved into position for a real offensive.

He also created a phantom naval bombardment to come close to El Alamein which made the enemy withdraw his forces back into the desert, which was of immense value at a critical time in the battle raging round the besieged city of El Alamein.

After a month of deception, it became apparent that the enemy was not responding to the false information as quickly as before and probably was in the process of working out that he was being duped, so the whole operation had a planned shutdown synchronized with the arrest of the agent near Reading in England and rescue of the hostages.

When the Major was interrogated, it was found that the enemy agent had selected him because he was the cypher officer and privy to many of the top secret documents. He had been abducted from his billet for twenty four hours over a week end to set up the blackmail and establish a meeting place for the exchange of information in the 'Revelation Night Club', which the Major was already visiting regularly to see one girl who he favored. The unfortunate girl had later been blackmailed by the enemy agent into becoming part of the conspiracy in that she was forced to agree to make the pretense of 'performing' with two men and not disclose anything about the lengthy discussions and handing over of documents that took place in the private room.

Mike searched round the burnt out car for clues on what had happened to Susan and found foot prints in a patch of soft earth indicating that she had been taken by two men and dragged towards the road, where there was easy access up the embankment.

Close to this place, there were tyre marks where a heavy vehicle had pulled off the road and stopped with more of Susan's foot prints where she had probably been forced into the vehicle. The vehicle had then moved off towards Newport.

As Mike was about to leave, he smelt diesel fuel and looked down. There were marks where a few drips of diesel had fallen while the vehicle was stationary, so it looked as though one of the tankers from the Newport distributor had been used in the abduction.

He went back and hid the bike in the old house and went to a cafe where he could observe the fuel distributors yard and sat with his coffee near the window for a while and then had to move around while he observed.

Both trucks were out so he had to wait for one to return and check if it had drips coming from its discharge valve.

Late in the afternoon the local delivery truck returned and was parked just inside the chain wire fence surrounding the depot.

Mike put on an act of being drunk and staggered towards the fence and made a show of vomiting against the fence.

The truck had a slowly dripping discharge valve!

So it was likely that Susan was being held in one of the sheds in the fuel distributor's yard.

There was a hardware store at the top of the street so he went in and spent some time looking at hand tools and slipped a pair of pliers, with wire cutters on the side, into his pocket, selected a claw hammer and some nails and paid a black market price for the hammer and nails at the counter.

As soon as it was fully dark, he left the old house and went to the fuel depot. He had noted that there was a part of the fence that was in deep shadow from the one shaded street light and started cutting a large hole in the chain wire.

Some of the sheds had one open side but there were two that were fully closed in with locked doors. Using the claw hammer as a jemmy, Mike broke the padlock off one shed and crept inside. His pencil torch showed that it was a well-equipped workshop. He helped himself to a screw driver and slipped it into his pocket.

There were no partitions or small rooms and after a quick check round the benches he went out and started unscrewing the hasp holding a padlock on the door of the other shed.

This shed was used as a storeroom for tins of oil and accessories and there was a small office just inside the main door.

The office was locked. Mike tapped lightly on the office door in a familiar rhythm.

There was an answering grunt and scratching sound.

When looking for the door handle and lock, Mike noticed that the hinges were of the loose pin type and that it would be possible to pull the hinge pins out with the pliers and lift the whole undamaged door out of its frame. This was soon done and the torch's slender beam showed a very distressed Susan securely tied and gagged with bleeding hands and burns on her face, lying on the floor.

The bonds and gag were quickly removed, but Susan had such a dry and swollen mouth that she was not able to speak properly.

Mike told her not to try speaking and helped her out of the office so that he could replace the door, insert the hinge pins back into the hinges and leave no evidence of the intrusion.

It took a few minutes of chaffing her ankles and wrists to get Susan's circulation flowing again so that she could move normally.

As soon as the area had been wiped over with a rag to remove any blood or scuff marks, Mike helped Susan to stand and left her in the shadow between the two sheds while he screwed the hasp and padlock back into place.

They cautiously moved to the hole in the fence and went through. Mike then roughly twisted a few strands of wire together to close the hole and they crept through the shadows to the old house where the bike and Mike's knapsack were hidden.

It took a long time to bind up Susan's hands where her finger nails had been pulled out and to give her some food and water.

Now that the car was destroyed, they needed a bike for Susan so Mike went off again and 'borrowed' one that had been left outside the back of some shops.

When it was fully dark they moved camp to the first village along the coast road going north and hid in a tumbledown Fisherman's hut close to the road.

"Now that we are well away from Newport and can relax a bit, please tell me what happened."

"I drove along the South coast road, as the publican had suggested it was a nesting ground, and when I was at that bit of road, with a drop down to the rocks, a fuel truck suddenly pulled onto the road in front of me accelerating violently and charged me so that I was forced to swerve off the road and drop onto the rocks.

I hit my face on the steering wheel when the car landed and was shaken and bruised but not seriously hurt.

As I was still a bit stunned and was thinking about getting some basics out of the boot, two men grabbed me from behind and dragged me to the truck, one of them took a can of petrol from the truck and set fire to the car. They then took me to the depot and started to torture me while asking questions.

They wanted to know if I was an informer for the police or the Northern Irish Government, so after the bastards had removed half of my nails, I hinted that I worked for the Northern Irish Government and that seemed to satisfy their curiosity for the time being, so I was given some water, tied up and locked in the office."

"You have been a very brave girl, will you be OK for a while? Because now I must leave you here while I go and see if I can find where the big truck and driver rest when there is a 'sub supply run' in progress. You remember, we found that there was about eight to ten hours when the big truck must be waiting somewhere. That is the time when I will add Doc's potion to the fuel."

Mike went to the village and while going through an alleyway collided with a drunk who stumbled out of a small door.

The drunk was not hurt and begged for some money to buy another drink, so mike said that he had heard there was a truck parked somewhere near and that he could nick some fuel from it for his boat.

The drunk's watery eyes lit up like lamps at the sight of the one pound note in Mikes hand and he poured out a vivid description of how a truck 'with a big belly full o' fuel' came and stopped close to the house of Molly O' Shaunessy.

"She has the body of an angel and the whiles of the divil and could tempt the papish hi'self into the lustful ways o' the world!

T''is of't I see the truck driver having his wicked way wid' her, in the front room, be'gorragh."

He then gave directions to the place where the truck was usually parked.

Mike thanked the drunk and promised to give him some fish when he had got some fuel for his boat and parted with the pound note.

The drunk almost ran to the pub, still clutching the pound note.

Early in the evening, Mike heard the fuel truck coming up the hill and stopping. The driver got out and went into a house without knocking. As the drunk had said, it was possible to see into the house through the open window. The driver and a woman had a meal in the kitchen and then went into the front room and lay on a couch with much noisy lovemaking.

This was the moment, so Mike quickly climbed up onto the top of the fuel truck, released the filler cap and tipped one packet of the Doc's potion into the tank.

He wished that he would be able to see the stranded subs floating helplessly in the Atlantic.

Mike and Susan waited in the fisherman's hut till after midnight when they heard the fuel truck coming along the road, passing the hut and going on towards the headland. So the plan was working so far, and Mike wanted to be sure and follow the truck, but Susan talked him out of the idea.

"We still have five more packets of the Doc's potion, so perhaps you are right and that we can lie low here and give you a chance to recover for a few days?"

"Yes that would be good, but we will need some food. I noticed an overgrown garden just up the road with some potatoes and things that we could use but you will need to go to some shops in another village for groceries."

"That is OK I can do that. As it is not safe to go into Newport to check on the truck's movements any more, I will need to go and wait near where the truck parks every day to be sure that we can keep up 'doctoring the fuel', because there is the risk that when the first sub's engines fail that they may realise that the fuel has been tampered with and do some checking."

Susan said.

"Did the Doc tell you how the potion works?"

"Yes, he said that the chemicals only become active at the high combustion temperatures inside the cylinders of the sub's engine and create an oxygen rich combustion which causes rapid oxidation, or burning away of the exhaust valves.

After four or five hours of operation, under normal conditions, the exhaust valves become so eroded that the engine starts to lose power and finally stops and can't be restarted."

The supply runs became more frequent and Mike was able to use all the potions during the next ten days, so the mission was now completed.

They decided that the time had come to get out and used the bikes to go to where they could pick up a series of trains back to Belfast. They would not report the loss of the car.

Susan's hands were giving her a lot of pain and could be a giveaway so Mike bought a pair of men's leather gloves so that there was room for small dressings on Susan's damaged fingers. She used heavy make up to try to cover the cigarette burns on her face but they were still visible from close up.

During the ferry crossing, they sat in their cabin and worked out a carefully encoded message that could be phoned to London as soon as possible.

As soon as the ferry reached Liverpool they checked into a small hotel. They then slipped out via the fire escape and made the coded phone call to London from a phone box, which gave Richard a summary of the Saddle Headland operation and confirmed that the last six loads of fuel had been 'doctored'.

Mike and Susan stayed the night in the hotel in Liverpool, as they were very tired, and caught the first train to London in the morning.

One passenger in the carriage seemed familiar and Mike remembered that he had been on the ferry and realised that they were probably being followed. He waited till the man went out, presumably to go to the toilet, so told Susan and they quickly moved to another compartment.

The man soon found them and two other men then came into the compartment and all three men squeezed into the vacant seats.

Mike did not want to disclose the fact that they were going as far as London so said to Susan.

"I think our stop is very soon."

As the train approached Birmingham station he got their luggage down from the overhead rack.

The train stopped and they got off and walked slowly down the platform towards the exit barrier.

The three men were following some distance behind. When they were alongside a news agent's kiosk, Mike suddenly pulled Susan round the corner and pointed his revolver at the three man who were taken completely by surprise.

"Put your hands up or I will shoot."

Two men complied and the third started to run and was shot in the leg and collapsed.

A group of people was forming behind Mike so he asked two soldiers in uniform to go to the station master's office and phone for the police while he kept the three men covered.

Susan could not do much with her damaged hands so went to the kiosk and asked if she could come in and sit down as she was feeling faint. The motherly woman in the kiosk quickly opened the door and Susan was able to take off one glove, get her revolver out of her bag and cover the scene from behind the counter and said to the woman.

"The three men are suspect enemy agents and we need to get them picked up and interrogated.

Please just act normally, and thank you for your help."

The two soldiers returned with the station master and two aged railway porters and said the police were on their way.

Eventually the police arrived and the three men were taken off in a police van. The station master demanded an explanation so Mike and Susan followed him back to his office.

"Thank you for getting the police. We found that we were being followed on the train by known enemy agents and got off at the next station. My partner has recently been kidnapped and tortured by these men." Susan took off her gloves to prove the point.

The station master was suitably horrified and asked if he could do anything else to help.

"We would appreciate it, if you can arrange that there is no publicity about the events today.

Would you please phone this number and tell the operator what has happened today and ask that they send a man immediately to interrogate the prisoners at the local police station." He wrote down a special public relations number used by London.

After a devious train ride to London, Mike and Susan met Richard and gave him all the details of their trip to Ireland.

Richard said.

"You will be pleased to hear that we have a submarine hiding off the coast watching the Saddle Headland ready to land some commandos and grab the men actually doing the supply operation on the beach.

Because Ireland is technically neutral, we can't arrest the men working at the fuel distributor without an awful lot of publicity and red tape cutting so they have been put on a long list of known collaborators being kept under observation.

From now on, we will have to improve our surveillance of that coastline and keep a visible presence to bluff them into closing down and tighten up the availability of fuel.

There is a Royal Navy Base at Londonderry, called 'Sea Eagle,' and they can extend their coastal patrols farther down the West coast.

Having a supposedly neutral country alongside us has always been a chink in our armour and we should have been more careful. Particularly now that we have had a similar incident on the West coast of South Africa. German Subs were being supplied by German collaborators in a very similar operation, so that they could keep in the shipping lanes round the Cape to attack our ships going to the Far East.

Now in the greatest of secrecy, I will tell you that we are having no end of trouble with American oil companies supplying German subs and shipping crude oil from South America.

You see there is a strong anti-British minority and isolationist movement in America with a sympathetic Republican controlled Congress which is dependent on the support of the greedy oil companies to stay in power."

Mark, Sasha, Sally and Michelle were in the garden enjoying the sunshine when Annie come out and said that Raymond had phoned to say that Mr. Richard was on his way up from the lodge.

Richard was accompanied by the Doc. and joined them in the garden."

Mark said.

"Welcome to you both, it is a long time since we have seen you. What brings you here this time?"

"There are no new beams to be bent at the moment but we wanted to bring you up to date on the exploits of Mike and Susan in Ireland, also to discuss another project that we have in mind."

Richard gave a detailed account of the supply and refueling of enemy subs on the Irish coast and then said that the plan had been highly successful in that six enemy submarines had been disabled and were found by coastal patrol aircraft floating helplessly on the surface in the Atlantic. Five had put up a token fight with their small deck mounted guns and had been sunk or disabled, but the last one had not been found for over two weeks and the crew were already starting to die from starvation when they were found and the survivors surrendered. The sub had been towed back to a shipyard and provided a lot of vital information on their communications equipment and armaments.

Another team had been sent immediately to follow up on the Newport operation and had located the enemy agent who was controlling the operation and keeping radio contact with the subs and was scheduling the supply times.

He was posing as a junior curate and was seen going to the church, on his bicycle, at regular times carrying a small suit case. He was caught while actually transmitting from his suitcase radio connected to a permanent aerial concealed in the bell tower of the church.

That had been the last transmission that he would ever make!

Richard then continued.

"We are still encumbered with the US. Ambassador, Joseph P. Kennedy, who continues to use his diplomatic immunity and status to try to spread his defeatist and subversive views, so he is being totally bypassed and does not get access to any information. There was the hell of a row when it was confirmed that he was passing secret documents to the enemy and a member of his staff got the chop, but I think that he was set up by Kennedy as the scapegoat and had just been acting on direct orders from Kennedy. The sooner Kennedy takes his tribe of children back home the better.

Britain is now sitting on a razor's edge between survival and defeat and any form of negative behavior or subversion could swing the balance the wrong way. So we must continue to be fully alert and use every skill, subterfuge, scientific development and sheer determination to win the war.

Your family contribution to our survival is of immense value and we thank all of you.

The students coming from the 'riding school', as it is still called, have strengthened our Baker Street Irregulars or M I 5 as it is now called, as well as sending many well prepared M I 6 agents overseas.

On the home front, we have pulled in numerous enemy agents, who in many cases had been planted long before the outbreak of war and would have been impossible to locate without the better trained people who are now available from the riding school.

We have been able to decode some enemy signals relating to a planned invasion of Britain which Hitler was calling 'Operation Sea Lion,' but it appears that he had been talked into having a trial or mock invasion first, to test our defenses.

Hitler is so cock sure of his ability to conker Britain and the World that he has already drawn up new maps showing his idea of the 'New World Order Germanic Territories' and has also issued detailed plans for the operation of his 'New World Order.'

He is using 'Nazi psychological terrorism' in all the occupied countries to try to break down their last bit of resistance and national identity.

Arrival of the information about the 'Sea Lion' trial invasion did not give us much time to farther improve what meager forces we have available.

It has been known for some time that Hitler has a paranoid fear of fire, so the boffins were asked to use this fact to create the most effective defense system possible, with the very limited resources and time available.

A German armada of landing craft and makeshift barges was sent across the channel and when they got to within about half a mile of our shores, they were suddenly met by a wall of burning oil and petrol with devastating results.

A few well-armed Vosper fast patrol boats and MTBs were then able to use torpedoes, 0.50 cannons and machine gun fire to prevent any enemy vessels from escaping the fire and returning to base, so the enemy trial invasion was a total failure.

The boffins had devised a simple system of perforated hoses laid on the sea floor which could be pumped full of petrol and oil which came to the surface and was then ignited by tracer fire.

Charred bodies were being washed ashore for weeks afterwords!

This single, defiant act of defending our shores seems to have struck at Hitler's paranoia about fire and our radio interception people tell me that he has revised his priorities, for the time being.

We are still losing a devastating number of ships to enemy U boats, even in the channel.

Our agents in France have just found that one of their main U boat bases is under, what is claimed to be a bomb proof roof, and is located on the French coast at St. Malo.

Drawings of the whole complex were smuggled out of France by one of the local Engineers who had been forced to work on the project. The designs have been double checked and it is confirmed that the concrete thickness and steel structure are strong enough to resist even our largest bombs.

We thought about using divers from a submarine but they could not carry enough explosives to do more than localised damage. It would also be highly risky.

So we now need a plan to destroy their U boat base and as many U boats as possible and thought your explosives expert, Tad, may have some ideas."

"That is quite likely, as Gillie once said, he is as cunning as a wagon load of monkeys. Would you like me to send for him now?"

"Yes please, we need to take action as soon as possible."

Tad arrived, joined the group and had the challenge explained with the aid of a map and some aerial photographs.

"Wee'm had same sort'a trouble when a drive in one of the mines that were under the sea, and she started to cave in like, and would have flooded the whole mine, so wee'm had to send in a huge charge to make the whole roof collapse and block off the drive a'fore the mine be flooded back into the rest 'o the workings.

Weem' made a long pusher out'a poles and carefully forced a coup'a mine cars full of explosives with a long fuse set and pushed them into the half flooded drive and saved the mine from flooding.

But, you should be able to send in some boats with that new fangled 'lectric stuff to find the 'ole and get right inside 'afore you let 'er blow."

Richard became excited and said.

"That's it by God! Radio controlled boats loaded with HE sent in and guided from a 'Mother Boat'.

I must get a developmental team onto it right away. There is a team working on a dam busting project using radio directed bombs, but they aren't having any luck so far.

They are based at Conway in North Wales and use the wide part of the river upstream of the Telford Bridge to do their testing of trying to aim dummy bombs onto a pattern of buoys anchored in the river.

We only need a few powerful, high speed, small boats and the boys can rig them up with radio controls and start testing in a few days. Once we have the radio control systems working reliably, we can apply them to the operational size boats.

Well done Tad, and thank you.

Perhaps you would like to go and work with our team in developing how the explosive charges are to be placed in the sacrificial boats to give the maximum blast to wreck everything, including any U boats that are inside at the time. If you can start a fire as well, that would make sure that the whole base is put out of action.

Tad was pleased with the opportunity to apply his skill and experience with explosives to help win the war and was to await instructions on where and when to go.

About a week later there was a phone call followed by the arrival of a fast car and Tad was whisked away to Plymouth to start working on 'Operation Armadillo'.

The 'mother boat was to be an MTB equipped with two torpedoes and two belt fed machine guns.

Four powerful cabin cruisers were disguised to look like dilapidated old fishing boats which were then loaded with a cocktail of explosives as suggested by Tad.

A dynamite charge was first placed on steel plates to direct the blast upwards, this was followed by a triple layer of plastic explosive, PE3 wrapped round outdated armour piercing shells which should discharge in all directions and then there was a layer of incendiary bombs which would be showered far and wide.

Just to top off the cocktail a lot of two gallon tins of petrol and small barrels of tar were lashed to the deck and covered with old fishing nets.

After much cutting of red tape, Tad was allowed to go on the 'mother boat' as an observer.

As dawn was breaking and shafts of light lit up the surface of the water, the German sentries patrolling the outer part of the roof of the U boat base suddenly became aware that there was a group of fishing boats in the 'Verboten Zone' in front of the base and rushed to their guard hut to report.

Engines roared and the four 'fishing' boats leaped forward with each under the radio control of its personal director in the MTB 'Mother Boat' which started continuous machine gun fire aimed at all the likely gun emplacements defending the base.

One enemy machine gun started firing at the leading 'fishing' boat and it blew up just in front of the entrance with a dramatic display of pyrotechnics, leaving a large area of burning petrol and tar which reached up to the machine gun emplacements built into the rim of the roof.

Two of the 'fishing' boats were successfully directed into the U boat base and detonated with great sheets of flame and debris being ejected through the opening. The two torpedoes were then fired at the base but exploded in the entrance. There must have been some sort of deep under water barrier for protection against torpedo attacks.

The last 'fishing' boat lost radio contact after the blasts and charged out of control into a small jetty beside the entrance and blew up destroying the German 'Schnellboot' (Fast boat with three Mercedes diesel engines)moored there.

A second MTB took over to provide covering fire while the 'Mother Boat' turned and headed for home.

Tad looked back and could see clouds of black smoke pouring out of the base with the occasional explosion that sounded like torpedoes going off. Jerry would not be able to use the base for a very long time and had probably lost several subs that were in the base at the time.

Mark's brother, Hugh had been posted to Singapore and was billeted in an old house on the outskirts of the city that belonged to one of the wealthy merchants. The Malay house servants had stayed on 'to look after the Tuan's house' and were happy to treat the officers as house guests. The officers gave them regular tips and provided liberal supplies of Army rations.

His unit had to do regular patrols to the North up the peninsula to ensure that the Japanese had not made a secret landing or sent patrols through the jungle. This routine had continued for many months and suddenly there was news of a fast moving Japanese invasion coming down the peninsular while his unit was out on patrol.

On receipt of the signal, Hugh's unit had rapidly dug some trenches near a village and were prepared the repel any advancing troops coming down the road. They had then been attacked from behind by a much superior force that had been hiding in the jungle and emerged with guns blazing. The men in the patrol had either been killed or taken prisoner within a few minutes.

Hugh was cut about by shrapnel from a hand grenade and was concussed. He was then taken prisoner along with about half of the men in his unit.

They were tied up and left with some guards in the village for a few weeks while column after column of Japanese troops went through the village. They could then hear a battle raging in the distance, as Singapore was taken by the Japanese.

Sometime after the noise of the distant battle had ceased, a Japanese officer arrived in a commandeered army truck and started screaming orders at the prisoners. He finally got them tied together in a long line. He then made them walk to the old Changi prison on the outskirts of Singapore where they met hundreds of British and Australian men who had been captured when Singapore had fallen.

The men who had been in Singapore during the battle described how the Japanese soldiers went berserk as soon as they arrived in the city and wantonly slaughtered hundreds of civilians.

When they got to the hospital they had bayoneted or shot the patients, raped and murdered the nurses and stolen or destroyed much of the equipment and medical supplies.

They said the city was in a shambles, but that some of the residents had been evacuated by ship just in time.

Hugh then started a long period of near starvation, brutal cruelty, disease, seeing the agonizing death of many fellow prisoners and a feeling of utter helplessness under the impossibly harsh prison conditions.

There was much talk of escape plans, but even if a number of prisoners were seen talking seriously in a group in the yard or walking along the perimeter wire by a Japanese officer, he would fly into a rage and have the prisoners beaten, and or, put into punishment cages made out of wire netting and corrugated iron sheets and made to beg for water each day while crawling round the yard. Many men died of heat exhaustion and dehydration in the punishment cages.

William became more and more involved with monitoring enemy espionage which was rife in the Middle East.

Because the vast majority of the population were extremely poor, the promise of a few pounds could turn almost any of the locals into informers. But they were very street savvy and there was always the risk of an informer finding an enemy agent and selling his, or often her, services to the other side as well, to make a few extra pounds.

So the only safe answer was to tighten up security at all military establishments, which was very lax in many units, and ensure that no important information was leaked or stolen.

But to leak just a little bait of false or out of date information to keep the enemy agents busy transmitting, thus exposing themselves to the radio detection trucks which were becoming more experienced and proficient.

It was found that the enemy agents were paying their informers with counterfeit money printed in Germany, and when counterfeit notes were found it was often possible to use the discovery of the counterfeit notes to trace the agent.

Out of the blue, William was posted back to England, given fourteen days leave before he was to report to a unit near Portsmouth.

When Michelle got a phone call from William in London, to say that he was on his way home for fourteen days leave she was very excited and immediately started to make plans for their time together.

As usual in wartime, William's train was late and Michelle was becoming more anxious as the time got over an hour past the scheduled arrival time.

Eventually the train arrived and service men and women in uniform poured onto the platform.

William was in one of the rear end carriages and was immediately lost in a sea of khaki as he walked along the platform. Michelle spotted him and tried to push against the crowd but it was impossible, so she had to move to one side where she could stand and watch his progress along the platform.

They kissed and embraced as they met and walked hand in hand to the station yard where Sasha's car was parked.

Michelle drove home and William noted that some of the buildings were partly protected by sand bags and that everywhere looked drab and deserted and that there was some random bomb damage.

It was wonderful to be home and William was greeted like a returning hero by everyone.

After dinner Mark gave William all the news and then told him what George and Tad were involved with.

The next day William and Michelle announced their engagement and a small festive dinner was arranged by Sasha the same evening and Mark stood up and welcomed Michelle into the family.

It was becoming socially accepted that an engaged couple could be quickly married during leave from active service, so William and Michelle consulted Sasha and she was delighted with the idea.

Arrangements were made and the marriage service was held in the Village Church a few days later, so that the couple could have a few days honeymoon before the end of William's leave.

They used Sasha's car and planned to stay in the holiday resort town of Llandudno in North Wales, but they found that the whole town was full of Ministry officials who had been evacuated from the bombing in London, so they had to stay in the Station Hotel at Llandudno Junction a few miles away.

The newlyweds were able to relax and enjoy the start of their intimate life together and had long walks along the beach and explored the famous Great Orm's Head peninsular, which had been the site of numerous copper mines about two thousand years ago. They returned to Glendarvel one day before the end of Williams leave and found that Sasha had arranged that the newlyweds had the double guest room at the front of the house.

The leave ended just as William and Michelle were starting to get used to living together and it was a terrible wrench when they had to go to the station and kiss each other goodby. At least this time William would be in England and they should be able to meet occasionally.

As soon as Sally had removed the plaster off Angus's arm, he had gone back to the RAF base at Speke for a medical checkup and was back in the air flying a Spitfire a week later. There were fewer pilots available which meant that those who were still available had to fly more sorties, and just sheer fatigue became a major factor in keeping alert, and hence surviving.

At one pre- flight briefing the squadron leader said.

"The Jerries swarm round Liverpool like blowflies round dung, so we must keep up our maximum level of daylight patrols to detect any stray raiders and of course the squadron scrambles to attack the bomber formation raids on the docks are still our prime function.

On the latest aerial photographs that our people took of the Liverpool dock area there are so many bomb craters that the docks look like a close up picture of an unsociable disease. They must have dumped hundreds of tons of bombs on the dock area, not to mention the hundreds of bombs that they drop in the wrong places."

William was posted to a unit that was part of a special Coastal Defense Force near Portsmouth that was responsible for patrolling and defending all the highly secret and vital ship yards and shore establishments with particular emphasis on the Vosper shipyards where the fast patrol boats and MTBs were built and repaired.

There were numerous American bases a little farther inland as well as all the established naval establishments and shipyards along the coast that had to be patrolled and carefully checked for any subversive activity, from within or in the surrounds.

On a trip to Hastings to pick up some supplies, he came across several places where there were teams of workmen building dummy airfields which were complete with plywood aeroplanes.

When William got a forty eight hour leave, he arranged for Michelle to come down so that they could stay at a small hotel near Salisbury for the week end.

It was wonderful to see her, make love and relax together for a few hours, but the time for another parting came all too soon.

George had completed building his quota of floating Mulberry harbour modules long ago, and they had been towed away by tugs to a location in the Solent near the Isle of White and then had been deliberately sunk in shallow water to prevent detection by enemy reconnaissance planes and to be ready for refloating just before the big day.

The model tests that George had been involved with, for the effect of bombing dams, showed that the bombs needed to be exploded as close as possible to the base of the dam wall to have any certainty of achieving the desired effect.

This then presented a new challenge. How do you ensure that bombs dropped from a fast moving plane can be placed exactly at the base of the dam wall before they explode?

The boffins at Teddington came up with the idea of bombs that would skim across the surface of the water and sink against the dam wall, before they exploded.

Much experimenting was done on a long lagoon on the Dorset coast and eventually a delayed action bomb was developed that could be dropped onto the surface of the water from a very low flying plane.

The bomb would then skim or bounce along the surface to the dam wall, sink to the bottom and explode with its full force applied against the dam wall.

This technique required precision flying and amazing nerve to swoop down into a valley, set the plane at a very critical height, and release the bomb at an exact distance from the dam wall, swoop over the dam wall and climb out of a narrow valley, past a battery of AA guns!

A special squadron was formed from the most skillful air crews, and after intensive training, a series of raids was made on the reservoirs which supplied water to the German's steel industry in the Rhur Valley with amazing successes. The most notable was the breaching of the Mohr dam above the Krupp steel works at Essen.

William became aware that the invasion of Europe was imminent as more and more troops and supplies kept pouring into the area.

With his experience in deception, William could see that there were more dummy planes, trucks, landing craft and phantom tented camps close to Dover, with the real invading force spread out along the coast from Dartmouth to Shoreham.

There were even old trucks being driven round and round the mock up dummy units to make sure that there were fresh wheel tracks everywhere to make the deception look real from the air.

A huge deception was in progress! 'Une grand ruse de guerre!'

There was an intense sense of pending action with men keyed up with all the pre-battle emotions.

A period of uncertainty and pent up anticipation set in and there were some incidents of brawls between rival units that were packed closely together along the coast.

On returning to his billet one night, William was surprised to find a note from George suggesting that they met at a pub later that evening.

The pub was packed with men from every type of unit and it was difficult to get served. After a long wait they got their drinks and went out into the garden away from the cigarette smoke and noise.

George said.

"It is good to catch up with you in this mass of anticipation. How are you?"

"I am well, thank you, and how are you coping with your projects?"

"All my babies are still swimming in the Solent, waiting for the 'word'.

We don't know exactly how long it will take to rescue them, as we are dependent on the Navy swimmers to help connect them to the airlines. We know that all of ours will be easy, but the babies that were built elsewhere may not have been given the same special treatment. We have our fully equipped work boats ready to go out to do the rescue at a moment's notice, from our private jetty, which is across the harbour from your base.

When you think about the overall sequence of events on the 'big day', it is likely that our rescue operation will be the very first in the whole chain of action. The next will probably be the 'housemaids' to do the mine sweeping in the channel before the main show starts.

What are you doing when the action starts?"

"My unit has been allocated to one of your babies to provide twenty four hour protection from the beach. We also have another duty which is to help set up and look after the PLUTO terminal.

I think that they are waiting for the weather to improve before they blow the whistle because your babies and the small craft are not very good sailors."

George looked at his watch and said.

"Sorry I can't stay as I am due back at my base in half an hour and must be off now, so good hunting and good luck."

"I hope everything goes smoothly for you and all the best till we meet again."

They shook hands and parted with each deep in thought about their vital duties that would start 'when the balloon went up'.

Two days later, William called into his depot early in the evening to ensure that the next patrol was fully equipped and ready to take over from the previous shift when he heard the engines of George's work boats start up where they were moored at a separate jetty just across the harbour.

That meant that 'the balloon was in the process of going up'!

There would now be a very anxious twenty four hours before the invasion forces were called into action.

A large Navy truck driven by a WREN went past with about a dozen men and a load of gear in the back.

That would be the Navy divers going out to George's jetty with two divers and an airline minder allocated to each work boat.

Chapter 22

'OVERLORD'

(The operation that nearly didn't start.)

The work boats each had a large diesel engine driven air compressor lashed on the fore deck which would be connected with hoses, by the Navy divers, to the submerged Mulberry harbour modules to force the water out and refloat the hollow concrete structures.

The whole success of 'Operation Overlord' depended on the next twenty four hours of very difficult underwater operations by the crew of Navy divers!

William could not say that he knew that 'the balloon was in the process of going up', but decided to delegate supervision of the patrols to his 2 I/c and then took his light truck down to the work boat jetty to be ready to cover any emergencies that Uncle George might have.

He recognised George in the first work boat as it left the jetty and then the other boats followed and went out into the Solent. They each gave the thumbs up sign.

The WREN was still standing beside her truck at the end of the jetty so William parked alongside. There was the sound of radio static coming from the WREN's truck and he could hear George's voice giving the divers on the other work boats masked instructions on connecting up the hoses and the background noise of diesel engines.

The WREN looked as nervous as a long tailed cat in a room full of rocking chairs, as she listened to the radio and was obviously vividly living every move that George was describing in obscure terms.

William walked closer and said.

"Hello, will you have to keep in radio contact all the time that the work boats are out?"

"We are not allowed to say anything, Sir."

As the girl looked terrified he said.

"My name is William Oakhill and George Bridgeman, who is talking on the radio, is my uncle, so I already know exactly what is going on. I am responsible for shore defenses, so I am part of the show and am here to provide any assistance that you might require."

"I am sorry that I can't answer your question directly but I am pleased to meet you Sir, and thank you for offering assistance. I am WREN Lucy Bateman."

"I am very pleased to meet you Lucy.

My Uncle George supervised the manufacture of about half of the harbour modules and is confident that there will be no problems with the units that he made and is here to see that all his units are easily recovered, but he is unsure about the others which were made elsewhere by a contractor who has since gone broke.

George says that as the units were made over a year ago there is the possibility that the threaded connections for the air hoses, which are embedded in the concrete, will have corroded in the sea water and be difficult to open.

George insisted that he only used fittings made out of 'Admiralty Bronze', which is unaffected by sea water, which as a WREN you would know."

Lucy started to relax and said.

"Actually, I do know a bit about marine corrosion problems, because Daddy has a yacht and is always very careful that he uses the right sort of fittings."

"The divers have only been given twenty four hours to have all the deep sea dock modules refloated and ready for them to be towed across.

Which makes me wonder if you have someone to take over from your watch?"

"As there is so much secrecy about our operation, I am the only person, other than the diving crew, who was allowed to know anything, so I have to stay here till they are finished.

We just got a code worded message about half an hour ago to say that we were to come here immediately and that I am to stand by the radio."

"You poor girl, I suppose that you are hungry and did not have time to pick up any supplies?"

"Yes you are right, we had to leave in such a hurry that there was not time to pick up anything or have a meal.

I will need a coat if it gets cold tonight, even though it is June."

" I have arranged that my 2 I/c looks after my unit, so that I am free and available to help Uncle George, if needed, and can get something to eat and drink and a spare coat for you, if you like?"

"That would be wonderful, thank you Sir."

"As soon as I heard George's work boats start up, I knew exactly what was starting to happen."

William went back to his base and got the cook house to make up four portions of packed meals and a large thermos of coffee. He then picked up two thick windproof jackets and returned to the jetty.

Lucy thanked him for the food and tried on a jacket, which was much too big, and being khaki looked odd over her blue uniform.

She giggled and said.

"They will think that I have defected to the army! But it will keep me warm and thank you."

The radio was silent for several hours and William and Lucy were able to sit in the big truck and relax while they chatted about their respective family lives.

Suddenly the radio burst into life with Lucy's call sign and the officer in charge of the divers was on the air.

"Calling Tortoise two, Calling Tortoise two, come in Tortoise two, over."

"Your signal loud and clear, Tortoise two awaits your message, over."

"Report four babies fully recovered and two more improving rapidly. Stop.

Difficulty feeding some babies and need you to go to base and pick more specialist people soonest. Over."

William asked Lucy if he could reply and she nodded.

"Doctor William here with message for Uncle George. Stop. Please provide details of patient's condition. Over."

"Uncle George here, many patients having trouble drawing breath. Stop. Need extra nurses and stronger instruments to insert breathing tubes soonest. Stop. Pleased that you are available to help cure patients. Over."

"Wilco Uncle George. Stop. Tortoise two standing by. Over."

William said.

"Lucy, this is exactly what George was afraid would happen. From what George has said, the divers must be becoming exhausted from struggling with corroded fittings under water for hours and need a relief crew of divers and also need bigger tools that will apply more leverage.

Can you call your base on the radio?"

"Yes, I can change frequency to our base working frequency and call the duty officer. Would you like me to do it now?"

"Yes please, get your duty officer on the air as soon as possible."

A few minutes later the Naval Base duty officer answered 'en claire.'

William answered.

"Hello, this is Captain William Oakhill of the 'Coastal Defense Force' providing technical assistance for your operation Tortoise and we need your close attention to my requests. Please arrange a very urgent meeting with your Base Commander, repeat, Base Commander, and then meet me at the front gate in a few minutes. Over"

"Good evening Captain, I am not conversant with 'Operation Tortoise' so I will contact the Admiral immediately and then meet you at the gate. Over."

"Thank you Lucy, please keep on watch, as you have been instructed, and if there is any more important news you can call the duty officer at your Base again. When I have finished at your Base I will go and see my friends at the Vosper ship yards and try to arrange for them to send one of their MTBs or fast patrol boats here to ferry the extra divers and equipment out to where the 'Babies ' are being rescued.

Everything depends on what we can arrange in the next few hours. See you soon."

William drove to the Naval base and went into the guard house at the gate and asked for the duty officer.

The petty officer in charge of the gate house said that the duty officer was using the telephone at the moment and he would let him know that William was waiting.

The duty officer finished his phone call and introduced himself as John Allen. William asked John if he was aware of operation Tortoise.

"Pleased to meet you William. I was not informed about Operation Tortoise, but when I saw the Admiral just now, he knew all about Operation Tortoise and said that he will see you as soon as you arrive, so please follow me to his office?"

The Admiral's office was like a maritime museum with memorabilia and models of famous ships and miniature brass canons on every horizontal space and also in numerous glass cabinets and had a commanding view over the harbour.

The Admiral was a tall well-built man and had a friendly smile as he extended his hand in greeting when William came in and saluted.

"Please sit down Captain Oakhill and give me the details of what you want. I already know about Tortoise in principle but have not been given the details."

William explained the outline of the Mulberry Harbour plan and how that the modules were sunk in the Solent to hide them till they were needed, which is right now!

"I am in charge of the Coastal Defense Force in this area and have to keep tabs on everything going on and became aware this afternoon that the work boats, to be used to convey the divers and their equipment, were leaving their private jetty to go and refloat the harbour modules, known as 'Operation Tortoise', which of course is the vital prelude to putting 'Operation Overlord' into action.

A signal was sent from the Operation Tortoise work boats to their watch on the jetty about twenty minutes ago to say that they were having trouble connecting the compressed air lines to some of the modules, probably due to corrosion, and that the original divers are exhausted after struggling under water for about four hours and urgently need a crew of relief divers and some stronger tools.

So Sir, we need your intervention to call up about eight Navy divers to go to the Private jetty as soon as possible. I now plan to go to the Vosper yard and arrange for the tools to be made and see if they have a patrol boat available that can pick up the extra divers from the jetty and take them out to the site."

"Now that I am aware of the problem, I see the importance of your request and will do all in my power to get you the divers. If Vosper don't have a patrol boat available, let me know at once and I will send one of our fast small craft to wait at the jetty till the divers arrive."

"Thank you Sir, I will see that you are kept informed."

William saluted and hurried out to the front gate, jumped into his truck and went round to the Vosper shipyards.

As it was late evening, the administration staff had gone home and there was just a night shift working.

The night shift manager immediately under stood what tools were needed and ordered some Stillson wrenches to be modified with longer handles. There was a completed patrol boat available, waiting for the armaments to be fitted, but it needed the directors approval to take it out on an operation before it was handed over to the Navy.

After several phone calls, William was told that one director was on his way down to the yard to personally take charge of preparing the patrol boat for the operation and would arrive in a few minutes.

A Jaguar car swept into the car park and his friend, Stewart Hastings, got out and greeted William.

"It is a bit irregular for a boat to go out on an operation before it is handed over but we realise the importance of your request, so I will get a crew together and send it over to the jetty. How long do you think the boat will be needed?"

"That depends on how soon the Admiral can get the divers and how soon they can connect up the hoses, but we need to be prepared for at least twenty four hours, at a guess. Those poor bloody divers struggling with rusted on fittings in their rubber suits must be going through hell!"

"OK,William, it will take me about an hour to check that the boat is seaworthy and put a crew together, refuel and drive over. I will send the boat to the jetty as soon as possible, to wait till the divers arrive. The modified tools are being made and will soon be ready to put on board.

In case all else fails, I have also put out an air drill that works under water so that they can drill through the old fitting and then tap in a new thread and insert a new hose connection, but it will take time and skill to do that under twenty feet of murky water."

William went back to his Base and met his 2 I /c and explained that he would be involved with his uncle's project for a few hours and emphasized that the unit must be kept ready to go into their action mode at any time.

He then picked up more supplies, his rifle and revolver and plenty of ammunition on the way back to the jetty and found Lucy still sitting in her truck with the radio on and just emitting a bit of static noise.

William got Lucy to call the officer in charge of the divers and advise him of what was happening and was told that there was little chance of meeting the completion time unless all the items requested arrived immediately! The Admiral was informed of the situation.

There was nothing more to be done till the patrol boat and divers arrived.

Nothing happened till about 0230 Hrs. when the radio burst into life.

"Calling Tortoise two. Calling Tortoise two. Come in Tortoise two. Over"

Lucy was awake after a good sleep and quickly replied.

"Your signal loud and clear. Tortoise two standing by. Over."

"Need progress report, most urgent, repeat, and most urgent. Over."

So the panic had started and there would be no letup of top brass calls till all the dock modules were recovered and the 'Operation Tortoise Completed' code word had been sent!

Lucy called the work boat on their frequency and asked the officer in charge for a progress report to be advised that due to exhaustion and lack of instruments the work could not proceed till the request for personnel and instruments had been fulfilled!

William suspected that the reply was being monitored and suggested that Lucy relayed the work boat message verbatim, which she did and stayed on the air.

As expected, there were fireworks on the airwaves!

Within minutes a Navy staff car arrived at the jetty and the Admiral got out.

While William and Lucy were bringing the Admiral up to date, a fully armed MTB came up to the jetty and the Skipper jumped ashore and saluted the Admiral.

"Sir. We had just finished our patrol duty and docked at the Vosper wharf for radio repairs and some other minor repairs to find that there is a very urgent delivery job that has to be done, because the boat that Vosper was going to use was found to be still part way through a steering system modification, so we put their gear on board, refueled and came here as fast as possible.

We have brought one of the Vosper staff, who is a diver, and says that if the tools that he has made will not do the job, that he can drill and put in new fittings."

"Thank you Jenkins that was good thinking, well done.

I have sent out a man hunt for divers, but so far have only got two men on their way here. They should be here at any moment."

The Vosper fitter / cum diver came out on the deck of the MTB and William immediately thought of Jack Darlington, the blacksmith in the Village at home. The man was built like a tank with huge hands and arms. A similar build to Jack and just the man to fix the problem, if it is fixable.

There was no sign of the two new divers for about half an hour and then a small Navy truck arrived and an officer got out and reported to the Admiral that the vehicle bringing the two divers had been involved in a road accident and that the divers were being taken to hospital!

The Admiral said.

"We are running out of options and time, what do you bright young men suggest?"

Jim Jenkins, the M.T.B. Skipper, said.

"We were involved with an aerial attack last night and had to put two wounded crew ashore during the night so we need a radio and a radio operator and also a machine gunner to make up the ship's complement before we are fully operational. Sir."

William called Lucy over and asked if her radio could be transferred from the truck to the boat?

"It only took the signals man two minutes to plug it in and clamp on an aerial, so presumably it can be transferred to the boat without too much trouble. Sir."

William turned towards the Admiral and said.

"May I suggest Sir, that due to the extreme urgency, that the Vosper fitter transfers the radio from the truck to the MTB immediately, that WREN. Lucy Bateman be appointed radio operator for the MTB and that as I am experienced with machine guns that I assume the role of machine gunner and that we go to the site as soon as possible."

There was a pause while the Admiral mulled over the suggestion and he then said.

"Jenkins, do you think that the plan is workable?"

"Well Sir, there are some irregularities, but on your command, I will be pleased to put the plan into action, as it appears to be the only option."

"I order that Operation Tortoise Two goes to sea with all speed, and good luck.

When I can get more divers they will be sent out to you and I want you, Jenkins, to stay on station for the whole operation and provide surveillance and protection. Are we all agreed?"

William, Jim and Lucy all said "Yes Sir."

William went with Lucy to her truck and Jim sent the fitter, Sam Chenowyth, across with his bag of tools. The radio was soon transferred to the MTB and connected up. The Admiral stood and watched as Lucy put out a test signal to her Base and said that Tortoise Two was 'going to sea'.

The admiral shook hands with everyone as he wished them Bon Voyage and then went ashore.

He was still standing on the jetty as the MTB pulled away and went out into the Solent.

William wondered what was going through the Admiral's mind. He had suddenly inherited the responsibility for correcting a problem of immense proportions, which if not corrected immediately would have catastrophic consequences.

All caused by sloppy workmanship done by the other contractor who had built some of the modules. And largely due to the extreme secrecy, this had not come to light till the most critical time in the whole war!

There was a short chop as the Vosper MTB got out into open water and spray was thrown onto the deck as the powerful twin Thornycroft diesel engines drove the boat at over twenty knots towards the other side of the Solent channel.

The Mulberry Harbour dock modules that had been refloated looked enormous and dwarfed the work boats moored nearby.

William pointed out which work boat George and the officer in charge would be on and they went along side and tied up.

There were brief introductions and Sam was soon donning a diving suit and putting his tools into a netting bag before he was helped over the side and guided down by one of the exhausted and sweat stained Navy divers.

Bubbles streamed up to the surface as Sam sweated and strained to unscrew the rusted on fittings.

There were then three tugs on his airline to say that he was coming up!

As soon as Sam's sweat streamed face emerged from the helmet, William knew that the worst had happened!

"Bloody cheapskate, ignorant bastards only used galvanised fittings and did not anchor them properly in the concrete, so now that I can apply more force, the whole bloody pipe embedded in the concrete is turning and could break free!

The only way is to drill and tap the cap on the end of the pipe and screw in new fittings, so I need an airline for the underwater drill and the other bags of tools and fittings.

This is going to be a difficult and slow job!"

Jim asked.

"How long do you think it will take Sam?"

"Well, I don't want to risk using any more force trying to unscrew the fittings because the pipes could break free from the concrete, so the only safe way is to drill and tap each one.

Jim, you had better let your boss know that we will need up to another twenty four hours. If I can keep going that long!"

Sam took another bag of tools and went back into the murky water with an exhausted Navy diver to help him.

Paul Rosenberg, the officer in charge of the diving operation, said.

"I suppose it is my luck to be the one to inform the boss that they will have to postpone 'Operation Overlord' by twenty four hours. I expect the fan will get severely damaged when this news hits the airwaves!" He then went into the cabin and asked Lucy to call his Base.

William talked to the other divers who had just been served a cup of tea and sandwiches by Lucy.

They were exhausted and trying to regain the strength to go down, one at a time, and help Sam.

William realised that the sudden appearance of over twenty enormous concrete structures floating in the Solent would attract the attention of every enemy aircraft in the area which could then be followed up by an unwelcome visit from an enemy dive bomber, so he asked Jim to show him the deck mounted machine gun so that he could get it fully operational. When the covers were off, it turned out to be a 0.50 heavy machine gun on a swivel mounting which William was already fully conversant with. There was also a BREN gun and a special ammunition locker full of spare magazines close by.

Sam was able to complete one 'drill, tap and fit' operation each half hour, followed by a half hour break.

After Sam had finished his operation on each module it was necessary to move to another sunken module so that one of the other work boats could then use compressed air to force the water out, which then took another two or more hours.

Work continued through the night and everyone had to push themselves to keep going.

Lucy had curled up in the cabin and had had some sleep and awoke well before dawn. She went out on deck to see if the men wanted some breakfast and to get some fresh air.

Out of habit, from when she was on her father's yacht, she picked up the skipper's binoculars and scanned the horizon as the first shafts of sunlight came across the water.

"William. Quick. We have company!"

"What can you see? And keep in the shadow of the cabin."

"The low sun is reflecting off what looks like the lens of a periscope, over to the West!"

Jim was called and used the binoculars from inside the cabin to scan the horizon to the West. He soon spotted the sun reflecting off a periscope!

"There is a remote chance that it is one of ours and also we can't fire a torpedo from here because if we miss the overshoot will hit shore installations, we must wait and see what it does. Lucy, we need to check with base. Can you do that?"

"Yes. Sir."

"This is what I want you to say. 'Tortoise Two proceeding with all haste as directed and now have an unknown marine visitor. Stop. Please verify soonest. Over."

There was a long wait till the reply came. Calling Tortoise Two. Calling Tortoise Two. Continue to proceed as directed. Stop. We have no marine visitors in your area today. Over.

"Well, at least we now know it is a Jerry sub and can have a shot at it if it comes closer or we can move to get a shot from a different angle."

Jim decided that if he could move off quickly in an arc he could get a shot from a safe angle before the sub could get the periscope down and be lost under water.

The engines were warmed up, the torpedo tubes flooded and made ready to fire and William was in position crouching behind the machine gun on deck. The mooring lines were drawn in carefully by a man lying on the deck.

The twin engines roared as they achieved full power, the boat surged forward on the plane in an arc and as soon as the aim was right. Jim gave the order to fire the torpedoes.

Two lines of disturbed water and bubbles streaked off towards the periscope as it began to disappear below the surface.

There was then that anxious moment of a hunter's anticipation waiting to see if the quarry has been hit!

A loud underwater explosion confirmed one strike but the other 'tin fish' had continued on till it ran out of power and presumably sank in deep water. Jim slowed the boat and held it bow on to where the periscope had disappeared.

Lucy used the binoculars to search the surface and saw nothing for a while so handed the binoculars to Jim.

"We may have done a lot of damage to a sand bank in this shallow water. I can't see any signs of a wounded sub."

Jim kept searching with the glasses for a few minutes and then moved closer and saw an oil slick.

"Stand by, we may have hit the sub. Look out for any signs of it surfacing."

Suddenly the bow of a sub erupted out of the water at a steep angle and then the conning tower appeared followed by a still part submerged hull, well down at the stern.

The hatch cover on the conning tower flipped open and a German officer climbed down to the deck. He was quickly followed by some of his crew who made a dash for their deck mounted gun.

William waited till the men were all clustered round the gun, pulling off covers, opening ammunition lockers, loading and starting to slew the gun round before he opened fire in a long traversing burst.

The gun crew were all killed and blasted off the narrow deck into the sea. He then fired a burst into their ammunition locker till it started to explode like fire crackers going off.

The officer was still standing beside the conning tower with his pistol drawn, so William fired a short burst aimed at the deck close to his feet. The officer got the message and dropped his pistol and put his hands up.

William became aware that Lucy was kneeling behind the gunwale with his rifle aimed at the German officer in case he tried to use his pistol, and was impressed by her spontaneous action.

As Lucy closely watched the rest of the submarine crew emerge from the conning tower and assemble on deck she noticed that the first officer had put on what appeared to be an ill-fitting water proof jacket and became suspicious.

Using the X eight power telescopic sight on Williams rifle she saw the muzzle of a weapon poking out of the zipper opening of his jacket.

There was not enough time to alert William to use the BREN gun so she took careful aim at the man's chest and fired.

On being hit, the reaction of the German officer was to squeeze the trigger of the Schmeisser machine pistol as he stumbled and fell slowly backwards in to the sea. An arc of bullets sliced through the air as the 32 round magazine discharged all, or nearly all, its contents.

The Schmeisser machine pistol, with its folding butt, was the first choice of the Gestapo and many German officers and over one million were in service.

"Good shot Lucy, that was just in time. Please send a signal and say. 'Tortoise Two has a disabled marine visitor and requires assistance soonest.'"

Lucy quickly called up her base and gave them the message. She then wondered what the reaction would be when they realised that the MTB had 'bagged a sub'! ?

Jim went alongside the sub. and tried speaking to the German officer and found that he spoke a little English. William kept them covered with the BREN gun till another MTB arrived and took the prisoners on board.

Two men were then detailed to search the sub for stragglers and booby traps and they returned a long time later and said that they had only found two corpses and that the sub was slowly sinking due to damage in the stern. A message was sent for a salvage boat to be sent out to tow the sub away.

By this time, the Navy divers had had sufficient rest and were able to do more to assist Sam and as they became more experienced with the process, the rate of recovery improved.

Several progress report signals were sent to the Admiral and very soon ocean going tugs arrived and started to couple up to the Mulberry Harbour modules. William wondered what their final configurations would be to suit each beachhead on the French coast.

Operation Overlord started twenty four hours later than planned with the mine sweepers (House maids.) heading off well before dawn on the 6th of June 1944 to sweep a path for the hundreds of assault craft and other shipping that would go across in the next few hours.

The landing craft and assault vessels each had a designated route from their five starting points to go to a code named beachead on the French coast on the East side of the Cherbourg peninsula.

> Dartmouth to 'Utah' Beach.Americans.
> Portland to 'Omaha' Beach.Americans.
> Southampton to 'Gold' Beach. British.
> Portsmouth to'Juno' Beach. Canadians.
> Shoreham to'Sword' Beach.British.

All five beacheads were secured on the first day by 176,000 allied troops.

The work boats and divers returned to their jetty at Portsmouth. George and Sam were able to go home, completely exhausted, now that the 'Operation Tortoise Completion' signal had been sent.

Jim's MTB, with William and Lucy still on board, continued to keep station for the fully assembled Mulberry Harbours till they were towed away by tugs during the next night with an escort of destroyers.

The MTB then went back to Portsmouth and Lucy had her radio returned to her truck and

William was glad to be back on dry land.

As he was about leave, William complimented Lucy on spotting a sub and the quick action taken in dealing with the German officer before he could damage a vital part of a preliminary stage in Operation Overlord and her role in the success of the whole operation.

"Your arrival gave me confidence and I felt that I was part of the crew and was able to overcome my nervousness and work normally while you were there, and thank you Sir. I will never forget working with you on this operation."

The radio crackled and there was a message for William and Lucy to report to the Admiral's office immediately.

There were two other senior naval officers present in the Admiral's office and the atmosphere was decidedly tense.

"Please sit down and give us a complete report of what has happened in the last few days."

William took the lead and started with how the modules were built at two or more locations and then gave details of the recovery operation right up to when the modules were towed away.

He called on Lucy to describe her part in operating the radio, spotting the sub and shooting the German officer as he was about to use his Schmeisser, which she did with confidence.

The Admiral said.

"There are questions coming from 'above', so I need to establish how such a vital process was not given more attention to detail and that some 50 % of the harbour modules were supplied with defective fittings?

Without the spontaneous intervention by these two people, and others, a disaster would have resulted at what was probably the most critical moment in the war!"

He then looked questioningly at the two naval officers, who explained that the contracts for construction of the Mulberry Harbour Modules were handled by the Ministry of Supply, in great secrecy, and that no Navy personnel were involved till the order was issued for a diving crew to be formed to refloat the units about a month ago.

"Now is not the time for a witch hunt, but from what you say it was a typical lack of proper specifications and inspection before the units were delivered and then the shroud of secrecy covered up the faults till it was nearly too late. As it was, the main show was held up for twenty four hours, much to the embarrassment of the Navy and the extreme annoyance of Mr. Churchill and the Joint Commanders of Overlord.

Next time you are given an unfamiliar task, don't sit and wait, go and check what is involved so that you are fully prepared!" He then dismissed the two naval officers and said to William and Lucy.

"I apologise for having to call you in, but as you can guess, I have to satisfy my superiors on what caused the delay and what emergency measures were implemented.

I congratulate and thank both of you for acting above and beyond your normal duties in time of extreme urgency and danger thus preventing a further delay in the invasion, and for your parts in the destruction of an enemy submarine that was about to ruin the whole operation.

I will be recommending that both of you are awarded medals for your action in Operation Tortoise."

He then shook hands with both of them and wished them well.

As they were driving back for Lucy to pick up her truck, William said.

"You are very welcome to keep in touch and visit any time, and it has been a pleasure working with you. Good luck."

Lucy reached across, gripped his hand, kissed him on the cheek and said.

"Yes, I will be pleased to keep in touch and thank you for building my confidence and you keep safe for the rest of the war."

William returned to his unit to prepare to leave before dawn the next day on a landing craft and cross over the channel to the Mulberry Harbour site 'B' at Arromanches beach.

The landing craft had a most unusual 'sea gait' due to it's large flat bottom and did a lot of side slipping and thumping down on each wave rather than cutting through it.

They landed on a shallow sandy beach and their vehicles were able to drive down the ramp into shallow water, cross a firm sand beach and go into a pine plantation to keep out of sight from the Junkers 87s, or Stuka, dive bombers, which kept strafing the landing area.

The Mulberry harbour was already moored in position a few hundred yards out to sea and the engineers were erecting long sections of steel roadway on pontoons to join the dock modules to the beach and allow for tidal rise and fall. Amazingly, the roadway could support 40 ton tanks.

There were small recesses in the bulwarks on the sides of the outer dock module of the harbour for the 0.50 heavy machine guns that they had brought with them, to be mounted.

Use of these guns against dive bomber attack was to be one of their main functions.

William saw a bulldozer being used to haul heavy trucks up the beach and when it was not busy he asked the driver to make some shallow hollows in the pine forest to give his men and trucks more protection. They then pitched their small camouflaged tents in the hollows.

It could be many months before their current duty was completed, so they might as well make their camp area as safe and comfortable as possible.

Two AA gun emplacements were added to give more protection from the dive bombers.

Within two days the harbor was fully operational and supply ships started to arrive and were unloaded by men from an RAOC unit, with the supplies being quickly trucked away from the exposed beach.

The heavy machine guns had been mounted in position at the end of the harbour together with their ammunition lockers, but William was concerned that they were much too exposed and had little protection from enemy fire so he sent a sergeant and ten men in a truck to look round the nearest railway yards to collect plenty of spare sleepers. The thick timber sleepers were soon built into raised parapets and a roof with just a small opening for the machine gun. The whole area was then covered with tarpaulins and camouflage nets draped over the top.

The next day an odd looking ship came up to the harbour. It had a huge drum of special hose on the deck which was lowered into the water and rolled up the beach by the bulldozer while paying out hose.

A very deep furrow had been made by the dozer and the hose was immediately buried. This procedure was used all the way to the nearest village where a refueling terminal was established.

The line of the buried hose was then raked over and covered with natural looking debris.

This was 'PLUTO'. (Pipe Line Under The Ocean.) which would pump fuel from the English coast to the terminal (At 1500 PSI.) in the village and keep the whole of the Allied forces supplied till the local supplies became available, which could be months away. Petrol or diesel could be pumped through the 2 inch I/D hose and was soon being delivered at the rate of one million gallons a day. More terminals were established across France as the troops advanced.

A heavily fortified machine gun emplacement was built near the main fuel terminal and a twenty four hour duty roster was established for all the guns and the foot patrol on the beach.

There was a raid and nine of the 12 Stukas were shot down and several were severely damaged over the next month while the Allied troops were fighting their way across France.

Supply ships kept on arriving and the tanker trucks kept filling up in the village to keep the front lines supplied.

The Mulberry Harbour 'A' at the American's Ohmaha beach was not adequately moored and was severely damaged by a freak storm early in June so 'Mulberry Harbour 'B' at Arrowmanches was the only operational Mulberry harbour and became known as 'Port Winston.'

During the ten months of operation, 2.5 million men, 500,000 vehicles and four million tons of supplies were safely landed at Port Winston! This was an amazing feat of planning and engineering that was originally the brain child of Winston Churchill.

Chapter 23

A FIGHT TO THE FINISH

Mark's mother, Agnes, died and her faithful housekeeper / companion, Annie, went to look after her invalid sister, so Sasha suggested that Michelle and William could move into the self-contained suit and that Michelle could arrange for it to be redecorated into her preferred décor.

As soon as this was completed, Michelle moved in but continued to join in with all family activities and confirmed that her baby was due any day.

William had been able to hint in his letters to Michelle that he was going to France but could not say where, but as soon as George arrived home he had been able to provide all the details, including William and Lucy's part in destroying the German submarine and William's involvement in the use of the Mulberry harbour, and through his contacts in France, he had been able to keep informed on the success of the operation.

He said that after 'D' day, the allied advance across Europe was being fought against stiff resistance and counter attack all the way.

Keeping the Allied forces fully supplied was already critical, but as the supply lines got longer and more men and armaments were involved the volume being handled by Port Winston increased to a twenty four hour nonstop operation and that William's unit was stretched to the limit.

Richard came to stay at Glendarvel on one of his regular visits and said that William's spontaneous involvement in refloating the Mulberry Harbour sections had been explained to Churchill by the Admiral and that the 'old man' was duly impressed and confirmed that medals were to be awarded to all concerned. Mark and Sasha were very proud to think that their son had played such a vital role in the final preparation for D day.

The terrible plight of Hugh and all the men being held as prisoners by the Japanese was discussed. Information about the fall of Singapore and the conditions in Changi prison had been smuggled out of Malaysia via British agents hidden in the jungle and a control center at Kandy in Ceylon.

The first priority was to finish the war in Europe as soon as possible and then more resources could be applied in the Far East. The British nation was becoming exhausted physically and financially and it required every last ounce of determination to keep up the war effort.

Hitler introduced his new weapon which was soon christened the 'Doodle Bug'. These unmanned rocket propelled bombs were landing in the South East of England, mostly concentrated round London.

The rockets were launched from an inclined ramp and kept up their stuttering rocket propulsion till they ran out of fuel and then turned nose down and became a powerful bomb. The aim was very erratic and there was no apparent logic in the rate of fire so they did a lot of random civilian damage and consequently had a major psychological effect on the population as well.

Richard returned to London with that degree of fear and uncertainty that indiscriminate bombing or shelling creates. A direct hit by a V1 rocket was lethal within a 25 yard radius and if you heard the rocket motor stop it was only a few seconds before the powerful bomb exploded. This appeared to be an extension of Hitler's psychological warfare.

Rockets kept coming from June to September, and then the first launch site was located at Peenemunde and bombed, but very soon other launch sites became operational and the rockets started coming again. The Germans had also started sending over the more powerful V II rockets.

The RAF were able to shoot some of the rockets down and the fighter pilots also found how to fly alongside and use their wing tip to direct the rocket down so that it fell into the sea.

Britain started to retaliate by night bombing German cities which started to have a demoralising effect. The Americans bombed by day and the German people were rapidly becoming war weary and just wanted hostilities to end, but the German Army continued to fight till May the 8th 1945 when an unconditional surrender was signed.

When the port at Le Harve was operating William's exhausted unit returned to Britain and was sent on leave to await further instructions.

Michelle was so relieved and excited to see William home again and could not stop looking at him and smiling as he held the baby.

Mark and Sasha were delighted to have William home after so long and were very proud of his achievements and were delighted by the arrival of Michelle's baby boy.

All the stress and hardship during the war had aged George considerably and Anne persuaded him to retire from general consulting and just undertake a few assignments for the estate.

Angus had been posted to Bex Hill on the South coast for the last year and had been on almost constant fighter combat duties and as soon as he got some leave he married Sally and they planned on living in the village, so Mark arranged that Andrew's house would be renovated and extended for them as soon as things returned to normal.

The war in Europe had ended and there was much celebrating but there was still a very large military force left to sort out the confusion and devastation in Europe.

There was suddenly news of atomic bombs being dropped in Japan on Hiroshima on the 6th of August and Nagasaki on the 9th of August followed by the Japanese surrender on the 14th of August and the war in the pacific was over.

It was over three months before Hugh got home and Margret had great difficulty in hiding her horror at seeing the condition that he was in. He was still deathly thin and weak and on a special diet because of the damage done to his system in Changi.

He would not talk about his time in Changi when the girls were present but told Mark and William how they had been treated and how right up to the end the guards had jeered and goaded them with things like.

"White monkey enty lice sak on choptic."

Any signs of aggression to the taunts had always resulted in another beating or a session in the punishment cage.

Hugh still had terrible scars on his back from the numerous beatings.

It was early December before Mark and Sasha could get the whole family back home with life starting to return to normal, so a victory celebration was announced

It was decided to have the main event in the Village hall and the school principal made the school buildings available for use by the caterer.

A week before the celebrations were due to start, William received a very sad letter from Lucy Bateman saying that she had had no replies to her phone calls and letters to her home and when she had finally been able to return home on being demobilised she had found that her parents' home had been hit by a V1 rocket and that they were both killed and that she and was now having to live with her married sister and would like to accept William's invitation to visit some time.

Mark and Sasha recalled being told about how William and Lucy were thrown into the recovery of the Mulberry harbour near disaster and decided to invite her to the victory celebrations and asked Ann if she could arrange for her grandson, John, to meet Lucy off the train and look after her during the celebrations.

Richard and the Doc. had agreed to come and stay for the celebrations. Mike and Susan would call in for the day.

Admiral Fyfe, from Portsmouth, was an old university friend of Richard's and was persuaded to come with Richard, and both of their wives, which added a very welcome surprise.

Peace celebrations started at twelve o'clock and some two hundred people were packed into the village hall when Mark welcomed everyone and thanked all those who had served in the forces overseas in defeating the enemy. He also thanked all those who had contributed in so many ways on the home front.

Richard asked if he could say a few words and was welcomed by Mark.

"Ladies and Gentlemen, it has been my privilege to work in the background with Mark and a number of local people on some of the vitally important projects during the war and I give you all my heartfelt thanks and congratulations on a job well done. Thank you and good luck."

Admiral Fyfe then stood up and said a few words about William and Lucy's spontaneous action as part of Operation Tortoise, called them up, congratulated them and shook their hands while everyone clapped and cheered.

Jack Darlington responded on behalf of the local people and thanked Mark and his family for their help and leadership during the war and said that they all now felt that they were part of a proper community again.

During the evening, Mark and Sasha stood at one side and watched their family and friends mingling with the local people with much pride and recalled everything that had happened in their lives to reach this moment.